THE
DOG ROSES

NA FEIRDHRISEACHA

DAVID H. MILLAR

TITLES BY DAVID H. MILLAR

Conall: The Place of Blood: Rinn-Iru

Conall II: The Raven's Flight: Eitilt an Fhiaigh Dhuibh

Conall III: The Sisters: Na Deirfiúracha

Conall IV: A Brace of Eagles: Snaidhm Iolar

Conall V: Retribution: Díoltas

The Dog Roses: Na Feirdhriseacha

IN THE WORKS

The Blood Queen: A 'Bhanrigh Fuil

To a new arrival, my grandson Jaxon.
And to my granddaughter, Sasha,
who was the inspiration for Aoife.

ACKNOWLEDGEMENTS

The process of writing, publishing, and marketing novels is a team sport. Often times it is arduous, especially when faced with a blank page for days or weeks, and sometimes it is inspired. At all times a good sense of humour and a bottle of Irish whiskey within reach are essential.

I am always very appreciative of the international cast that comprises Team Millar. Thanks go to my editors (Kahina Necaise and Cecily Blench from The History Quill), my cover designer and internal formatter, Ida Jansson, Amygdala Design, and my very patient map illustrator, Chaim Holtjer.

Last, but certainly not the least, a big thank you to my beta readers: Authors Judith Fullerton and Jolie A. Reynolds, Lauren Millar, Susan Robitaille, and Brendan Sullivan.

CONTENTS

GAELIC PRONUNCIATIONS

The world over, everyone wants to be Irish, have an Irish heritage, or just celebrate St. Patrick's Day. After the initial glow, probably from Guinness or whiskey, they are faced with the obstacle of an unpronounceable Irish language—Gaelic!

I have long maintained that Gaelic only ever sounds wonderful when it is sung. Listen to Clannad or De Danann. To my ear, normal spoken Gaelic sounds quite harsh and guttural. To increase my readers' misery, I have tended, whenever possible, to use ancient Irish Gaelic, which sometimes does not equate with modern Irish Gaelic.

However, to ease your pain, I have provided, below, a guide to the most frequently used personal names used in the novel. I hope adds to your enjoyment of the tale. One of these days, I will post a comprehensive pronunciation guide on my website and Facebook page. Until then, pronounce the names in the way that gives you most pleasure. That is what I do!

Ailill Mac Máta	AHL-il mak MAWta
Aodh Mac Aodh	AWD mak AWD
Aodh Mac Eochaidh Fionn	AWD mak OHY-fin
Aoife	EE-fa
Aoibheann	AY-veen
Báine	BAWN-yuh
Beacán Ó Cathasaigh	B'YAG-awn o-KAS-akh
Brighid Ni Conall	BREED nee KON-ul
Cairbre	CAR-bryeh
Cass	KASS
Ceara	KYAR-a
Cet	KET
Cináed	KIN-awd
Conall Mac Gabhann	KON-ul mak GAWN
Conchobhar	KRU-hur o-
Crónán Mac Dedad	CROW-nawn mak DAY-da
Cúmhaí Mac Aodh	koo-VEE mak DAY-da
Danu Ni Conall	DAH-noo nee-KON-ul
Daráine	dar AWN yeh
Draighean	DRYNE
Eithne	EN yeh
Fainche	FINE-kha
Flann	FLAN
Glaisne Mac Aodh	GLASH-neh mak AWD
Iasg	EE-ask
Labhraidh	LA-ra
Maine	MAN yeh
Maolán	MAYL-awn
Medb	MAY-ve
Mongfhionn	MUNN-yung
Mórrígan Ó Cathasaigh	Moe-rig-gAHn o-KAS-akh
Naomh	NEV

Neasán	NYAS awn
Nuadha Ó Dubhghaill	NOO-a o DOO-l
Onchú Ó an Cháintigh	UN-choo Awn HAWN-tyg
Scolai	SKUL-lee
Sláine Mac Sláine	SLAWN-yah MAK SLAWN-yah
Torna Mac Dedad	TUR-uh-na mak DAY-da
Uallachán Ó Dubhghaill	OOL-akh-awn o DOO-l
Úna	OO-na

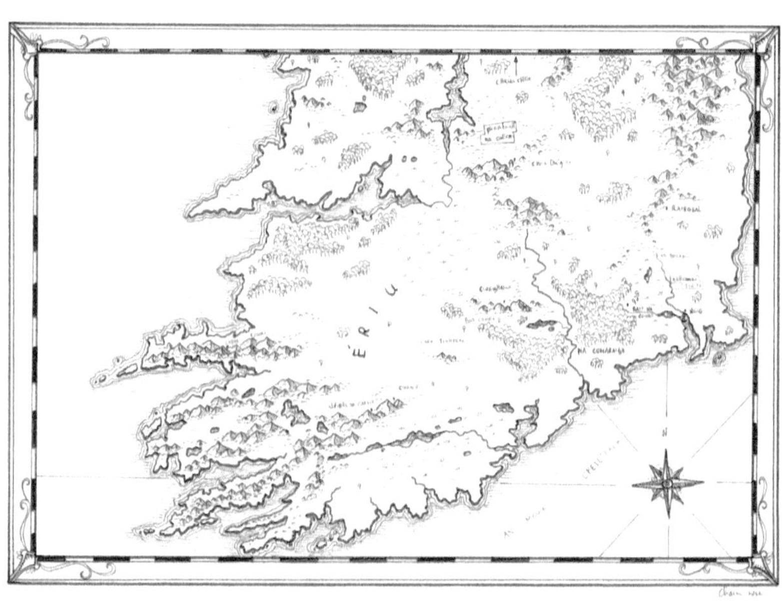

ÉRIU

CHAPTER 1

394 B.C.—Midsummer

At seven, although she would insist almost eight, summers old, Aoife loved her sheltered cove. Unlike her older siblings, she had few chores, leaving her lots of time for adventure and exploration. Carefree, she spent as much time as she could walking barefoot in the soft white sand or splashing in the perpetually chilly waters of Ériu. She did not mind the temperature, whether summer or winter, considering it a small price to pay for the pleasure she enjoyed. Aoife loved the feeling of the wind messing up her long black hair and laughed with every gust.

A cheerful child, only the thought of growing older and being unable to visit her bay made Aoife sad. In her prayers, she asked the Goddess to forestall that future. Sacrifices, precious to her, were dropped into the stream that ran past her family's small farmstead near the settlement of Niúig.

The Goddess sympathised with Aoife's plight and greatly valued her gifts. Still, she knew that only death would give Aoife her desire, and that was unacceptable. Thus, she restrained Fate and held back the *bean-sidhe*. On this day, as compensation, the Goddess gave Aoife a memory she would never forget.

✶✶✶

Brighid Ni Conall, Princess of Clann Ui Flaithimh, leaned forward and firmly gripped the ship's bow rail. Tails of braided auburn hair flicked cheeks burned red by sea and sun on the long voyage from the Great Sea port of Massalia. As she gazed in the direction of Ráth Na Conall, the ancestral home of her family and clann, mixed emotions of joy and trepidation filled her.

The smell of rotting seaweed and the sounds of screeching seabirds and gently crashing waves soothed her senses. Not so much, the ring of iron striking iron and shouts of warriors. With a loud gulder, she alerted her sister, Danu, who stood stiffly at the prow of a second trireme. *Is she ready for this? Has she recovered sufficiently from the wound?* Ever since her almost mortal injury, Danu, whose nature tended towards quietness and introspection, had become more withdrawn. Brighid smirked. *She could also be a stubborn bitseach.*

A pleasant throbbing in her chest drew Brighid from her musings. Even when apart, twins instinctively know what the other feels. Brighid and Danu were different. They were linked forever, in life and possibly death, by the mystical *feirdhriseacha*—the dog roses—imprinted on their cleavages. Yet only the Sidhe, Mongfhionn, knew the full extent of the roses' power, and she had kept that to herself. Thus, Brighid knew her sister was aware that all was not well at the hillfort. That was confirmed by Danu's shout. "Disembark your riders! Form up on the beach." The command was unnecessary. Brighid was already barking orders to sailors and warriors.

Danu, marginally the eldest of the twins, smiled at her sister. *This will be good for her.* She visualised the black *feirdhris*—dog-rose—between her sister's breasts. The rose's colour seemed to mirror the dark presence that wrapped its talons around her sister's heart, and its pink tips became blood-red in battle. *She thought I was dead, and she left alone. Can I blame her for loving me so much?* Danu's jaw set. It was a remarkable semblance of her father, Conall. *We will defeat this darkness, Brighid.*

* * *

Breathless after scrambling up the steep dune, Aoife flopped down on a patch of stiff grass. "Ouch!" she exclaimed as a green spike stabbed her arse. Eyes, the colour of lapis, grew wider and wider as she watched three ships glide into the cove. She had never seen boats this big. They dwarfed the *currach* used by her da and older brothers for fishing.

Black sails tumbled to the decks as the triremes cut through the final stretch of calm water and came to a halt alongside the wooden jetty. Aoife watched as one of the females, who looked quite young, pointed to the sandy coastline. She heard shouts of, "Disembark! Beach and secure the ships. Pytheas will not be amused if we let his precious children drown." *Who was Pytheas? And what a strange name.*

The senior helmsman, his face dark mahogany and the texture of boiled leather from a lifetime in the climate of the Great Sea, cracked a rare smile at Danu's concern. Triremes were very efficient and powerful, if costly, vessels. The woods used in their building became waterlogged if left in the sea overlong.

Danu watched as, with practised efficiency, one hundred fully armoured men and women rested oars, grabbed weapons and shields, and jumped from the second ship into the shallows. Many swore as the cold water quickly soaked through plaid *triubhas* and soft boots.

Aoife giggled at their complaints. She did not know of the warm waters of the Great Sea or that the air, even in midsummer, was filled with balmy breezes or that the skies were blue and cloudless. The warriors splashed forward, coming to a halt on the packed, damp sand. Iron-rimmed oak *sciatha* painted red and emblazoned with a swooping black raven clashed as the shield-wall formed. Javelins at the ready, they awaited orders.

The second trireme docked but only as long as it took another hundred men and women to disembark. These were the mounted warriors and chariot teams. Their horses, two for each rider and four for each chariot, were in the third ship. Space was limited on the vessels. Hence the need for a third to carry mounts, stores, and equipment. Emptied of its warriors, the second ship slipped back into the cove's waters to allow the final trireme to moor at the jetty.

Entranced, Aoife watched as teams of men and women carried the *crets*, wheels, and fittings of five chariots down the gangway. Once on firm sand, they began their assembly under the glare of the chariot group's white-haired commander. Next, clip-clopping down wooden ramps that flexed unnervingly with each step taken, came the horses.

Aoife gasped, thrilled at the sight of so many beautiful horses, and instantly wished she could ride one. She clapped and shouted enthusiastically when the midsummer sea churned white as the mounts grasped that they were no longer captive and could stretch cramped muscles. Yet the beasts sensed that all was not as it should be and put up little resistance when their riders guided them into two ranks alongside the shield-wall.

✳✳✳

The princesses' *caomhnóirí*—personal guard—had been chosen by their da and ma, Conall and Mórrígan. The protectors, two hundred battle-hardened veterans and five chariot teams, were a microcosm of Clann Ui Flaithimh's army. Both the foot and mounted warriors were as expert with slings and bows as with axes, maces, spears, and swords. They were commanded by the wily Flann, a tall, hard-muscled veteran of many campaigns.

Íar Mac Dedad, the clann's best horseman and breeder, had selected the horses. Íar's ancestral home of Curraghatoor was a day's ride north of Ráth Na Conall. Danu looked forward to visiting the fort and had messages to deliver on Íar's behalf. The charioteers and drivers had been picked by Gràinne Ni Fearghal, the fearsome *Cinn Péinteáilte*—Painted Ones—queen from Northern Albu. However, unlike the cavalry mounts, the chariots' horses were bred from the smaller, hardier horses of north-western Albu.

"I think we are discovered, sister. Perhaps we are already in danger?" Startled, Danu followed the line of Brighid's pointed finger. A wide grin quickly replaced concern. Caught by Brighid's sharp ears, Aoife's shriek of delight and clapping had revealed her position.

Caught between fleeing or standing her ground, the child stood, uncertain. *What would my da do?* "The Hag!" muttered Aoife. The Goddess smiled.

Danu called the chariots' leader, Báine, to her. "I have an important mission for you." The charioteer cocked an eye and then grinned at her orders. "Make sure the child gets home safely."

⁕⁕⁕

As a rule, each chariot team consisted of a driver and a warrior. Traditionally, the cret's colour and design reflected the warrior's personality. Aoife watched the gaily coloured vehicle, banners flapping in the breeze, effortlessly climb the dune to the grassy crest of the shoreline. Then her eyes widened as the *carbad* swept around in a wide arc and headed in her direction. She considered running, but at the speed the chariot was travelling, that was a foolish notion. Once again, she wondered what her da would do and exclaimed, "Shite!"

Báine's blue eyes looked down at the beautiful child dressed in a worn green *léine*. Aoife's gaze twinkled with adventure, mischief, and a touch of defiance. *The child has a bold streak in her.* "May I escort you home? These are perilous times, child, and I'm sure your ma and da will not want you wandering around as sunset approaches."

"My name is Aoife, not child."

The chariot driver played with the horse team's reins and chuckled at Aoife's solemnity and chastising tone. Yet there was no hesitation as she grasped Báine's outstretched arm and, with a scream of delight, was lifted into the cret.

"Hold on to me tightly. This will be a bumpy ride."

The smile on Aoife's face and her shouts of happiness did not stop until the chariot drove into the farmstead's yard. And neither did Báine's.

⁕⁕⁕

"Is this foolishness, sister?" asked Danu. "We've never led warriors into battle. What hubris made us think we can put down a rebellion and free the people? What if they don't want to be freed? Will we force them to exchange one tyrant for another—us?"

Brighid looked at Danu with a mix of puzzlement and concern. "This is not the time to be having second thoughts. Our ma and da did not want us to take on this quest, but we prevailed and won the argument. And we were supported by wiser heads than us." Brighid looked at the force assembled. "Even if *you* have doubts, that can't be seen by our caomhnóirí or those in the ráth. They look to us for an example. We've overcome adversity before and will do it again."

"Do *you* have doubts, Brighid?"

Brighid turned her mount around to face Danu and, with a hint of exasperation in her voice, said, "No—but then I was never one for looking more than one sunset ahead. You're the thinker; I'm the blade. That is why we make a good team. The Goddess willing, you'll figure it out. Besides, we have our uncle, Beacán, to counsel us."

***

The ranks tramped northwest, and it being Ériu, were soon greeted by light rain showers. Fortunately, the land before them was one of gentle slopes, forests, and verdant farmland, and they made good progress. Soon, Ráth Na Conall, silhouetted against the Na Comaraigh mountains to its west, came into view. Brighid and Danu walked their horses ahead of the warband, although still within two paces of their shadows—the four burly veterans tasked as their shield-men. The twins slowed to a walk at the snorts of a second pair of horses cantering alongside.

"None of us know what we're walking into or whose side we should take. It would be prudent for Iasg and me to scout ahead," said Beacán Ó Cathasaigh. He looked in the direction of his slender companion, who signalled her agreement.

"Agreed, uncle. But, from the clamour, the ráth does appear to be under attack," replied Brighid. An impish smile lit on her lips. She pointed to the fort and added, "Technically, that is our property. So either we support the residents to repel the attackers or expel them as unwelcome squatters." Beacán sighed. The stubborn set of his nieces' jaws reminded him of their father. They had already made up their minds.

✳✳✳

Onchú Ó an Cháintigh, Rí of Carn Tigherna and the guardian of Ráth Na Conall, slammed a cracked shield into his foe's face. The raw strength behind the blow crushed the man's nose, prompting a gush of blood and snot. The thrust of a gore-encrusted spear into the man's gut quickly followed. Shouting curses at Onchú, the attacker fell from the rickety scaling ladder and onto the stakes populating the fort's perimeter ditch. In response, Onchú spat a glob of bloody phlegm that tracked the man's path.

"That one will not fight again. And if he has not been diligent in his sacrifices to the Goddess, he will have a long and painful death before the bean-sidhe accepts his spirit."

Alongside Onchú, Conchobhar Ó Deargáin—the taciturn commander of Ráth Na Conall's garrison, or at least of what remained of it—nodded in agreement. Attrition had reduced Conchobhar's command to less than a score of warriors still able to fight. Onchú's fighters, seconded from Carn Tigherna's garrison, had suffered similar losses. Both men, thankful that the besiegers had decided to give up the attack, placed blood-stained hands on the wooden fence and breathed harshly.

"Spineless bastards!" grunted Onchú. "They had the numbers to finish us off."

The skirmish, the fourth in as many sunsets, had been short and fierce, and the list of those unable to fight increased. From the laboured breathing around the walkway, the fort's defenders were spent. Whether they had the strength to fight on the following sunrise was in the hands of the Goddess. Yet the ráth stood… bloodied but defiant.

The inner wooden stockade had not been breached, although that seemed only a matter of time. Fire-hardened snouts of rams had cracked much of the outer stone walls, and large portions were little more than rubble, exposing the pine and oak wood fence behind.

Perversely, the debris helped bridge the perimeter ditches, making the battlements easier to attack. Many summers of neglect by the fort's civic leaders had contributed to the rampart's state of disrepair. Gold for upgrading defences could always be spent elsewhere.

"You have done all that is possible, Onchú. Leave. Return to your family in Carn Tigherna. Ráth Na Conall will fall and probably by the next sunset. We will take as many as we can with us, but there is no sense in giving Uallachán your head to decorate his doorpost."

Although reluctant to concede, Onchú saw no path forward. He groaned in despair and vehemently cursed the hand behind the mercenaries. Yet, in his heart, he knew Conchobhar was right. His death would be a sacrifice with no gain. Furthermore, his defence of Ráth Na Conall, although noble, had weakened Carn Tigherna. He needed to ready his home's defences for the inevitable reprisal. That he had not seen his hand-fast partner, Eithne, or his sons and daughters, in several cycles of the moon made him grimace. Onchú remembered Eithne's harsh words and accusations of neglect when they last met.

"Warriors approaching the south wall!" The cry of alarm abruptly cut short both men's contemplations.

"The Hag's hairy arse!" Onchú cursed as he ran to the seaward wall and peered in the direction of the coast. The well-ordered ranks of warriors, cavalry, and chariots moving steadily towards the fort sent a chill up his spine. "The bastard has hired more mercenaries!" he snarled. Ráth Na Conall's defenders were in no shape to face another battle against fresh warriors. Onchú looked to the sky in hope, but the sunset was still far off. With resignation, he turned to Conchobhar. "Prepare to defend the southern wall."

✳✳✳

Danu called the force to a stop one hundred paces from the ramparts. "Cúscraid would certainly disapprove of the defences," said Brighid. Yet she was unaware that the clann's famed Master of Defence had overseen their construction—albeit a score summers past. She tapped her sister's arm and pointed to two figures at the centre of the defenders.

"We should unfurl the banners." Then, tongue firmly in cheek, she added, "Let's speak with our subjects."

The young women, both on the cusp of eighteen summers, guided their mounts forward, stopping twenty paces downhill of the crumbling defences. In a moment of anxiety, Brighid touched her sister's arm. "At this distance, we're dead if they have throwing spears or bows."

Danu snorted. "Advice is only useful if it is timely, sister."

"Bitseach!" Ignoring Brighid's emerald glare, Danu breathed deeply to settle her rising anxiety and then exhaled slowly.

Beacán shook his head. The twins' youth made them too arrogant and impetuous by far, and he foresaw many arguments in the near future. Yet the blood of Conall and Mórrígan flowed through their veins. At their age, Conall and Mórrígan had fought the might of the Connachta to a standstill before escaping through the Black Pig's Dyke.

A small hand on his forearm brought a smile to Beacán's face, and he turned to face Iasg. "Trust them. They will do fine." Beacán's musing came to a halt as Danu called out.

"I am Danu Ni Conall, and this is my sister, Brighid. We are the daughters of Conall Mac Gabhann, Rí Ruirech of Clann Ui Flaithimh, Hand of the Goddess, Rí of Ráth Na Conall, and Conqueror of Rome. Our mother is Mórrígan, queen of Clann Ui Flaithimh, also known as *An Fiagaí Dorcha*—the Dark Huntress."

As if signifying the Goddess's approval, a brisk wind lifted the gold and red banners of tribe and king, making them flap and crack like whips. Danu surveyed the grime- and gore-encrusted faces of the fort's defenders and the broken walls stained with blood. She turned on the thick *dillat* that covered her blue roan's back and loins and signalled for the Ráth Na Conall envoy to come forward.

"Your envoy was eloquent and persuasive in describing your plight. Perhaps you would accept our assistance." Silence followed until Danu added, "We also bring provisions—beer, wine, and food." At that, a loud cheer rose from the stockade.

"Thank the Hag that we brought food and drink. They look so gaunt and may have been tempted to eat us," said Brighid, looking a little less anxious.

✳✳✳

A small hillfort with an enviable location, in peaceful times Ráth Na Conall's garrison totalled fifty warriors. Most were the third and fourth sons and daughters of farmers. A lack of space had forced the fort's founding community of artisans and trade workshops to vacate the inner courtyard long before the current troubles. Many chose to set up their enterprises against and around the ráth's walls, leaving the fort to the garrison, their families, and the trades needed for war—the armourers, blacksmiths, and fletchers.

The business structures, constructed mainly of wood, were the first to be burned to the ground by Uallachán's forces. And the artisans and workers were the first to flee or die. The charred ruins of small farmholdings in the fields around Ráth Na Conall testified to a similar fate. Fire had also consumed much of the stronghold's barracks and accommodations. Thus, the twins' caomhnóirí set up camp in the forests south of the fort.

To Danu, the state of disrepair of the building, affectionately known as the Great Hall, reflected that of the fort. Although not entirely from the stone-lined firepits that blazed down the room's central aisle, the smell of woodsmoke hung in the air.

She dipped her head and smiled at Onchú. Seated at the end of a long oak table, Onchú tugged at a scruffy beard and made little effort to disguise his scrutiny of the twins. Since their arrival, a constant procession of artisans, tradespeople, and the fort's defenders had come to pay their respects and pledge their loyalty. Only one civic leader, Neasán, remained within the ráth's environs. He seemed troubled rather than delighted by the princesses' arrival.

According to Onchú, the fort's residents and families from the surrounding farmstead, excepting the warriors and armourers, had fled north to the dense forests or east along the coast.

The civilians' flight was sensible and unsurprising. They rightfully feared that Uallachán Ó Dubhghaill, Rí of Caher Conri, and his brother, Nuadha, would inevitably breach the defences and slaughter everyone. Onchú explained that death would be preferable to the likely depravities that Uallachán would visit on any survivors, especially the younger men and women.

As Onchú observed them, Brighid's and Danu's demeanours spoke of assurance and sympathy. Both were wise enough to make no commitments save those that pleased but were of little consequence. Both were similar physically, although Brighid had a slighter build. Like their da and ma, both were of above-average height. They had the deep emerald eyes of their mother and the auburn hair of their father. Compared to the local people's milk-white skin colour, the twins' skin had a soft golden tone. *They'll soon lose that colour here.* Onchú chuckled, shaking his head at the princesses' inquiring glances.

In fact, and as far as Onchú could tell, apart from their physiques, the only discernible difference between the sisters was the highlights in their long tresses. Threads of silver-blue for Danu and golden blonde for Brighid. Onchú saw pain in Danu's eyes and something sinister in Brighid's. He shivered at the latter. Brighid brought to the surface long-buried memories of a young Mórrígan.

"They will be fine. Never doubt their courage or skills."

Beacán sat down beside Onchú. He indicated Danu. "She took an axe to the chest while fighting alongside me. She lives only by the Goddess's hand and the Sidhe, Mongfhionn's healing powers." Onchú shivered. He well remembered the Sidhe and the terrible power she wielded. "Both fought with honour and bravery alongside their ma and da and the cream of Clann Uí Flaithimh's fighters when Gaiscedlach assassins came to murder the tribe's nobles and children. Many of the tribe's youth owe them their lives."

With a nod in Brighid's direction, Beacán continued, "Brighid is a fierce and passionate, if somewhat impetuous, young woman. Like her ma, she is a deep well. In a fight, you could do no better than having her beside you, and she was the one who pulled the axe blade from Danu's chest. Being here will be good… for both of them."

Beacán reached for another horn of beer, and his face broke into a wide grin. "Of one thing, I am sure. The Hag help any who are foolish enough to challenge either of them. They have been trained by the best of Clann Ui Flaithimh, and they and their tutors have the scars to prove it."

Onchú wanted desperately to believe Beacán and share his confidence in the twins, but his manner held doubt. "They have never led, Beacán, and that's what the people will expect." Beacán shrugged, although the flush on his cheeks signalled irritation.

"Worst case, you have one hundred fresh, well-armoured warriors and over one hundred riders and chariots."

"That's true, and for that, I, and everyone in the garrison, are very grateful."

Feeling the eyes of Brighid and Danu on him, Onchú looked up and forced his lips into a smile. If their eyes had been steel-blue, it could have been Conall holding his gaze. They were evaluating him as much as he was them. Beer raised, he nodded to them.

"How fare my old friends? I assume your ma and da are well." Danu nodded. "What about Cúscraid, Íar, and that rogue, Fearghal?" The sadness that appeared in both girls' eyes at the mention of Fearghal negated an explanation.

"Fearghal died a hero at the Battle of Rome," said Danu quietly.

"I'm very sorry," replied Onchú. "He will be missed by many."

"Were our family's dead treated with respect?" asked Danu, hoping to divert the topic to something less painful.

Onchú's eyes glowed in approval of Danu's words. "The dead of your family and the others of the community slaughtered by Eochaidh Ruad and the Roman, Cassius Fabius, were burned until only ashes remained. Not far from this ráth, there is a mound and a copse of oak trees. That marks their final resting place. In the morning, after you have broken your fast, I will take you so that you can pay your respects."

Danu dipped her head and then whispered in Brighid's ear. "When we have concluded our meal, and before we retire, we wish to walk the defences. It will signify our commitment to those who remain in Ráth Na Conall." Then she turned to Beacán and Iasg. "I know we have just arrived, but your talents are more useful to us outside the ráth. Please determine the enemy's strength."

Brighid whispered in her sister's ear, and both smiled unnervingly. "My sister also suggests that you sow some seeds of fear in their camp." Danu sighed. "If only we had the Sidhe with us… or even our ma." Then, as if something had jolted her thoughts, she looked at Conchobhar. "Do we have wolfhounds? Are they well-trained?" He nodded to both questions. "Good. Send half of the hounds out tonight. I want our 'friends' to have a fitful sleep—if any."

Danu turned back to Beacán. "Uncle, I suggest Iasg and you make friends with the hounds before you depart. There is likely little salve remaining in the fort for bites." Those around the table chuckled, appreciating Danu's effort to introduce some levity.

"Finally, light all the torches and braziers. I want Ráth Na Conall lit up as if it were the festival of Bealtaine. Uallachán needs to learn that times have changed—and not in his favour."

∗∗∗

The crews of the triremes sat around blazing driftwood fires, eating, drinking, and telling tall tales of amazing adventures, journeys to foreign lands, and great sea monsters. As Danu slipped from her horse and approached, the senior helmsman and commander of the small fleet, a Greek named Thrasius, stood and walked to meet her.

"I have a request," said Danu. The sailor smiled and dipped his head. His orders from Pytheas were clear—obey all reasonable petitions.

"I would like two ships to return to Massalia at first light. Please prevail on Pytheas to fill the triremes with weapons and armour—enough for one hundred warriors. The garrison in the ráth is pitifully equipped," said Danu. "I am aware that there is always a contingent of Clann Uí Flaithimh's warriors and equipment in the city. In addition, the fort of Ráth Cavares is a short journey along the Rodonos River. So our request should not be too demanding."

As if uncertain of her subsequent request, Danu hesitated. "Can a message be delivered to Gaius Aurelius at Lugudunon?" Thrasius tilted his head to one side, waiting for Danu's request. "My sister and I would be delighted if a team of ballista instructors and the iron fittings for ballistae could accompany you on the return journey."

The helmsman looked with concern at Danu. "Is it that bad in the fort?"

"Yes, and it will get worse." Danu's lips pursed, and she gripped the sailor's forearm. "Please ask Pytheas to relay a message to our da and ma. Inform them we have arrived safely… and all is well." At the raised eyebrow from the helmsman, Danu shrugged. "They have enough worries and burdens without us adding to them."

***

A shadow detached from the wall and glided towards Danu as she approached Ráth Na Conall's rear gateway.

"Is all well, sister?"

"The ships will leave at first light."

"How long?"

"Two cycles of the moon. Maybe three, depending on the weather. We should plan on staying alive for the longer period without any additional support." Danu hesitated. "I think it would be best that those in the ráth did not know this. There's no sense in raising or dashing hopes."

Brighid inhaled deeply. "Who doesn't like a challenge?"

CHAPTER 2

Concealed by the creeping gloom of dusk, Beacán pointed to the enemy's camp and reluctantly conceded that the encampment was well-situated. The expression on his face told Iasg that something other than the site's location bothered Beacán, and she mouthed, "What?" He wanted to move closer and touch her, but instead, his lips parted, and he shook his head. They had a job to do. "It's nothing." Neither he nor Iasg believed the words.

The encampment lay in a clearing between the lush, entangled wildwood and the beginning of the ancient forest with its widely spaced tall pines and gnarled oaks. The sun still reigned in the narrow ribbon of land, bordering the woods and beyond the sunlight-smothering canopy of the trees. Bursts of wildflowers broke the green carpet, and a profusion of mint, pine, and rose scents refreshed the air, enhancing an already soothing vista.

Only the smells of woodsmoke, roasted flesh, and stale beer struck discordant notes. As the flames of many campfires licked at its edges and spat glowing embers into its depths, a sensitive soul could detect the nervous trembling of the forest. None of the four hundred who sat around the fires, eating, drinking, and sharpening weapons, cared about the woods. To them, the trees were no more than firewood. They were mercenaries with few morals and fewer scruples. Their sole interest was the gold promised to them and, once paid, they would move on to another employer.

The band's leader glanced around the camp. A tall, brawny, and single-minded veteran, his presence radiated intimidation. A half-cycle of the moon ago, the band had entered the campaign against Ráth Na Conall. There were five hundred warriors at that time, and all had been in good health and spirits. As they sat around the fires, he knew many of the warband questioned his ability to deliver on the agreed contract. Given the reputation of their employer, their anxiety was understandable.

As dusk fell, the Leader sat alone, chewing on roasted rabbit flesh. Grease made his large hands slippery, and he wiped them on his triubhas. Lost among many previous stains, the new blemishes made little difference. A quick survey of his band confirmed that a quarter of those remaining had injuries. Most were minor, but a tithe would hear the cry of the bean-sidhe soon. Yet by his estimation, supported by the tales of those who had surmounted the stockade before being thrown back, Ráth Na Conall had less than two-score defenders. Furthermore, the fort's garrison and defences had been degraded substantially.

From past battles, the Leader knew that the besieged always had the advantage. Still, surely, he had enough warriors to take the ráth in one final assault. He called his three burly lieutenants to his side. "Double the guards. Ensure the camp lookouts stay awake. I don't expect trouble, but why take chances?"

***

It was an assassin's night. The moon skulked behind slow-moving clouds while the stars shone elsewhere. The camp's night of misery began with the barking of wolfhounds. On their hind legs, the massive beasts stood taller than a man and weighed more. Coats of short, wiry hair in muted tones of grey and brown made the dogs practically invisible. Jaws that could snap a man's thighbone and teeth to rip out his throat worked in harmony with a muscled torso and legs that propelled the hounds at speeds well beyond other beasts and humans.

The snuffling and low growling of the hounds woke the Leader, and he sat up, momentarily confused. A shriek shattered the stillness of the night. The man's cry brought unwelcome clarity, and sleep fled everyone. The victim had chosen his sleeping place too far from the fires. Dragged, screaming, into the wildwood by the dogs, he would never be seen again—at least not in one piece.

"War dogs!" roared the Leader, and the refrain was swiftly taken up. "Stay close to the fires. Remain alert." The mercenaries were not the usual mob of thugs and brigands held together by the promise of gold. They were a well-drilled cohort of warriors. Still, the endless howling and shadows, real or imagined, moving through the wildwood shredded the fabric of their sleep and gnawed at their minds. Around the camp, the air rang with the cries of the bitten and the cries of those dragged beyond rescue.

At a soft whistle from the wolfhounds' master, and with snouts masked in blood, the dogs drifted away from the camp and bounded in the direction of Ráth Na Conall.

***

Beacán scowled and ran his fingers repeatedly through his shoulder-length red hair. His trade relied on his ability to take in and interpret small signs, and yet something eluded him, refusing to come under his control. A hand on his arm brought him back to the current task, and he looked upon Iasg.

With his face covered in dirt and charcoal, Beacán appeared no more than a set of white teeth floating a man's height above the ground. Iasg resisted the urge to chuckle and instead checked the knives sheathed in two broad leather belts that formed a harness across her chest. *It will be a pity to lose my blades. I hope there's a good blacksmith in the fort.*

Finally, she examined the two throwing axes tucked into her belt and the handful of daggers sheathed in her boots. Since their need was for speed, neither she nor Beacán was constrained by armour. Iasg smiled at Beacán and whispered, "I'll take the right flank." Before he could respond, the gloom had swallowed her.

Beacán did not carry as many weapons as his partner. Iasg preferred combat at the distance of a knife or axe throw. Beacán's skill was that of a spectre, and, most times, this required being close enough to touch the target. His tactics were surgical, and his victims rarely saw his face. Only the sting of a razor-sharp blade drawn across a vulnerable neck or piercing a vital organ announced Beacán's presence.

Of late, it increasingly troubled Beacán's spirit that he was exceptionally talented at his profession—murder. Few doubted that he was the best assassin in the clann and possibly in Albu, Ériu, and Gaul. Only Iasg kept him from being overwhelmed by its inevitable darkness.

That worried Beacán. Before asking Iasg to be his hand-fast partner, he had been a solitary soul. Yes, he had family and friends, but few understood the loneliness and torments of his profession. Only Iasg was willing to talk openly and honestly about it. That said, Beacán was not overly comfortable with the path that had taken Iasg from a young girl in a Northern Albu fishing village to the companion of an assassin. Was he dragging her to the Otherworld with him?

In the deep night, the light cast by the campfires was a gift to Iasg. Men and women silhouetted against the flames shrieked and fell, struck down by Iasg's knives. She carried ten in the crossed belts, and ten targets dropped to the dirt. Iasg rarely threw her axes, although, as with her knives, her accuracy with them had few rivals—not even Beacán. They were for when she faced an enemy and had no room to throw. The size of the axes suited her tiny hands. With her stock of blades expended, Iasg gripped the hand-axes and retreated silently from the enemy camp.

Iasg's diversion provided Beacán with the time and room to manoeuvre. He smiled in the darkness and then shook his head and grunted. He had work to do before the sun rose above the horizon.

✳✳✳

Long fingers, with scarred knuckles, used to gripping axe and spear, scratched a beard in desperate need of trimming. His long hair had been copper-gold in his youth. Now steel threaded the braided tresses. Some said this gave him gravitas but that he would gladly trade for fewer years and fewer aches in the morning. As had been his habit for many summers, Conchobhar stood on the parapet, watching the sun rise above the horizon. He enjoyed seeing the sky cast off its purple and grey tones and embrace pink and orange flushes.

The creak of wood piqued his interest, and he turned. Hazel eyes flecked with green tracked the princesses as they climbed the rickety ladder to the narrow walkway. *They're so young. How can they lead warriors and some with more summers of fighting than they have lived?* Yet both were impressively armed and armoured.

A tightly buckled cuirass protected each princess's upper body. The breastplates, made from layers of boiled leather bonded together, were engraved with ornate swirling designs and painted. Moonlight-blue for Danu and red-gold for Brighid. The armour, moulded to emphasise the young women's figures, was more dramatic in Danu's case. Under the cuirasses, sleeveless blouses of chainmail rested on their hips. Each lay on a light chemise of soft hide. *They carry the weight well.*

Plaid triubhas—cerulean blue for Danu and red-gold for Brighid— were tucked into calf-high leather boots laced along the calf with leather thongs. Patches of chainmail were stitched onto the pants to protect their thighs. Danu and Brighid held plain conical helmets, each with an attached mail neck guard. The coverings' only embellishments were short horsehair plumes. These were matched to the colours of their breastplates and triubhas and sprang from the helmets' acorn-shaped nubs.

Conchobhar admired the broad, ornately engraved leather belts resting on slender hips. Each was brought together with a large gold and silver clasp. The veteran grunted. Along with the bands of copper, gold, and silver on the girls' upper arms and braided gold torcs, each twin was worth several summers' labour. He scowled. Why make yourself a target and a prized piece of plunder in battle? Then he muttered, "Stop this nonsense." Which warrior did not enter combat carrying his wealth?

A pair of short-shafted axes, each with wickedly sharp double blades and vicious spikes that protruded from each end of the haft, hung from leather loops on the belts. Each carried a sheathed, short, double-edged sword similar to a Greek xiphos and several knives to complement the axes. Conchobhar's eyes drifted downwards and applauded what he saw. The strips of sheepskin wrapped around each shin held more daggers. *I hope they fight as impressively as they look.*

Yet, to Conchobhar, perhaps the most disturbing feature of the twins' armour was something he had not noticed in the gloom and flickering rushlights of the Great Hall. In the dawn sun, the swirling indigo-blue designs on their faces and arms appeared in constant motion. Every indication pointed to the curling shapes being permanent, not painted, and not constrained to visible flesh. They were so striking that once seen, they would never be forgotten.

"Shite!" mumbled Conchobhar. He was well-acquainted with the legend of An Fiagaí Dorcha. Did her daughters follow in Mórrígan's footsteps? In Ráth Na Conall's current predicament, would that be good or bad?

Conchobhar's train of thought was disturbed by the heavy slap of boots on the walkway. This time, Onchú climbed the ladder and stepped onto the wooden parapet. Four burly, heavily armed giants followed him but ignored both men. They walked up to the twins, bowed, and handed over two small round shields. Each was made of oak, covered in hide, and had a boss and rim of iron. Each was painted with a swooping black raven on a field of blue for Danu and red-gold for Brighid. When the *sciatha* were handed over, the men set two bow staves, several quivers of arrows for each bow, and eight javelins against the stockade. Then, with immense pride, they lowered their heads briefly and, spear in hand, took up positions five paces away.

"Shite! The six of them are better armed than the rest of the fort put together," exclaimed Conchobhar in a voice that held tones of awe and envy. Conchobhar ruefully examined Onchú and his torn clothes and battered armour. "The armour and weaponry of Conall's army have advanced significantly since he was last here."

⋆⋆⋆

Danu and Brighid looked the two veterans up and down with the same scrutiny a *ceannairí céad* gave new recruits. Under the stare of deep green eyes, both men found it a challenge not to flinch. Despite the condition of the tattered clothing and armour, Danu noted that both men's weapons were well maintained.

Sensing Onchú's embarrassment, Danu remarked, "We brought additional armour. Yours has served you well, but I doubt it provides much protection." Turning to face Conchobhar, she said, "Perhaps you would assign some men to retrieve the supplies from the ship in the harbour."

Conchobhar nodded before sighing deeply and exchanging a knowing glance with Onchú. Yet Onchú imperceptibly shook his head, and his lips pursed in disagreement. The veteran turned to the twins and, with a bow, said, "I relinquish my command. The fort and its garrison are yours." With another dip of the head, he stepped back a pace.

"Why? Are you not competent at your job?" Brighid peered at the veteran more closely. "Perhaps you are injured. Should we fetch a healer, sister? Are there any in the fort?" Brighid's rejoinder startled the warrior, and Conchobhar appeared lost for words. Anger flushed his face. His demeanour did not improve at Onchú's obvious amusement.

"I have commanded this fort for a score of summers and held it for two against overwhelming numbers. Were I a gambling man, I would not have wagered on the ráth lasting a cycle of the moon against Uallachán's forces. So yes, I am good at my job. *Bloody good.*" Feeling as if he should also mention the bravery of others, he added, "As are Onchú and those warriors who remain alive. The dead's sacrifice speaks for itself."

Danu nodded approvingly. *He still has fire.* Then she looked at Onchú and smirked. "He reminds me of Grandpa Fearghal. Always cranky in the early morning." Then she looked at Brighid. "I see no reason to replace our Battle and Garrison Commander. Do you, sister?"

At Brighid's deliberate shake of the head, Danu turned to Conchobhar. "My apologies, but no, you do not have our permission to resign. What made you conclude we would replace a man who has fought and served so well? My sister and I will need all the help we can get. Onchú has his responsibilities at Carn Tigherna. We need a veteran here in Ráth Na Conall because grim times are certainly ahead."

For the first time, Conchobhar's craggy face split into a smile. Then, he turned to Onchú and said, "Was their da as sarcastic?"

Onchú nodded and, looking at the twins, added, "And their ma could be a frightening bitseach."

***

After a circuit of the fort's defences, Danu turned to Conchobhar and Onchú. "The ráth's location on this mound endows it with long sight-lines, and it is protected to the west by the Na Comaraigh mountains. However, in its advanced state of disrepair, a half-competent warband chieftain could besiege and seize the fort. Why have they not?" Not knowing if they had just been insulted, Conchobhar and Onchú looked at each other uneasily.

"Danu favours our da," said Brighid. "She is an excellent *fidchell* player and thinks about strategies and tactics. I'm more impetuous. Just point me at the fight and who needs killing." Brighid swept her arm across the fort and the landscape. "My sister and I do not question your courage or fighting skills, but even I can see that Uallachán is playing with Ráth Na Conall as a feral cat would with a mouse. Thus, there is more to Uallachán's design than is currently evident."

Brighid acknowledged the perturbed looks on Onchú's and Conchobhar's faces and added, "We assign no blame to either of you. You have fought hard and desperately for a long time with one goal—survival. In that, you have been successful, although at a high cost. Now is the time to lift your eyes and discern the bigger picture."

Danu nodded in agreement. "We need to kick the rat's nest and see what transpires and that may not be difficult. Once Uallachán knows we are in Ráth Na Conall, he will have real targets for his anger—not just crumbling walls and exhausted warriors." Danu looked at Conchobhar. "You and I will oversee the repair of the ráth's defences. Brighid will take command of offensive strategies and tactics. Like our ma, Brighid is quite adept at inspiring terror. Her task will be to keep our enemies distracted while Ráth Na Conall once again becomes a stronghold."

Danu faced Onchú. "Concerning the defences, I have something in mind, but I will need labour—and the sooner, the better. We should speak with Neasán and prevail on him to entreat those who fled their farms and workshops to return. Inform those who come back that we will help them rebuild the workshops and farms pillaged by Uallachán." Onchú dipped his head.

"One more item, Onchú. We need strong allies and friends. You have been a loyal friend to Ráth Na Conall, but perhaps it is time you returned to Carn Tigherna. Things can unravel quickly in the prolonged absence of a king. Apart from anything else, an estranged family will only breed discontent and distract from what needs to be done. I would rather have a strong king on my flank than one preoccupied with internal troubles."

"Mmmm…" The group turned to face Brighid, who appeared to be having a private struggle. Finally, she sighed and said, "Where are the druids? It's bad enough that we do not have the protection of a representative of the Aes Sidhe. Surely we can attract some spiritual support and preferably a few with healing skills."

As Conchobhar and Onchú walked away, Brighid turned to face Danu. "I have no issues with your orders, whether to Thrasius or Conchobhar and Onchú. But *we* should have discussed this before their issuance. We're a team, and you are only a fraction older than me." The flush on Danu's cheeks was not mitigated by Brighid's "all is well" embrace before she strode away.

✻✻✻

The leader of the mercenaries fumed but resisted the urge to rage at his band. He had lost a dozen warriors to the blades of an assassin. Some claimed it was a faerie who had delivered death. Although close to the truth, their reward was to have their jaws bruised by the Leader's fists. Yet his ire was aimed not at the dead but the camp's missing sentries. Had the cowards deserted? If the hounds had carried the guards off, would he not have heard their screams?

"After we've broken our fast, we'll attack Ráth Na Conall. Today the fort will fall, and its treasures will be ours. The men and women will be dead or enslaved." It was a confident delivery, but the sleep-deprived band's response was sullen and muted. Yet what else could be done? They still far outnumbered the ráth's garrison.

CHAPTER 3

Brighid watched Beacán and Iasg jog up the long dirt track to the fort's gateway. Their clothes were stained red, which, given her fighting style, was unusual for Iasg. However, from their freedom of movement, neither appeared injured, which was a relief. Separated from the counsel of the Sidhe, Mongfhionn, and her ma, Brighid felt that only Beacán understood her inner turmoil.

The pink-tipped black feirdhris imprinted on her chest throbbed sympathetically with her simple trust in Beacán as her mentor and deliverer. Brighid shivered, knowing that there was another leaf to that *seamair óg*—her executioner. She turned to face Danu, who, sensing Brighid's trepidation, offered an understanding smile and nod but held back from physical contact. Danu had been hurt by Brighid's assertion of not involving her in decisions.

The twins had always had a sense of each other's presence from birth. Still, since Danu's near-death experience in the forested foothills of the Alpes, a mystical element had been born. Brighid felt the throb of her sister's dog-rose and the response from her blossom. Unlike Brighid's petals, Danu's flushed pink with black tips. If forced together, only the Goddess knew which feirdhris would dominate.

"Our uncle and Iasg have returned. What next, sister?" asked Brighid.

***

Four sat around a small wooden table and broke their fast with a meal of hot oatmeal, fruit, cheese, and milk chilled in a nearby spring. Danu spoke first. "My sister and I have taken stock of our situation." She looked at Conchobhar and Onchú. "The garrison of Ráth Na Conall is brave and loyal. They are, however, in no condition to fight—not today and possibly not for many sunsets. Therefore, their role will be to guard the southern wall. If our plan works, they will not have to join the upcoming battle." Danu nodded to Brighid.

"Beacán and Iasg estimate the force we face is about four hundred strong and well organised. From what I gather, they had little sleep, and my uncle tells me that he left a surprise for them. Although, being insufferable, he did not expand on what that might be." Brighid paused, took a long gulp of milk, dragged the back of her hand across her chin to remove several smears of cream, and then licked the back of her hand.

"My uncle thinks that the force will break camp and attack once they have satisfied their bellies and fortified their courage with strong beer. We will encourage the enemy to assume the garrison remains few in number, in poor condition, and exhausted. Danu's shields will remain out of sight on the walkway. I will position my chariots and riders on the southern side of the hill."

"Will the sailors fight?" asked Onchú.

Danu shook her head. "Only one ship remains and the crew is already at half-strength. The shield-warriors and riders doubled as oarsmen for the journey from Massalia. I cannot risk their number decreasing more." At Onchú and Conchobhar's furrowed brows, Danu quickly changed the topic. "Brighid." Brighid peered at her twin with one eyebrow raised. "I want prisoners. Uallachán needs his invincibility challenged and a message delivered."

Brighid sensed Danu's feirdhris darken and shivered. *Perhaps the taint of darkness is not constrained to me.* To Conchobhar and Onchú, Danu's mien was unnerving, and her tone of voice sent chills up their spines.

That it also brought a perturbed pursing of Brighid's lips surprised both men. Danu took a gulp from her bowl of milk, purring at its rich creaminess.

"Thank the Goddess, we still have a few milking cows."

The levity was welcomed. Changing the topic with seamless ease, Danu looked at Onchú. "Assuming all goes to plan, I suggest that, after the battle, you return to Carn Tigherna. My sister and I would like to visit your home and meet your hand-fast partner, Eithne, and your sons and daughters, but that may be two or three cycles of the moon away."

"What of Curraghatoor? And Clárach? What of the hillforts to the north and east? Surely not all of southern Ériu's kings cower before Uallachán." Brighid's interjection and the topic surprised all at the table. "Íar Mac Dedad remains at my father's side, but he is still Rí of Curraghatoor. My da told me that Íar's father was a good friend and ally. Yet you avoid mentioning that hillfort. Can we count on the support of Curraghatoor? Likewise, the Rí of Clárach and his allied nobles came to our da's aid in the fight against Eochaidh Ruad."

The flush of anger on Onchú's face told a story that needed few words. "Curraghatoor is a bastion much stronger than either Carn Tigherna or Ráth Na Conall and likely Clárach. Apart from a garrison of two hundred, most of its army is mounted. However, I believe they also have a handful of chariots. When Íar's father lived, he was a strong defender of Ráth Na Conall and its people. After his death, Íar's two half-brothers took command of the fort, its garrison, and its five hundred mounted warriors."

Onchú paused to dampen down the bile that rose in his throat. "The brothers have no love for Ráth Na Conall. They remain angry that neither were made rí and, even in his absence, the title, sword, and ring were given to Íar." Onchú scowled. "It was a slap in the face from beyond the veil. Thus, few were surprised when, to spite Íar and besmirch their father's memory, the bastards allied with Uallachán."

Conchobhar cut in, if only to let Onchú simmer down. "Clárach, and the cluster of nobles who support it, have always kept to themselves. They fought beside Conall, out of self-preservation, not because the cause was just. The old rí passed beyond the veil several summers ago.

"He had three sons, and the eldest, Aodh, sits on Clárach's throne. I have no idea whose side Aodh and his aligned chieftains favour. There are rumours that the middle brother, Cúmhaí, covets the throne. The youngest brother, Glaisne, keeps his head down, so not much is known about him or his loyalties. As for the other ríthe to the north and east—who knows? There wasn't much socialising before Uallachán's rebellion, and there's even less now."

"It seems that Curraghatoor needs a lesson in loyalty. Once we have dealt with our immediate problem, we can consider our strategy for Curraghatoor and Clárach. Perhaps visits to Carn Tigherna, Clárach, and Curraghatoor will come sooner than anticipated. A strong Ráth Na Conall will attract the attention of others. Whether that will be in our favour or not is in the hands of the Goddess." Danu rose, signalling an end to the discussion, but halted at Brighid's raised eyebrow. "What?"

"Have sacrifices been made to the Goddess?" Brighid held Danu's gaze. "Our ma and da often had disagreements with the Goddess but always were faithful in their gifts—especially before battle and trials. We should continue that custom." Danu nodded approvingly at her sister, although she wondered at Brighid's sudden religious fervour.

A great golden eagle swooped and soared in the skies above Ráth Na Conall. The Goddess laughed. "They play the game well. These two have potential."

✶✶✶

Meán lae—midday—approached as the mercenaries' leader marshalled his band. Cheeks flushed by beer and a brisk northerly breeze, the group tramped through the wildwood. Some, unsteady on their feet, cursed as they tripped and stumbled into the tangle of brambles, nettles, and thistles. Woollen *triubhas*—trousers—gave little protection against barbs that penetrated thin cloth and tore flesh.

North of Ráth Na Conall, and until it crossed the Abhainn na Siúire river and merged with the forest, the land was mainly level. Ribbons of gentle *droimníní*, small mounds, and copses of oak gave it character. The exception was a long, chest-high ridge that followed the northern bank of the stream. Until Uallachán's raids, the plain had been fertile cropland or grazing land for cattle.

The distance between the woods and Ráth Na Conall was not huge. A fit man, rising at sunrise, could be in the fort well before meán lae. As they crossed the river, the band's leader stopped and gasped at the sight that greeted him. "*Na tuilithe*—the bastards!" he spat. Arrayed before them were the heads of his missing sentries. Each had been spiked on cut branches planted into the soft dirt. Hollow eyes stared accusingly at their former comrades. Always a succulent treat, the eyeballs had been plucked from their sockets by ravens. The same birds now took to the air, protesting loudly at the interruption of their feasting.

The effect was sobering. Until that moment, the sellswords had controlled the battlefield. No one had brought the fight to them. However, the Leader was canny and, seizing the chance to turn unease into an advantage, shouted, "Forward! Kill the bastards who slaughtered our comrades." His words were disingenuous. Few mercenaries cared about anyone other than themselves or anything other than plunder. However, confident of victory, they marched forward shouting for revenge.

Close enough to discern the faces of those who manned Ráth Na Conall's stockade, the Leader's curiosity was piqued at the new and unusual array of banners adorning the battlements. The emblems cracked like whips as they flapped in a brisk breeze. At fifty paces closer to the hillfort, it was possible to discern the swooping black ravens adorning the red flags. Yet the design brought no recognition. The apparent sparsity of warriors on the ramparts raised the Leader's confidence, and he shouted, "*Ionsaí*—attack!"

* * *

On the northern wall, Flann, the caomhnóirí's commander, a tall, hard-muscled veteran of many campaigns, stood and rubbed calloused palms on the rough wooden stockade. He cursed the gentle, heavily forested incline to Ráth Na Conall, which gave the enemy cover. However, at two hundred paces from the walls, the mercenaries were fully committed and within range of his warriors' bows.

"Now!" Flann bellowed.

One hundred warriors stepped forward, nocked arrows, and sent the first volley into the attackers. At a count of one shaft loosed for every six breaths, the quivers on the walkway were soon empty. For a short but furious time, the air filled with black-shafted missiles striking trees, shields, and, from the shrieks and curses of the enemy, flesh. Flann glanced at Danu, who grunted as she sent a final arrow to its target. "We didn't do very much damage, but they'll be more cautious, and we can use that." At his shout of "Javelins!" each of Flann's warriors hefted a throwing spear.

To his credit, the Leader recovered quickly from his shock and disbelief at the missile attack. Bows were used for hunting, not fighting. Still, and of more concern, where had the ráth's reinforcements come from? His band's injuries were slight, if only because of the trees. He felt fear rippling through the men and women, but his enforcers kept them going forward.

"To the forest edge. Use the trees for cover. We'll rest and attack in the gloom before dusk."

Danu turned to her commanders. "It seems that our adversary is not altogether stupid." Then she frowned. "I hope Báine and Brighid restrain their usual impetuosity. I'm not sure whose temper is the more brittle."

Conchobhar shrugged broad shoulders. "Whoever the mercenaries' leader is, he knows he has one chance to rush our walls and take the fort." The Battle Commander of Ráth Na Conall glanced up at the sky and observed the first grey clouds forming on the horizon. "My guess is that he'll attack before dusk or when the sky darkens enough to give him cover. It's what I would do." Conchobhar pointed to places where the fort's stone walls had crumbled and bridged the ditch. "That's where they'll target. We should each take one." He scratched at his whiskers before turning to his men. "Bring braziers, cauldrons, and torches to the ramparts."

It was *ardtráthnóna*—mid-afternoon—when the Leader judged the sky dark enough to support his attack. The rain had steadily increased from an annoying mizzle to a heavy shower. Wet clothes were an annoyance, but of more concern, the downfall made the ground slippery, challenging his band's ability to make a fast sprint to the walls. He looked up at the darkening grey expanse and flinched at the flashes of lightning that starkly illuminated the landscape.

Battle cries always start as enthusiastic shouts, taunts, and curses bellowed from warriors' throats. However, they quickly descend into an incoherent, amorphous growl as if the force had merged to become one great beast. Danu watched the mercenaries stumble and slip as they sprang from the forest cover—yet they kept going. She glanced to her side and smiled. Having no need of her protectors, Brighid had ordered them to Danu's side. Behind them, a score of men and women stood ready to defend her chosen stand.

"Javelins!"

Conchobhar's shout was taken up instantly by Danu, Flann, and Onchú. Danu's eyes misted over as another cry sounded out. "*Na Feirdhriseacha*—the Dog Roses!" Hefting one of the six spears set against the stockade, she threw the weapon as a man came into range and heard his cry. Volleys of spears were flung at the attackers until they gained the walls and were effectively out of sight.

"Empty the cauldrons!"

Many sighed in relief as the great smoke-blackened vessels were emptied over the stockade. Standing next to the simmering and smoking vessels filled with oil, water, and embers produced red-rimmed eyes and tears. Most were happy to suffer minor burns as they tipped the containers over. The shrieks of the mercenaries whose flesh burned, boiled, and sloughed off rose, together with the unpleasant stench of cooked meat.

Danu quelled her stomach, gripped her double-bladed half-axe, settled her shield on her arm, and steadied her stance. Amazed that anyone could overcome the defences, she felt brief admiration for the warrior whose head appeared before her. A flashback to another forest and skirmish made her chest tighten. She hesitated. The skull suddenly exploded in a gush of blood and bone.

"Kill them, or they'll kill you," growled her shield-man as he yanked his leaf-shaped spearhead free. His tone did not hide his disappointment and anger. Embarrassed, Danu bit her lip until it bled and set her jaw. She felt her feirdhris throb and overwhelm the painful memory. With a scream, she swung her axe at the next attacker's face and saw the woman's head cleaved from brow to chin. Hot gore splashed Danu's countenance, and she quickly dragged the back of her hand across her brow to clear her vision.

"Much better," came the voice of her protector.

Rickety scaling ladders, iron hooks on thick ropes and even the rams previously used to batter the hillfort were flung at the wall. Ráth Na Conall's stockade was little more than two men high, so many used comrades' shoulders in a desperate attempt to find purchase and surmount the barrier. Valiant as their efforts were when heads and chests appeared over the fence, they found only the shield-wall. The few who gained the walkway faced a red barrier as unmovable as the stockade. Blades slashed, blood flowed, and men and women screamed.

The Leader cursed Ráth Na Conall's new defenders. *Who are they and where did they come from?* His attack faced defeat, and if he waited much longer, his band would be degraded beyond recovery. Another assault would prove impossible, and the spectre of being executed rather than paid haunted him.

"Retreat!" he roared. "Assemble at the bottom of the hill."

On the ramparts, rivulets of blood and rain trickled down Danu's face and onto the walkway. To her shield-man, she said, "Blow the horn. It's Brighid's turn."

***

Three hundred mercenaries broke from the forested foothills and ran to a small mound nearby to regroup and consider their next move. The other hundred were either too injured to move or dead. Yet the Leader consoled himself that his number remained sufficient. Having taken the measure of his enemy, all he had to do was devise a new strategy. An unearthly scream to his right and the shrill blasts of hunting horns on his left made him reconsider his optimism.

To the west of Ráth Na Conall, the Na Comaraigh mountains ran parallel to the fort's stockade. While narrow, the valley between the hill-fort and the crag was wide enough for several chariots with war scythes to pass side by side. An unearthly scream from a white-haired bean-sidhe echoed off the fort's wall and the mountainside as Báine's chariots raced to the far side of the mound.

"I hope she stays safe," muttered Brighid.

The princess cared for Báine much more than she liked to admit. She turned on her dillat, grinned ghoulishly, and addressed her riders. "It's our turn. Danu has had her fun, and Báine's chariots' scythes should be far from our horses." Brighid slipped booted feet into the leather loops hanging from the broad girth belt and, using her knees, nudged her black mare into a walk. "Try not to kill everyone. Danu wants prisoners." The ripple of laughter was soon drowned by the battle cries of the warriors.

***

"Shite!"

His band of three hundred now seemed insufficient against the horses charging towards him and the chariots who had cut off his retreat. "Stand firm. They'll dismount to fight," he shouted. The Leader had every confidence in his command since tradition held that warriors always dismounted to give battle. One-on-one, his mercenaries were a match for anyone. His eyes widened when the riders pressed their horses to an even faster gallop instead of breaking their pace.

Brighid screamed an order and, without breaking their stride, a volley of javelins was hurled at the mercenaries. Each horse carried six throwing spears in sheaths bound to their flanks. The pace, however, did not allow for a second barrage and the mounts climbed the grassy mound. Broad shoulders bludgeoned mercenaries out of their path. Faced with maces, axes, slashing swords, and bony horses' hooves, the Leader had little choice and yelled, "Scatter! Retreat!"

Chariots operate best in the chaos and space of disrupted battle lines. Thus, as the mercenaries scattered, they inadvertently handed Báine a gift. Long knives spinning on axle hubs, the five chariots weaved in and out of the fractured ranks. Báine's strident howling sent shivers along the spines of an already rattled warband. The *carbaid* were hard to miss as all were painted in a riot of colours and designs, and tribal banners streamed from long poles.

Báine's spinning scythes carved a bloody path through flesh and bone, leaving a trail of limbs and broken warriors in their wake. Simultaneously, Brighid's riders battered and slashed through the confusion with ruthless and brutal efficiency.

Resigned to his fate, the Leader grasped a spear, balanced his *scíath* on his arm, and sought the enemy's leader. Perhaps her death would turn the battle in his favour. A horse's snort made him swing around, and he stared into a mask of swirling symbols. The cruel smile on the young woman's face chilled his heart, and her club's iron fist propelled him into unconsciousness.

✳✳✳

Stripped and plundered of any valuables, although that proved a meagre bounty, the remnant of mercenaries sprawled on the grass mound. The Leader sat in numbing, bone-deep pain. Brighid's mace had left one half of his face a mass of raw flesh and clotted blood. A flap of skin, torn from forehead to chin, hung limply from his jawline. A good friend would have put him out of his misery.

The night passed miserably, painfully, and slowly for the mercenaries. No herbs or salves were proffered for the injured, and no one spared a blade to end the suffering of the mortally wounded. Bellies rumbled from hunger, and only rainwater slaked their thirst. Yet apart from curses and ridicule, the guards were well-disciplined and showed no interest in using the prisoners for more sadistic pleasures.

As the sun rose on a new day, the Leader looked up at the sound of Ráth Na Conall's gates opening. Accompanied by a score of warriors, four walked down the dirt track towards the prisoners. Conchobhar and Onchú both wore red mid-thigh-length tunics and triubhas. Glimpses of steel-grey chainmail showed that wool was not their primary protection. The Leader recognised the men, but who were the two young women that accompanied them?

"Are you the leader of this rabble?" asked Danu. The Leader nodded, gasping in pain at the effort. "I am Danu Ni Conall, and this is my sister, Brighid." Danu saw no hint of recognition in the man's eyes, although the blow to his head might have affected his mind. "Perhaps you know of my father and mother. We are the daughters of Conall Mac Gabhann, Rí of Ráth Na Conall, and his queen, Mórrígan, also known as the Dark Huntress."

"The Hag preserve me!"

Around campfires, *seanchaithe* told stories of the battles of Conall and An Fiagaí Dorcha. Mothers sent their children to sleep dreaming of fulfilling heroic *geasa* or, when disobedient, threatened them with a visit from the Dark Huntress. However, conquering *ríthe* and *rígana*, more often than not, die young in battle or in their beds from knives wielded by covetous kin. Thus, after a score of summers, all but a few fanatical believers thought the tales gross exaggerations and the king and queen long dead.

Furthermore, throughout Uallachán's dominion, all were forbidden to mention Conall's or Mórrígan's names from the youngest to the oldest. Torture and death were the rewards for transgressors. The shadows that fell upon the Leader told him that the famed rí and rígan were not only alive but thrived. He smiled, for he knew two kings who would not be pleased.

"You find something humorous in your situation?" asked Brighid. "A sober reflection on your current peril would be more appropriate."

The Leader shook his head very slowly and, slurring his words, said, "I wish I could see the faces of those who receive the news of your arrival." He smiled at the young woman. "I assume that I will not have the dubious honour of being that messenger."

Danu shrugged dismissively. "You chose your employer badly," she said and then turned to Flann. "This is not a task worthy of your rank, but I need to be sure it is completed. Bind these men and women and walk them to the end of the valley that follows the southern slopes of the Bod Carraig bluffs. There you know what to do." Flann dipped his head. "Take as many men as you need to ensure your safety."

Danu then looked to Brighid. "Select a score of your riders to accompany Flann." Brighid turned to walk away, but a firm hand on her arm restrained her. "Be careful, Brighid. I have no wish to lose my sister in a stupid skirmish this early in the game."

"I am not altogether stupid, sister." Brighid bristled, and her nostrils flared.

"I'm sorry. I didn't mean to offend."

Conchobhar and Onchú looked at each other uneasily. The lightning-fast smile that opened Brighid's lips and her embrace of Danu seemed a tad insincere.

CHAPTER 4

"Oh, my ma's tits!"

The small band of scouts were on the verge of returning to Caher Conri when they stumbled on the horrific tableau. Curious about the unkindness of ravens soaring in the grey sky, the band's leader had pushed his party closer to its source. Now, they cursed the fervour of one who, seeking to impress Uallachán, had led them into territory well beyond his orders.

Belatedly, the inexperienced leader realised and then regretted his folly. Some things are best left undiscovered, unseen, and untold. A few of the younger patrol members—most were under sixteen summers old—lost control of their stomachs, bent over double, and threw up. Several lost the authority over their bladders and bowels. For them, the march back would be uncomfortable.

Spread across the narrow valley were threescore warriors. All sat upright. From a distance, it looked as if they rested against wooden poles. The misinterpretation was understandable as all had had stakes driven into their arses before being dropped into forearm's-length holes. Customary with the punishment, each victim's legs had also been broken.

Yet escape was likely the last thing on each of the men and women's minds as the pale travelled slowly but relentlessly through vital organs and displacing bones before eventually erupting from their chests. The young leader winced at the expressions on what remained of the executed's faces. Their countenances bore witness to the agonising pain suffered and the long time it took to die. Bite marks and chunks of meat ripped from the bone testified to one final indignity. In their last moments, they had served as food for beast and fowl.

The lead scout was untried but not stupid. *The Hag if I'm going to be the bearer of this news.* He eyed his retching companions and, in a voice he hoped spoke of command and persuasion, said, "I require a volunteer to return immediately to Caher Conri. Uallachán must be informed of this atrocity."

A cough drew the leader's attention to a winsome, if skinny, girl of sixteen summers whom he intended to rut—willingly or not. He followed the trajectory of her hand, which pointed to an object stabbed into the soft, damp dirt. It had been overlooked in the preliminary examination of the brutal scene. He walked closer to examine the object—a wooden scíatha, painted red and embellished with a swooping black raven.

"The Hag!" he muttered. *There's no bloody way I'm taking this news back to Uallachán.*

***

Many forts dotted the craggy headlands of Ériu's southwestern coastline. The most impressive was the stone-built fortress of Caher Conri, which nestled at the foot of a rugged mountain range and a promontory constantly lashed by waves. Oceans and cliffs protected the ráth from attack on three sides.

The fort had been burned and razed to the ground by Brighid and Danu's father in the war with Eochaidh Ruad, but the bastion had risen defiantly and stronger from the ashes under Uallachán. Of Caher Conri's buildings, only the Great Hall, which doubled as the residence of Uallachán and his brother, Nuadha, was of note. It stood a tall, thick-walled stone tower, similar in construction to the brochs of Northern Albu, although rectangular. The Hall was Caher Conri's last line of defence. However, Uallachán considered Caher Conri impregnable, and few disagreed with him.

To its north, a high berm of dirt and stone guarded the fort against the presumed weakness on its northern flank. The embankment had a single entrance cut into it. Caher Conri's thick walls and earthen dyke also featured deep, stake-filled ditches on the outer side of the barriers. Hence a besieger had little choice but to attack from the north and overcome Caher Conri's formidable battlements.

As the messenger entered the Great Hall's large reception chamber, her eyes were drawn to the two thrones. Uallachán's gold-painted, gem-encrusted chair rested on a raised plinth of black granite. The carved seat, more elaborate and infinitely gaudier than those of much more powerful ríthe, screamed of insecurity and hubris. Many called it a tasteless display, but few uttered such truths openly.

In Uallachán's domain, orators of contrary opinions, and their families, provided sport for Uallachán's depraved appetites. After serving that purpose, they were executed. Those with the resources had long distanced themselves from the excesses of Caher Conri or purchased their security by other means. Unfortunately, the poor had no such path to sanctuary.

Uallachán, a tall, heavyset man with rounded shoulders and a fat belly, carried an air of cruelty and excess. Those of a mystical bent claimed that Uallachán had absorbed the evil of the ráth's previous occupant. They were misinformed. Uallachán had nurtured and finessed that malevolence to unheard of depths of debauchery.

As a boy, Uallachán was the one who slowly and deliberately pulled the legs and wings off fat blackflies, watching the insects' struggles with perverse pleasure. Bolstered by his ma and da forever insisting he was special and born to lead, Uallachán became as bitter and twisted as his parents, whose ambition to lead their community had been thwarted by the twins' grandfather. Uallachán's temperament led him to become a bully. Yet, mocked mercilessly by his younger and older peers, Uallachán's sphere of influence quickly diminished to one—his brother, Nuadha.

In an early battle for Ráth Na Conall, a spear thrust had cost Uallachán the use of his left arm. The stump hung a withered, useless appendage, and the bitterness of its loss festered into an intense hatred of Conall and any who bore his name. Adding kindling to his anger, Conall had also spurned Uallachán's demand to be declared Rí of Ráth Na Conall.

Still, it was unwise to underestimate Uallachán or the motivation his sense of entitlement fostered. He had a native cunning and a mind for the long game. Yet, after twenty summers, Uallachán felt frustrated that his strategies had not come to fruition and his just rewards eluded him. The time was overdue to spread his disease more aggressively across the south-west kingdom and consolidate his power.

His kingdom and campaign had the support of Maine Athramail, Rí Ruirech of the powerful northern Connachta. That should have pleased Uallachán. Welcomed at first, now it seemed to emphasise his weaknesses and inability to fully assert his will across the land. That his accomplishments could be claimed by another grated on Uallachán. Was he no more than a plaything for a more powerful ruler? The idea that he was a mere pawn in someone else's game served only to increase his malevolence towards those unable to defend themselves.

Adjacent to Uallachán's seat, although not raised on a plinth, was Nuadha's smaller and less ostentatious throne. The younger by four summers, Nuadha was rí in name only, and he and everyone in the kingdom knew it. A permanent scowl had taken up residence on his face, and he slouched in his chair. It was his puerile rebellion to demonstrate annoyance at Uallachán's ongoing domination. Still, all knew that Nuadha was bound to Uallachán with chains stronger than iron. Indeed, the poor wretches in Caher Conri's dungeons had more freedom.

A paunch of indolence spilt over Nuadha's belt, more noticeable than Uallachán's due to him being a hand shorter. While his brother was remarkable for the ugliness of his character and physique, Nuadha had a nondescript mien with a victim's mentality and could easily walk unrecognised in any crowd. His bearing spoke of unfulfilled opportunity.

Draped over the thrones and scattered on the floor around the seats were magnificent bear and wolf furs—although none had met their end by Uallachán's or Nuadha's hand. A small group of naked girls and boys, none more than thirteen summers, huddled and whimpered on the hides. They were the latest batch torn from their mothers' arms, waiting to be despoiled by the brothers. It was perhaps the only activity the brothers enjoyed together, although Nuadha preferred young boys.

The room's upright oak beams divided the Great Hall into three aisles. Firepits were sunk into the stone floor in a row down the middle lane. Augmented by many freestanding braziers, the room avoided the deep cold of winter. Since Uallachán deemed them a potential weakness, the building had no windows. Hence, the room was perpetually gloomy and an apt metaphor for the evil that resided within its walls.

Numerous rushlights, fluttering in iron sconces, were supplemented by the light from sunken fire pits. Wood and blue peat smoke curled upwards, escaping through the hall's thatched roof. Hung from the heavy oak rafters, sides of beef, ham, venison, and pink fillets of fish swayed on iron hooks as they cured in the rising fog.

The chamber's walls were draped with heavy tapestries featuring Uallachán's heroic exploits, which were few, and lewd pastimes, which were many. In front of the curtains and a pace apart stood one hundred of Uallachán's guard. Hard eyes stared forward, and stony faces gave no clue about their true feelings.

★★★

For commoners, an audience before royalty is generally something to be remembered and treasured. An invitation to the Great Hall of Caher Conri had a better than even chance of being followed by a death sentence—and rarely was it a quick and painless demise. The messenger stood before Uallachán, considering that her impetuosity might be fatal. She muttered, "*Tuilí*—bastard!" recalling the expression on the leader's face as he graciously accepted her offer and declined the "honour" for himself. Belatedly, she grasped his relief at having passed this task to another.

The young woman inhaled and exhaled several times to compose herself before commencing her report. Her opening delivery was terse and without embellishment—save to cast aspersions on the group's leader. It was a petty act, but if it landed the arsehole in the shite, then good. Uallachán's unblinking stare, his eyes the colour of moonstones—pale blue on a milky white background—flustered her. She tripped over her words as she grew increasingly nervous in the oppressive atmosphere.

She concluded her tale, exhaled a sigh of relief, and bowed. With a glance for approval, the girl walked forward and laid the red scíath, face-up, at the feet of Uallachán. Both men recoiled at the black raven as if attacked by a viper. Nuadha's face drained of blood, and he appeared close to tears. It was as if a long-lost spectre had stepped from his nightmares and stood before him. Uallachán glared at the young woman. Rage and anxiety filled his eyes. Something else also lurked in his stare—a visceral need to cause pain. The messenger knew her life was over.

"Strip the lying bitseach!" screeched Uallachán.

Two guards held the girl while a third tore the clothes from her body. From their economy of effort, it seemed this was not the first time they had obeyed this particular command. "She's not much to look at. Too skinny by far, although my brother might want to indulge himself." Uallachán looked at Nuadha, but the younger sibling was deep in his thoughts and ignored his brother. "It seems that no one values your message or your body."

Tears of humiliation rolled down the young woman's cheeks. Having little to lose, she straightened up. Anger flared in brown eyes as, with head held high, she spat defiantly at the throne. "The Hag curse you, Uallachán of Caher Conri, your brother, Nuadha, and all within this fort. The Goddess has rejected you. The ravens will feast on your eyes and the wolves on your balls."

"You have a sharp and impetuous tongue," said Uallachán. To the guards, he commanded, "Tear her tongue out! It offends me."

The young girl gasped, "No!"

"Gouge out her eyes, too. They are too pretty a colour to hold such anger." A twisted smile took up residence on Uallachán's lips as he said, "And since I do not have the use of my arm, neither should she."

The girl's agonising screams echoed off the chamber's walls as the guards carried out the sentence. Her tongue, torn from its roots, left the messenger only able to make a bloody, guttural croaking. The last vision her eyes beheld was her left arm lying beside her tongue on the stone floor and her blood seeping between the cracks.

The girl slipped into unconsciousness as her heart faltered and then failed. The Goddess, having deemed the envoy had suffered enough, allowed the bean-sidhe to call her name as Uallachán gave his final order. "Drag her to the barracks. Some might want to use her while her body is still warm. After, throw her to the hounds."

Nuadha stood and whispered in his brother's ear. Uallachán nodded and signalled to the captain of his guard. "No one will speak of this. Find the others who were with this liar. Blind them, rip their tongues out, and cut their throats."

* * *

Brother faced brother in the empty chamber. "We have to do something. Ráth Na Conall rises as it did in Eochaidh's time. We should negotiate terms," said Nuadha. The hard slap caught him by surprise, splitting his lip. Uallachán's subjugation of his brother was total but had not been physically violent to date. Nuadha stumbled backwards. Catching the edge of a wolf skin, he tripped and landed on his arse. With more courage than he had exhibited in many summers, he looked up and blurted, "It's a message. We cannot ignore it."

"Conall and Mórrígan are dead," snapped Uallachán.

"If you truly believe that, then you're a fool." The sudden presence of a spine in Nuadha startled Uallachán. "Who staked the mercenaries for us to find and left the shield for us?"

"Who indeed, brother?" *And whose gold paid the sellswords?* Uallachán's stomach churned, and his Adam's apple bobbed up and down as he considered the most likely answer to his unspoken question. Had his sleeping partner awakened? And what did that mean for him? Uallachán sensed other forces had entered his game. More urgency was needed.

Uallachán reached out a hand to help Nuadha regain his feet, but his brother recoiled, slapping it away. There was no apology or regret in the offer, and Nuadha knew it. "Leave me. I need to think." As the doors to the Great Hall closed, Uallachán reached for a cup of wine. His hand trembled, and the green liquid splashed over the rim. He chose to ignore the omen. *It's just an overfull goblet.* Perhaps using one of the young girls in the cells below would calm his temper.

CHAPTER 5

"Ráth Na Conall is built in the wrong place," said Danu.

It was early morning as the small group stood on Ráth Na Conall's battlements. Danu shielded her eyes from the rising sun and pointed to the hill's highest point on its eastern side. "That is where we will build a new fort with much better sightlines, steeper slopes, and natural exits to the east and the south. There is more than enough space to build a ráth three hundred paces in length along each wall. Wood is plentiful, and I have plans for the rock and rubble from the old Ráth Na Conall."

To bolster her argument, Danu added, "All the buildings can be built with eastern-facing entrances to make full use of the sun's path." Both statements took Conchobhar and Onchú by surprise, mainly because they had never considered the subject. Constructed where the twins' family and community lived, the fort was built out of necessity and in the face of an impending attack.

It sat on the west side of a vast, thickly forested hill and, at that time, its location made sense. The western slopes were gentler, making goods produced by the settlement easier to transport to nearby farmsteads and villages. Moreover, the mound was large—about fifteen hundred paces from east to west and about the same from north to south. Space was not an issue.

"That would give us space for a garrison of five hundred warriors plus essential trades such as blacksmiths, fletchers, and leather-making," said Conchobhar. He tugged at his beard, which looked much more presentable since he had taken a bath and trimmed his whiskers. Refreshed and in new armour, colours, and weapons, he looked ready for battle. "We could corral the horses in the woods to the south of the fort. Building riders' quarters close to the mounts would also be sensible."

Danu's countenance relaxed at Conchobhar's mounting enthusiasm, but she decided a cautionary note was needed. "I know what I want. I've seen it in the Carnutes' city of Cenabum where my uncle Bricriu is the Oracle." Danu's name-dropping was deliberate, and Conchobhar's raised eyebrow her desired response. Conchobhar and Onchú needed to grasp how much Clann Ui Flaithimh had grown. She needed them confident to forge ahead, knowing the reach and strength of the tribe.

"My vision for the fort can be rebuilt much more rapidly than a stone fortress." Danu sighed. "The weakness in my plan is that we will need a large workforce."

Shrugging broad shoulders, Conchobhar looked at Brighid. "Brighid has encouraged the healthier, if not fully fit, men and women and Neasán to borrow the cavalry's spare mounts. All except Neasán have ridden out to find those that fled Ráth Na Conall and the surrounding farms." The veteran frowned. "Neasán's inclination to procrastination and raising objections is discouraging."

Danu's brows knitted. "My sister and I will seek an explanation for Neasán's aversion to action." She fell silent, deep in thought.

"Perhaps we should keep the braziers and torches burning at night and build a great bonfire on the peak. That might attract the curious— good and bad," said Conchobhar, "but it could be a half-cycle of the moon before we get a response."

"Can we move the conversation along?" Brighid gave an exaggerated shiver. "It's chilly, and I need to piss." An impromptu jig followed to emphasise her need for relief. Danu and Conchobhar laughed. The recent spell of action had long lost its shine, and an impatient Brighid constantly complained of boredom.

"How strong is Uallachán's army?" asked Danu. Brighid growled at the apparent dismissal of her question.

"At Caher Conri, Uallachán has around two hundred warriors, but he can likely call on another thousand warriors from the coastal forts on the headland. Added to this are the nobles of the southwest. They ally with him either by choice, bribery, or because he holds their sons and daughters hostage. Thus, the total could easily swell to about three thousand warriors."

Conchobhar scratched at his skull with great deliberation. With a grunt of satisfaction, he squashed something between his fingers before flicking it over the stockade. Danu and Brighid caught each other's eyes and barely held back gasps of "Ewww!" Oblivious, Conchobhar said, "Of course, and as we have experienced, there are always mercenaries looking for work. So we should count on about five thousand fighters."

"And we have two hundred. That hardly favours us," said Danu.

A cough made the quartet turn to face Beacán, who had been quietly observing the conversation. "Speaking of mercenaries, something has been bothering me since Iasg and I visited their camp."

"Well?"

Danu's and Brighid's impatience surfaced, but to their chagrin their uncle just chuckled. However, soon his lips thinned in disapproval. What had they missed? "What did *you* observe about the mercenaries? Their tactics, their organisation…" Beacán paused and then added, "… their accents."

Danu clapped a hand to her mouth—"The Hag's arse!"—and looked at Brighid.

"As usual, my sister was right," said Brighid dryly.

Conchobhar shook his head. "Will someone enlighten this poor warrior?"

"The mercenaries had Connachta accents. As my sister surmised, there is more to this conflict than a simple rebellion. Another, perhaps more dangerous, piece is revealed on the fidchell board."

"Rut the Hag!" exclaimed Conchobhar.

Feeling the need to divert the conversation until she had considered the topic further, Danu turned to Brighid. "Our ma terrorised the Arverni nation with a band of two hundred. Do you think you could do likewise to Uallachán? He remains the immediate threat." Brighid's emerald eyes sparkled. Danu put up a hand. "However, until the fort is rebuilt, you may only take fifty riders and spare mounts. The rest of the cavalry and chariots are needed to patrol closer to home and guard those who return."

Disappointment briefly dimmed Brighid's eyes, but the opportunity to be free from the chores of strategising and ráth building was much too tempting to pass up. She nodded her agreement.

"Good, choose your targets carefully, Brighid. In the end, we need Uallachán's people to rise against him."

"When should I start?"

"Why are you still here?"

Brighid grinned at her sister. About to descend the walkway's ladder, she stopped, smirked, and pointed to the snow-covered Na Comaraigh. "Whoever *they* are, they must be freezing their arses off. Should I take care of them first?" The others followed the line of Brighid's arm. Against the stark white landscape, it was just possible to spot a small group watching from a rocky outcrop that jutted from below Na Comaraigh's snow line.

"Shite!" exclaimed Conchobhar, annoyed at himself. "We need to post lookouts on Na Comaraigh." Then he smiled at Brighid. "You have a hawk's eyes."

Danu opened her mouth to speak, but the touch of Brighid's finger on her lips stopped her. "Still, perhaps, *that* one is of more interest." Once more, the small group followed Brighid's gaze, but this time to the dark, shimmering figure who stood on the highest peak. Only the white background made the figure visible. Danu wondered whether that was deliberate.

On the mountain top, and apparently immune to the cold, the tall, black-cloaked figure chuckled.

✶✶✶

"Yer getting soft."

The insult was delivered in the soft burr of those native to the low-lands of Northern Albu. It was Iasg's response to Beacán's grumbling at being cold and wet as the pair scrambled further up the eastern slope of Na Comaraigh. To Brighid's disappointment, Danu had assigned the mission to Beacán and Iasg. The couple departed the ráth shortly before meán lae, accompanied by a cacophony of blaring horns and pound-ing hoofbeats as Brighid's riders galloped towards the Bod Carraig valley. Beacán had rolled his eyes at the diversion, but Brighid's actions were an effective distraction, and he was thankful.

Beacán had hoped for a sunny day, clear skies, and the advantage of the sun at his back. Instead, the day started grey, with cloudy skies and intermittent showers. *At least the rain is light.* Using the foothills' cover of oak, ash, and alder, he and Iasg climbed to the higher slopes. There, only purple heather, and yellow gorse provided cover. Thus, they kept to the northern side of a ridge of steep bluffs, paralleling their target, the snow-covered plateau. The ascent was long, if not overly taxing.

In a shallow hollow aseated around a blazing fire, the group's con-versation was loud and good-humoured as if they were friends on a hunting trip. Beacán glanced at Iasg and shook his head. From the tenor of the discussion, which carried clearly in the mountain environment, it sounded as if most were young. Their tone suggested they took the task light-heartedly and beneath their status. *Fools!*

The fair-haired young man at their centre laughed at his compan-ions' complaints, although the brittleness in his voice seemed odd to Beacán. Confident they remained unseen, the group had not posted guards. Occasionally one or two would leave the comfort of the flames to piss or peer across to Ráth Na Conall.

Beacán shook his head. *Amateurs!* Tapping Iasg on her shoulder, he mouthed, "Kill or capture?" Both knew it would be much easier and less of a risk to slay the five and leave their bodies as a sacrifice to the mountain. With a shrug of resignation, Iasg held up four fingers and drew one across her throat. Without waiting for Beacán's response, she scrambled off in a wide arc to take a position diagonally opposite her companion.

The rock, lobbed high into the air, landed with a crash, scattering burning brands and throwing embers into the laps of the watchers. Veterans would have suffered the minor burns, unsheathed weapons, kept low, and waited for the enemy to make their next move. Instead, the group jumped up, cursing, and swearing revenge on the unseen foe who had disturbed their solitude.

When they realised their folly, it was too late. Razor-sharp blades punched through thick furs and into unwary chests and backs. Wild-eyed, the young leader spun around and watched the two figures approach. "We're friends!" he shrieked at the tall, red-haired man who loped towards him.

"Then you're a fool and should have knocked on the front door," said Beacán before his fist carried the young man into oblivion. "Bind him, Iasg. I'll take care of the others."

It is never easy cutting through bone, flesh, and gristle to cleave a head from its body. Perhaps the corpse feels it has to resist, giving the perpetrator time to reflect on his deed. Beacán had performed the gruesome act so many times that it meant little to him. *Still, who needs to be haunted by the spirits of the dead?* If the young man spoke the truth, Beacán would regret the wasted lives and drink a few extra beers.

A moan teased Beacán's ears and he glanced behind him. The eyes of the young woman—she looked younger than Danu or Brighid—fluttered open. Blood seeped from full lips that fought to smile in the hope of mercy. Hers was the final body he had to deal with, but now the option to save her raised its head. Sadness filled Beacán's eyes, and he whispered a heartfelt "Sorry," before plunging his blade into her heart. Wearily, he looked at Iasg.

"Her wound was mortal, and ye know it," said Iasg. "There is no guilt, and she is in Mag Mell." Iasg was right, yet her words gave Beacán little comfort.

⋆⋆⋆

"Well, we've just slaughtered the Rí of Clárach's people. So much for making friends and forging a partnership with a potential ally." Danu looked to Conchobhar. Frustration and helplessness were written across her face.

"It could not be helped. They spied on us, assessing our strengths and weaknesses. That is not the behaviour of a friend. The responsibility is on Aodh's head, not ours. And no blame can be attributed to Beacán or Iasg."

"At least we have *him*," said Danu, looking at the young man, still bound and gagged. The unexpected guest from Clárach squirmed in his seat under Danu's gaze. "Unbind him, feed him, and let's hear his tale." *He is tall, quite handsome, and a few summers older than me.* Her guest paused his eating, met her eyes, and smiled as if hearing her thoughts. The smile appeared honest to Danu, and his grey-green eyes were undoubtedly attractive. *Brighid has her liaisons. Why not me?*

Danu's lips parted to show her teeth, and the welcome spread to her eyes. Feeling her cheeks flush, she dropped her gaze and berated herself. *Focus, Danu.* "Time to talk. I will start. I am Danu, Princess of Clann Ui Flaithimh, daughter of Conall Mac Gabhann, Rí Ruirech, and Mórrígan, An Fiagaí Dorcha. My twin sister, Brighid, accompanies me, but she is away, causing trouble for Uallachán. My sister and I intend to rebuild Ráth Na Conall, unite the kingdom, and destroy all who oppose or betray us." Danu dipped her head towards her guest. "Your turn."

The young man sighed, set his cup aside, placed both hands on the table, stood, and bowed to Danu. The wine was excellent. Much better and more robust than the piss they drank in Clárach, and so he had watered it to avoid the embarrassment of falling over drunk. "I am Glaisne Mac Aodh, the youngest of three brothers. My eldest sibling is Aodh

Mac Aodh, Rí of Clárach.

"My other brother, Cúmhaí Mac Aodh, undoubtedly covets the throne but has neither the support of enough nobles nor the skills of an assassin." He looked at Beacán. "Were you for hire, Cúmhaí would make you a wealthy man." Beacán smiled and nodded, wary of how quickly Glaisne disparaged his kin to strangers.

"Thank the Goddess, we didn't kill the brother of the Rí of Clárach. That could have complicated matters," said Conchobhar. "But what do we do with him? Aodh sent him to reconnoitre and assess us, which is not a friendly act. Still, given the quality of the scouts, I seriously doubt Aodh expected much." Conchobhar nodded to Glaisne. "No offence meant."

"Were any of your companions noble or wealthy?" asked Danu.

Glaisne shook his head. "They were acquaintances. I barely knew them." The sadness in his eyes seemed honest to Danu, and she warmed to the young prince. Her charity was short-lived.

"A suspicious person might deduce that our guest was not meant to return to Clárach… alive," said Beacán.

"Shite! Brighid and I have enough to contend with. We will not get involved in family squabbles." Danu glared at Glaisne. "What do you say?"

Glaisne pointed to his seat. "With your permission." Danu nodded, and he sat silently for a short time with brow furrowed. As if reaching a conclusion, he responded. "Your immediate need is to strengthen this ráth's defences. However, I very much doubt that you have the labour. It is unsurprising that your subjects have fled." Danu's brief dip of her head supported Glaisne's contention. He paused to sip his wine.

"My brother, Aodh, will not pay a ransom for me, but he might trade my safe return for workers. I am not my father's heir and, unlike Cúmhaí, pose no threat to Aodh. Also, if I may be immodest, I am well-liked. Clárach's allied chieftains would be unhappy if Aodh left me to rot and die here.

"Aodh has no love for Uallachán, and sees his actions as none of Clárach's business. However, having a friend in Ráth Na Conall might gain his interest. Providing you with workers for a cycle of the moon would cost Aodh little and please the nobility. Besides, once assured of your lineage, I doubt he will be foolish enough to make an enemy of the daughters of Conall Mac Gabhann and the Dark Huntress."

"You will remain our guest for another sunset."

As pleasant as Danu's smile was, suspicion settled in Glaisne's eyes, for he knew this was not a request. Sensing his unease and not wanting to risk a potential friendship, Danu said, "No shackles, no gags, or blindfolds. Feel free to explore and ask questions." With a smile, she added, "I will be delighted to be your guide."

✶✶✶

"That could be dangerous, Danu," said Beacán as Glaisne departed the room. "We know nothing about him save what he has told us. All the other witnesses are dead. And he neatly avoided answering your question."

"The risk is acceptable. We have two sunsets to convince Glaisne that our cause is just. That will equip him better to convince Aodh to lend us the workers. If needed, we might sweeten the arrangement with a small portion of the gold we brought." Beacán dipped his head, looked at Iasg, and turned to exit the chamber. Iasg lagged. He looked at her questioningly, but she signalled him to continue. Once out of earshot, Iasg turned to Danu.

"It is dirty and dangerous work ye send yer uncle to do. He will never complain or refuse, but some respect for his counsel would not go amiss." Iasg turned on her heels and walked away.

"Well, that's me put in my place," said Danu.

Conchobhar chuckled. "That is a very protective lady. Given her talent with knives, best not to get on her wrong side."

✶✶✶

Maine Athramail, the eldest son of Ailill Mac Máta and Medb and recently crowned Rí Ruirech of the Connachta, was of average height, passably handsome, and not the sharpest blade in the armoury. Yet his lack of intelligence proved no hindrance to consolidating his position as the Connachta's new Rí Ruirech.

As a rule, leaders and rulers who consider a wide diversity of ideas, opinions, and options often find themselves baring their necks before a replacement who has but one goal—to take power. Maine had no such limitations. Indeed, there were strong rumours that he had hastened his father's journey to Mag Mell. His limited intellect permitted him to focus on a limited number of challenges simultaneously.

The Connachta army was arguably the strongest in Ériu. Only the Ulaid's famed Cróeb Ruad warriors in the north could challenge that assertion. With no one to contest him, and his kingdom protected from a northern invasion by bogs and the Black Pig's Dyke, Maine was a bored king looking for an enemy. Thus, he looked southwards.

The curse of the Gaels is to have long memories, an unwillingness to let go, and a fondness for vengeance. Maine set himself the goal of wiping clean the stain of his father's perceived humiliation at the hands of a young Conall. At the time, his father, Ailill, considered the result an honourable draw. Still, among the nobility of the Connachta, the skirmish was considered a humiliating defeat.

The bitterness of that humbling festered among Maine and his six brothers. All had sworn to exact a terrible retribution if given the opportunity. As princes of the Connachta, and without their father's approval, Maine and his brothers had supported an inconsequential southern rí— Uallachán. His rebellion and mischief-making provided the perfect vehicle for Maine to meddle in the domain of Ráth Na Conall. Still, while Uallachán saw himself as an equal partner and friend of Maine, the Connachta *prionsaí* saw Uallachán as a disagreeable but useful puppet.

On this day, the Rí Ruirech of the Connachta received a messenger from the south whose report angered him. Sitting on his throne in the stronghold of Chrúachain, he pondered the future while awaiting the arrival of his brothers. Maine looked up and smiled as the doors of the Great Hall swung open. As usual, Cairbre led them into the chamber.

Once they were seated, Maine stood. "We have two things to discuss. Firstly, a messenger has just informed me that the daughters of Conall Mac Gabhann have taken up residence in Ráth Na Conall. They have already defeated the mercenaries paid with our gold. Secondly, Uallachán did not inform me of this event."

Maine scowled at each of his brothers. "The mercenaries are of no consequence and we have saved the final half of their fee. However, it may be time for us to take a more active part in Uallachán's affairs. At the least, our dog needs reminded who is his master."

CHAPTER 6

Onchú's horse trotted along the riverside track skirting the ringfort of Carn Tigherna. The stronghold was a minor fort and well-defended by deep ditches and circular ramparts of stone and earth. Its garrison had fallen to about fifty warriors—there was no excess gold to pay for more. Of that number, Onchú had seconded roughly half to defend Ráth Na Conall. Onchú's strength, and perhaps his weakness, was his honour.

Hence, Onchú was delighted that Conall's daughters had arrived and looked forward to devoting more time to his partner and children. Before his last departure, Eithne had threatened to have a druid dissolve their bonds and take his children from him because of his neglect. *What other choice did I have?* Yet the wounds of inattention were deep and needed healing. Onchú smiled and guided his mount along the dirt track that wound its way up the hill to the broad grassy and forested plateau where Carn Tigherna sat. He felt optimistic and looked forward to sharing recent events with his family.

He frowned as he considered the situation at Curraghatoor. In the absence of its rightful king, Curraghatoor had fallen into the hands of Íar's half-brothers. The siblings' first deed was to abandon their duty to protect Ráth Na Conall. Onchú vehemently disagreed with Curraghatoor's current occupants and knew they could readily provide men to protect Ráth Na Conall. Still, Onchú considered them misguided rather than enemies.

Downwind from Carn Tigherna, Onchú caught the smell of horse shite—not something usually associated with his home. That the scent was strong caused his brow to furrow. Only a handful of mounts were stabled at the fort during normal times. This stink pointed to a much larger herd.

Had Curraghatoor, a day's ride northeast, sent mounted men to Carn Tigherna? What disaster needed Curraghatoor to come to his ráth's aid? Panic rose in Onchú's belly, and he feared for his family. Urging his mount into a canter, he neared the ringfort, only to be met by another smell—woodsmoke.

Silhouetted against an obscenely glorious sunset, Carn Tigherna burned. Onchú swept his sword from its sheath and encouraged his horse into a gallop. About to exit the tree-lined farm track and enter the meadows, Onchú found himself unceremoniously pulled from his mount. He hit the earth with a force that knocked the breath from him. Instinct made him pull a dagger from his belt and cast around for his sword.

"Put your blade away. I am not your enemy." From the darkness of the forest, Brighid emerged. Laying a hand on Onchú's shoulder, she said, "We must talk."

In the campfire's light, the anguish on Onchú's face made Brighid's feirdhris burn with anger and the painted symbols on her face flow like a molten black river. As Brighid related what she and her band had witnessed, Onchú tore clumps of hair from his mane of steel and red.

Her riders had been well past Carn Tigherna and about to enter Uallachán's domain when one of them spotted the red glow in the night sky. By the time they had retraced their steps and were within sight of the ringfort, it was in flames. Shouts of anger from warriors and screams of terror from partners, mothers, and children had filled the air.

"We must attack now and kill the bastards," said Onchú.

Brighid shook her head. "No. It is night, and we do not know how many we face. My scouts identified two substantial forces: one is likely from Caher Conri and the other, Curraghatoor. It seems my sister was right. Ráth Na Conall may not have been Uallachán's primary target. A strong piece needed removing from the fidchell board—you."

"But my hand-fast partner, my sons, and daughters. I can't just abandon them," rasped Onchú.

"They have value to Uallachán. He's not stupid enough to throw away future leverage—especially if you remain alive." In her heart, Brighid hoped that what she said was true. To those around her, she said, "Rest. We make our move before sunrise."

As the riders drifted away to find soft beds among the forest debris, Brighid called her second-in-command, the stocky, dark-haired Maolán, to her. Nodding in Onchú's direction, she said, "Watch him. Make sure he does not attack the ráth on his own." Brighid smiled grimly. "That does not give you licence to go with him." *The Hag! I'm starting to sound like my sister.*

✳✳✳

Danu tossed and turned in her cot. Foreboding filled her sleep. With a start, she sat up, making the sweat pooling between her breasts trickle down her belly. Her feirdhris pounded, and its colour seemed more crimson red than pink. "Shite!" Rolling from her bed, she ran to her bedchamber's door and flung it open, startling the two guards in the hallway.

"Alert the fort. Gather our forces. Post lookouts on the highest peak of Na Comaraigh. I want Conchobhar and the ceannairí céad in the small chamber… *now!*" As the sentries rushed away to carry out her orders, Danu padded back into her room. She looked down.

"Shite!"

One of the guards smiled as he ran down the hallway. Among Conchobhar's men, he had won the wager as to whether the princess's sigils covered all of her body.

✳✳✳

As morning broke, Brighid and Onchú stared at the smouldering ruins of Carn Tigherna. Along the curve of its front-facing wall, the fort's defenders had been nailed to the stone and disembowelled. The fortunate ones were dead before the evisceration, but from their death masks, that was a pitifully small number. Behind Brighid and Onchú, hardened Clann Ui Flaithimh veterans cursed. The female warriors, less restricted by manly convention, wept for the dead. All promised revenge.

Weapons in hand, the band walked cautiously through the fort's shattered gateway. "No!" bellowed Onchú, falling to his knees at the horrors before him. Scattered around the citadel's round tower were bodies, from babies to grandparents—the families of the ráth's garrison. In war, kings and commanders sometimes sanction terrible deeds, deeming it for the greater good. The sight that greeted Brighid and Onchú went far beyond such explanations.

In the greyness of a dawn mizzle, a complete listing of atrocities was impossible. All were stripped of clothing. Pregnant mothers with babies in their wombs and arms were speared and spitted like raw meat awaiting the fire. Congealed blood bore evidence of the multiple rape and sodomy of males and females. Many had been flayed alive, and some set alight for cruel pleasure.

Brighid fought to keep an iron grip on her stomach. Calling Maolán to her side, she ordered him to search the fort for anyone alive. She knew it was a faint hope. Then, in a quieter, colder tone, she added, "Send riders to track where these animals journey. Also, send a messenger to Ráth Na Conall. My sister must be informed." Brighid took a deep breath and walked across the yard to Onchú. "We need to know if your family is among the dead. My men and I don't know them. I'm sorry."

Moments later, a howl of anguish rent the hearts of all present, and Brighid had the answer she feared most. She found a sobbing Onchú kneeling before the massive oak doors of Carn Tigherna's Great Hall. He stared at the remains of his young sons. Nailed to the entrance, the skin had been peeled from their flesh, likely while they were still breathing. Beneath the two, on the blood-soaked earth, lay ribbons of skin, coils of guts, and their manhoods.

Brighid stood at Onchú's side and placed a hand on his shoulder. "I am truly sorry." She hesitated before asking, "Are your hand-fast partner and daughters among the dead?"

Onchú looked up at Brighid, tears streaming down his face, and shook his head. "Better if they were than in Uallachán's hands."

"No!" snarled Brighid. "Alive, they will witness our retribution on the tuilithe that did this." She watched as Onchú's tears were replaced by the fires of vengeance in his eyes and breathed easier. *Better this than madness.*

Between dawn and meán lae, Brighid's riders gathered the dead of the fort and laid them on several pyres. It was a sign of respect, for the spirits of the dead had already been escorted to Tír Tairngire and Mag Mell. With the fires fading and the deceased honoured, the scouts returned to the ruins of Carn Tigherna. Brighid walked over to Onchú, who stood, hands clasped before him, staring at his sons' funeral bonfire.

"I never really knew them, nor they me. I hope they can forgive me."

"If they had anything of their father in them, they did," said Brighid.

"Thanks." Onchú inhaled deeply before speaking. "Did your scouts bring news—good or bad?"

"The attackers broke into three bands—two large warbands and a smaller one. The larger groups are Uallachán's foot warriors and mounted fighters from Curraghatoor. About five hundred on foot and three hundred mounted march or ride in the direction of Ráth Na Conall. If that is their destination, they will arrive by the next sunrise. There are also signs that others march to join them. This was well planned and executed."

"The other group?"

The ghoulish smile on Brighid's face sent shivers along Onchú's spine. "Fifty men on foot, escorting three female prisoners. I have no information on the physical state of your partner or daughters, but they are alive. Mounted, we can intercept them well before Caher Conri."

Onchú nodded. "We need to warn Danu and Ráth Na Conall."

"Trust me. My sister knew of this when I did." Another ripple coursed along Onchú's spine. "However, a rider was sent at sunrise and may already be at the fort."

"Mount up. I will be with you shortly," said Onchú before turning and walking towards the round tower.

After a while, Brighid turned to Maolán. She let out a loud breath and asked sharply, "How long should we give him?" Moments later, Onchú emerged, helmet, shield, and spear in hand.

"Now that makes a statement," muttered Maolán, and Brighid nodded. It was not the armour or weaponry that caught the attention of both, but the shaven head and face of Onchú.

"I think his blade needs sharpening," said Brighid.

CHAPTER 7

Sunrise was not far off, yet the sky and room remained obstinately dark. That had little to do with the additional rushlights and braziers lit to dispel the gloom. The intimate chamber chosen for the meeting had no windows. Thus, darkness and shadow were its natural state. Danu's insistence on the additional light aimed to raise the spirits of those attending. Although laudable, it came at a cost—the rancid smell of burning vegetation. Hence the door was left ajar.

Glaisne entered the chamber, dipping his head to each of those assembled around the table. At one end, a short, stocky man stood up. "This is Thrasius, the commander of our trireme fleet." Once more, Glaisne nodded. "It seems you might be with us longer than anticipated," remarked Danu. The genuine smile and brightness of her eyes suggested that she was not unhappy at the delay.

"That is no burden," answered Glaisne, immediately taking up the vacant seat on Danu's left.

The fleeting touch of their hands was missed by all in the room except a sharp-eyed Beacán. The assassin frowned, growled low, and pondered whether he should engineer a believable accident. He scowled again, but this time the expression was aimed at himself. Only his gut doubted that Glaisne had anything but friendly intentions towards Danu.

Perhaps, as the others seated around the table thought, it was an innocent and likely short-lived infatuation. Glaisne was young, not unattractive, and appeared just as smitten with Danu as she with him. However, no matter the explanation, the timing troubled Beacán. Brighid and Danu had a challenging job to accomplish. Needless distractions would only delay or imperil the task given to them. And whereas Brighid moved, with abandon, from lover to lover, Danu tended towards being more selective and sought a deeper commitment.

"Trust her," whispered Iasg in Beacán's ear, knowing he was exceptionally protective of the girls. His response was a muttered grunt and a broad smile at Glaisne, which was totally at odds with his thoughts. That Glaisne's response was an unreserved beam did little to allay Beacán's misgivings. Once again, he considered the possibility of a tragic accident.

Turning to Thrasius, Danu gave her first order of the day. "I will not have our remaining ship captured. It could be our only path of retreat. You will ensure the vessel is ready to sail at all times." Conchobhar peered at Báine and Flann. His questioning look was plain, but if either of them had answers, they had no intention of revealing them. And so, they shrugged and focused on Danu.

Danu steadied her breathing to compose her thoughts. "A rider from Brighid entered the fort a short time ago. Curraghatoor has betrayed us, and Carn Tigherna lies a charred ruin. Its garrison and people were slaughtered and desecrated. The only good news is that Onchú's hand-fast partner and daughters are captured but alive. His sons were hideously tortured and executed." Gasps of "The Hag!" "Shite!" and "Bastards!" rippled around the room.

"I believe an attack on this fort is imminent."

Danu's eyes set on Báine. The chariot warrior's eyes were a deeper blue than the lakes of the Alpes. Danu held them with a gaze as dark as obsidian. "Until Brighid and Maolán return, you will take charge of both riders and chariots. Of necessity, your force will remain outside of the ráth." Báine's eyes gleamed. Danu shook her head and pondered how Brighid had chosen someone as impetuous as Báine as a leader… and maybe more.

"Subdue your natural inclination to recklessness. I cannot afford to lose any warrior needlessly, and you will report to Conchobhar regularly. You will strike hard and fast but retreat faster." Danu smiled. "I am, however, still relying on your talent for causing mayhem. As a priority, I suggest you send a few riders to the ends of the valleys north and south of Na Comaraigh." Báine dipped her head and slipped from the room.

Next, Danu turned to Conchobhar. "You and I will speak after this meeting. In the meantime, triple the number of lookouts on Na Comaraigh to cover the southern and northern approaches to Ráth Na Conall. Between Báine and yourself, I want to know the numbers and path of the enemy." To Beacán and Iasg, she said, "Our weakness is a lack of intelligence. Do what you can to counter that position."

Finally, Danu turned to Glaisne, resting a hand on his. "This is not your fight. With a good horse, you could make it back to Clárach before the battle commences. Should you choose to leave, there will be no ill will, and we will provide several fast mounts." Danu paused and smiled. "We have known each other a brief time, but I would like to list you as my friend and Ráth Na Conall's ally." Across the table, Iasg winced at the hand that suddenly clamped her thigh. She turned to protest but stopped when she saw the look in Beacán's eyes.

Glaisne shook his head. "Whether my brothers choose to believe it or not, if Uallachán can destroy Carn Tigherna and Ráth Na Conall, then Clárach is likely high on his list for conquest. My home's strength is that it sits on the summit of Sléibhe na Clárach, which has steep bluffs on all its sides. That said, apart from the mountain, its protection is a single circular bank of dirt and a labyrinthine web of paths to the top."

Rubbing his chin ruefully, Glaisne continued, "Generations of Clárach kings were quite tight-fisted. They saw little point in spending gold on more solid defences or a bigger garrison. Clárach is larger than Carn Tigherna, but its fighting force is less than Curraghatoor or Caher Conri. Aodh relies on levies from the local chieftains in times of trouble, but that takes time to organise."

Glaisne dipped his head to Danu and Conchobhar. "If you allow, I will stay and fight alongside you and Clann Ui Flaithimh. However, if you can spare a rider, we should alert Clárach." Danu nodded and was about to speak when Glaisne, to raised eyebrows, added, "But maybe not Cúmhaí. He may have other priorities."

As she listened to Glaisne and gave her assent, Danu felt her heart beat faster, and her cheeks flush. Glaisne smiled and gestured at his clothing. "I'm not, however, exactly dressed for battle." Conchobhar beamed at Glaisne and slapped him on the back.

"We'll find you armour suitable for a prince. I'll meet you after Danu and I discuss our strategy."

Danu's brow furrowed as if she had recalled a thought. Yet neither option sufficiently described the origin of the idea. *It was just a dream.* Finally, she shook her head and said, "Do blackthorn bushes grow around the ráth?" The strange looks from those remaining in the chamber were unsurprising. However, they confirmed that the plant was prolific on the hill and the surrounding landscape.

On Na Comaraigh, the black-cloaked figure tapped her blackthorn staff on the frozen ground and chuckled.

***

The leader of Uallachán's warband was a brute with limited intelligence. He was also a fool who dismissed any possibility of a counterattack. Who would dare oppose the king's men? Hence, he led his warriors towards Caher Conri at a leisurely pace and along a meandering path of rutted farm tracks and through forests and farmland. Perceiving no danger and seeing no need to make haste, they made frequent stops in small villages and farmsteads.

They would brag of their exploits at each stay, demand food that their hosts could ill afford to spare, and slake their thirst until the stocks of beer were gone. Like a plague of grasshoppers, they stripped the land of its vitality and robbed the residents of gold, crops, and animals.

Not content with wealth alone, they bullied peaceable hand-fast partners and fathers into surrendering their women and daughters. Protests resulted in severe beatings or death. The females, left without protection, were violated multiple times by foul-smelling and foul-mouthed men. As sunset approached, a scout brought news of a small farmholding in a hollow beyond the next rise. "Perfect," beamed the mob's leader and waved his men forward.

One scout returned to Brighid, leaving her companion to track the small warband. According to the rider, Uallachán's band was close, and Onchú's family were alive. Urged, by Onchú, to provide more detail on his partner's and daughters' condition, the messenger's diplomatic evasions caused the frustrated Rí of Carn Tigherna to stomp away angrily. Brighid swore. Not at the envoy or Onchú but at what had been left unsaid.

As the sun rose, Brighid, Maolán, and Onchú surveyed the tidy farmstead from a grassy mound to its east. A chest-high dry-stone wall enclosed three roundhouses and a large wooden barn. The houses were positioned at the centre of a sizeable yard with the barn off to the side. Uallachán's raiders had divided into two approximately equal-sized groups.

One section apportioned its members among the two largest roundhouses. Those remaining guarded the wall. From the loud and indignant conversations, the latter group's complaints were about favouritism, the unfair allocation of duties, and the lack of access to the females. The shrieking and screaming from inside the dwellings confirmed that Onchú's family were imprisoned in one of the buildings. Their treatment clearly did not accord with that customarily given to the nobility. Brighid ground her teeth.

✳✳✳

Brighid thanked the Goddess for the dawn. Restraining Onchú while he heard the pitiful cries of Eithne and his daughters proved a challenge. In the still night, the heart-breaking sounds had carried clear and far. Hence Brighid's relief to finally turn and say, "Now is our best time to attack. I doubt the early morning will find the tuilithe alert."

One final time, Brighid, Maolán, and Onchú surveyed the farmstead. Tapping Maolán on the shoulder, Brighid pointed. "Take half of the band, circle around, and position your riders where we can set up a crossfire. On my signal, kill as many as possible with your bows." Maolán nodded and moved away. Ten summers older than Brighid, the strapping warrior moved as silently as a large *lincse*.

Onchú gripped Brighid's forearm. "There are innocents in the farm buildings—and not only my family."

Brighid brushed his hand away and shook her head. Holding Onchú eyes with a glacial green stare, she said, "Until Uallachán's subjects fear *my* wrath more than their king, only the dead are innocent." Then she added, "When we have rescued your family, *I* will judge the rest."

Onchú bit back a retort. It would have been a waste of words as none of Brighid's riders would have taken his side. He watched as staves were unsheathed, bowstrings attached, and the signature red and white feather fletches on black shafts smoothed. Onchú smiled grimly and observed Brighid nock an arrow, select her target, and loose the missile in one fluid movement. Forty-nine others followed it. Immediately a second arrow was put to the string and released.

The time of day matters little to the dead. Struck down with silent efficiency, men and women fell. Some passed beyond the veil but more writhed, shrieking and bleeding in the dirt. To them, the pink morning sky became an abomination. Some, seeking shelter from the hail of barbs, ran to the far side of the farm and the barn's protection. Others pleaded for help with those in the roundhouses but were ignored. After several volleys of missiles, none were left standing in the open yard. Dark crimson splashes splattered the buildings' wattle and daub walls and the wood of the outbuilding.

"Mount up!" shouted Brighid. As one, the riders walked their mounts to within a few paces of the farmstead's perimeter wall. Perched on the backs of tall horses, they were a noticeable and frightening sight.

Brighid called Maolán, "Select ten to take high positions. Watch for trickery. Kill any who try to escape."

"Am I to have any say in the proceedings?" asked Onchú.

"Of course," answered Brighid sweetly and pointed towards the buildings. "You will identify who is in charge and negotiate the warband's surrender."

"Ah, so you deem me as disposable," said Onchú, this time with a wry smile. "Do you intend to release them if they surrender?"

"Of course," replied Brighid. Disbelief was written over Onchú's visage. Only a fool negotiates with criminals.

****

Secure within the farm buildings and their minds dulled by beer, rutting, and sleep, the rest of the warband ignored the cries of their wounded comrades. A hoarse shout, as if from a crushed larynx, called out. "You two, check what is going on." The group's leader gained a scant reaction to his order. A slap of fists on flesh yielded several yelps of pain, and two half-naked men pushed aside the roundhouse's door covering. Each held a naked, listless child as a shield as they warily stepped outside. The blood that stained the abused's thighs and arses told of the horrors visited on them.

"Shite!" gasped one of the outlaws.

His eyes finally accustomed to the sun, he saw the riders surrounding the farmstead. Tossing the girls aside, both men jumped back into the roundhouse. The cries of the girls' mother were rewarded with the brutal slap of a calloused fist to her face. It was instantly followed by the sound of a table crashing and pottery breaking. One of the girls staggered to the stone wall and was quickly lifted over it. The other lay prone on the dirt.

Barely containing his anger, Onchú guided his horse to the farm entrance and shouted, "Who speaks for this rabble?" Shoved reluctantly through the doorway, a man snarled at his comrades. He walked several paces before a black arrow shaft pierced his throat, and another thudded into his chest. Propelled backwards into the roundhouse, the man fell heavily, pulling the hide flap down. His comrades cursed the blood that splattered them and kicked him aside.

"How often do you wish to repeat this before your true leader stands forth?" asked Onchú.

Six dishevelled men armed with spears and shields exited the larger roundhouse shortly after. One who, by the size of his belly, liked his beer too much walked at the centre of the men. "I speak for these men. We serve Uallachán, Rí of Caher Conri and Carn Tigherna. Depart from here, and no more will be said," he blustered.

If there had been a speck of mercy left in Onchú's heart, the mention of Carn Tigherna squashed it. A flicker of movement in the corner of his eye was quickly followed by a cry of pain and a dropped spear. He shook his head and glared at the group's leader. "You are wrong. *I am Onchú Ó an Cháintigh, Rí of Carn Tigherna.*" The man before him blanched, and swore to punish those tasked with checking that the Carn Tigherna's king was among the dead.

Onchú pointed to Brighid sat astride her black mare. "This is Brighid Ni Conall, daughter of Conall Mac Gabhann, Rí Ruirech of Clann Ui Flaithimh, Rí of Ráth Na Conall and ruler of the lands from Caher Conri to Ráth Na Conall. You may also have heard of her mother, Mórrígan, or An Fiagaí Dorcha."

Shudders of fear rippled through Uallachán's group at the last name. Onchú allowed himself a cruel smirk. "The princess is said to favour the temperament of her mother. As you may have heard, she is a fervent advocate of staking as a punishment for criminals." A crescendo of argument and cursing swept through the small group and those in the roundhouses.

"Quiet, morons!" Then, with unjustified bravado, the leader exclaimed, "We have the women. We are in control." The man spat in the dirt and smiled crookedly. "Go away. We'll set the women free at the next village. You have my word."

Onchú leaned forward across his horse, and in a voice colder than the ice on the highest peak of Na Comaraigh, he said, "You are going to die and everyone, man and woman, with you. That is not in doubt. Only how you die remains to be decided. If it were up to me, I would peel the flesh from your skin, stuff your balls and cock in your mouth, and leave your guts steaming in a pile at your feet. Just as you did to my sons." Onchú paused and then, with a primaeval snarl, said, "Send the women out, unharmed, *now.*" Fearing for their lives, the men scrambled back into the roundhouse.

"He's not going to give up the hostages," said Brighid, sidling up next to Onchú. "Do you trust me?"

Onchú rolled his eyes. "Do I have a choice? Do what you think is best. But know this, I will never forgive you if harm comes to my partner and daughters due to your actions."

"That's fair enough," said Brighid. Turning around on her thick dillat, she called out one word to Maolán. "Fire."

✶✶✶

Splattered with mud and flesh torn by brambles, the lookout had run at full pace down the slopes of Na Comaraigh and then up the hill to Ráth Na Conall. Wheezing and coughing with lungs spasming and heart thumping, her ability to speak had long since fled. "If you were a horse, I would put you down," remarked Conchobhar. Instead he offered cold water and milk. "Inhale and exhale, slowly and deeply. Calm yourself, and then give us your report."

"One thousand foot warriors march from the west. Today, they are just beyond Clárach. They will likely take the Bod Carraig pass north of Na Comaraigh." At the mention of Clárach, Glaisne's face took on a concerned mien. "Two hundred horses canter from the north-west to join those who attacked Carn Tigherna. The riders will be here before sunset if they continue on their current path. The infantry will take another four sunsets, even at a hard march." As reports go, it was succinct, but what else could or needed to be said?

Danu looked around the table. "I hope Brighid resists the temptation to pillage and returns to Ráth Na Conall this evening. Even with the combined riders and chariots, the odds do not favour us." Then she smiled and lifted her goblet. "At least we have four sunsets to prepare for Uallachán's army. On the fifth, we'll burn Uallachán's dead. *Sláinte mhaith.*"

Red pottery cups and jugs slammed down on the oak table. Some shattered, spilling their contents over the wood and neighbours. "Perhaps I should ask Pytheas to send more chalices, or we'll soon be supping with our hands." Ribbons of laughter curled around those at the table. All knew the picture looked grim, and the *mná-sidhe* gathered. "At least the seanchaithe will immortalise our stand," Danu murmured.

"We have two hundred against fifteen hundred," said Conchobhar and then winked at Beacán. "Seems surprisingly good odds to me." Then he looked at Danu, whose face carried a look of unease. "Apart from the obvious, what troubles you?"

"We're missing something. The force is too large by far. Uallachán knows our strength, either by observation or his spy in the fort." Eyes widened at Danu's last words, and she smiled. "I always assume the worst." She looked at Glaisne. "Except in some areas." Then she continued, "Gold is a great temptation for most men and women. Threats of death, dismemberment, and the violation of family members can make even the most loyal subjects sell out those they have served faithfully."

"Perhaps, since the defeat of the mercenaries, Uallachán is unsure of our real strength. This could be his final push," posed Beacán.

Danu sighed. "If only we had brought ballistae with us." Conchobhar and Glaisne looked strangely at Danu. She wondered why and then smiled. "War machines—mounted bolt-throwers. They are gaining in popularity in the nations of the Great Sea."

"The Hag's arse!" exclaimed Conchobhar.

Danu stood. "Uallachán's forces appear poorly coordinated. His horses will arrive four days before those on foot and that makes no sense." Unable to discern Uallachán's strategy, Danu exhaled sharply in frustration. Then, accepting defeat, she switched focus. "We'll make our sacrifices to the Goddess at meán lae. We need all the help we can get. Then we'll take our places and wait."

Beacán and Iasg held back as the others exited the room. Danu's eyebrow raised. "Have I forgotten something, uncle?" Beacán shook his head and smiled broadly. Typically Beacán was a man whose face was unremarkable. Yet when her uncle beamed, Danu thought he looked the handsomest man in any room.

"Iasg and I are more effective outside. With your permission, we will depart the ráth, reconnoitre the battlefield, and take an advantageous position in the forests. We will bring death in the dark hours of the night."

Danu shook her head. "Not this time. I need experience by my side. I respect Iasg's and your skills, but against such odds, the risk of harm, even your death, is too high. You will stay and fight by my side."

"As you wish."

Beacán grasped Danu's hand. "This is a tough first command. I doubt anyone in Lugudunon anticipated the snake pit you and Brighid have stepped into. If they had, no matter how much you protested, your ma and da would never have allowed you to leave. At the least, they would have sent a much larger force. You and Brighid are doing well. I'm proud of you, and so would Conall and Mórrígan be." Danu smiled as Beacán walked to the doorway. Before Iasg joined her partner, Danu held her back.

"Take care of him, Iasg. I will not lose my uncle or you. Ráth Na Conall is not worth that price." Iasg opened her arms and embraced Danu.

"We'll be fine, and so will ye."

∗∗∗

At the door of her chamber, Danu's neck hairs stiffened. She whirled around, knife in hand, and stared into Glaisne's smiling face. "Not exactly the welcome I expected," he said with a chuckle and looked at the blade pressed against his belly.

"You surprised me," said Danu. Her tone was challenging.

"That was the intent. I thought we could spend some time alone before the fighting starts." He pushed against the blade until it was withdrawn. Danu felt his arm around her waist, pulling her closer, and watched as his lips parted and his head dipped. A finger placed on his mouth stopped the manoeuvre.

"This is not a suitable time." Danu sensed his body tighten and saw his jaw clench. Releasing her, Glaisne dipped his head, turned abruptly on his heels, and strode down the hallway, brushing aside Danu's guards. They shook their heads at the unpleasant scowl on Glaisne's face.

CHAPTER 8

A cloud of arrows arced high into the air, marking the pale blue sky with trails of grey. All struck the sun-faded, roof of the barn. It was not an extraordinary feat, for even a novice bowman could hardly miss such a huge target. The roofing, damp from recent rainfall, at first resisted, producing only tendrils of white smoke.

Laughs and jeers erupted from the roundhouses. When the second volley of arrows struck the thatch, the smoke turned black as the small fires came together as visible flames. The roof transformed into a raging inferno, raining burning straw inside the barn. Anxiety crept into the group's demeanour.

Horses, cattle, and men screamed as dry hay and forage were set ablaze. Thick smoke filled the air. Soon, the barn doors burst open as five men, choking and gasping for air, sought to escape the inferno. Arrows thudded into their chests, propelling them backwards. Stomped on by fleeing animals, they died, and the mná-sidhe escorted their spirits to the Otherworld.

Brighid signalled Maolán, and another volley of fire-arrows gouged the sky. The target was the smallest of the roundhouses, and likely a store for equipment, food, and seeds. Uallachán's captain exhaled when no villains burst from its entrance. Helpless, he had watched his band reduced to a third of its original size. The rest were dead or gravely wounded.

The circular buildings had no doors or heavy window shutters. Only pieces of cloth or scraps of inferior quality hides kept the weather at bay. Behind the door covering of the larger roundhouse, Uallachán's man watched with heightened anxiety. Carried by a soft breeze, embers and thin brands from the storehouse flew ever closer to the steeply sloped thatches of the last two roundhouses.

More showers of arrows sped towards the second-largest home. By its size, the dwelling could have slept fifteen people and several animals. Burning missiles plucked at the egress coverings while others penetrated the thatch. Brighid watched with grim satisfaction as the barbs swept away or burned the flimsy entrance and window drapes. From the shrieking inside the building, some had found flesh—but whose?

Onchú gripped his sword, his knuckles white with anger, despair, and helplessness. The cries of men and women from inside the building intensified his emotions. Were the voices those of his hand-fast partner and daughters? He looked at Brighid, but her face held no trace of emotion. *Is she that heartless?*

Gasping for breath, their faces smeared with ash, men, women, and children exited the roundhouse. All were naked. Brighid's lips thinned. *Someone among them has a brain.* Without the means to distinguish between farmer and brigand, did she have any choice? She nodded to Maolán, and the men fell—dead or injured.

Stunned, the women and children stared at those prone on the dirt. They prayed to the Goddess that the cooling corpses were their despoilers and not their lovers, partners, and brothers. Two females, however, were wolves and quickly grabbed the youngest of the children as shields. With blades held against soft throats, the pair edged slowly towards the final roundhouse and sanctuary. Mothers and siblings bawled hysterically.

Yet one, her family destroyed, and she degraded many times, had reached the end of her tether. Screaming, "No more!" she picked up a discarded spear. In hands calloused by farm work, she held the shaft as if wielding a pitchfork, shouted "Bitseach!" and lunged at the trailing female. Spitted by the leaf-shaped spearhead, the warrior released her hostage as her eyes sought comprehension. From the grimace on her death face, the Otherworld was her destination.

The knife in the second warrior's hand bit into soft flesh, and she screamed, "Stand back!" The child cried out for her ma as droplets of blood trickled down her neck. An arm tightened around the small child's chest. She whimpered, and her mother shrieked. The fighter glanced around in desperation. Although only a few paces away, the distance to safety seemed unattainable.

Mesmerised, she watched her comrade's slayer place a foot on the torso and, with deliberation, wrench the gore-covered spear from the corpse. She saw strings of flesh hang from the spearhead and smelled the stench of piss and shite released in a final indignity. The warrior's eyes were wild with fear, and her movements uncertain. Having no children of her own, she had no concept of a mother's relentless determination to protect or avenge her offspring.

Focused on the vengeful mother, the female miscreant lost sight of the larger picture. Frantically, she looked around and then froze, captured by the merciless eyes of the rider with long plaits of auburn hair. "No!" the warrior gasped as the arrow sped towards her. Another shaft followed quickly in its path.

The arrows pierced both eyes, exiting her skull in a gush of blood, brain, and bone. She released the child and for a moment stood motionless before the force of the arrows flung back into the burning roundhouse. Her hope of rest in Mag Mell was dashed when she joined her comrade at the maw of the Otherworld. The Goddess did not favour any who spilt the blood of innocent children.

"I learned that from my ma," remarked Brighid, turning to face Onchú. She pointed to the remaining dwelling. "Once more, it's your turn to negotiate with those tuilithe. I estimate there's eighteen of them in the remaining roundhouse, along with your partner and daughters." Onchú winced as Brighid gripped his forearm. For one who looked quite fragile, Brighid's strength was undeniable.

"If need be, I will end this, and if the price is your friendship, I will accept the toll." Onchú scowled and walked his horse to the farmstead's gateway.

* * *

"Over thirty of your band are dead or injured. Surrender and release your captives. Or, as the Hag is my witness, I will visit unspeakable pain upon your miserable bodies. You will beg for the bean-sidhe to give you release, but she will laugh in your face and delight in your suffering."

"Your approach to negotiation is reminiscent of my da," said Brighid, rolling her eyes. "Neither he nor my ma were noted for their diplomatic skills." Loud arguments increased in ferocity within the roundhouse. "The rats turn on each other," snorted Brighid. Further discussion halted when a shout came from the building.

"We'll send the woman and the children out—and our leader. In return, you will agree to let us go." Shouts of "Fools!" were stemmed by the smack of fists on flesh.

"Agreed," called out Onchú. "Send the females out first." He turned to Brighid. "Their leader is mine. You can have the rest."

Brighid nodded. "Agreed, although I doubt you will inflict as much pain and suffering as I could." The deep green eyes, now almost black, sent a shiver along Onchú's spine.

Three naked females stumbled out into the farmyard. All rubbed their eyes and squinted in the strong sunlight. The many bruises and bloodstains that covered their bodies drew a loud moan of anguish from Onchú. He dismounted and walked to meet them. At his back were Brighid and ten guards.

The girls, aged thirteen and fifteen summers, spotted their father but did not recognise the fierce, shaven-headed warrior. Onchú smiled, scratched his scalp, and, arms opened wide, went down on one knee. With a scream of "Da!" they ran towards him and leapt into his embrace. Tears of relief cascaded down the faces of father and daughters.

"Ma is not well," said the older girl, looking at the tall, dark-haired woman standing in the centre of the yard.

"It is understandable, but you are all safe now. Go with my friends, and I will join you shortly." Onchú stood and watched as his daughters were wrapped in blankets and led away. He sighed as he walked towards his hand-fast partner. She looked at him, but hazel eyes, flecked with amber, held no recognition until he said one word. "Eithne."

"Tuilí! You murderous, uncaring bastard!" screeched Eithne. "You deserted us and left us helpless to defend ourselves. *You* killed my sons and left my daughters and me to be raped and sodomised—over and over. What kind of heartless man are you?"

Those watching the scene stood uncertain, not knowing whether recognition had returned to Eithne or her sanity had deserted her. Screeched curses rent the air, swiftly followed by slaps and punches. Onchú said nothing and did nothing. Yet only the blind could miss his shoulders slumping. Attempts to embrace Eithne resulted in more profanities, accusations, and blows. Focused on Eithne, Onchú did not hear Brighid arrive beside him.

"Shite!" exclaimed Brighid. She looked at the crazed woman and shook her head in disbelief, although perhaps that was due to her lack of years. "My lady, I grieve for your loss and the treatment of you and your daughters, but there are other events and priorities in play. This is no time for histrionics. Please, gather yourself up and see to your daughters." The words had no impact and Eithne continued her tirade.

Brighid said, "I'm sorry."

Onchú looked at Brighid without understanding. The fist caught Eithne under her chin, snapping her head back, and she collapsed senseless to the dirt. Brighid called two riders to her. "Clothe her, bind her, gag her, and tie her to a horse. I'll deal with the consequences at a later time."

Brighid held Onchú's gaze. "You need to put an end to this swiftly. Danu needs us at Ráth Na Conall."

Shoved out of the roundhouse's entrance, the leader of the thugs snarled at his men. His face was bloody, lips were swollen, and diseased gums had several new spaces. Stupidly defiant, he leered at Onchú. "Your partner prefers my company to yours. I'll buy her from you. That said, she's not worth much now. Most of us took turns rutting her… and your daughters." However, his mocking could not disguise an involuntary tic of fear, and he made one desperate plea. "Fight me. Warrior to warrior."

"A murderer, torturer, and despoiler of women and children has no rights." Onchú called two burly riders to him. "Strip him, bind him, and secure him to the wall." The men nodded. Soon the sound of a hammer striking iron sounded out, accompanied by shrieks of pain from the recipient. Onchú looked at the men questioningly. They shrugged. There was no rope or chains to bind the man to the wall. What else could they use but iron spikes? Onchú stood before the shocked outlaw and pulled a long, wickedly curved blade from its sheath.

"I used this blade to shave my head. You can still see the blood because its edge is dull."

The man screamed as the tip of the blade was drawn slowly along the seam of his ballsack. The envelope parted, exposing his balls as they fell and dangled loose. He gasped in excruciating pain as Onchú wrenched his cock forward and sliced it at the root. The newly created eunuch whimpered as Onchú tossed the body parts aside. The predator felt his thighs slick with warm gore.

"Not so much fun when you're the one on the receiving end, is it?"

In one movement, Onchú sliced deeply and slowly across the man's abdomen. Purple-grey coils of intestines slapped the earth. Onchú turned and walked away. It was less than the man deserved, but animals would finish the tuilí. He would suffer long and die slowly.

As Onchú walked and stood ten paces beyond the entrance of the last roundhouse, a group of men, and several women, emerged into the farmyard. "We had a deal," shouted the band's new leader. The look in Onchú's eyes froze the man.

"I do not make deals with bandits and rapists," said Onchú and looked at Brighid. "They're all yours."

Brighid turned to her riders and called out her orders. "Behead the dead. Bind the living. Check the injured. Leave those who can't walk to the mercies of the farmers' women."

As the remaining women and children emerged from their captivity, Brighid leant over her black mare's shoulders and stared at them. In a voice laden with menace, she said, "This land belongs to Clann Uí Flaithimh and its Rí Ruirech, my father Conall Mac Gabhann and his queen, my mother, Mórrígan. Spread the news. Any who give succour to Uallachán, and those who take his gold, will face the wrath of my sister and me. There will be no mercy."

"Are we returning to Ráth Na Conall?" asked Onchú as Brighid cantered towards him. She nodded.

"There is a stream not far from here. Take Eithne and your daughters. Let them bathe, put on dry clothing, and eat. I will take ten riders to accomplish my task. I will be back by the time you have finished. Then we ride hard for Ráth Na Conall."

She put a hand on Onchú's arm. "I am truly sorry for what you and your family have suffered, but my feirdhris tells me that Ráth Na Conall is in peril." Brighid held Onchú's gaze and, in a cold voice, said, "No harm had better come to my sister. Else, I will make this land run with blood—and I will not care whose it is."

Onchú shivered, for he had no doubts that Brighid would keep her vow.

＊＊＊

The dirt track ran through the middle of a series of rolling hillocks. From its width and heavily rutted surface, it appeared to be the primary path for artisans, traders, and farmers travelling to Caher Conri. Five paces apart and spaced on a ridge across the track, twenty men and woman whimpered. The excruciating agony of the staking had passed, and shock had set in. Until the forest's predators came to feed, there would just be a deep unbearable throb.

Three red shields, each with a swooping black raven on a field of red, hung from three cut branches before the staked miscreants. At each end of the line of the executed, red and black, and gold and black banners of king and clann flapped in the wind. The daughters of Conall had thrown down the challenge.

"I had hoped to be closer to Caher Conri, but I think this should underscore our previous message," said Brighid to Maolán. He responded with a savage grin.

CHAPTER 9

394 B.C.—Lugnasad

Autumn had just begun and yet Danu shivered and wished Ériu's climate was more like the Great Sea's. Hoping to draw its warmth closer, her cold fingers fumbled with the heavy wolf fur draped over her shoulders and the ornate clasp that drew its edges together. Alone on the ramparts, Danu organised her thoughts, running through countless stratagems and dismissing most. She wondered how Brighid fared and prayed for her swift return.

To the west, snow and fog cloaked the heights of Na Comaraigh. In the fields around the ráth, patches of white mist floated over the ground, gently rising and falling in tandem with the light morning breezes. The vista was beautiful and ethereal. The sun, shimmering on the horizon, foretold the scene's demise.

The fort had become a hive of activity, which, while appearing chaotic, moved forward with purpose. Ráth Na Conall's northern, forest-facing rampart had taken most of the damage during the past four seasons' battles. Sustained attacks had left the stone wall breached and crumbling. The inner wooden stockade had many gaps where the massive piles had been pulled down or burned. Many of the fence's timbers lay in the perimeter ditch.

Hearing Conchobhar's shouts, Danu looked to the source of the noise and smiled. His allocation of work duties caused ripples of good-natured complaints among the gangs of warriors. One group focused on clearing the ditches and replacing the sharpened stakes. Another was tasked with filling the gaps in the stone facing walls. A final band cut down trees from the nearby forest to replace the missing timbers.

Danu anticipated a strong cavalry attack. Hence, the final workgroup also placed felled trees at the foot of the mound, with the branches sharpened and angled outwards. The labour was purposeful, and few complained, yet all knew they were attempting to make a pig look like a wolfhound.

✳✳✳

"There's a messenger from Ráth Na Conall who wishes to speak with you. He says Glaisne sent him and offered this as proof." Aodh, Rí of Clárach, reached out to take the ring from his shield-man. "He rode an imposing horse with an equally fine spare. Better than any of Curraghatoor's stock by my reckoning." Aodh examined the ring carefully but instantly recognised it as one of three his father had given to Glaisne, Cúmhaí, and himself. *Into what pit of trouble had Glaisne fallen?* His mission to observe the new occupants of Ráth Na Conall was straightforward and not overly challenging.

Aodh examined his green woollen shirt and plaid green triubhas for signs of his early-morning meal of oatmeal and berries. Satisfied he was presentable, he said, "Send him in… and let's keep this to ourselves for the moment." The shield-man, who had been at Aodh's side since the king's childhood, read between the lines and nodded. His expression briefly spoke of disappointment at Aodh's struggles with his siblings.

The envoy, a young man of no more than twenty summers, stopped a diplomatic distance from Aodh's throne and bowed deeply. "Your brother sends you his greetings and wishes you to know that he remains at Ráth Na Conall as a guest with no limits on his freedom." Aodh raised bushy eyebrow. "The princesses, Brighid Ni Conall and Danu Ni Conall, who are the daughters of Conall Mac Gabhann, Rí Ruirech of Clann Ui Flaithimh and Mórrígan Ni Cathasaigh, send you greetings. They hope to meet you in person at a less turbulent time."

"I thought that bastard and his *bitseach* partner were long dead." Only the glimmer of a smile on Aodh's face prevented the messenger from taking offence. "Now you inform me that Conall's daughters are at the fort? Why?"

"An ambassador from Ráth Na Conall was received by the Rí Ruirech at his stronghold in Gaul and pleaded for help in resisting the rebellion led by Uallachán, Rí of Caher Conri."

"Now there's a real *tuilí*, and his brother too," snarled Aodh. "Why didn't Conall come? It's his mess to clear up. He was the one who snubbed Uallachán and shamed him by exiling him to Caher Conri." The envoy bowed and walked through the opening presented to him.

"At the time, Conall was bound by a *geis* from the Aes Sidhe, which prevented his, or any male offspring's return to Ériu… ever."

"Bloody Aes Sidhe! It'd be hard to find a bigger bunch of interfering women in this world or the next," snapped Aodh. His shield-man nodded in agreement. "So Conall declined because of a promise made to a witch?"

"There were other circumstances. Conall was also about to lead his army into a battle with Rome," said the envoy.

"Battle?" Aodh snorted, and his shield-man chuckled. "I have heard tales of Rome. Its might is well known, even in far-flung Ériu. Surely you mean skirmish?"

The ambassador from Ráth Na Conall smiled and dipped his head. "With respect, I hardly think an army of ten thousand shield-warriors, two thousand cavalry, and two thousand Cinn Péinteáilte is necessary for a 'skirmish'. With his allies, Brennus, the Rí Ruirech of the Senones and Celtillos, the Verrix of the Arverni, Conall slaughtered the Roman legions and conquered Rome." The envoy paused to enjoy the consternation on Aodh's weather-beaten face and the worry on his shield-man's pursed lips.

"Shite! With that army, he could land in Ériu and be declared

Ard-Rígh—High King—instantly."

Aodh's hazel eyes held the messenger's gaze. Neither man flinched until the ambassador considered he had made his point and averted his eyes. Aodh smiled. He was growing to like the young man standing before him. "Well done. You tricked me into letting you demonstrate why it would not be wise to get on the wrong side of Conall's daughters. Now tell me what you have omitted from your message."

"Carn Tigherna is destroyed, burnt to the ground by the combined forces of Uallachán and Curraghatoor. Onchú's sons were defiled, tortured, and cruelly executed, and his hand-fast partner and daughters taken captive and violated." The envoy paused. "Five hundred riders from Curraghatoor ride for Ráth Na Conall. A thousand of Uallachán's foot warriors march in the direction of the fort."

"That is disturbing, and I grieve for Onchú's loss. It shows that Uallachán does not care or fear Conall, his daughters, or his allies. But unless you're holding something back, this is not Clárach's fight." Aodh paused and stroked long blond whiskers. "My garrison is not so large that I could make a difference even if I were disposed to interfere. I thank you for your report. Should the princesses survive, I will be delighted to receive them at Clárach or visit with them at Ráth Na Conall."

The envoy bowed. "Apologies, but I have one final piece of information. Alone, the riders from Curraghatoor far outnumber the garrison at Ráth Na Conall. The mounted force plus the foot warriors appear excessive."

Aodh's eyes narrowed, and lines furrowed his brow. Danu's emissary judged it time to make his final statement. "I'm not sure what your scouts have informed you, but as I stand here before the throne of Clárach, Uallachán's thousand currently camps within striking distance of Clárach. I do not wish to spread alarm, but it would be remiss of me not to counsel that Carn Tigherna had no warning of an attack." Aodh's mien darkened. "Ráth Na Conall has no wish to see a friendly neighbour… and possible ally removed from the fidchell board."

"Please stand to the side. I wish to talk privately with my advisor." The envoy bowed and walked away but not so far that he could not hear. "There is a heavy stink of pig shite in the air," exclaimed Aodh. "Whose watch is it in the valley today?"

"Cúmhaí."

Aodh shook his head. "I know he covets the throne, but surely he would not betray his people to get it." The burly shield-man shrugged broad shoulders. "How many can my brother count on?" asked Aodh.

"Fifty at the most. The army doesn't like him that much… yet."

Aodh glowered at his shield-man and rubbed his hand over the pommel of his sword. "Do I have a problem in *this* room?" The tall guardian's laughter echoed off the chamber's walls. To Danu's messenger, it was not the mirth of a dishonest man.

"The Hag, no. But *you* should have taken care of this much sooner." Aodh growled at his shield-man's chastising tone. "By all appearances, Glaisne accepts you as Clárach's king, although, following this night, we may need to re-examine our previous assumptions. However, Cúmhaí has made no secret of his desire to sit on Clárach's throne." The veteran paused to suck at a morsel of meat trapped in his teeth. "At least Cúmhaí has demonstrated a level of honesty—if misguided."

The burly shield-man scratched his full beard as if thinking, an affectation, since he always understood the fort's defensive position thoroughly. "We have two hundred loyal warriors. Even if we can resolve our internal problem, we do not have many to counter Uallachán's thousand, and that is with Clárach sitting on the top of a mountain."

"Secure the gateways. Keep a watch on Cúmhaí's men when they return and guide them to where they can be corralled and disarmed. Send my brother to me when he arrives and triple the guards everywhere."

Aodh stared at his second-in-command's back before turning back to the messenger. "Has anyone ever told you that you are a bloody trouble-maker?" Ignoring the hand raised in mock protest, he added, "You have a choice. You can remain here and see what transpires or get something warm in your belly and ride back to Ráth Na Conall. If you choose the latter, tell the princesses that Aodh, Rí of Clárach sends his greetings… and his thanks."

* * *

"Riders to the north. They've stopped on the northern bank of the Abhainn na Siúire, beyond the ridge that follows the river. The water is not deep this far upstream, and they can walk the horses across with no problems. At a fast canter, they could be here well before meán lae." The lookout from Na Comaraigh was exhausted, although not as much as on her previous visit. She had begged Báine for one of the spare shaggy-haired chariot ponies and was delighted that the horse loved the challenging mountain slopes.

"We're about to see how good our makeshift defences are," said Danu to Conchobhar. "Do you have a plan?"

"We're on an elevated hill, but the long inclines will cause no great problems for horses. The fort has high walls, albeit needing repair. In our favour, horses were never meant for sieges, and the riders will have to dismount to attack. Also, our hundred and twenty-five shield-warriors are all veterans and know how to hold a defensive position.

"Báine's chariots and riders can harass them while we hold the fort. I have to believe that our mounts and cavalry are more experienced and better equipped than theirs. The blades on Báine's chariots will put the fear of the Hag into Curraghatoor's riders." Conchobhar sighed. "But I wish Brighid were here—every little helps." He coughed. "Báine tells me she has a plan." Danu rolled her eyes.

"You haven't mentioned the real threat—Uallachán's thousand warriors."

Conchobhar shrugged well-muscled shoulders, although the effort was more to adjust his newly acquired chainmail. "What can we do about them? It is what it is. The Goddess will choose whom to favour."

Turning to the warriors arrayed along the walkway, Danu lifted her shield and javelin high and shouted, "We will hold the wall. *Ní ghéillfear, nó cúlú*—no retreat, no surrender!" Around the walls of Ráth Na Conall, spears slapped shields, and the war cry of Clann Ui Flaithimh rose.

* * *

Midway between the grassy ridge and Ráth Na Conall, whatever plan had been devised by Crónán Mac Dedad and his half-brother, Torna, began to unravel. From the highest peak of Na Comaraigh came the ululating invocations of the Sidhe. Perhaps, bored with the inactivity—those of the Aes Sidhe were not known for their patience—she had decided to intervene.

A cold, northerly wind rose and howled through the forests. Early hail fell from clouds that had ominously darkened. The wailing and complicity of the weather unsettled the minds of man and beast, and the riders from Curraghatoor began to falter.

"What the Hag's arse is going on?"

Conchobhar referred not to the unexpected, if welcome, contribution from the Sidhe. Rather, he pointed to the two hundred riders who had split from the main body. Veering to the left, they came to a halt on a ridge one thousand paces to the east of Ráth Na Conall. There they steadfastly ignored angry shouts from Crónán and Torna to re-join the attack.

"Curraghatoor is not as united as we thought," said Danu. "But will they fight or watch?"

Conchobhar's and Danu's musings were interrupted by a full-throated howl and the blare of trumpets. From behind the hill, banners flapping and long, bronze blades spinning, Báine's chariots charged. Side by side, the five carbaid drove at the advancing cavalry. One hundred paces behind—a distance reluctantly agreed by the riders—fifty mounts galloped.

Synchronised to the thunder of hooves, the red foxtails fixed to the nubs of otherwise unremarkable helmets whirled and bounced. Each rider grasped a javelin in his right hand and a smaller version of the oblong, shield-wall scíatha in his left. Each had five other throwing spears and various weapons held in sheaths strapped to the horses' flanks. All screamed curses and taunts at the Curraghatoor force, but the words were whipped away by the wind.

Undoubtedly, the chanting of the Sidhe and her unearthly intervention unnerved Curraghatoor's riders. The desertion of their comrades rattled them further. Yet, above all, the sight of war chariots, led by a white-haired warrior, hurtling towards them at reckless speeds struck terror into the minds of the bravest of the mounted warriors. Too late, many began to wish they had joined those who had chosen not to fight.

To the west, a howl from the mouth of the Bod Carraig valley brought a huge smile to Báine's face. *Great timing, Brighid.* The visages of Crónán and Torna and Curraghatoor's riders fell. Even the stupidest among them could sense the jaws of a trap closing. Far from having overwhelming numbers, the balance of strength moved in favour of Ráth Na Conall. The would-be ríthe swore as cheers and war cries from the fort thundered across the plain.

The chariots struck first, slamming into Curraghatoor's forward line. Spinning knives shuddered, and horses screamed as legs and tendons were sundered. One blade snapped and spun through the air. Hot blood spurted from decapitated torsos, showering those around in gore. Others, perhaps less fortunate, were merely maimed by the missile.

Chariots, however, have poor suspensions—if any at all. Thus, when Báine's vehicle hit a wrinkle in the land, it momentarily took to the air like a gaily coloured raven before swooping downwards and crashing into the mass. Frightened mounts tossed riders to the ground; many were crushed as injured steeds fell on them.

Báine's teams, unable to forge further, ground to a halt and were quickly surrounded. After exhausting their supply of arrows, darts, and javelins, they took up axes, clubs, and swords, swearing to avenge Carn Tigherna. Just in time, the two wings of Clann Uí Flaithimh's cavalry came to Báine's relief, hurling volleys of javelins and heavy darts.

Then they, too, switched to their favoured long-handled axes, maces, and swords. Brighid's riders, facing the right and rear flanks, dismounted, and proceeded to empty quivers of arrows into the midst of the Curraghatoor mass. Barbs exhausted, they remounted, hefted heavy maces, and, to the accompaniment of bloodcurdling wails from Brighid, charged.

Crónán's and Torna's riders had previously overwhelmed a defenceless Carn Tigherna. Now, they faced experienced fighters, and neither Crónán nor Torna were shrewd tacticians nor experienced in battle. It eventually dawned on the false ríthe of Curraghatoor that the selling of Curraghatoor's assets had not prepared them for the desperate fight they had started. The foolishness of not waiting for Uallachán's warriors flooded their minds. Courage deserted the half-brothers, and they ordered the horns to blast out shrill calls to retreat. Fleeing the battlefield, they recrossed the Abhainn na Siúire and entered the safety of the forest.

∗∗∗

Cúmhaí's arrangement with Uallachán was simple. Uallachán would attack when it was Cúmhaí's rotation to guard Clárach's entrances, and they would stand aside. In return, Cúmhaí would pledge loyalty to Uallachán, and his reward would be the throne of Clárach. That Cúmhaí accepted Uallachán's word at face value was a measure of how much he coveted his brother's seat. Equally, it was clear evidence that Cúmhaí would make a terrible king.

Clárach's defences, a single circular defensive berm, three spears high, of dirt, peat, and stone, were, by most measures, crude and based in antiquity. There were four entrances, positioned north, south, east, and west. Heavy oak gates secured all. A tortuous web of narrow trails from the foot of Sléibhe na Clárach to the fort's earthen walls were the only viable access to the fortress's gates. The rest of the mountain was sheer rock bluffs. Hence, for generations, the ríthe and garrison of Clárach slept easy in their cots.

Accompanied by a guard of ten tall, beefy warriors, Cúmhaí strode through the northern entrance of Clárach. A tap on his shoulder drew

Cúmhaí's attention to the absence of his men among the sentries, provoking a frown. That the number replacing them had tripled further raised his concern. While not known as the brightest of his father's sons, Cúmhaí's instincts told him something was amiss. Anger, however, prevailed over thoughtful analysis and, indignant that anyone would countermand his orders, Cúmhaí stormed across the muddy yard to the Great Hall.

Clárach's Great Hall stood a rectangular block of stone, twenty-five paces long and twenty paces wide. The roof was thatched, there were no windows, and the doors were thick oak slabs, swung on substantial iron hinges. Cúmhaí pulled up, startled at the presence of guards on either side of the doorway. His brother had never been overly concerned about security—until now. Physically, Cúmhaí was a powerful man. Cheeks flushed red in anger, he pushed the heavy doors open with enough force to slam them against the inner walls. He strode up the central aisle to where Aodh sat on the carved oak throne.

His brother did not rise to greet him, forcing Cúmhaí to advance as if a supplicant wishing to plead his case. Cúmhaí ground his teeth until his jaw ached. Aodh's sober mien provoked a rising concern, as did the presence of the score of warriors who stood along the longer walls. There was, of course, the king's usual shield-man towering over the throne. As he got to within a few paces of the royal seat, Cúmhaí saw in his brother's eyes the look of a spider whose dinner had just set the web vibrating.

"Who replaced my men at the gates? And why?" demanded Cúmhaí. With the wind taken from his sails, his voice held a tone of uncharacteristic unease.

Aodh stroked his whiskers deliberately and slowly clasped his hands before speaking. The simple act infuriated Cúmhaí. "I wonder why your scouts did not inform you of the thousand warriors from Caher Conri, who stand at the foot of Sléibhe na Clárach." Hazel eyes stared hard at Cúmhaí, making the younger brother flinch. "Or perhaps they did. In which case, the question becomes, *brother*, why did you not inform me?" Cúmhaí opened his mouth, but a raised hand stopped him.

"In fact, the only reason I am informed of this unusual turn of events is via a message sent from Ráth Na Conall by our brother, Glaisne."

"Nothing good comes from Ráth Na Conall," snapped Cúmhaí, "or anything truthful from Glaisne."

"I might have agreed with you—until the boots of Uallachán's army ventured into Clárach's territory without *my* permission." Aodh bent towards Cúmhaí, and his eyes locked onto his brother's. "Did you sanction this incursion? In which case, likely you have a reasonable explanation. If so, now would be an appropriate time to unburden yourself." Aodh smiled, and his posture now resembled a viper about to strike.

"Or should I just proceed to your execution for treason?"

Cúmhaí's reputation as the best swordsman of Clárach was well-deserved. His weakness was his inability to anticipate. Aodh's shield-man did not have that flaw. The sword that appeared in Cúmhaí's hand travelled rapidly towards Aodh's neck. The weapon met the blade of Aodh's shield-man swung with equal speed, preventing Aodh's demise. Sparks flew as Cúmhaí's weapon scraped the stone floor and was stamped down to the hewn rock. The sharp pain of his wrist twisting made Cúmhaí gasp. His discomfort was temporary, ending when a calloused fist met his chin and laid him out beside the steel blade.

When he awoke, Cúmhaí's long hair was grasped and twisted painfully tightly by Aodh. Teeth bared, Aodh hissed in his brother's ear. "I overlooked your many plottings to usurp the throne our father entrusted to me. I had hoped that time would temper your ambition. That was misplaced loyalty to my family." Aodh signalled the warriors from the walls. "These faithful guardians will take you to join the other traitors on the ramparts."

Aodh turned to his shield-man. "Order every man, woman, and child who can hold a spear to the walls. And think about how, should we survive the next sunset, we thank Ráth Na Conall. I will not be in any man's or woman's debt."

* * *

"Shite!" gasped Uallachán.

In the gloom of the mist that hovered above the mountain, the human torches that had previously been Cúmhaí's men burned brightly. The smell of pitch and roasting flesh tumbled down the slope. Uallachán breathed harshly and grabbed a thick tree branch to steady himself. He was not a fit man, having long foregone exercise. Hence, the long climb to the summit of Sléibhe na Clárach had winded him and gave him a sharp pain in his side. Hubris drove him to the top of the mountain. That, and a desire to gloat over Aodh.

Cúmhaí, however, was not among the candles. Nailed to the oak doors of the northern entrance, Uallachán dupe's eyes had been gouged out, and his throat cut. Still, his fate was undoubtedly less severe than Uallachán had envisaged once Cúmhaí had outlived his usefulness. With a snarl, Uallachán ordered the two hundred men with him back down the mountain to re-join his main column. Clárach might still fall, but not without a higher level of bloodshed. He had much to ponder.

CHAPTER 10

Danu was delighted to see Brighid back in Ráth Na Conall, although it saddened her to hear of Onchú's personal troubles. The hillfort was a small community, and gossip travelled as fast as a whisper. Hence, the schism between Onchú and Eithne became widely known—and all took sides. As a gaunt, shaven-headed Onchú walked the walls, from sunrise to sunrise, the sympathies of the ráth's garrison and their partners were firmly with him and his daughters. Many stopped to give Eithne a "piece of their mind", but the lady's eyes held a glimmer of madness and walls of anger imprisoned her.

Danu sorely missed Onchú's wise head as she peered around the table. The small group had evolved to become Brighid's and her *Chomhairle*—Council. "Tactics? Can we expect another assault from Crónán when they have broken their fast? Do we defend or attack?"

"Bring all the warriors, horse and foot, into the fort and make Crónán attack. The advantage is ours. We have walls, battle-hardened warriors, a large stock of weapons, and the trades to make more." Conchobhar spoke in between mouthfuls of hot oatmeal, cheese, berries, and long slurps of milk. "Without overwhelming numbers, Crónán would be an eejit to attack us."

"Agreed, but when they join with Uallachán's men, Curraghatoor's riders will have the numbers they need. Confining our horses and chariots to the fort will weaken our position and reduce our flexibility," countered Danu.

"Attack them with our chariots and cavalry before they reorganise. We have better horses, armour, and weapons." Brighid looked to Danu for support, but her sister shook her head.

"No. Only the seanchaithe like tragedies of heroic but doomed assaults. At best, it would blunt our only advantage."

"Bitseach! Will you ever consider any of my suggestions?" Brighid's nostril's flared, and her lips curled as she glared first at Danu and then Glaisne. "Does *his* counsel find favour with you but not your sister's?" An awkward silence fell as Brighid stormed from the room, slamming its door in her wake.

Danu took a deep breath to settle her irritation at Brighid's outburst. She looked at Glaisne and gave him a weak smile of apology. He had the expression of a cat that had just feasted on a pink fillet of fish. Did her sister have a point? She shook her head dismissively. "Apparently, I'm not such a great fidchell player. We still have two forces to contend with."

"What will be the mind of Crónán after being forced to retreat?" asked Beacán.

"Why don't we ask those of his warriors who refused to fight?" suggested Flann. "They've been kicking their heels since the battle. On the one hand, we don't know whether we can trust them and, on the other, they can't go back to Curraghatoor. Whether they made a brave or foolish choice needs to be resolved quickly."

As the meeting broke up, Beacán held back. Worry etched his face as he placed a hand on Danu's arm. That she flinched at his touch drove his concern higher. *Were they too young for the responsibility?* He looked into Danu's eyes and worried that their usual brightness had diminished. A cough cleared Beacán's throat. "Brighid's suggestion was good. She did not deserve such a brutal dismissal delivered by you and before the Chomhairle."

Danu's face flushed deep red, and she opened her mouth to retort, but Beacán had turned and exited the chamber. "The Hag. What am I doing?" Danu's feirdhris throbbed painfully, but she chose not to examine its roots for fear of what might be revealed.

In Brighid's private quarters, her rose pounded like a second heart. Not even Báine's touch and soothing words were a salve.

✲✲✲

Draighean wore a deep track in the snow as she pondered her recent impetuous and out of character meddling in the affairs of men. She had long been an opponent of the Aes Sidhe's current predilection to forge deeper connections with humans. Was it not the ancestors of man who banished the Aes Sidhe to the Mounds and underground dwelling places?

Many of the demi-goddesses, herself included, disapproved of tainting the purity of the Sidhe with human contact. Even worse, two of the Aes Sidhe, Mongfhionn of Clann Ui Flaithimh and Medb of the Connachta, had taken human partners and borne them children. Draighean ground her perfectly white teeth, for she knew they were unlikely to be the last to drink from that chalice.

The irony of her current mission was not lost on Draighean. It was on the orders of Mongfhionn, who paradoxically had become a much more powerful voice among the Aes Sidhe, that Draighean stood on Na Comaraigh. Draighean was aware that she followed in Mongfhionn's footsteps as she looked down on Ráth Na Conall.

She harkened back to her intervention in the cavalry battle. *I was bored.* Ennui seemed the only rationale for her actions and was more palatable than other reasons. Still, there was little doubt that Draighean had enjoyed the frivolity of exercising her powers. Her realm was the winter with dark threatening skies, cold winds, and hail and snow. In the lands of the Aes Sidhe, she was just one of many with limited opportunity to flex her otherworldly muscles. She found the freedom exhilarating—and dangerous.

Draighean sighed long and deep and decided to sleep on the matter.

That was simple procrastination. The Aes Sidhe had no compulsion or need to lay their heads down.

***

"I am Fainche. I speak for the riders from Curraghatoor."

"A striking woman," muttered Conchobhar beneath his breath. It was an apt description. Fainche was as tall as any of those present and beautiful. Her body, garbed in a rider's boiled leather cuirass and worn triubhas, appeared muscular without being angular. As was common in Ériu, her skin was the colour of white smoke. The exception was her face. Due to the weather and a love for riding at every opportunity, Fainche's high cheekbones had a permanent and pleasing blush of pink.

Gossip among the riders at Curraghatoor had it that Fainche found horses much better company than men or women. Yet all this was not what classified Fainche as "striking". Long, arse-touching tresses of ash-grey hair, highlighted with shafts of black, crowned her physical appearance. Oddly, the rare colouring was the perfect complement for her face—and the grey she rode.

"Will you fight with us?" Danu saw no point in prevaricating.

"Are we welcome?" responded Fainche, matching Danu's gaze and brevity.

"You turned once. What is to say that you won't turn again?" Brighid remained angry at Danu but smirked at Danu's riposte. It was like watching duellists test each other's temper.

"Íar Mac Dedad is our rí, not Crónán or Torna," snapped Fainche. Incensed at Danu's insult, her cheeks flushed.

"Íar is not here," retorted Danu.

"That does not make him any less our rí or mean that we should not follow his or his father's customs." Fainche smiled at Danu. The contrast with her sober mien charmed all around the table. It proved to be a false dawn when she struck. "Conall Mac Gabhann, Rí of Ráth Na Conall, is not here. Does that make him any less the rí?"

"First game to Fainche," chuckled Beacán, and was promptly kicked in the shins by Iasg.

"You would be under my sister, Brighid's command. Does that cause you any challenges?" said Danu.

"Not unless her orders are stupid or dishonourable," smiled Fainche, dipping her head at Brighid. "My riders have had their fill of poor leaders."

"Maybe I should kill you now," countered Brighid.

"You could try," responded Fainche, "but you would not learn anything about Crónán or Torna, which, as you and I know, is the only reason I am standing here."

"And the battle is won," muttered Beacán, quickly moving beyond the range of kicks from Brighid, Danu, and Iasg.

***

Sitting on the thick dillat, Brighid felt much more at ease as she walked her mare along the line of Fainche's riders. At seventeen hands, Brighid's horse was a hand taller than the Curraghatoor mounts. Brighid growled at the one exception. It had to be Fainche's horse, a steel-grey mare, which stood equal in height and appeared a perfect match to her rider. Brighid noted that Fainche's grey was a much better beast than the others.

"I trust that the quality of your horsemanship is better than that of your mounts." Brighid dipped her head to Fainche. "With one exception." A touch exasperated, Brighid tugged at the ends of her long braided hair. "What happened to the horses of Curraghatoor? Íar Mac Dedad would be angry and ashamed."

"Torna was in charge of the horses. He sold the best of the herds to the Connachta, the Ulaid…" Fainche gritted her teeth and spat the next phrase out, "… and Uallachán. Gold is Torna and Crónán's only interest." The rising rumble of discontent from the Curraghatoor riders who judged Brighid an arrogant and indulged princess worried Fainche. "Each mount does not lack courage and will ride until their hearts burst. They will die for their riders."

98

"We'll see," said Brighid, who, still upset at Danu, missed the warning signs. "I don't have enough spare horses to change, and perhaps that is for the best. There is little time for you to befriend a new partner." Brighid examined each rider. "I do, however, have enough spare armour, weapons, and clothing to make you at least look as if you belong in *my* cavalry." She paused and looked to the sky. "It is almost meán lae. Eat, re-equip, and meet me on the plain north of Ráth Na Conall. I will introduce you to my riders, and you will practise *our* way of fighting."

***

Torna Mac Dedad was neither the cleverest nor most observant of men. Still, even he could not miss or ignore the fear that had taken up residence in Crónán's eyes. In truth, things had come easy for the half-brothers. Most bastard sons of kings found themselves outcasts or dead. While decidedly unfaithful to their mothers—or indeed any female—their father had indulged his progeny.

Finding themselves the overseers, but not the ríthe, of Curraghatoor, proved to be a poisoned cup—a moment of whimsy from the Goddess. Íar was unlikely ever to return. Hence, the half-brothers could have managed and grown the wealth and power of Curraghatoor. Instead, they evolved from pampered adolescents to spoiled men, filling their drinking vessels from the bitter jug of jealousy and their pockets with gold.

Everything they did was designed to bring ruin upon Curraghatoor while enriching themselves. Worse, with the attack on Carn Tigherna, Crónán and Torna crossed the line from being simply insufferable to evil. They had enjoyed and willingly participated in burning the hillfort and violating its men, women, and children. Blind and foolish, they aligned with Uallachán.

Sunrise lightened the skies, and with it came a disturbing realisation. The brothers' chaotic retreat from the smaller Ráth Na Conall force showed that others were willing to stand against them… and Uallachán. Unless they acted swiftly, their life of privilege would cease. However, neither brother was an expert at much and certainly not war. The best of

Curraghatoor's warriors—"All ungrateful bastards," muttered Torna—had switched sides at the first opportunity.

Torna sighed and supped his first beer of the day. He and Crónán would wait safely on this side of the river until Uallachán arrived. Then, with overwhelming numbers, they would destroy Ráth Na Conall. Thus, as the sun rose, the sound of blaring horns, the whooping of riders, and the howling of the red-haired apparition who led Ráth Na Conall's mounted forces was a nasty surprise. Scolded by Beacán, Danu had acceded to Brighid's plan.

It was dawn, and the host from Curraghatoor was in the midst of their morning repast. The half-brothers had posted no lookouts. Why should they? Torna dashed across the camp to his brother, shouting, "What do we do?" His fear and panic were mirrored in his sibling's eyes. "Useless bastard!" screamed Torna. Around them, warriors craved leadership but found none.

Desperately, Torna searched for an escape route but saw none. Water splashing and the crunch of bony hooves on pebbles told him that Ráth Na Conall's riders had entered the river. The enemy would be in the camp before he could find his horse. Retreat as an option was gone. For perhaps the first time, Torna, finding some measure of courage, lifted his sword and turned to face his enemy.

* * *

"You were right. They are not experienced at much," said Brighid, wiping the back of a blood-streaked hand across her forehead. Fainche shuddered. The mask of gore appeared to suit Brighid, and the trail of red was quickly consumed by the dark, curling sigils covering her face. "No stockade, traps, or anything defensive. Did they genuinely think we would ignore them?"

Alongside Maolán, whose company she found more comfortable than Brighid's, Fainche walked the corpse-strewn river plain. Truthfully, she felt more pity for the dead and maimed horses. It would break her heart, but she would not flinch from ending the latter's suffering with the blade gripped in her hand.

As to her former comrades, many of whom lay beside their mounts, they had made their choice, and it proved a poor one. A hundred riders from Curraghatoor were dead or injured. Likely they were the best of the three hundred, and Fainche thought that a pity. She knew that Ráth Na Conall desperately needed warriors.

The wounded would soon cross the veil for Ráth Na Conall had no accommodation for prisoners. The feral look on Brighid's face made Fainche doubt the princess envisaged any other end but death. A remnant of the horsemen and women fled in the direction of Curraghatoor. "I know the commander of Curraghatoor. He is an honourable man and, freed from the pretenders, won't open the ráth's gates. The riders' only sanctuary might be Uallachán, but would he be pleased with their incompetence?"

Maolán dipped his head as if listening to Fainche. Truthfully, he just took pleasure in her company.

* * *

There was no compassion for Crónán and Torna. In desperation, Torna chose to stand and fight, whereas his half-brother took to his heels and ran—although not far enough. Bruised and bloody, both were bound and now walked and stumbled, tied behind two horses. Crónán, finally finding a measure of audacity, threatened his captors with the vengeance of Uallachán. Only taunts and laughter were his reward.

Torna rasped, "*Dún do bheal*—shut your mouth!" He took comfort in the expectation that their destination was Ráth Na Conall. When the fort fell to Uallachán, they would be set free. Yet as he felt the burn of the sun on the back of his neck, doubt and anxiety slowly penetrated his mind.

Brighid's riders journeyed not south but westward along the Abhainn na Siúire river. The sun was halfway to the western horizon when the group stopped at the tip of the Bod Carraig range. Dragged kicking and screaming, Crónán found himself thrown on the crest of a grassy hillock. Torna, acknowledging the futility of resistance, shrugged off his guards and walked to stand beside his brother.

On their knees, both men watched Brighid stride towards them. They shivered as eyes of the deepest, coldest green held their gaze. "You are doubly fortunate that Onchú, Rí of Carn Tigherna, is not among this band, and I have little time to spare. Your guilt is plain, and your demise will be painful."

"Release us, bitseach," snarled Crónán. His eyes held no confidence that the creature who stood before him might obey his command.

"You should know your judge and executioner. I am Brighid Ni Conall, daughter of Conall Mac Gabhann, Rí Ruirech of Clann Ui Flaithimh, and Rí of Ráth Na Conall. In my father's name and with the authority given to me by Íar Mac Dedad, Rí of Curraghatoor, I sentence you to death."

"No!" gasped both men.

Tears streamed down Torna's face, and he pleaded for mercy. Crónán refused to accept that there would be no rescue until he felt the sharp end of a stake against his arse and heard the hammer strike the wood. The half-brothers' screams rent the valley's pastoral calmness. Left bloody and whimpering, in their final moments they watched an obscenely glorious sunset.

"Time for us to return to Ráth Na Conall. The next battle will be more challenging," said Brighid. Her brow furrowed as she observed the oddly matched duo—one stocky and the other tall. Maolán appeared captivated with Fainche, and by her responses, the admiration was mutual.

"Awww, shite!" murmured Brighid. "We could all be in Mag Mell in a few sunsets. Why shouldn't they take what pleasure they can?" The frown reappeared when she thought of Danu and Glaisne. Shaking her head, she muttered. "No, I just don't like that tuilí."

CHAPTER 11

It was meán lae and a pleasant day… until now. Uallachán swore as he viewed the staked corpses of Crónán and Torna. Nuadha blanched at the horrific scene. His squeamishness was remarkable, given he had witnessed his brother's atrocities and participated in many. Chunks of flesh were missing from the bodies, and their eyes were little more than hollow black holes. Uallachán recovered his composure and laughed at the sight and his brother's retching.

"Brighid Ni Conall's work, no doubt. She would make the perfect queen for me. Perhaps I will spare her life after I make her watch her sister's violation and execution and raze Ráth Na Conall to the ground."

That this was the only hint of levity since leaving the domain of Clárach troubled Nuadha. Until this moment, Uallachán's ranting about the Clárach debacle and the endless stories of Brighid's warband terrorising his lands and people had dominated the journey. It was intolerable to Uallachán, that his people had become more frightened of the red-haired bitseach than of himself. Repeated threats to re-educate *his* subjects about their proper place in *his* kingdom when he had overwhelmed Ráth Na Conall wearied Nuadha.

Yet, of his brother's gushing threats and condemnations, all that Nuadha absorbed was a single word—"his". After the battle for Ráth Na Conall, it might be time to review his place in Uallachán's domain. That he even entertained such treasonous thoughts, for that was how his brother would see them, made his hands tremble. But why wait? Why not escape now? Nuadha's hands shook more.

"I'm a coward," he muttered.

Since boyhood, his brother's will and whims had dominated him. He did not know which frightened him more—a life away from Uallachán or the comfort of continued subjugation. However, deep inside, Nuadha knew his sibling would inevitably tire of his presence. Uallachán's paranoia at a potential, if unlikely, rival to Caher Conri's throne would eventually rise to the surface. Nuadha needed an escape plan.

***

"The column passed Bod Carraig at meán lae. It travels slowly but will be at Ráth Na Conall's gates in two sunsets. I estimate the army is about one thousand strong and appears to have the usual mix of veterans and youth. Uallachán will see the young as nothing more than a shield for his experienced warriors." The messenger bowed to Danu and Brighid and coughed. "I would like permission to remain in the fort. One extra sword may not be much, but it is yours." Then she bowed and stepped back a step.

Danu smiled. She had grown to like the young messenger but shook her head. "For the moment, we need you and your companions to remain on Na Comaraigh to inform us of our enemy's progress." Danu noted the disappointment that settled into the scout's eyes. "However, choose two from your group. They will remain on Na Comaraigh—even during the siege. You and the rest will return to the fort in two sunsets—before the assault begins."

Delight painted the envoy's face, yet that saddened Danu. The only certainties about battles, large and small, were death, pain, and the cries of the mná-sidhe. A shrill blast of a horn disturbed the princess's thoughts and caused a rumble of swearing around the table. Scuffling outside the chamber's door was quickly followed by a fist banging on it. Danu nodded to Conchobhar, who rose, unsheathed his sword, and went to the exit. He returned quickly. "A messenger from Clárach wishes an audience."

Glaisne inspected the ambassador and signalled to Danu that he knew the man. On seeing Glaisne, the envoy bowed and said, "My Lord." The young Clárach prince acknowledged the messenger with a curt greeting and indicated that the messenger should address Danu. However, the young man had orders from Aodh and would not deviate from them.

"Aodh, Rí of Clárach, wishes to inform you that your brother, Cúmhaí, was found guilty of treason and executed. He desires that you return to Clárach—for your safety."

"Well, there's a vote of confidence in us," huffed Conchobhar.

"I meant no offence. We are aware of the talents, both in battle…" The envoy paused and looked at Brighid. The ends of his lips lifted in an approving smile, "… and in other areas that reside within Ráth Na Conall."

"I sense a 'but' coming," snorted Conchobhar.

The messenger dipped his head and looked at the princesses. "My rí sees no path to victory for those within this fort. He pleads with his brother to ride back with me. Clárach can spare no men to support Ráth Na Conall. Aodh put fifty warriors to death because of Cúmhaí's rebellion. A score more have ridden to raise the levy of chieftains and nobles loyal to Clárach. Once Uallachán has taken this fort, Aodh believes his attentions will return to Clárach."

"It's only one thousand against us, and we have a good position," growled Beacán. "The armies of Clann Ui Flaithimh have faced and overcome such odds in many battles. I'll take your gold if you wish to wager against us."

The envoy shook his head. "Not so. The number against you is much greater. Uallachán has a second force of equal size, moving under the canopy of the coastal forests to the south of Na Comaraigh." Observing the stern glance sent by Danu to the young messenger and the flushed cheeks it prompted, Aodh's envoy again shook his head.

"Your scouts on the mountain could not have seen them. The forests are dense and they have been careful to eliminate any sign of their presence."

The man scratched his beard. "Underestimating Uallachán can be fatal. My guess is that one force was to conquer Clárach and the other Ráth Na Conall. Once his ambitions for Clárach were disappointed, Uallachán pointed both armies at this fort."

"The Hag's hairy arse!" The exclamation came from Flann, but only because he pipped the rest of the table.

∗∗∗

Before dusk, a guard ushered Beacán and Iasg into the small chamber. Torches flickered, and a wood and peat fire roared in the stone pit at the centre of the room. In all, it was a pleasant and warm atmosphere dominated by the sweet smell of peat. Danu, Brighid, and Conchobhar sat at an oak table laid with meat, cheeses, bread, and a selection of drinks. The looks on the twins' faces told they were about to ask something unpalatable.

"The answer is yes," said Beacán. Beside him, Iasg nodded her approval.

"What?" exclaimed Danu.

"You are about to ask Iasg and me to do something, but you'd rather not. You and Brighid have wrestled with the problem but can see no alternative. Am I right?" Beacán smiled. "Iasg and I thank you for your concern. But these are tough times that need awful and unpleasant decisions taken."

Taking a deep breath and then exhaling slowly, Beacán said, "You are not only my nieces but also the representatives of the Rí Ruirech of our clann. That comes with a heavy burden—and many times, a price to pay. I will give you the same answer I would give Conall—yes. Now spit it out. What do you need from Iasg and me?"

"We need an edge, an advantage that upsets the balance," said Danu.

Brighid nodded and bit her lip until it bled. For Brighid, it would be disastrous to be without her uncle's counsel. Danu paused, feeling as if she were about to hand out a death sentence. "Without leaders, our enemies will flounder, if only for a short time. But that time could be precious. We want you to sow confusion among Uallachán's force. Kill as many of Uallachán's chieftains as you can."

* * *

The door had just closed behind Beacán when it opened again, and a soft "Uncle" was heard. Smiling, he turned to face a teary-eyed Brighid. "I cannot lose you, uncle. Take me and some of my riders with you. We are well-acquainted with your tactics and can protect you." Brighid's eyes brightened as she thought of a more practical argument. "A larger party could cover both of Uallachán's divisions. Alone, you will have to choose one and leave the other untouched." Brighid's jaw set, and Beacán smiled.

"You know this makes sense, uncle."

"Yes, it does." Brighid beamed but only for a moment when Beacán shook his head. "But no. Your place is with your sister." A glum Brighid exhaled. She knew by her uncle's tone that he would not change his mind. "However, what you say is correct. Iasg and I cannot cover two armies. Choose two from your riders who are well-versed in stealth. They will accompany us."

As they crossed Ráth Na Conall's yard and walked towards the gateway, a long shadow detached itself from the wall. "I am going with you, as is my friend." In the flickering light of torches, Beacán looked into Onchú's eyes and saw grief and a desire for vengeance. He also observed that the Rí of Carn Tigherna would not be persuaded to stand down. Beacán looked at Iasg, exhaled and bared his teeth.

"Let me be clear. Iasg and I are in command of this mission, and you will do as we direct. This is *not* a quest for personal vengeance. Our task is to give Danu and Brighid more time to prepare Ráth Na Conall." Beacán breathed deep and, in a grim voice, added, "Make no mistake. *I* will end any who disobey or jeopardise our goals."

107

Turning to Iasg, Beacán looked uncharacteristically uncertain, and resolved to a course of action not of his choosing. "You will ride with Maolán and Fainche to the southern forest; I will ride with Onchú and his comrade to Bod Carraig. Onchú knows the territory better, so that makes sense." To Maolán and Fainche, he added, "Iasg is your leader. Defy her, and you will face me."

✳✳✳

Iasg looked at her companions. "Confusion or stealth?" Maolán chuckled but more at Iasg's native brogue than the question. At times, the burr in Iasg's voice was so strong that understanding her was a challenge.

"Once we start, there will be mayhem no matter the plan," said Fainche. "My advice is to start the way we wish to proceed and keep it simple."

"The tents of the chieftains are easily identified by the banners of their *finte*." Iasg paused as the pieces of her plan became more apparent. "Can the two of you create a diversion? Once the confusion begins, ye'll be ma shields."

The enemy camp sprawled across the forest floor. Even in the darkness of *meán oíche*, it remained a hive of activity. Arrogance and the excitement of imminent battle, combined with beer and rutting the camp whores, lulled the warriors into a false sense of well-being.

It also fostered lax security—no fences or traps were set. During Uallachán's reign, no enemy gave them much of a fight. Hence, while it was stupid, it was also unsurprising that the chieftains assumed the combat at sunrise would be little more than a formality. The garrison of Ráth Na Conall would be slaughtered, and Conall's *bitseacha* despoiled, along with any other females. After the massacre, life would return to Uallachán's interpretation of normality.

Only their location at the centre of the encampment protected the leaders of each *fine*. Apart from boiled leather cuirasses—and in the darkness, the armour was unseen—Iasg's group dressed as the enemy. Thus, the interlopers passed through the camp, heading steadily towards the clutch of pavilions. Only drunken challenges and offers to rut slowed their progress.

As they passed a campfire, Maolán and Fainche sheathed their longer-bladed cavalry swords, picked up several burning brands, and tossed the torches into the first chieftain's tent before moving on to the next and the next. As it was autumn, the shelters' material was light and easily set alight. In their wake, Iasg's steps were measured and unhurried. Soon the air was filled with the brimstone smell of burning shelters.

Gael society was relatively egalitarian, and women fought alongside men in battle. Indeed, many claimed females were the better, fiercer warriors. That philosophy, however, rarely reached the command structure. Hence, in the upper echelons, men dominated. As their tents burst into flames, naked men ran from them shouting and bellowing curses.

Maolán had never seen Iasg in action, although he had heard stories of her talent. With admiration, he watched the petite assassin calmly select her targets. The blur of blades leaving her small hands was quickly followed by the thud of the weapons penetrating flesh and grunts of pain. Clutching bleeding chests, the *fine* leaders were welcomed by the mná-sidhe, who took their spirits. If they were fortunate, Mag Mell would be their destination. If not, the maw of the Otherworld awaited them.

"The Hag preserve us!" mouthed Fainche, in awe of Iasg's skills. Her supply of knives exhausted, Iasg made clear that she did not consider her mission concluded. Pulling two throwing axes from her belt, Iasg charged toward isolated chieftains. Although not as proficient as Beacán in close combat, her whirling axes took a dreadful toll on any who crossed her path.

Fainche shouted, "To Iasg's side! Protect her."

In the chaos and a background of burning tents, the small chevron of warriors slashed through the camp. That stopped when, hands on her knees and panting harshly, Iasg paused for breath. Her pale face smeared with blood, she looked up at her companions and smiled. "I think we've reached the limit of shock and surprise, and we cannae fight off a thousand of the bastards."

"Perhaps ye could find us a way out of here."

* * *

Struck in the shadow of Bod Carraig, the second camp was a much more sober assembly. This was unsurprising and totally due to the fear and paranoia that Uallachán inspired. No one wanted to risk any form of behaviour that attracted the attention of the capricious tyrant. Thus Beacán's group were unable to take advantage of the chaos typically found in a large military encampment. Additionally, the heavy presence of Uallachán's guards and enforcers virtually eliminated the trio from ghosting through the crowd.

The circumstance did not overly disturb Beacán. On the other hand, Onchú and his friend were vessels filled with roiling emotions, barely controlled aggression, and thirsting for revenge. *This will be a challenge.* Beacán's unease focused on managing his companions long enough to get the job done. As far as Beacán was concerned, once he had despatched a sufficient number of leaders, it was every man for himself.

On this night, the Goddess favoured the trio—if only for a short time. Lightly armed and with weapons, clothes, and exposed skin darkened with a mix of ash, charcoal, and dirt, the men chose their entry points. Calloused hands clamped over mouths. Blades drawn across throats were the final memories of unwary sentries. After penetrating the outer defences, the group moved deeper into the camp.

Beacán had no compassion or mercy for his targets. The chieftains had chosen a foolish path and leader. In the deep darkness between meán oíche and dawn, many regretted their folly, but death gave them little time to dwell on their lack of judgement. Beacán's blood-soaked clothes stuck to his skin as he emerged from the third tent.

He mouthed a fleeting "Sorry" to the innocents, but were any genuinely blameless? Those who slept beside and rutted the chieftains knew their character and either ignored it or did not care. Now, they lay silent forever.

In contrast to Beacán's stealth, Onchú and his companion had every intention of creating mayhem and slaughtering anyone who crossed their path. They strode forward, jaws set, eyes burning with hate, and thirsting for retribution. Each gripped two short swords and carried a shield strapped to their backs. Disregarding Beacán's orders, they had just one target—Uallachán's pavilion. Neither harboured any hope of surviving, and as long as Uallachán paid with his life, they did not care.

"The Hag's hairy arse!"

Beacán swore at the increasing outcry that roused the camp. "Bloody eejits!" Yet the distraction drew attention away from his activities. Muttering, "They're big and ugly enough to look after themselves," Beacán moved on to his next target. He counted ten chieftains killed before a nagging itch in his mind forced him to circle around to the central pavilion.

Beacán watched as Onchú, and his companion, cut a bloody path to the main tent. They fought back-to-back, increasingly surrounded by the enemy. In their wake, the fluttering light of torches and campfires showed a trail of the maimed and the dead. Unlike many in Uallachán's camp, both warriors were powerful veterans. They fought with an economy of movement to conserve their strength.

Still, massively outnumbered and with many blade slashes, blood wept from minor cuts and flowed from the deeper gashes. Onchú's companion fell first, brought down by a slashing blade that hamstrung him. However, Onchú kept going, viciously slashing and stabbing anyone who stood in his way. He relished the cries of those that fell before him.

A single purpose, retribution, kept the shaven-headed, gore-drenched Onchú going forward. Yet that became increasingly difficult as scores of experienced warriors stepped into the gap between him and the main tent. Without his companion to guard his back, he was vulnerable. The sharp pain in his back took his breath away, and the blow to his head sent him into the arms of darkness.

***

Beacán's blade, made from the finest steel, remained wickedly sharp and cut through the inner and outer walls of the spacious domed pavilion with contemptuous ease. Once inside, Beacán stood still and slowed his breathing to a murmur. As his eyes adapted to the darkness and torchlight, he thanked Onchú. The tent's occupants gathered at its entrance to watch the spectacle and remained unaware of his presence.

Green eyes with flames of red swept the shelter. Outside, the crowd's raucous cheering as Onchú fell disguised Beacán's activities. His target stood at the entrance flap, sandwiched between two burly guards. Grabbing a heavy bronze jug, Beacán moved swiftly and silently and brought the pitcher crashing down on the man's skull. Feeling their charge slump to the dirt floor, the sentries turned.

One, Beacán immediately stabbed in the neck, slicing through the artery and larynx, and he fell to the dirt. The other showed her lack of experience and attacked with a spear instead of shouting for help. Years of hunting human prey had taught Beacán the importance of watching his opponent before acting. It had taken many years to drive impulsiveness from his fighting style.

Beacán waited, moved inside the spear thrust, grabbed the pole, and yanked it towards him. He thrust his dagger up and under her chin and twisted the blade. Blood splashed his hand as the blade pierced soft flesh and travelled quickly to the brain. She was likely in Mag Mell before the knife emerged from her skull.

A moan from the floor took Beacán's attention away from the warrior, and he discarded her body. Tearing a strip of cloth, Beacán rammed it into his captive's mouth. "On your feet. You will walk from this camp, or you will die. Make your choice," rasped Beacán. The two stumbled from the tent and into the darkness.

As a new day dawned, the pair rested by a spring. Under the best of circumstances, it was a two-sunset trek to Ráth Na Conall. His fleshy prisoner was in no condition for a forced march, and Beacán's shape was not much better. It had been a hard battle to escape Uallachán's camp, and his wounds took a severe physical toll. He looked at his prisoner, shook his head, and pulled the gag from the man's mouth.

"Tell me, Nuadha, where is your brother?"

CHAPTER 12

394 B.C.—Two cycles of the moon after Lugnasad

Dawn brought the unwelcome, if not unexpected, sight of two hordes converging on Ráth Na Conall from the north and south. At meán lae, Uallachán's armies had the hillfort in their jaws, and an assault was imminent. Danu paced the walkway with Conchobhar, Flann, and Glaisne. All but Glaisne frequently stopped to share a jest or offer encouragement to the one hundred and twenty-five warriors who stood alert. The eyes of those closest to the smoke-blackened cauldrons, filled with embers, oil, and water, wept and smarted.

Danu's defenders were well outnumbered, but they wore superior armour and wielded better-quality weapons than the majority of the enemy. Boiled leather armour, strengthened with small, rigid iron scales affixed between the multiple layers protected torsos. A smaller number, including Danu, Conchobhar, and Glaisne, chose the protection of the relatively new armour of chainmail. Each type of protection had its advocates and critics.

All wore helmets of bronze and iron, and all were smoothly utilitarian in design and construction. Most fought to constrain unruly tresses of red, blonde, and black hair. Conical and tapering to a small, flattened oval nub, the helmets had metal flaps to protect the ears and a broad ribbon of chainmail to shield the neck. For some, the only embellishment was a finger-width, twisted rope of copper and bronze that trimmed the headdress. Apart from Danu's blue horsehair plumes, the garrison's plumes were uniformly red and black.

Oblong, waisted shields that protected from neck to knee rested against the stockade, as did javelins, spears, and the larger clubs. Swords, longswords, and axes were carried in sheaths on broad leather belts and baldrics or hung from simple leather loops. Knives, ranging in size from short blades to small swords, were slipped into belts and boots. Grim-faced men and women, all veterans who had fought with the princesses' father in his campaigns, faced their enemies and swore to make them pay a high price.

Danu wondered where Brighid, along with Báine and Fainche, had chosen to position the horses and chariots. When asked, Brighid shrugged and walked away. *Had Brighid considered the question an insult? Her sister had never been overly sensitive. Perhaps it was she who was insensitive?* Danu growled. "I have no time for sibling squabbles."

She looked across the expanse of the battlefield and knew it was perfect for riders and carbaid. The landscape was predominantly level south of the high ridge and river, interrupted only with gently rolling *dro-imnín*. Each of Brighid's riders carried an armoury on their mount's back. "It's our only advantage," Danu murmured. To Conchobhar's questioning look, she added, "Brighid's force. Three hundred riders can hurt foot warriors badly."

"Do you think *they* are alive?" asked Conchobhar.

Danu knew to whom he referred and nodded. "My uncle is a hard man to kill and exceptionally talented at his profession, as is Iasg. I would not lay a wager against them returning." Yet Danu offered up a quick prayer to the Goddess.

Conchobhar chuckled. "Indeed, that would be a waste of gold." A frown replaced his grin. "Eithne appears less dramatic. She found out about Onchú's mission when her daughters wouldn't stop crying. The bitseach probably realises that if he is dead, Carn Tigherna will remain in ashes, her lifestyle will be gone, and she will be destitute. Many will offer to adopt the girls, but few will care a wit about her future, including me."

***

The loud banging on the front gates resounded like a peal of thunder, shocking everyone in the fort. Those posted in the gateway's guard posts looked at each other, dumbfounded. *How could anybody strike that hard?* Their next thought was, how could anyone ride the length of the long farm track to the hillfort's entrance unseen?

Self-preservation became the next priority. Who would Conchobhar or Danu blame? What would be the punishment for not seeing or challenging the black-cloaked and hooded rider? Sitting on a huge dark-red mare that sported a long crimson mane and tail, they were unquestioningly a striking pair.

"Are you going to open the gates, or do you wish me to destroy them?" Draighean surveyed the defences and was unimpressed. "Given your circumstances, that would be a poor choice." The rider's voice was low, slightly husky, and richly accented, although none could place its origin. Still, no matter how pleasant it was to hear, the authority within her words suggested a low tolerance for disobedience.

"Escort the lady to the Great Hall and see that she, and her horse, have food and refreshments." Danu turned to Conchobhar. "We should greet our visitor, for better or worse. Please send a messenger to Brighid. She should be here."

"Please be seated." Danu indicated the carved chair opposite her. The smile that accompanied Danu's words was regal and, given the lady's intimidating presence, took considerable effort to maintain. Brighid just scowled at the inconvenience. Danu reminded herself that this was not their first experience of a Sidhe. She and Brighid were wards of the Sidhe, Mongfhionn, and had known that force of nature all of their lives. Mongfhionn was a woman of terrible beauty and power, except in the persona of the Hag, when she was simply terrifying.

The Sidhe who stood before Danu, although no less beautiful than Mongfhionn, appeared a stark contrast. She was taller than any in the room and possibly in the fort. Long, pale fingers reached up to remove her hood and released thick tresses of black that fell across and over her shoulders. In the torchlit room, the flames picked out contrasting thin auburn braids that accented her hair. Draighean's highlights were perfectly coordinated with the shades of her maroon lips and fingernails.

"High maintenance," muttered Conchobhar.

"I prefer to stand," responded Draighean in answer to Danu's offer.

"That figures," snorted Conchobhar. His words elicited a throaty, feral growl from the Sidhe, an admonishing look from Danu, and the broadest of grins from Brighid.

"I am known as Draighean. As you likely have deduced, I am of the Aes Sidhe."

"It gets better. A Sidhe called Blackthorn." Conchobhar, obviously not a fan of the Aes Sidhe, shook his head and wondered if the circumstances at Ráth Na Conall could get worse.

Draighean held the glimmer of a smile at bay. The veteran's brash words and thoughts were honest and refreshing. She nodded. "Oh, circumstances could become much worse." Then she smiled sweetly at Conchobhar. "While I respect different opinions and may tolerate a level of brashness or audacity, my mercy is not limitless." Danu looked quizzically from warrior to Sidhe but got no explanation from either. Draighean turned her attention to Glaisne. He squirmed under the stare.

"Your presence is neither needed nor wanted. Go."

As the door closed behind a deflated Glaisne, Draighean turned to Danu. "Feirdhriseacha from me would have had different hues and, under my oversight, may yet change. I sense that neither of you understands your gift. The sooner you appreciate its promise, the better." She smiled as Danu bristled at her words yet kept her temper under control and nodded approvingly as Brighid tensed to defend her sister.

"Fight, girls, fight. Let no one, not even a Sidhe, trample on what you believe and hold dear. You are young, but you are also royal. Act like it." The sisters were unsure whether Draighean had admonished or complimented them.

"Why are you here, my lady?" asked Danu, the fire in her cheeks having subsided to a pleasing pink blush.

"I am here at your Lady Mongfhionn's command." The tone of irritation in Draighean's voice was undisguised. "Blessed by the Goddess, she wields considerable influence among the Aes Sidhe—even though she bears the taint of humans." This time it was Danu's turn to growl like a mountain lincse.

That seemed to please Draighean, and she continued. "Corrupt kings, despots, and tyrants eventually are removed by others of a similar nature or by revolution. In which case, the Aes Sidhe do not interfere. That is the realm of the Goddess and Fate.

"However, there are those who do not recognise or care about the value of blood. These men and women are truly evil, and upset the balance of things below and above ground. The Aes Sidhe are long-lived and do not bleed—much. Humans are short-lived, and blood is a treasure. Those who spill blood without consequence, along with their philosophies and adherents, must be purged. Uallachán has fallen into this group."

* * *

The two orphans were sisters. Naomh, the eldest, was fourteen summers, and the other, Úna, had recently turned thirteen. For as long as they could remember, they had been abused by those who should have cared for them. Sadly, their one piece of good fortune was not being counted among the lengthy list of those defiled by Uallachán and Nuadha.

Throughout their brief lives, numerous others—men and women, kin and strangers—had taken advantage of and profited through them. In Uallachán's camp, they had less value than cattle and had no voice or choice in who rutted them. They heard rumours that the princesses of Ráth Na Conall were young and wondered how, under other circumstances, their lives might have been different.

Naomh looked up when she heard Úna cry out as her long hair was grasped, and she was dragged away, bent over a log, and penetrated. The shriek was not fear, although many of Uallachán's men imitated the cruel perversions of their king. It was more of surprise at the abrupt interruption of a pleasant daydream and her only escape from whoring. Naomh heard the grunt of a climax as, with dispassionate efficiency, the warrior expended his seed, pulled out, tied up his triubhas, and walked away. The older girl felt her sister's disgust and helplessness.

"Tuilí!" muttered Naomh. The man had left no payment, not even a crust of bread.

The camp was anxious, although not because the enemy was within sight. Everyone expected the battle to commence once the warriors had broken their fast and fortified their courage with beer. Naomh glanced across to the two men bound naked to tall poles. Those who passed the prisoners taunted them and added more knife cuts. Some pissed on them or threw shite. Both were coated in a veneer of gore and excrement. She knew one was alive, but only because he moaned, albeit infrequently.

Camp gossip told of a third who had escaped, which was the source of the encampment's anxiety. Was he still in the camp, waiting to strike? The strengthened guard around Uallachán, who had entered the encampment at dawn, was proof of that concern. The three assassins from Ráth Na Conall had killed a score of chieftains and many minor warband leaders. Rumour also had it that a female demon had visited death on the other army. Furthermore, Uallachán's brother, Nuadha, had not been seen since meán oíche.

The older sister's brow furrowed. *Arseholes!* Even she could comprehend that the threat was gone—and so was Nuadha. A calloused hand smacked Naomh across the face, splitting her lip. The violence was utterly unnecessary. How could she resist? Yet she knew some men needed to dispense pain to the helpless. Without it, their manhoods remained flaccid, which brought greater brutality and even death. She winced in pain as her arm was almost wrenched from its socket, and she was dragged away.

It was the same stump used for Úna's violation. She felt the hard, selfish thrusts ram her slight body against the rough tree bark. While being despoiled, she looked up and saw one of the prisoners lift his head a little. Pity overwhelmed her, and tears left tracks on her dirt-ingrained cheeks. She promised to give him water once the battle commenced and the camp emptied.

✱✱✱

"Any word from Beacán or Onchú?" asked Iasg.

Iasg was a fearsome wee woman. Yet when her beloved and long-time partner Urard died, it had initiated a downward spiral into depression and starvation. Beacán had rescued her from that fate and became a father to her children. Since then, Iasg had filled out nicely. She would never be a voluptuous siren like Báine or Fainche. Still, Iasg's lithe figure married well with her chosen profession.

As she looked at Iasg, Danu passionately believed that her uncle and Iasg were good for each other. Before Iasg, Danu had worried about the loneliness of Beacán's lifestyle and how it was grinding him down. Or worse, driving him deeper into that dark place, which seemed to be a family curse. *What can I say that will give her succour?*

The fear written on Iasg's bruised and blood-smeared face was unmistakable. The thin trickle of blood from her lower lip was due to nervous biting, not battle. Unusually, Iasg's body looked as if she had bathed in gore. *It must have been fierce fighting.* Her blades were gone, and the single hand axe remaining was encrusted in dried blood. Maolán had told Brighid that at least ten leaders met their end by Iasg's blades. The body count would grow if those injured succumbed to infection and passed beyond the veil.

Danu exhaled and shook her head. "No news yet."

Taking Iasg by the shoulders, Danu looked into eyes whose depth of colour matched her own. "I am certain that's a good omen. You and I know that Uallachán would take immense pleasure in displaying Beacán, dead or alive, before our walls." Then, needing to divert Iasg's attention, Danu took a pace backwards. "I need you at my side on the ramparts."

Danu sniffed and grinned. "But first, you stink! Take a bath, rinse the blood and grime away, rest a little, eat and drink, put on new clothes… and armour."

⋆⋆⋆

"For one so young, your skill at inspiring others to do what you want or need is impressive."

Deep in thought, the movement at her shoulder startled Danu. "*He* is our uncle, and *she* is our friend and our family. Neither are fidchell pieces," snapped Danu. "But what are *your* plans, my lady?" Footsteps on the walkway announced the presence of Conchobhar and Flann. Discomfited by the Sidhe, Glaisne chose to remain what he considered a safe distance away. From the expressions on their faces, all were interested in a demonstration of the Sidhe's powers and preferably one that destroyed the enemy's armies.

Draighean's skin had taken on an attractive, if faint, pink hue in the rising sun. No one could determine the Sidhe's eye colour because the shade was so deep as to appear obsidian. A shout of "They're attacking!" rang out around the hillfort, averting a direct response to Danu's question.

With frustrating timing, as signalled by Draighean's expression, the shrill blare of hunting horns announced that Brighid's and Fainche's divisions had taken the field. Those on the battlements watched as horses galloped and chariots drove at breakneck speeds from the foothill's forest cover towards Uallachán's left flank.

Draighean raised an eyebrow. "In future, discuss all battle plans with me. Your tactics have restrained my talents. A battlefield of ice and mud is no friend to horses and chariots." An enigmatic smirk fluttered on red lips as Draighean looked at Danu. "I hope you obeyed my orders, or we could be in trouble."

"What bloody orders?" snarled Danu.

Draighean ignored the question. "I suggest you position your defenders to the southern and northern walls. I will choose my place."

Ignoring Danu's scowl, she added, "I trust Brighid's horses are not jittery." Then, with a swirl of her cloak, Draighean turned and strode towards the nearest guard post. Climbing the ladder to its thatched roof, she straddled the covering's apex. Settling her stance, the Sidhe reached upwards with her hand and the blackthorn staff.

No earthly voice made the ululating invocations, which started low, quickly rose to a crescendo and never waned. Those in the fort shivered. Fearful of the Sidhe, they were also thankful she was on their side. As the chanting swelled, the veils that in normal times protected frail minds were shredded. Synchronised with the howling, gusts of bone-chilling winter winds swirled across the plain, and lightning forked across a sky that had become an oppressive grey.

"I'm impressed," said Conchobhar, his voice barely audible above the storm. Danu looked at him curiously, and in answer, he leered mischievously. "She's naked under the cloak." Perched like a great raven on the guard tower's roof, Draighean's lips opened wide and she laughed heartily. Danu rolled her eyes but chuckled.

With a dip of his head to Danu, Conchobhar slapped a helmet on his head, turned around and bellowed, "Check armour and weapons! Ní ghéillfear, nó cúlú!"

"*Striapach!*"

The sight of Draighean silhouetted against the sky drew screams of rage and whines of unfairness from Uallachán. It could never be a straight fight with Conall or his bitseacha. On horseback, he roared at his chieftains to keep their warriors charging forward while ignoring the howling in his mind that kept repeating, "*Cúlú*—retreat!"

* * *

Brighid, Báine, and Fainche had agreed on the plan of attack. However, that was before the howling began and the onset of weather more suited to winter. The full force of riders and chariots would attack Uallachán and the northern battalion. "She could have warned us," grumbled Brighid, her teeth chattering. "We would have worn winter clothing."

Draighean's ululations and the sudden change in the weather caused Brighid's and Fainche's horses to falter. They slowed to a trot, assessing the new conditions. Reassured that the creature in the fort was on their side, their pace quickly recovered. Soon the canter picked up, and once again they galloped across the grassy terrain.

A cavalry's advantage is its mobility. Thus, the strategy against Uallachán's foot warriors favoured hit-and-run tactics. The three hundred riders charged the nearest flanks, slowing to a walk when they were within the distance of a javelin throw. Once the volley of missiles was released, the riders peeled away in a sharp arc. Then they circled back, repeating the cycle until the projectiles were exhausted.

Infuriated at their refusal to engage face-to-face, those on Uallachán's flank cursed the mounted warriors. Brighid's and Fainche's cavalry refused to come nearer than a spear or dart throw. The latter— lead-weighted darts—were flung at the enemy once the javelins were depleted. It was a tactic introduced by Clann Ui Flaithimh's Thracian cohort and unfamiliar to Uallachán's warriors. Thus, it caused an uproar in their ranks.

Angry at the incessant sting of thrown barbs, small groups broke from the column and charged the riders. It was the opening for which Báine had waited. The foolish quickly discovered they were no match for chariots' spinning knives. Attempts to assemble hedges of spears were unsuccessful. Uallachán's warriors did not have the discipline or fortitude to accomplish this and keep moving towards the fort.

Brighid observed Uallachán's ragged, bloody flank and the growing number of fallen with grim satisfaction. Yet the main body of the enemy steadily tramped towards the fort. As Brighid's riders dismounted, taunts and jeers rose from Uallachán's left flank. Thinking they were finally about to make an enemy that stung like a swarm of wasps suffer, several large groups broke off from the main body.

With the efficiency of an exercise ingrained into muscle memory, bow staves were unsheathed and strung, red and white fletches smoothed, and arrows nocked. A hail of iron barbs found their adversaries. Brighid relished the cries of agony, and the black feirdhris between her breasts throbbed happily. Yet each quiver carried only thirty black shafts, and soon they were used—apart from the two that Brighid held in her hand. The princess scanned the field for her target.

Uallachán deemed running with his men undignified and thus was one of the few on horseback. Whether due to cowardice or tactics, he took up a position at the rear of the army, surrounded by trusted guards. Brighid watched and nocked an arrow as he came within range. In the chaos of the charge, their eyes met. Brighid gave a feral snarl and loosed the arrow. A second followed in its trail.

Panic saved Uallachán. As he pulled frantically on his mount's reins, the beast rose up on its hind legs. The arrows took the horse in the neck, tearing an artery and causing it to stumble. Thrown to the ground, Uallachán cursed the animal that had saved his life.

"Shite! The bastard must have a witch protecting him," seethed Brighid.

As she remounted her mare, her scowl was replaced by a smile. Chariots need space, and Brighid's flaying of Uallachán's flanks had provided it. The wailing, white-haired spectre of Báine wheeled her chariots around to attack the fraying rear of Uallachán's army. Travelling at speed, the momentum of a chariot makes it a terrifying weapon. Wheels rimmed with iron broke and crushed bones, and long spinning blades cleaved limbs as a farmer scythes hay.

All chariots are teams of horses, drivers, and warriors: the driver directs the horse teams to position the vehicles to do the most damage, and the warrior hurls javelins and darts. Her missiles exhausted, Báine gripped her longsword with a gore-splattered hand and swept the weapon from its sheath. Others chose long-handled axes, maces, or swords. For Uallachán's rear, the torment continued.

For Brighid, it was a victory of sorts. The battlefield was splashed in gore and littered with body parts from fingers and toes to arms and legs. Fear rippled through the ranks of Uallachán's army. But cajoled, kicked, and threatened by the king's brutal guards, the central bodies of the southern and northern divisions continued to move steadily and relentlessly towards Ráth Na Conall. The jaws of Uallachán's trap were about to close.

Brighid railed against the heavens at her impotence. She fumed at her sister, whose orders were explicit in one area. She was not to throw away her riders for a glorious but useless victory. Swallowing a taste as bitter as *caisearbhán*—dandelions, Brighid signalled, and the trumpets sounded. Ráth Na Conall's mobile forces retired to a safe distance from the battlefield. There they would wait for another chance to fight.

✳✳✳

"I think it's our turn."

Conchobhar nodded to Danu, secured the straps on his helmet, and, along with Flann, strode along the walkway to take positions on the southern wall. Danu had elected to command the northern rampart. Four huge bodyguards left no room at her side for an irritated Glaisne. Perched on the guard post, Draighean, voice undiminished, maintained her incantations and directed the winter's elements. With the riders and chariots having left the arena, the Sidhe felt at liberty to unleash rods of rain and hail the size of a child's fist on their enemy.

Danu paced back and forward, watching the besiegers overcome the barrier of trees at the bottom of the hill. Sharpened branches, slivers of wood, and gorse and brambles stabbed the attackers. She ground her teeth at the yelps of pain and curses but reluctantly admired their persistence. Still, the obstacle had done its job and the momentum of Uallachán's attack wavered.

Danu waited for the besiegers to break from the treeline and come within range of her bows. Before long, every muscle in Danu's right arm burned with the continual nocking and shooting of arrows. She had sixty black shafts in two quivers and had only used one. Grimacing, she continued until she had loosed all the missiles. Bleeding bodies carpeted the killing ground—their final resting places marked by fluttering red and white feathers.

In battles, those behind show no patience or sympathy for those before them and curse the slowness of the advance that endangers them. Furthermore, the front rows are usually populated with callow youth and glory seekers. Yet knowing the fate that likely awaited them, there seemed to be no lack of young men or women to fill the forward lines. *What made them sell their lives so cheaply?* A battle was an unlikely place to make a stand for the invulnerability of youth.

Danu wondered whether Uallachán might have become a respected leader if he had not taken the path of a depraved tyrant. *Instead, he forces his people to fight and me to slaughter them.* Danu scratched her arse and sniffed her fingers before smoothing the blue plumes on her helmet. She looked upwards. Meán lae approached, but since the sky remained overcast, that observation was based on the rumbling in Danu's belly. She smiled at the rude comments her actions provoked. It might be their last joke before Mag Mell.

Uallachán's divisions had run or trotted since they had broken their fast. They had suffered under Brighid's riders and chariots. The cold blasts of winter rain and hail from Draighean continued to sap their strength—and spirit. A roar of "Javelins!" broke Danu's train of thought, and she hefted a throwing spear.

With no bridges, the only path waiting for the first to crest the berm was downwards. The front ranks tumbled into a ditch two javelins deep and two wide, and onto sharpened stakes. Danu ground her teeth at the cries as flesh was rent by the pales. To her ears, the voices were mostly of young boys and girls. Her nostrils flared at the first faint smell of bowels loosed in death.

"Hold your javelins!" she shouted. "Let the ditches do their work." She looked to several who held bows and stood beside braziers. "Now would be a good time." Lit arrows arced and fell into the ditches. Poured barrels of pitch and bales of hay covered the bottom of the trench. The gully burst into flames and curls of thick, choking black smoke rose. Then, another smell took its place on the battle menu—roasted flesh. Danu winced at the shrieking, and a tear rolled down her cheek. Her mind roared, *"Tuili!"*

On the southern wall, Conchobhar grinned. *She's learning.* Above the gatepost, Draighean nodded her head in approval of her protégé and decided it was time to take her place on the walkway.

✶✶✶

Apart from whores and a small group of guards, the camp was deserted. The *striapacha* had considered fleeing the encampment. After a battle, men are much more brutal, especially the vanquished, and the women knew the casualty and death tolls among them would be high. As for the sentries, they were mainly drunk or rutting the whores.

The sisters kept their wits sharp and eyes open as they crept closer to their target. Úna had objected to Naomh's design and where her sympathies lay. While charitable, it seemed dangerous to even bring the prisoner water. Yet she conceded because her sister had always taken care of her, and Úna owed her that loyalty.

From a distance, the prisoner looked appalling. Up close, his condition made the girls throw up. How could anyone be this cruel? The man's body had too many lacerations to count. Scabs closed many but a sizeable number, the final acts before Uallachán's warriors departed for battle, bled freely. "Perhaps, like his friend, the bean-sidhe came for him," said Úna. Looking at the man, she thought death would be a mercy.

Their question was answered as the man spasmed and coughed raggedly. A mouthful of blood splashed his chest. "Help. Please help." His strength spent, he slumped against the wood. At that moment, the girls' plan faced their first obstacle. They were small, and the man was huge. Plus, he had been raised up on a tall pole and tied to a crosspiece to keep him in place. Even to give a sip of water from a skin would be challenging.

"The Hag! This is impossible!" exclaimed Úna.

Despite Úna's reliance on Naomh for comfort, protection, and survival, the younger of the sisters was the cleverest and the most sensitive. Perhaps it was why she suffered more from the abuse and forced rutting. "If we're to give him water, one of us will have to climb the stake." Úna breathed in and exhaled slowly. "I'm the better climber." Naomh nodded and handed over the skin of water… and a knife. Blue eyes opened wide, and Úna's head tilted to the side.

Naomh said quietly, "His life is in your hands."

At the top of the tree trunk, Úna took a few breaths to quell her belly. Her hands, feet, and clothes were stained with blood and gore. He, and now she, smelt of death and shite. How had the man lost so much blood and yet still lived? She looked to the sky and prayed to the Goddess for guidance. At that moment, the man's eyes opened.

The whites of his eyes had splashes of red from numerous broken veins. His deep brown irises held sadness and kindness in equal measures. When his mouth opened, he spoke one word hoarsely through cracked lips. "Please."

"The Hag's arse," Úna mumbled. *Why me? Why do I have to make the decision?* She looked down on Naomh, muttered, "I hope the Goddess favours me," and started sawing the ropes that bound Onchú. Below, Naomh smiled and cut the thongs and twine that bound his feet and legs. The man fell heavily when the final rope severed, almost crushing Naomh. That he had not moved since the fall raised the girl's anxiety. After all their effort, had they killed the stranger?

The sisters looked around in desperation. Good fortune had accompanied their efforts so far, but that well was not bottomless. "Give him some water. Maybe he'll be able to move—if he's not dead," said Úna.

Naomh looked at her sister curiously. In her eyes was something unseen in many summers—hope. "Tend to him. I'm going to look for a path out of here."

The younger sister looked down at the man. Even in his horrific state, Úna could see his arms, chest, and legs were heavily muscled, and he was tall… very tall. She shook her head, and dark, lank tresses flared out. They certainly could not carry him. Could they even drag him? Anxiety overwhelmed her. Her heart pounded, and she fought to breathe. If discovered, Uallachán would have them raped to death. It was his nature.

Her misgivings made Úna want to run, but she stayed and encouraged the man to sip the water. She told him her sister was scouting a path from the camp and would be back soon but did not know if he could hear or understand. Since he no longer hung on the stake, his breathing sounded more regular, and his chest rose and fell steadily. From his moans, the effort caused him pain—likely, he had broken ribs. Overwhelmed, Úna wept for the man, her tears carving valleys in the gore that covered his face.

Hearing the bushes rustle, Úna started and grabbed the knife. She would not be taken without a fight. Relief flooded her when Naomh appeared. "We are closer to the Abhainn na Siúire than I thought. Once through the riverside foliage, the riverbank slopes steeply downwards to the water's edge. If we can drag or roll him down to the river, I think the current will take us away from the camp."

"I wonder what he's called and where he lives. I hope he's a good man and worth saving," said Úna.

"Onchú."

The man gasped the single word through teeth clenched in pain. Eyes open and finally able to think, Onchú wondered how two fragile girls not much older than his daughters had freed him. When they grabbed him under his arms and dragged him over the dirt, he tried to help, but his legs refused to cooperate, and every move was agonising. He thanked the Goddess for his rescuers and prayed they would have a quick death when, inevitably, they were caught.

★★★

Theoretically, those behind walls, defending an elevated position,

129

hold the advantage. Danu knew that a small contingent of her da's army had held the stronghold of Lugudunon against thirty thousand. That said, Lugudunon's towering stone walls and ramparts were vastly superior to the patched-up defences of Ráth Na Conall—and they had ballistae. Danu wondered if the triremes had reached Massalia and delivered her messages. Yet, even if they were on the seas and returning, it would be no help against the horde converging on the hill.

She heard the dull crump of trees thrown across the ditch. Ironically, by cutting down the massive boles for their defence, they had provided the means for Uallachán's hulks to bridge the trench. Men grunted on the narrow walkway as the great cauldrons were lifted and tipped over. Red hot embers, boiling oil, and scalding hot water cascaded down on those attempting to get purchase on the stockade.

Shrieks filled the air as skin blistered, boiled, and sloughed off. Disfigured, many would take their lives rather than suffer the indignity of begging and a lifetime of pitying looks. Alive, they would become outcasts, for who wants to look in the face of defeat? Those on the ramparts hurled javelins; the attackers watched in shock as iron spikes punched through flesh and bone.

Inevitably, Uallachán's warriors gained the wooden walkway. The timbers trembled as hundreds joined in a macabre ballet of death on the ramparts. Ráth Na Conall's garrison was the fresher, but the enemy had the advantage of numbers.

The two, a boy and a girl, each no more than fourteen summers old, were friends. Together they heaved a sigh of relief. They had avoided Brighid's riders and chariots and overcome trees, ditches, and the stockade. Confronted by the mask of curling sigils on Danu's face, they shuddered at something they did not understand.

Cajoled and pushed by those at their backs, the duo attacked. A memory of how Bláithín Ni Neill, a queen of Clann Ui Flaithimh, had almost died at the Battle of Dún-an-Rí because she hesitated saved Danu. Battering the boy with her shield, she swung the short-handled, double-headed axe at the girl. She felt the blade tremble as it carved a deep fissure across the young warrior's skull and grimaced at the splatter of warm blood, bone, and brains.

Before the girl's corpse hit the walkway, Danu was already swirling around. The boy had no armour, not even a leather breastplate. Danu's axe cut through clothing that offered no resistance. Shocked at the blood-spewing diagonal gash across his chest, the boy was spared further pain by the blow that cleaved his head from his neck.

A glance to Danu's right saw Glaisne holding several attackers at bay. His skill with coordinating scíath and sword was impressive. Evidently his father had not been tight-fisted when preparing his son for battle. Time and again, his chainmail turned away the points of swords and daggers, confounding his foes and leaving them open to the slash of his heavy double-edged sword.

Danu smiled. Glaisne was economical, efficient, and deadly. That he appeared to enjoy killing raised a brief frown, but there was no time to dwell on an observation made in the heat of battle. A macabrely joyful scream to Danu's left drew her attention.

Draighean whirled in circles, wielding two single-edged knives with wicked forward-curving blades. Yet that skill was not her only advantage. As the Sidhe twisted and turned, the black cloak parted and flared out, revealing the dark designs swathing her body. That she was amply endowed distracted the foolish, sending them into the arms of the mná-sidhe. Danu shook her head as if to confirm her eyes. Under the dark sky, Draighean's skin now had a faint blue hue.

"How many do you want to kill?" asked Draighean, despatching several warriors with ruthless efficiency.

"What?" The Sidhe's question caught Danu unawares.

"It is a simple question. Your shields are impressive and have held the walls, but numbers and tiredness will eventually tell. Do you wish the seanchaithe to tell tales and sing poems of the brave defence of Ráth Na Conall that became a tragedy?

"Thus, my question is twofold. Have you killed enough, and do you wish me to intervene?" Draighean paused as if to consider another option. "Of course, since my mission is to protect your sister and you, I could simply remove you from the battlefield. Uallachán could be eliminated later by stealth."

The Sidhe smiled. "Well?"

"Are you telling me that you could have stopped this senseless slaughter? What kind of a heartless being are you?" exclaimed Danu, her eyes molten green with anger.

"Men and women, kings and queens—even princesses—need to know the cost and consequences of their actions. Otherwise, why should they stop? Bloodshed tempers the plans of wise rulers. Uallachán's iniquity is his disrespect for and the low value he sets on blood." Draighean held Danu's stare without the slightest hint of flinching or guilt.

"Your parents understood this. Again, I ask. What would you have me do? Make your decision—quickly." As Danu opened her mouth to respond, the Sidhe held up her hand. "But remember. *You* will bear the cost of your decision. I am simply your weapon."

"Stop this madness. Do what you can," snapped Danu.

"Here's hoping you obeyed my instructions," smirked Draighean.

"What bloody instructions?" shouted Danu, but the Sidhe had focused on other matters.

"Oh, the Hag's tits!" exclaimed Danu. Around the ramparts, many echoed her sentiment.

Across the hill's slopes, masses of blackthorn shrubs with wickedly long thorns burst through the earth. Suddenly filled with *straif*, the perimeter ditch became an impenetrable barrier of spikes, preventing Uallachán's force from advancing.

Those who had gained the defences found they had no path to retreat and fell to the blades of the garrison. Besiegers screamed as an enemy they could not resist stabbed, encircled, and strangled them. Men and women slashed furiously at the bushes, hoping to carve a path to the bottom of the hill and safety.

As the blackthorn bushes slowly but inexorably crushed Uallachán's army, the sky gradually became summer blue, and the storms of thunder and lightning retreated. Once more, Draighean's skin flushed pink. In the chaos, the chastised force fled towards the Abhainn na Siúire, hoping to escape along its western river plain. They were pursued by Brighid's riders and chariots, astounded at the gift they had been given. Uallachán's misery had not ended.

As sunset neared, a sweet and heavy musky fragrance reminiscent of rutting arose from the proliferation of the blackthorn's flowers. To Danu, the scent seemed horrifically inappropriate but served to mask the decay of the dead. As Danu surveyed her victory, she remembered her dream about the straif bushes.

"Shite! Did I do this?"

"Yes," came the answer.

✳✳✳

Nuadha watched Beacán grimace as he bent over to skin and spit a rabbit. *He must be in great pain.* One arm hung helpless, and its shape pointed to at least one break. Yet, even with one arm and wounds that seeped dark stains into his tattered clothing, Nuadha did not doubt that Beacán could kill him. *I am pathetic to be cowered by a gravely wounded man.* He wondered how the friend he once knew had become the ruthless assassin who moved like a ghost and killed with impunity. And then he thought about his own life and wondered who should be pitied the most.

The smell of roasting flesh made Nuadha's belly rumble. It had been three sunsets since the night of horrors and since he had eaten. Thankfully, thirst was not a problem. There were many small springs and streams. This night, they perched on an outcrop of Na Comaraigh, shielded from the wind and unfriendly eyes. In the distance stood Ráth Na Conall and his fate.

Nuadha watched his brother's army retreat and pondered the implication of his indifference. Mulling over recent events, Nuadha was uncertain whether the defeat of his brother was good or bad. Did he wish to return to Ráth Na Conall? He snorted. *As if I have a choice.* His life would likely end very painfully at the hillfort. Was that such an awful prospect? In death, he would be free of Uallachán forever.

Nuadha coughed and dipped his head towards the spit. A thin stream of drool dribbled down his chin, and his belly rumbled again but louder. Beacán's laugh chilled his bones. *Had he ever known this person?* A grease-dripping leg and thigh were flung in Nuadha's direction, landing in the dirt at his feet. Bound hands clumsily grasped the food. He ignored the charred meat and pieces of earth. His stomach was much too empty to be fussy.

"We move at first light." They were the only words spoken by Beacán that evening.

CHAPTER 13

A relieved Beacán allowed himself a thin smile as the gates of Ráth Na Conall loomed large in his vision. His many wounds tore and wept as he forced the pace back to the fort. His ferocity, as well as his threatening demeanour, cowed Nuadha. So far, Beacán's childhood acquaintance had complied with his orders.

In Beacán's favour, Nuadha's decadent lifestyle had bequeathed him a body that was obese and plainly out of condition. However, Beacán's strength diminished with each passing sunset. Nuadha was not blind, and even he would soon realise that Beacán's fortitude had reached its limit.

"Beacán!"

The scream brought a smile to his blood-smeared and dirt-ingrained face. Iasg, having recovered from her mission and the recent battle, had kept watch faithfully on the battlements from sunrise to sunset. On this day, the Goddess rewarded her steadfastness as Beacán's haggard figure stumbled the first few steps on the track to the fort's gateway. Behind him staggered the bound figure of Nuadha.

Gripping the hand not taken by Iasg, Brighid allowed herself a smile and sent a heartfelt "Thanks" to the Goddess as she walked beside the litter. "Your long absence distressed us, uncle."

Beacán lay in pain, exhausted, and his wounds offered a temptation that disease and infection would find hard to resist. Brighid cursed the absence of druids in the fort and wondered if Draighean had talent as a healer. Trying to lighten the sombre mood, Brighid sniffed and looked to Iasg. "He smells worse than horse shite and piss. I'd advise you to bathe him." Then she winked. "But I wouldn't recommend more intimate behaviour. He'd likely not survive that." Iasg chuckled and dipped her head.

"Onchú?" queried a breathless Danu, who had hurried from the Great Hall on hearing the news.

As much as Brighid looked to Beacán as her confidant and counsel, Danu increasingly saw Onchú as her advocate. Thus, she was very reluctant to accept the possibility of his death. The shake of Beacán's head depressed her, making it hard to hold onto hope and the smile on her lips. Who would tell Onchú's daughters? Or Eithne? Her shoulders sagged. *I suppose that's on my plate.*

Beacán coughed as he summoned the strength to speak more than a few words. "He did help me capture a prisoner. I don't think you have met Nuadha Ó Dubhghaill—Uallachán's brother," said Beacán.

"Shite!"

✳✳✳

The boy, captured by one of Báine's patrols as dusk fell, was no more than eleven summers old. He was exhausted, his clothes were torn, and his arms and legs bled from thorns and brambles. According to his tale, he had left the coastal settlement of Niúig three sunsets past. Seated at a small table, he devoured the rabbit meat, bread, hard cheese, and milk. It was a stark change from the berries and spring water that had sustained him since he had escaped.

Yet what concerned Danu, Brighid, and the others in the room was the boy's insistence on only speaking with Báine. How did he know the name of the charioteer? And why did he want to talk to her? A disconcerted Báine, having arrived back in the fort from her patrol, was commanded to go immediately to the small chamber. Once in the room, she noted the perturbed looks on the faces of those gathered. *What the Hag have I done?*

It was then that Báine noticed the small boy. He stopped eating, looked up, and studied her intensely. Then, with a cry of relief, he jumped up and ran to wrap his arms around her. For someone relatively small, his grip would have shamed a bear. Tears streamed from his face as he sobbed sorely and repeated, "You've got to help her."

"This gets curiouser," said Danu, relieved to see Brighid concur. Things they agreed on seemed to be few and infrequent recently. "Perhaps, Báine, if you can get the boy to settle down, we may get some answers." Having gathered her wits together, Báine inspected the lad with equal intensity. His features were masked by dirt and scratched by brambles. Yet the dark, almost black hair, the deep blue eyes, and the shape of his face struck chords in her memory. Her eyes widened as the revelation hit her.

"You're one of Aoife's brothers," said Báine. The lad nodded, and instantly, Báine's expression became one of alarm and panic. "What's wrong? Is Aoife all right?"

Danu smiled, recognising the name of the little girl on the beach. "Well, at least that solves one mystery." She looked at the puzzled faces of the others and said, "Later." The atmosphere in the room thickened, and it seemed as if the temperature dropped dramatically when the boy spoke. He said just one word.

"Slavers."

✶✶✶

Báine took Aoife's brother, Cass, to a chamber to rest, promising him that she would come back in a short while. When she returned to the meeting room and before she had entirely crossed the doorstep, Báine thundered, "We have to do something. Aoife and her family can't be left to the mercies of slavers." The lack of enthusiasm from the group in the room flushed her usually pale cheeks red.

Both Brighid and Danu were startled at Báine's reaction. Setting aside her frightening behaviour and penchant for recklessness when

137

in a chariot, Báine's personality tended to pragmatism and not letting others get too close. The only exception was her growing intimacy with Brighid. Had Aoife impacted the charioteer that much? Brighid's eyes opened wide.

"That's why you asked me for a horse. You've been visiting Aoife and her family." Báine nodded, and Brighid looked disappointed. "You could have told me. I would have come with you."

"Sorry." Tears welled up in Báine's eyes.

"I had a family once, but they were killed in an Averni border raid. My brothers, sisters, parents, and grandparents are all gone. I survived only because I was fighting elsewhere." The strain on Báine's face was unconcealed as she fought to regain control of her emotions. "I can't and won't desert this family. No matter what is decided, I leave for Niúig at first light."

Truthfully, slavery was an awkward subject for those seated around the table. All grew up in households that had, and still had, slaves. Even in Ráth Na Conall, the menial chores were undertaken mainly by the indentured. Apart from the odd cruel master, the lives of the enslaved were often better than many peasants and labourers. They had regular care, food, shelter, and clothing.

Debt and criminal activities forced many into bondage, but most were enslaved after battles. For many rulers, it was a way to recoup some of the costs of expensive wars. That said, the most despised of people were the slavers, who wrenched innocents from their homes and villages for profit. The slavers' response to civilisation's moral dilemma was simple. If there were no demand, there would be no slave trade. It was their way of saying, "Stick your hypocritical principles up your arse."

The room fell silent as Báine's ire simmered, and each of those seated considered their conflicting emotions. Danu had no doubt that her chariot commander would attempt some foolishness. Given the cause, she would likely find sympathy and support among the chariot teams and riders. And it was inevitable that Brighid would stand with Báine.

Still, having just survived one battle, Danu was reluctant to weaken her garrison. Construction of the new fort proceeded at a snail's pace. She was deeply disappointed in Neasán's endeavours. Despite repelling Uallachán's assaults and the promise of protection, the level of labour attracted was miserable. Furthermore, Onchú remained missing, and Beacán needed time to recover from his injuries.

"Which one of us would choose to be a slave?"

It was Glaisne who broke the silence. Danu smiled. The fresh scar on his right cheek had stripped him of any traces of boyishness and, in its place, bequeathed an air of authority. None would argue that he had not fought bravely, so he had slipped deeper into her good graces, if not her bed. "The people of Niúig are not the victims of war. They were attacked. Ráth Na Conall is their neighbour and their friend—is it not?"

"Quite clever and a likely path to Danu's cot," murmured Draighean. Danu glared, and Glaisne scowled at Draighean's brutal observation. Both had no impact on the Sidhe.

A pair of hands slapped the oak table, making everyone jump except Draighean, who always appeared infuriatingly calm. "Face it, we know what we're going to do," exclaimed Brighid. Then she looked at Danu and grinned. "Since this would be an offensive campaign, that puts me in charge, doesn't it?"

A hand raised by Danu curtailed Brighid's initial enthusiasm, and petulance settled on the younger twin's lips. "According to Báine, Niúig is at the end of a long estuary and is guarded by a small promontory fort. Cliffs protect the ringfort on its northern and western flanks, a steep slope and marshland to its east, and an earth and stone bank and ditch to its south. The settlement is a half-day ride from here, and that assumes you find a ford across the Abhainn na Siúire. It's also a similar distance and time by sea."

Danu looked around the table, and her eyes settled on Thrasius, who had been summoned to the gathering. "Prepare your ship to sail at dawn. I will assign fifty shields for the voyage under Flann's command.

Your mission is to prevent any slave ship from escaping and entering open seas."

The fleet commander beamed and nodded his assent. He was no friend of slavers or of their crews who disgraced the name of seamen. Next, Danu turned to Brighid. "Take fifty riders…" Danu paused and looked at Báine, whose cheeks had lost some of their heat. "I expect we would have to chain and lock Báine in a cell to prevent her from joining you, so her chariots will accompany you."

Once more, turning to her twin, Danu said, "We lag four sunsets from when the slavers attacked Niúig. I doubt we have more than a sunset before they are gone forever." She stopped, dipped her head, and smirked. "Now, you may take command of your forces, Brighid."

✳✳✳

The three ageing penteconters had been stripped down to the essentials. Their timbers held the smell of death and the likelihood of more since their destination was the far shores of the Great Sea. The original crews of fifty oarsmen per ship were delighted to relinquish their oars. In their places, men, women, and children were bound with chains and locked into iron shackles.

The slaves would propel the vessels until exhausted. If their condition was judged irredeemable, they would be replaced and tossed overboard. Since the community of Niúig had provided more victims than the contract required, those who died on the journey would not be missed—at least by the slavers. Any of the surplus who survived would be the honey on the bread.

The commander of the slavers, a Greek named Pidytes, relished the women's wailing, the men's futile curses, and the mewling of the young children. "That's the sound of gold," he muttered and laughed aloud. Those closest to him were quick to join in the merriment. This would be a good trip. The slaves had been kidnapped to order with half of the payment provided in advance.

Moreover, the residents of Niúig, and its surrounding lands, were mainly artisans, farmers, and peasants. The poorly garrisoned ringfort offered little resistance. Consequently, Pidytes' men had only suffered bruises and a few broken bones. A movement on the periphery of his vision distracted Pidytes from mentally counting and spending his profit.

He cursed the tiny, black-haired bitch who had avoided all attempts to snare her. Even on the one occasion he had managed to land a punch on her fleeing back, she still escaped capture. In their pit of despair, she was a burning brand of hope to those in chains. Pidytes knew that it would only take a few slaves to embrace her belief, and he would have trouble on the return voyage. He roared at the child and, once again, called on his men to capture her.

Aoife's response was to lift up her léine, flash her arse, and shout, "*Póg mo thoin*—kiss my arse!" Before turning to evade her pursuers yet again, she made what he assumed to be an obscene gesture. Where on earth did the child learn such things? As Pidytes watched Aoife's pale arse disappear into the gloom of dusk, he smiled. The ships would be gone before meán lae on the next day's high tide, and the little bitch would be left alone to deal with the wolves.

✳✳✳

Aoife crouched in the cave that had been her home for four sunsets. Her stomach growled with hunger, and she was very thirsty. Lonely at not being with her ma and da and siblings, she sobbed. During the day, she put on a brave face, but at night, she wept uncontrollably until she finally slept. She was afraid for her family and herself and terrified at the scuffling and snuffling noises from creatures who saw her as their next meal.

But every sunset, before she fell into the arms of sleep, she faithfully prayed to the Goddess and called out Báine's name. The Goddess heard her, and in her fitful sleep and dreams, so did Báine.

✳✳✳

Brighid cursed in frustration, and Báine howled. At the first hint of dawn, the chariots and riders had raced through the gates of Ráth Na Conall, turned eastwards, and then settled into a fast canter along the

Abhainn na Siúire river. In the distance, they could see the ringfort of Niúig and the three penteconters anchored at the bottom of the cliffs. But the waters in the estuary were too wide and deep to cross, and the tide was racing in. They had no choice but to cross the river further upstream and follow its sister, the An Bhearú, until they found a suitable crossing.

At the helm of the trireme, Thrasius savoured the rhythmic pull and splash of almost two hundred wooden blades and the grunts of hard-muscled men and women. There was little wind and the distance to travel was not overly far, so oars alone propelled the ship. In the calm waters of An Mhuir Cheilteach, it was much more efficient to use muscle-power rather than sails. As with the riders, the ship had commenced its journey just before dawn. Unlike Brighid's force, the vessel made excellent time.

As meán lae approached, the vessel swept in a wide arc before entering the estuary that led to Niúig. The quiet waters of the bay, the tide, and the shallow draft of the trireme favoured the vessel, and it made swift progress towards the settlement. As the ship came within sight of Niúig's ringfort, its lookout called out. Two slave boats had begun their journey down the estuary. "Warriors to the upper deck," shouted Thrasius. Oars were pulled in and secured as fifty shields quickly changed from rowers to fighters. That still left over one hundred oarsmen at their posts, and the ship continued to cut through the water.

Poorly manned defences meant that terrorising and capturing the people of Niúig had been easy work—until now. From his vantage point on the walls of the ringfort, Pidytes stood aghast as he watched the trireme draw closer to his two ships. The trireme dwarfed his vessels. It was four times longer and twice as wide as the penteconters and had three times the number of oars—and hence, the number of men. Pidytes could list no advantage his ships had over the new arrival in the wide estuary.

The slaver cursed. Was a rival about to steal his cargo? What other reason could there be for the vessel's presence? Trapped onboard the ancient ships, his men were caught in the worst position. Had they delayed their journey for even a short time and stayed within the ringfort, the dirt and stone ramparts would have protected them. Pidytes' disposition worsened when his northern lookout shouted, "Riders approaching from the north."

Pidytes envisaged the tiny thorn in his side dancing with glee on the hillside. "The little bitch," he muttered. Feverishly and with rising panic, the slaver considered his options. He could recall his men from the third penteconter and make a stand at the fort. That option he quickly discounted. Instead, he grabbed his gold and abandoned his men. Scrambling down the hillside, Pidytes laughed at his men's curses. He could buy other ships and recruit desperate men to crew them. There were many more isolated communities to raid.

As the trireme slipped between the two penteconters, a bellow of "*Luí síos*—get down!" came from Flann. Startled at hearing their native tongue, the captives onboard did the opposite and stood. Jaws dropped as they saw rows of warriors line each side of a vessel that towered over the one to which they were chained. Each hefted a javelin ready to throw.

"Luí síos!" This time the shouts came from the captives, and as one, the prisoners dropped or were pulled to the ship's timbers. At that moment, the slavers fully realised their peril.

Theoretically, the slavers outnumbered the Gael warriors two-to-one. However, that advantage disappeared with the first volley of javelins. With their height advantage, Flann's force could choose their targets. The first to die were the ships' helmsmen, and sergeants who were swept into the estuary's waters, leaving the vessels leaderless and rudderless.

The second volley reversed any superiority of numbers. Crippled, the ships drifted until Flann's warband threw ropes across. The captives quickly grasped the cables' purpose and secured them to benches or iron rings. Flann's warriors leapt across and into the captured penteconters as the hulls clashed.

Knowing their probable fate, a few slavers showed no remorse and drew blades. They were no competition for veterans of the shield-wall whose faces showed an absence of mercy. Those remaining alive, and that was few, found themselves in chains. "Free enough captives to row the ships. I'll send two helmsmen aboard to guide the vessels to Niúig's harbour." The command came from Thrasius and was met with a broad grin by Flann.

On impulse, Flann roared, "Is the family of Aoife aboard this vessel? Stand and be recognised." The veteran smiled as a small group rose, uncertain of their fate. Were these warriors just more trouble? Then, loud enough that all could hear, Flann said, "This settlement owes a great debt to Aoife. Without her, your fate was a life of slavery far from Ériu." Flann rubbed his chin and remonstrated with himself. "Her brother, Cass, too. He ran to Ráth Na Conall with nothing more than berries in his belly for three sunsets."

***

"No!" bellowed Báine, pointing to the lone figure running and stumbling down the ringfort's long eastern slope.

"The rat seeks to escape," said Brighid. "My riders can take care of the pitiful remnant from the third ship and any in the ráth. Surely your chariots are not so slow as to allow him to escape?" The feral look on Báine's face caused Brighid to pause. "Remind me not to get on your bad side." Báine's quick smirk was followed by a scream. She tapped her driver's shoulder, and the chariot leapt forward. The two-horse team, bred from hardy Northern Albu stock, devoured the terrain before them.

Feeling every bone in her body ache with each bump and hollow over the rough terrain, Báine swore as she watched her quarry gain the edge of the marshland. She watched him turn and wave and envisaged the triumphant sneer on his face. Pidytes knew no chariot could follow him into the boggy land. With a snarl and her face red with anger, Báine snapped an order to her driver.

"Take me as fast and close as you can risk and turn the chariot around hard and sharply."

Mystified, the driver nodded, and the vehicle leapt forward. At the apex of the turn, using the vehicle's momentum, Báine leapt into the air. She prayed to the Goddess for a patch of firm earth. At first, she was disappointed as both feet sank into dark, peaty waters. Then she smiled—it was only ankle deep.

Sword in hand, Báine splashed in the wake of Pidytes, who realised his nemesis closed on him. Had he discarded his heavy bag of gold, perhaps he would have made a successful retreat across the bog. Instead, weighed down by his treasure, the marshy terrain fought him for each step. Báine's breath on his neck brought a shiver of fear. "Not so fast, tuilí."

The sharp pain Pidytes felt was the blade that hamstrung him. He stumbled and watched his treasure slip below the bog's waters. It was another piece of torment, although not his last, before Báine's blow rendered him senseless.

***

"I suppose hanging is our fate," said Pidytes, now held between two of his surviving crew. Báine's blade had bitten deep into the back of his thighs, and he could not walk without support. "At least it's a reasonably quick death."

Brighid shook her head. The smile perched on dusty pink lips sent shivers up the man's spine. "No. Hanging is for pirates, and your profession is much, much worse. I think I can devise a more appropriate death with much more suffering." Brighid watched a chariot draw close, and the tall, milk-pale warrior with long white braids jump off and stride towards her. There was no mercy on Báine's visage.

"However, before *I* settle your men's fate, my friend wishes to reward you for the pain you caused her small friend and family. She has wagered that she can flay the flesh from your body by tying you to her chariot and dragging you up and down this pebble and shale beach. The wager is how many cycles it will take, and will you still be alive for me to have my fun?"

Sadly for Pidytes, while his flesh was as bloody as raw meat, he remained alive when Brighid's warriors nailed him to the cut tree trunk and disembowelled him. Thirty slavers accompanied him, and all were arrayed along the edge of the estuary's cliffs as a warning to others. It was a slow and painful death, with their final indignity being shat on and their eyes pecked out by seabirds.

✱✱✱

A tearful Báine, whom Aoife's family had adopted, reluctantly returned to Ráth Na Conall seven sunsets later. Brighid was unsympathetic, suggesting Báine stop moping and pitch in with the fort building. Yet the smile behind her harsh words told a different story. Brighid both knew the value of family and treasured her friendship with Báine. *Perhaps I've been too hard on my sister.*

A shout of, "Men approaching from the east!" prompted Brighid and Báine to grab weapons and run to the ramparts, where they joined Danu.

"The Hag's bony arse! Is this another attack?" asked Danu.

Further along the ramparts, a Draighean gave a great belly laugh and stamped her blackthorn staff on the wooden boards. "A good deed has its reward," said Draighean as she turned to Danu and Brighid. "I believe a new friend wishes to speak with you." After a brief pause, she added, "You will have queenly decisions to make." Full maroon lips formed into an infuriatingly knowing smile.

Báine's shriek of delight shattered the group's musings. She had spotted Aoife perched on her da's shoulders, waving madly, and shouting greetings to the warriors on the battlements. Behind them were about four hundred men and women from the settlement of Niúig.

It was a sensible decision, yet Aoife's father, who remained a farmer at heart, was uncomfortable at his elevation to Niúig's Civic Leader. However, and having survived their recent tribulations, the community agreed that there was no one better to lead and direct its future. They also approved his contention that they were in Ráth Na Conall's debt and needed to repay the obligation.

Cináed gripped his daughter Aoife's hand as if needing her support as they entered the Great Hall. Facing him were Danu and Brighid, and sitting alongside were Báine, Beacán, Conchobhar, Draighean, Flann, Glaisne, and Iasg. Danu smiled at the awkward bow and indicated a chair for Cináed. Aoife immediately ran to Báine and sat on her knee. "We're not much for ceremony here, so speak plainly and honestly."

"I am called Cináed. I, especially, and those from Niúig, owe you a debt that will be difficult to repay. Aoife tells me that you need labour for a new fort." Danu nodded. "That we can help with." The broad smiles on the faces of those before him told of their pleasure and relief. Cináed inhaled deeply and then exhaled.

"However…"

The sudden sharpening of the features and eyes of those before him unnerved Cináed. He held his hands up. Whether in defence or to assure his audience all was well, it was left to others to judge. "You may have noticed that our partners and children accompany us. Most of us are farmers; others are artisans or have useful trades. We ask for your permission to settle the lands around Ráth Na Conall. Rumours suggest you are open to this."

Cináed took several gulps of water to help assuage the sudden dryness of his throat before making his final request. "We also wish to join Clann Ui Flaithimh and swear allegiance to your father, Conall Mac Gabhann, as our Rí Ruirech." He looked at Brighid and Danu. "And to you as the Rígana of Ráth Na Conall."

"It seems we are officially queens, sister," said Brighid as a broad grin spread across her face. Then, in a quieter tone, she added, "This is welcome news, given our recent troubles." Danu nodded, finding it a severe challenge to keep her delight under control.

Danu looked around the table and smiled. "I am unsure of the proper protocol, if there is one, for becoming part of Clann Ui

Flaithimh—apart from swearing your loyalty to our da… and ma." With a final look to measure any objections, Danu stood and reached out her hand. She was followed by Brighid. "On behalf of my sister and I, welcome. The feast of Samhain is still far off, but perhaps we can devise something more formal and celebrate at that time.

"In the meantime, there is much work to be done. And that brings me to another issue. Until we end Uallachán's rebellion, I must warn you that I expect he and his allies will continue to cause strife across the land. My army will protect whenever possible, but these will not be easy or peaceful times."

***

"I thought *you* would teach me," pouted Aoife, looking askance at Brighid. In turn, Brighid glared back, although not at Aoife but at Báine, who had volunteered her. The issue was who would train Aoife, and her brother, to ride the two ponies gifted to them by the rígana.

Báine laughed. "I know she looks fearsome, but she does have younger brothers and sisters who adore her. You will be safe in her hands, and there's no better rider in Ráth Na Conall. When you're older, and if you still want to ride chariots, then I will take over your training."

Aoife frowned, but it was not in her nature to remain petulant for long. An impish smile spread across her face, and that made Brighid wary. "So, how good are you?" With a howl, Brighid accepted the challenge and galloped across the pasture.

"Will she teach me how to yell like that, too?" Báine laughed and hugged Aoife.

***

Onchú groaned as his bones and broken body felt every bump of the wagon's solid wheels. Hauled by a team of oxen, it rolled slowly up the long track to Ráth Na Conall's gateway. Uncharacteristically, Onchú felt a high level of trepidation. Almost a cycle of the moon had passed since his capture, torture, and eventual escape from Uallachán's camp. During that time, his rescuers, and constant companions, had been the two young camp whores. Most at the fort, including his hand-fast partner, Eithne, and daughters, probably thought he was dead.

The Rí of Carn Tigherna had no qualms that he owed his life to Naomh and Úna, who sat on either side of the wagon's driver. Naomh's use of the river currents to escape had proved successful but took longer than expected. Mainly, this was due to his appalling physical condition and a lack of any salves or medicines. Úna, however, had identified some plants that mitigated his pain. Onchú smiled. That one had a future as a healer… or a witch.

Eventually, the river's flow had washed the trio up on a sandbank close to Niúig, and there, their fortunes changed. Spotted by farmworkers from Niúig, they were taken to Cináed. Onchú was regaled with the story of Aoife, Báine, and the slavers and informed of the settlement's move to Ráth Na Conall. Cináed tempered his guest's enthusiasm for a quick return to the hillfort. The journey would likely take two sunsets, even in a wagon. Onchú's poor condition ruled out early travel.

Still, the people of Niúig promised to keep Onchú's location and health challenges a secret until he could face those at the hillfort. Today, as the sun began its descent to the western horizon, Onchú drew closer to the gates of Ráth Na Conall. "Naomh, Úna, please help me stand."

"I don't think you're well enough to stand while the cart moves," said Naomh. Onchú smiled and stroked her hair. Naomh had shepherded and mothered him and Úna since escaping Uallachán's camp and showed no sign of relinquishing that responsibility.

"It's a man thing," answered Onchú.

"Do you think they'll like us?" Onchú nodded. *Most will but maybe not one.*

Supported by the girls and gripping the rim of the cart, Onchú stood and called out to the guard posts, "I am Onchú Ó an Cháintigh, Rí of Carn Tigherna, may my companions and I enter?"

"Shite! He's a rí," exclaimed Úna before turning to Onchú and, in a scolding tone, said, "You might have warned us."

Word of Onchú's return spread like wildfire around Ráth Na Conall. Not knowing whether to be frightened or happy, the girls jumped down from the wagon and stared wide-eyed as the garrison mustered around them. Then, as one, the warriors cheered and bashed swords against scíatha.

Brighid and Danu rand from the Great Hall. Stopping short of the wagon, they smiled and then looked puzzled. "Are you not staying, Onchú?" The rí looked sheepishly at the distance from the cart to the ground.

"I think I may need some assistance," said Onchú. Danu noticed the pain in his eyes.

Naomh bowed to Brighid and Danu. "He was severely injured and near to death. I think his honour and pride have been satisfied by entering the ráth on his own feet. However, now, it would be a kindness to help him." She wondered if these were the red-haired bitseacha that Uallachán often raged about. It seemed a very unfair insult.

"Conchobhar and Flann, get men to assist Onchú and carry him to his quarters in the Great Hall." Danu turned to the girls. "You will accompany my sister and me." The sisters gulped and nodded. "We will hear your story, and I will have every detail."

As the party moved towards the Great Hall, a scream of "Da!" pierced the hearts of all in the fort, and they watched as Onchú's daughters raced to hug and kiss him. The ashen look on his face told how much effort it took, but he would not be stopped from kneeling and holding them. Onchú looked to the burly men standing at his side, and they helped raise him up.

The Rí of Carn Tigherna saw the worry in his children's eyes. "I will be fine. I just need rest." Then he called his rescuers over. "This is Naomh and Úna. Without them, I would be dead. They will be living with us from now on—as part of our family."

"Striapacha!"

The shriek resonated around the hillfort as Eithne emerged from the shadows. "I will not have whores in my home." The fierceness of her look made Onchú's daughters grip their father's legs, and Naomh and Úna cower behind Brighid and Danu.

"You have no home, lady. It burned to ashes in Carn Tigherna. You live here only by the grace and compassion of Brighid and Danu, and I suspect their tolerance of your behaviour has reached its limit." Onchú pointed to Naomh and Úna. "These girls saved my life and will live with my daughters and me as one family. If you find that distasteful, leave."

Onchú laughed through gritted teeth. "You can have half of my property. Since that does not amount to anything, perhaps it will be *you* who becomes the striapach." Onchú's face seemed to moderate, and in a softer voice, he said, "None of us chose or desired the path we now walk, and I, too, grieve for our sons and how you and our daughters were violated." Then, in a more sober tone, he added, "Your behaviour is unacceptable, and my patience is not limitless. Make your choice. Stay or go."

As he crossed the entrance to the Great Hall, Onchú smiled as Beacán emerged. "Do I look as bad as you?" asked Onchú.

"Worse," said Beacán. Both men held each other in painful embraces "Let's celebrate our return with a few jugs of beer," said Beacán. Looking over Onchú's shoulder at a smouldering Eithne, he bit a retort back, saying instead, "You look as if you need several." Then Beacán looked to the two warriors who held Onchú between them and smiled. "Perhaps you would accompany us, lest we fall flat on our faces."

* * *

The Civic Leader of Ráth Na Conall, a wispish and opinionated man named Neasán, liked his status but had an air of perpetual pessimism. The current source of his misery was Cináed, whom he regarded as a threat. Cináed was clearly favoured by the princesses—or queens, as most acknowledged them. Hence, any complaint would be seen as simple jealousy, which was not far off the mark. After several sunsets, Neasán devised a suitable stratagem and asked for a meeting.

"Do we have to do this?" Brighid whispered in Danu's ear as Neasán entered the chamber. "I find the man obnoxious. He is narrow-minded and has an inflated sense of his importance." Seated on either side of the girls, Conchobhar and Glaisne chuckled. Draighean stood behind the twins, quietly observing. Danu sympathised with her sister but put on a mask of queenly neutrality.

"Welcome, Neasán. To what do we owe the honour of your presence?"

"I am troubled, my queen. Very troubled." Neasán's sober demeanour emphasised his mood.

"Perhaps we should recommend a purgative, sister. Perhaps his bowels are in need of release." While low and pitched to Danu's ear, Brighid's words were clearly meant to be heard by Neasán. The red flushes on Neasán's cheeks and ear lobes bore witness that the counsel had been received. Danu shook her head in silent admonishment of Brighid as she fought to hold back an unqueenly smirk.

"Please, Neasán. Unburden yourself."

"I am informed that you have given the community of Niúig permission to settle the lands around Ráth Na Conall."

Danu dipped her head. "You are well-informed… and correct."

"These lands belong to the people of Ráth Na Conall who have farmed and worked them for generations. That is unfair."

Two pairs of green eyes narrowed and stared at Neasán without blinking or flinching. Maintaining her mask, Danu asked, "Where are your people, Neasán? It has been over three cycles of the moon since my sister and I arrived. Yet I see none of *your* people in the fields planting crops. I do not hear the sound of quern stones grinding corn or the rattle of looms making cloth. I do not smell bread baking or meat cooking. The great cauldrons lie cold and empty of soups or stews. As for the fort, apart from yourself and several blacksmiths, there are only warriors—*my* warriors."

Danu paused, took a deep breath, and continued. This time, her visage was cold and stern, and anger coloured her cheekbones. "Tell me, Neasán. Where are *your* people? Are you such a poor leader that you cannot persuade your artisans, farmers, and tradespeople to return? Perhaps the fault is not with them but you."

Danu glared. "Perhaps they are unwilling to pay the bribe of gold you demand from them."

The precariousness of his position finally dawned on Neasán. Flustered, he opened his mouth to protest, but an imperial wave of Danu's hand stopped him. "Listen, Neasán. Listen. What do you hear?" asked Danu. "I hear the sound of men and women, warriors and civilians, building a new stronghold. But they are Cináed's people and my soldiers—not yours.

"You have failed my sister and me and are in no position to bargain or lecture. The lands around Ráth Na Conall are plentiful, and there is more than enough for *any* who wish to settle here. Cináed has delivered on his promise. You have not. Do not request another audience until you have made good on yours."

As a chastened and humiliated Neasán retreated from the room, Brighid turned to her sister with approval. "You can be a real bitseach when you want."

CHAPTER 14

Dawn broke, and, with barely a splash of oars, two triremes entered the bay south of Ráth Na Conall. The helmsman of the leading vessel shivered in a northerly wind that foretold a chilly winter. It was in stark contrast to the balmy climate of Massalia and the Great Sea, from whence the ships had departed several cycles of the moon past.

The seas had become increasingly stormy as the vessels navigated the freezing waters of the north. Hence the seaman's prayer of thanks offered to Apollo for their safe arrival. Had he delayed the voyage by even a half-cycle of the moon, it was doubtful whether they would have made it. Triremes were not strictly ocean-going or designed to conquer large waves.

Alongside the helmsman, Aulus Horatius Pulvilla sensed the sailor's relief at arriving safely and slapped him on the back. "Congratulations. You and your crews have earned a rest and much beer and wine. Put that on my account." Aulus looked around at the shield-men and chuckled. "From the sickly pallor on these warriors' faces, I'm certain they will be delighted to stand on dry land and rest their bellies from puking." As the acrid smell of vomit wafted into his nostrils, Aulus' belly churned, and he shook his head at the foolishness of his words.

"Serves the bastard right."

The *craic* from the shield-men was light-hearted, but, like all Gaelic humour, the words held a bite. Aulus, a veteran centurion under Gaius

Aurelius Atella, had been placed in command of the warriors on board the two ships. That Gaels were under Roman control was a strange and infrequent circumstance. Yet Conall and Gaius had agreed on the choice, and none of the shield-warriors demurred. The Romans had been with Conall for almost five summers, had fought bravely alongside the Gaels, and were considered part of the clann.

Standing at the prow, Aulus turned to face the men and women and called out, "Disembark! Form up on the beach. Charioteers, assemble your vehicles. Pick up the sacks of ballistae parts." Aulus grinned. "It's only a short march to Ráth Na Conall. If Apollo or your Goddess favour us, we should be at our destination in time for meán lae and a hot meal."

A good-natured ripple of complaints and curses followed Aulus' words. Still, most were happy to be on firm land and not a deck that frequently rolled in two directions simultaneously. Soon after disembarking, one hundred shield-warriors, five chariots with horse teams, and a small grove of druids set off for Ráth Na Conall.

Blasts of horns alerted the ráth to the landing party's presence. Soon men, women, civilians, and warriors flocked down the slopes to greet the new arrivals. The growing size and status of the ráth meant it could also sustain a handful of whores. Sensing an opportunity, they too joined the throng.

As she watched the reinforcements climb the long track to Ráth Na Conall, Danu whispered a heartfelt, "Thank the Goddess." Likely, they also brought stores of armour, weapons, shields, and, importantly, ballistae fittings. Alongside Danu, Brighid muttered her disappointment that no horses and riders were among the new arrivals. However, that quickly dissipated when she reflected that her force had tripled recently with the addition of Fainche's group. As for Báine, she could not resist a triumphant jig at having increased the number of chariots under her command.

* * *

Danu smiled as the Roman entered the chamber, took off his bronze Corinthian-style helmet and smoothed the long red plumes flowing from its crest. The act was deliberate, but many seasons of practice made it appear natural. He slapped his fist against a moulded bronze breastplate and bowed deeply. Brighid bent her head to Danu's ear and whispered, "I wonder if he is as muscled as his armour suggests." Danu rolled her eyes.

Aulus' burnished cuirass and greaves were complemented by a short red tunic and a heavy crimson winter cloak attached to shoulder clasps. A short sword and several knives were sheathed and hung from a broad leather belt. Danu assumed that a bronze shield completed the bronze ensemble. She smiled wistfully and heaved a sigh of longing. Aulus brought memories of her home in Lugudunon, her parents and younger brothers and sisters to the fore.

The Roman bowed to the princesses and then to the others present. "I am Aulus Horatius Pulvilla, a centurion in Gaius Aurelius Atella's command. I am delighted to greet the daughters of Conall, Rí Ruirech, and Mórrígan, Rígan of Clann Ui Flaithimh. I bring messages from your parents, family, and friends…" Aulus' eyes twinkled at the hint of disappointment in the twins' faces, "… and, of course, warriors, weapons, armour, and stores." Dipping his head again, he said, "I formally hand over my command and am at your disposal."

Danu stood and held out a hand. "Welcome to Ráth Na Conall. Please be seated, Aulus Horatius. Eat and drink," she replied and indicated Conchobhar. "My garrison commander, Conchobhar, has made arrangements for your men to be fed and assigned accommodation."

In a measured tone, Danu said, "As Gaels, we believe in being respectful of status at Ráth Na Conall but are relaxed about the need for ceremony. I apologise for the condition of the accommodation, but we've just fought a battle." Aulus studied Onchú and Beacán. *By their posture and scars, it must have been a fierce engagement.* The Roman knew of Beacán's reputation, and the intense dark eyes that examined him caused

Aulus to shiver. With a blink, he refocused his attention on the twins.

"With the help of our new workforce, the building of a bigger and better-positioned ráth is underway." Danu inhaled and exhaled. "I'm afraid my sister and I can offer you, and those who accompany you, nothing but hard work. The hillfort must be completed before the festival of Samhain and the onset of winter." Danu chuckled. "Tonight, however, we will eat, drink, and celebrate.

"But first, my sister and I must leave you and visit Thrasius and his crews. I'm afraid I will bring the helmsman and his seamen no good news. The trireme crews will also have to become builders and carpenters if they wish pleasant lodgings for the winter."

"May I have a private word?" asked Aulus. Danu and Brighid nodded warily as the others left the chamber.

***

"Your father and mother are gravely concerned about your circumstances. If you will recall, neither were enthusiastic about you undertaking this quest." The sharpening of deep green eyes and setting of jaws made Aulus pause but he did not shrink from what he had to say.

"My orders are to send one of the triremes back to Massalia after your festival of Bealtaine with a report. Your father has arranged with Dionysius of Sikelia for a small fleet of quinqueremes. Two thousand warriors and riders stand ready to embark from Massalia. You have only to request them."

"Shite!" exclaimed both girls as Aulus smiled, bowed, and exited the chamber. The room was silent for what seemed a long time, with each sister deep in her thoughts.

"The Hag, no!"

The outburst from Danu startled Brighid. It was neither shriek nor shout, but its declaration was unequivocal. "I am not a child and will not run with my tail between my legs to my da and ma. I have a duty to Ráth Na Conall and its people. If needed, I will fight Uallachán, the Connachta, and anyone else. I will win, or I will die."

Danu's feirdhris pounded, her eyes smouldered, and the symbols on her face and body throbbed with awakening power. Unseen to Danu, the colour of the flower had deepened from rose pink to ruby red. Brighid, however, was uncharacteristically subdued, a mite anxious, and a wee bit irritated.

She hoped and prayed that, at last, Danu was free from the memory of her awful wound. Yet her sister's selfish focus and lack of including her in the declaration irked Brighid. But when her black rose pulsated in harmony with Danu's, she, too, felt an unknown potency. She smiled and took hold of Danu's hands.

"I'm with you, sister. If our minds are as one, the bastards have no chance."

Outside the chamber door, Aulus chuckled and walked softly down the hallway. *Conall and Mórrígan understood their daughters perfectly.*

Further along the hallway, Draighean stepped from the shadows. "I agree, Roman."

✳✳✳

Uallachán's rage since his retreat from Ráth Na Conall had not abated. Even his abuse and execution of those he deemed culpable for the debacle and humiliation failed to quench his ire. That said, execution implied some semblance of justice. Uallachán's victims and their families suffered indescribable torment, eventual evisceration, and dismemberment. Indeed, it was only the intervention of the Goddess who cried "Enough!" and sent the mná-sidhe that relieved the victims' tribulations.

Each day, rumours of rebellion, this time against his rule, made Uallachán's ears burn. Messengers relayed news of chieftains and ríthe from the east to the west coasts, seeking to align with the striapacha of Ráth Na Conall. The wind appeared to fill Danu's and Brighid's sails. That a new fortress neared completion further fuelled his anger.

Uallachán dismissed as fanciful gossip reports that massive war machines were being built. Still, not since he had rebuilt Caher Conri and began his revolt against all things related to Conall had his power been so contested. Now he sat on his gilded throne and fretted that the tide had turned against him.

Truthfully, the only element that Uallachán did not miss was his brother, Nuadha. He had no idea if his sibling was dead or alive or where he might be. And, if he was frank with himself, he did not care. If asked, he had no intention of paying a ransom. "A waste of gold," he mumbled. In fact, the bitseacha of Ráth Na Conall might have done him a favour. Nuadha was one less burden to carry… or remove.

As if Uallachán needed more trouble, an envoy from Chrúachain awaited an audience. The timing of the messenger's appearance appeared ominous. Did Maine Athramail know of his defeat? That the ambassador travelled with one hundred well-armed warriors ruled out the possibility of Uallachán disposing of him and pleading ignorance.

"The Connachta ríthe and I have a common bond," murmured Uallachán. That this was not reassuring troubled him. Uallachán called his shield-man to him. "Permit the Connachta envoy to enter the chamber." Then, in a lower voice, he added, "Clear everyone else from the Hall. I want no witnesses to the discussion."

Head held high, the ambassador, a tall, lean man of about forty summers, strode down the central aisle, neatly skirting the sunken fire-pits. His demeanour spoke of arrogance buttressed by the strength of the Connachta ríthe. Yet experience had made him a cautious man and well-acquainted with Uallachán's love of random violence and cruelty. Thus, he was accompanied by ten burly guards. Ninety more stood outside. He stopped ten paces from Uallachán's throne, and his lips curled in a deliberate sneer at its garishness. Then, he dipped his head, but only the absolute minimum required.

"My Rí Ruirech, Maine Athramail, is displeased." Uallachán scowled. Apparently, there were to be no diplomatic niceties or weasel words. He signalled the envoy to continue. *As if the tuilí wasn't going to—permission or not.* "You did not advise the Rí Ruirech or his brothers that the daughters of Conall Mac Gabhann had taken up residence in Ráth Na Conall."

Uallachán's eyes widened, and he made a mental note to search out the Connachta informants.

"Furthermore, without the king's permission, you attacked Ráth Na Conall and by all accounts were totally embarrassed—by two girls. That does not reflect well on the rí's choice of 'partner'." The back of Uallachán's neck reddened at having to endure the ambassador's admonishments, and he swore to make the man pay.

The envoy had not finished. "You also did not inform Maine Athramail that a representative of the Aes Sidhe stands with Conall's daughters. That he sees as a grave, possibly mortal, mistake on your part." Uallachán's eyes narrowed. *Had the messenger just threatened him with death?*

"You will accompany me to Chrúachain—immediately." The envoy smiled at Uallachán's impotence. "You may bring a guard to match my own one hundred. Should you be allowed to return to Caher Conri, they will serve as your escort."

***

"Yes!"

Danu looked over the new Ráth Na Conall and fought hard against the urge to dance joyfully along its ramparts. The fort had been completed a half-cycle of the moon before the festival of Samhain. To the west lay the remains of the old ráth. Much of the fort had been repurposed in the building of the new stronghold.

Sitting on the highest peak of the hill, the new ramparts were a series of massive timber boxes filled with earth and stone and tied together with hardwood beams. Each wall was approximately three hundred paces in length and enough for three hundred shield-warriors to stand shoulder to shoulder. The double-faced stockade was five paces wide and three spear lengths in height. Three spear lengths deep and three in breadth, a ditch ran parallel to the fence. A protective berm on the trench's outer edge was built using the excavated dirt. Both ditch and berm were liberally planted with sharpened stakes and, to Draighean's delight, blackthorn bushes.

The ráth had three fortified entrances. One faced the eastern slope, one looked to the west, and the third guarded the northern rampart. A small gateway had been set in the southern wall. Guard towers jutted from the ramparts at each corner and on each side of the gateways. Each tower sported a heavy ballista, a small cohort of archers, and a squad of shield-warriors. All were positioned to throw down a deadly crossfire on attackers. Dispersed along the walls were the smaller, mobile bolt-throwers. Along each wall, shield-warriors stood alert. One-third of the garrison was always on watch duty.

Inside the ráth, two buildings dominated. The Great Hall, with its adjoining accommodations for Danu, Brighid, and Conchobhar and suites for visiting nobles, sat at the western side of a large square. In peaceful times, the yard would become a marketplace and auditorium for musicians and seanchaithe. The next largest building was the barracks for the fort's garrison and an adjoining armoury.

Around the main buildings, varying sizes of roundhouses sprouted like mushrooms. These housed blacksmiths, armourers, fletchers, bowyers, bakers, and hunters. The intolerable stench from their processes meant the tanners and leatherworkers were located near water but downwind of the fort.

Danu sighed. The Gaels were a society that appreciated art, music, and epic poems and tales. She constantly prayed to the Goddess for peaceful times when the ráth would become a gathering place for the local community and not a military camp. A light breeze wafted the smell of freshly turned land into her nostrils, making her smile. North of the fort, much of the plain had been ploughed and made ready for new crops. *How on earth did the farmers do this and help build the stronghold?*

A movement on the pastures drew Danu's attention, and she grinned broadly. Brighid whooped and yelled at her riders while Báine drilled her chariot teams. *They'd better stay away from the tilled fields.* A frown caused Danu's brow to furrow. How long would it be before blood fed the land and crops were trampled by warriors' boots and hooves?

Her depression lifted when she spotted a golden pony and its rider, who faithfully attempted to follow Brighid's instructions. Brighid incessantly grumbled about Aoife's presence but sneaked smiles of pride in her apprentice told a different story. Danu wondered how their newest sister in Lugudunon, only a summer old, fared. How long would it be until she bounced the child on her knee? Homesickness reared its head, but she shook her head and stamped on it.

CHAPTER 15

The folly of supporting a lowborn southern despot to destroy the legacy of Conall Mac Gabhann finally dawned on Maine and his brothers. Now the actions of Uallachán, including the recent debacle, saw the brothers ridiculed inside and beyond their kingdom by kings and peasants.

Maine was keenly aware that no wall of steel was impenetrable, and an assassin's blade could end his reign. He looked around the table at each of his brothers and wondered which of them plotted to dethrone him. Probably all of the bastards! Cowards! In their place, he would not merely consider the opportunity—he would have acted. *That's why I'm the king, and they bow to me.*

A cough from Cairbre, the next in line to the Connachta throne, brought Maine out of his reveries. "What?" he snapped before adding, "Sorry." An apology at any time was uncharacteristic of Maine. Instantly, the postures of the six brothers exhibited an alertness previously absent. It was followed by an exchange of glances and an almost imperceptible tipping of heads. Maine missed neither sign.

"According to *my* informant in Ráth Na Conall, more reinforcements arrived in the fort, and Danu Ni Conall has built a new, more defensible stronghold. Brighid Ni Conall's tactics have encouraged many nobles and chieftains to switch their allegiance to Ráth Na Conall. The spy also talks about great war machines, but I give that little credence. As I do her claim that Conall is a now a great rí ruirech with tens of thousands of warriors." Maine snorted. "I suspect her usefulness is over. The bitseacha have obviously uncovered her activities and are feeding her nonsense."

"What is our plan? We can hardly continue to play this game at arm's length. Apart from anything else, our tool—sorry, ally, Uallachán, appears incompetent. Our gold has bought us nothing and may now be working against us." Cairbre looked at Maine for an answer.

"Uallachán will arrive within the next few sunsets. We will hear what he has to say and then decide our strategy." Maine paused. "A direct Connachta incursion into the southern kingdoms may have undesirable consequences. In the southeast, the Rí of Ráthgeal, Labhraidh Loingsech, has a sizeable army and a formidable mountain fortress."

Cairbre stroked his long, braided red whiskers. Concern furrowed his brow. His brother's usual plans entailed using a club to crack open an egg. Force, not finesse, drove Maine's actions. Why was he now considering tactics and strategies? Perhaps the prospect of facing Conall's daughters dredged up memories of their father's battle—and doubts.

＊

"What do we do about *him*?"

The subject of the conversation squirmed in the hard, uncushioned seat. It had been a cycle of the moon since his capture, but during that time, the Rígana of Ráth Na Conall had been preoccupied: Danu with the rebuilding of the hillfort and Brighid with terrorising farmsteads and settlements across Uallachán's territory.

With the new fort completed and the feast of Samhain on the horizon, the surrounding pastures were a hive of agrarian activity. A steady flow of artisans and tradespeople and their families entered the kingdom. The clang of iron hammers, the thump and bangs of looms, and the scrape of quern stones brought warm feelings of satisfaction to the twins.

Now, attention finally turned to a slimmer Nuadha. Food at Ráth Na Conall was sufficient but sparing for one who tended to gluttony.

Much to Nuadha's chagrin and bruised ego, few considered him a threat or worthy of being imprisoned. Thus, shadowed by a single guard, he roamed freely around the old and new forts. His brother, Uallachán, had not sent envoys to demand his release or offer to ransom him. That rankled Nuadha. *Am I that worthless and of no consequence to anyone?* The question was rhetorical, but the answer was an emphatic, "Yes!"

"Will any present speak on his behalf? He should have an advocate," asked Danu, looking around those seated at the long table.

She looked at Scolai, the most senior of the grove of druids, but he declined. Danu growled in frustration. She was very appreciative of the healing skills of the clutch of priests. Most of the fort's injured, even Beacán and Onchú, were well on the way to a full recovery. But the leader of the druids had made it clear his duty was twofold: to administer and interpret the *Fénechas*—the Law, and to heal the sick. It was not to get involved in politics or war.

"I will speak on Nuadha's behalf."

Eyebrows, some bushy and some thin, were raised at Beacán's words. Iasg nodded her approval, as did Scolai. Draighean scowled. Her proposed solution was to drape Nuadha across a thriving blackthorn bush and let the thorns judge.

"Thank you," said Nuadha.

Beacán addressed the table. "I knew Nuadha when he and I were much younger. Even then, he lacked the fortitude to stand against his brother, Uallachán. At that time, youth excused the flaw. Certainly, he would have had a much different life had he accompanied his brother Torcán and followed Conall. Instead, Uallachán, whose arrogance and cruel nature were well known even in his early days, bullied Nuadha into acquiescence."

Beacán paused and rubbed a lightly bearded chin. "Perhaps Torcán bears some responsibility for the creature before us. Maybe he should have applied equal pressure to save his younger brother. But he was young and bull-headed. Good sense and a steadying hand fast partner came to him later." Beacán looked at Nuadha and shook his head. "Torcán would be greatly disappointed in you."

Nuadha's countenance flitted between anger and humiliation, as Beacán continued. "Nuadha became what you see before you. Undoubtedly, he is guilty of the abominations and depravities told of Caher Conri. He is as culpable of rebellion against Conall and Clann Ui Flaithimh as Uallachán—if not the mind who plotted its path. The number of his accusers would encircle this ráth more than once."

Beacán paused and looked at Nuadha with eyes that held sympathy but no mercy. "In conclusion, yes, he is guilty, but he is a weak man, easily led, and to be pitied. Our judgement should consider that."

"The Hag's arse!" exclaimed Conchobhar, angrily thumping the table with calloused fists. "He has been party to murders, tortures, and untold debaucheries against those who could not fight back. What say you, Onchú? You have suffered more than any at this table."

"What punishment will bring my sons back from Mag Mell? Or my hand-fast partner's sanity and love?" asked Onchú, shaking his head and scratching the stubble on his recently scraped head. He had vowed not to grow his hair until Uallachán was caught and executed. "Will I feel better watching a stake driven into his arse and hearing his death cries? Perhaps. I don't know. But at the least, he would never commit any more crimes."

"Have you wealth or property with which you can pay compensation—an *eiric*—to those you have wronged or murdered? Can their number be counted and their names told?" Danu spoke, and her words drew a rare smile from Scolai.

"I have no wealth, possessions, or property. My brother owns all." Nuadha shook his head as he spoke, fully accepting for the first time that indeed he was worthless and none would miss him.

"Get rid of this creature. Cast him out. He is pitiful and not worth the effort to stake," said Brighid. "Drive him from the fort. Let him walk back to Caher Conri. Let the people he, and his brother, harmed, despoiled, and persecuted be his judges and executioners."

"No," whispered Nuadha. "Please, no."

* * *

Before Uallachán sat the seven kings of the Connachta. Maine, as Rí Ruirech, sat on an ornately carved throne at the centre of his brothers. Not as disposed to follow their elder brother's example by smiling, the others wore severe demeanours. They considered Uallachán beneath them. He was an earwig to be crushed underfoot and deserved chains and a dungeon cell rather than an audience. Maine, however, had his own game to play.

"Welcome, friend Uallachán Ó Dubhghaill, Rí of Caher Conri. Be seated, eat and drink." Uallachán bowed and sat in the chair indicated. His uppermost thought was not of the peril he might have placed himself. Or the condescending demeanours of Maine's brothers—all of whom were much more powerful kings than he. Rather, it was how his throne at Caher Conri was much more elaborate and statelier than Maine's.

His ego fed and satisfied, Uallachán glowed until Maine asked, "Does your brother, Nuadha, accompany you?" Uallachán shook his head, his lips thinned, and his paranoia rose. Why the interest in his brother? "No. That is a pity. We would have liked to have greeted him." Maine looked to Cairbre on his right and smiled knowingly. Uallachán should have read the warning signs instead of basking in deluded self-importance.

"What is the state of Ráth Na Conall's defences? How many warriors are garrisoned there? Do they have allies who will come to their aid? Who?" Maine's questions fell like hail on Uallachán's head. Yet, of more concern, Uallachán had the impression that Maine already knew the answers.

A bead of sweat rolled down Uallachán's brow and over the flattened bridge of his nose before dropping with a plop into his wine. Were these the questions of an ally and partner? But then, given that

Uallachán had more experience of oppression and subjugation than making friends, he had little on which to base a comparison. More probing from Maine raised his pulse rate to even higher levels.

"If I am to commit thousands of Connachta warriors to support you in conquering the southwestern kingdom, we should know our ally's strength." The smile on Maine's lips reminded Uallachán of a lincse toying with a mountain hare. "How many warriors do you have? How many nobles have given you their oath and will provide men?"

The food and wine in Uallachán's belly soured, and his gullet burned at the realisation of his profoundly weak position. The Connachta armies numbered in the tens of thousands. Even with their children as his "guests", Uallachán would be hard pushed to raise five thousand fighters from the chieftains and nobility of southwestern Ériu. It had taken all of Uallachán's cunning and threats to muster two thousand for the recent and unsuccessful attack on Ráth Na Conall.

"It is apparent to my brothers and me that you have an overwhelming numerical advantage over the garrison at Ráth Na Conall. If that is so, we wonder why you have been unable to conquer the hillfort." Maine's blue-grey eyes locked onto Uallachán's and refused to let go. "Perhaps *you* are incompetent in the art of war. Your defeat at the hands of two girls pretending to be rígana suggests ineptness… or design. Which is it? Should we consider the need for your replacement?"

More beads of sweat rolled off Uallachán's brow, and the back of his shirt felt damp. He fervently prayed the wetness between his thighs was perspiration, not piss. Too late, he realised he had never been in charge and that the wolves before him were assessing whether to devour this lamb.

∗

"We have to attack. It's too good an opportunity to ignore."

Brighid fervently believed her words and glared at those before her, hoping to intimidate them into agreement. Given her audience, and regardless of the merit of her argument, that endeavour had little chance of success. Therefore, grumbling and using very unqueenly language, she resumed her seat beside Danu.

The meeting of the Chomhairle and Glaisne convened by Danu was prompted by a message from Cnoc Duíginn. The small but strategically situated fort sat on the summit of a domed mountain, straddling the border between the Connachta lands and those of the southwestern kingdoms.

To its northeast were the marshes of Phortaigh na Cullen. To the west and north were the main pass and river plain leading to the south and eventually Ráth Na Conall. Cnoc Duíginn was cleverly located, and its ríthe had amassed considerable wealth from the nearby silver mines. The current rí, Sláine Mac Sláine, named after his father, was considered as eccentric as the previous ríthe of Cnoc Duíginn. Whether he was as duplicitous had yet to be tested.

"It appears that Uallachán has journeyed to Chrúachain, likely to account for his defeat at our hands." Danu beamed at those seated around the table. "It's my guess he will want to enlist the direct help of the Rí Ruirech of the Connachta. Yet that strategy likely holds as much peril for Uallachán as for us. He will be like a mouse before a feral cat."

Danu's brow furrowed. "It is no secret that Maine and his brothers seek revenge on my father. Although, from what I've been told, Ailill Mac Máta and our da deemed the result of their confrontation an honourable draw and parted on friendly terms. Yet time and egos can twist the truth. Additionally, their hiring of mercenaries points to them being already committed to direct action. Perhaps Uallachán has always been Maine's puppet."

Danu took a sip from a cup of spring water, relishing its coldness. "According to the envoy from Cnoc Duíginn, Uallachán passed their fort seven sunsets ago and would reach Chrúachain in another three sunsets." Brighid fidgeted in her seat and unapologetically scratched her arse. It was her comment on the meeting so far. Danu grinned. "Patience, sister, the time for action will come." Then, addressing the remainder of the room, she said, "By my reckoning, Uallachán will not return to Caher Conri for at least a half-cycle of the moon. How can we take advantage of this?"

The ensuing discussion seemed interminable and doomed to go in endless circles until Onchú banged on the table. After his tribulations, Danu was glad to see signs of Onchú regaining his former demeanour. In this, she was very appreciative of Naomh and Úna, who had aided him and appeared to have become like sisters to Onchú's daughters. A frown fluttered on Danu's lips. Eithne remained a problem. Although, and perhaps at the realisation of what severing the braid of her hand-fasting would mean to her lifestyle, she had become less brooding.

"If we assume Maine is our real adversary, then an army of ten thousand well-trained warriors descending on us is not to be dismissed with bravado," said Onchú. "The good news is that they will probably not journey south until the winter is gone. That gives us between the feasts of Samhain and Imbolg to gather allies and draw up a plan to confront a Connachta incursion."

Onchú turned to Brighid and smiled. "Secondly, imprisoned in Caher Conri are many sons and daughters of the nobles of the south-western lands. Release them from captivity, and at worst, Uallachán's support will diminish and at best, we may gather allies."

"Yes!" Brighid jumped up in delight.

Danu smiled. "Speak with Conchobhar, Flann, and Onchú about a plan. And remember, this is a raid. The goal is the release of Uallachán's prisoners—noble or peasant. We do not have the numbers to garrison and defend both Ráth Na Conall and Caher Conri. I think, however, that you can still enjoy yourself within these constraints."

Danu turned to Glaisne. "Rather than sending a messenger, perhaps it would be better for you to return to Clárach and inform Aodh of the situation. Samhain is not far off. Implore your brother to join us for the celebrations, and we can show off *our* fort."

Glaisne's eyes held a knowing smile, but Draighean's eyes narrowed, and her full lips pursed. *Be careful what you say, Danu. Others may take a meaning you did not intend.* Once again, taking up the reins of the meeting, Danu addressed the table. "I want messengers sent to the major hillforts in this kingdom and those in the east. Invite the ríthe to celebrate Samhain with us."

As the last member of the Chomhairle exited the chamber, Brighid turned to her twin. "There is no *'our'* fort unless it is yours and mine. You would do well to remember that Danu." At the troubled look on her sister's face, Brighid smirked. "The Hag, Danu. Rut him if you wish." Then, in a much colder tone, she added. "But know this, I will end anyone who comes between us and the clann, whether in this world or the next."

CHAPTER 16

The steep stone steps were accessed through a door behind Uallachán's throne and led to Caher Conri's cages. Concealed by heavy drapes, the entrance's location made perfect sense. It was convenient should the need arise to present groups of his "guests" quickly to family members as proof that they were alive. There was even a small cell with a bathtub and sets of clean, dry clothes to make the hostages presentable. The stairway also granted Uallachán access for the nefarious abuses of his captives.

Not wishing to spend gold on separate accommodations, a single large cellar had been divided into small cells enclosed by wooden poles and bars. The chamber had a milieu of decay and degradation, and stank of unwashed bodies. Human waste slopped over the rims of wooden pails, spilling onto the dirt floor. Food, which the fort's pigs would refuse, barely gave sustenance, and certainly did not promote strong limbs or whole bodies. The only sounds in the chamber were of young ones crying, noses snuffling, and ragged coughs. Disease and infection ravaged the imprisoned. That the death toll was not higher was miraculous.

The faces of the broken had long given up hope of release or rescue. Whether their parents cared for them or not had little impact on their existence. Some had been imprisoned for several summers and most considered themselves abandoned.

In one dark corner, a young girl wept as dirt ingrained hands traced the growing swell of her belly. Yet she was not the only one to suffer the indignities visited on them by Uallachán and his guards. Because of their noble birth, many of the victims' only consolation was that they were not as disposable as others. Yet whether that was mercy was debatable.

Prayers and curses, in equal measure, rose to the Goddess. Pierced by the distress of her children, on this day, she smiled. Her avengers approached.

✳✳✳

Thrasius guided two triremes past the long sandbank, which jutted into the bay and towards its beach. As the ram of the vessel crunched against the shingle, Flann, followed by one hundred shield-warriors, leapt over the ship's rail and into the surf.

Iasg followed, gasping as she entered the water. Its coldness reminded her of the seas she had swum in during her youth in Northern Albu. She cursed that the depth barely breached the waists of the warriors but soaked and stiffened her nipples—and not pleasurably. She thought of the disappointed look on Beacán's face when Danu informed Onchú and him that they were not recovered sufficiently for this mission. Neither had taken the judgement well, but Iasg had whispered a whole-hearted "Thanks" to Danu.

Protected by mountains and seas, Caher Conri's headland location was enviable. However, a long and deep depression in the rock began just beyond the beach and ran south to north. The natural gorge led directly to the foot of Caher Conri's southern wall. It was along this trail that Flann and his warriors jogged. The blind spot had escaped the usually cunning Uallachán's paranoia. But then, in Ériu, few expected or had the ships for an assault from the sea.

A broad strip of farmland and dense oak forests bordered the coastline on the promontory's northern side. Brighid and her riders rode at a fast canter along tracks rutted by trading wagons. They abandoned the trails, keeping to the forest when the outer defences came into view. As a wan late autumn sun reached its apex, the band arrived at Caher

173

Conri's defensive berm.

Brighid snorted at Fainche and Maolán. "Flann's band have it easy. A quick journey along the coast and a leisurely mountain walk." The duo rolled their eyes. Both knew her diminished role in a raid, which she claimed, and with some legitimacy, as her idea, galled Brighid. Both pitied anyone they came across on the return journey to Ráth Na Conall.

With a scream, Brighid charged towards the earthwork's entrance, stopping an arrow's flight from the gateway. Behind her, the riders dismounted, unsheathed, and strung bow staves. Each warrior searched for targets in the two guard posts and on the rampart. "We need to find a way to ride and shoot on horseback," muttered Brighid. Maolán shrugged. He agreed, but they were stuck with simple girth loops for now.

The guards in the towers on either side of the entrance were astonished that anyone would attack the berm. The last assault on Caher Conri had been in Conall Mac Gabhann's time. Once they got over the initial shock, they responded with condescension, jeers, and bare arses. There was only one entry through the berm and one dirt bridge across the ditch. On either side were deep trenches populated with fire-hardened stakes.

First to fall was the overconfident eejit who stood on the broad, flattened apex of the berm, shouted insults, and waved his manhood at the attackers. Two arrows caught him. One removed his voice, and the other his balls. Few of his comrades regretted the arsehole's passing, but all were stunned by the mode of his death. In Ériu, bows were used for hunting and were not typically considered weapons of war. It was a salutary lesson for those who survived the ensuing volleys of missiles. For the philosophers among them, it was a glimpse into a frightening future.

Fifty warriors manned the rampart. Until now, it had been considered an assignment to reward kin and favoured friends. Twenty who did not react quickly enough were never to enjoy the privilege. As Brighid inspected the entranceway, she saw gates that appeared heavy, solid, and likely made of oak. She looked at Maolán and pointed to the entrance. "With a distraction, I could climb them." Maolán smiled and tramped over to speak with the riders. Several fires were lit, and volleys of flaming arrows peppered the gateposts.

"I hope the wood isn't too wet; it's almost winter," said Maolán.

"Fire or smoke, either will be sufficient," replied Brighid and then shouted, "Five with me. The rest, kill anything that moves."

The spearhead carved a deep track down the backplate of Brighid's cuirass, splitting the leather. She grimaced at the sting of the long cut and flung a string of curses at the defenders. In Ráth Na Conall, Danu, under a strange compulsion, scratched her back. As Brighid surmounted the gate and dropped to the dirt on the other side, the choking smell of woodsmoke filled the air. In the gateposts, guards coughed harshly as lungs filled with fumes and smoke. The few who tried to make a run for it met the blades of Brighid's group.

Once the gates were pulled and pushed partially open, the rest of the riders remounted and charged through. Javelins were hurled at any of Uallachán's men who foolishly broke cover. Then, wielding axes, swords, and clubs, they climbed wooden steps to the crest of the berm and the guard posts. Maolán glowered as his mace swept another from the rampart but smiled as Fainche's sword glinted in the other tower.

A snapped order from Brighid ended the wounded's lives with a knife drawn across their throats. Stripped and bound, those who remained watched the riders methodically search, strip, and behead the dead. The corpses were tossed into the trench, but fifteen, in good health, remained. They shivered uncontrollably in the cold, and fear made them lose control of their bowels. Uallachán discouraged the rumours, but all knew the gossip of the red-haired witch with a fondness for staking her enemies.

"Leave ten to guard the prisoners and the gateway." Brighid looked at Maolán and gave a half-hearted shrug. "We've had our fun. Let's go follow orders."

Maolán chuckled and dipped his head. With a shriek of "To Caher Conri!" and horns blaring, forty riders galloped towards the stone walls of the promontory fort.

***

At three spears high and one in breadth, Caher Conri's stone walls were a formidable barrier. However, the gaps and fissures caused by winter freezing and thawing had not been repaired in a long time. Thus, foot- and handholds were plentiful, and Flann's heavily armed warriors climbed steadily upwards.

Traditionally, the permanent garrisons of most hillforts were counted in the hundreds. In times of conflict, the fort's rí would call on his nobles and chieftains to contribute warriors to swell the numbers. Due to Uallachán's parsimony only a hundred foot soldiers remained in Caher Conri. None were veterans, for those had travelled with Uallachán to Chrúachain.

Brighid made surmounting the wall easier for Flann. Her screaming riders and blaring hunting horns caught the garrison's attention, drawing most to the northern defences. Showers of iron-tipped barbs swept the parapet clear. Those with a more developed sense of self-preservation took cover and prayed the storm would soon cease. They cursed the attackers and their comrades on the outer defences in equal measure.

The handful of defenders remaining on the southern wall had no chance against Flann's heavily armed veterans, who quickly swarmed the battlements. Those not battered from the rampart by shields fell to spears and swords. Their dying cries alerted their comrades on the northern fortifications. At that moment, the Commander of Defences, a fancy title earned by nepotism, realised that cowering behind his shield was no longer an option.

Flurries of early snow danced on the Great Hall's stone steps as, hands on her hips, Iasg surveyed the front of the edifice. At her back were two rows of shield-warriors. The shield-wall stood resolute with javelins hefted. The weapon was held not for throwing but to stab anyone who got close.

Still, few of Uallachán's force showed any enthusiasm to engage the warriors. The garrison's commander reckoned that at some time, the attackers would have to turn their backs, if only to escape the way they entered Caher Conri. "That's the time to strike," he muttered.

Iasg looked up at the towering Great Hall. "The Hag!"

Flann laughed. "I hope you've a head for heights. Without a ram, we're not getting through that bloody oak door."

"I'll hae to go in through the roof," said Iasg.

"Be careful. We don't know how many guards are inside."

"What choice is there?"

After a final check of her weapons, Iasg placed pale hands on the stonework and began to climb. Iasg might have looked frail, but that gravely underestimated her physical strength and spirit. Flann marvelled as, like a pale spider, she crept closer to the building's summit and disappeared.

Using her throwing axes, Iasg hacked at the building's thick thatch. The lack of care given to the roof made her labour easier, and now, astride the roof's apex, she paused to catch her breath and wipe sweat from her brow. "Stupid tuilí." Uallachán obviously didn't like spending gold on maintenance. She sighed in relief as she broke through the rooftop. Iasg paused to rub burning arm muscles, before tiny toes felt for the rafters and crossbeams. With a muffled grunt, she felt her way across one of Great Hall's beams.

It was doubtful whether the two hefty guards, standing on either side of Uallachán's throne, knew anything about the knives. Pitched from above and with deceptive strength, the blades plunged into their chests. *Thank the Goddess, they're not wearing armour.* Carefully, Iasg descended one of the room's supporting columns.

When her feet felt the stone floor, she sagged against the upright beam. Then, thankful at having suffered only minor grazes and punctures from splinters, Iasg walked unsteadily to the front entrance. Her strength almost depleted, she pushed and dragged the heavy wooden locking bar over its iron fittings, jumping back as it crashed to the floor. "I need ma toes," she muttered.

"I could do with ten of yer men if ye can spare them," she said as the door swung open.

Flann smiled at the petite woman covered in dust, scratches, and spiders' webs. "If you weren't Beacán's partner, I'd ask you for a dance at the Samhain festival," he said before ordering ten to follow Iasg.

As she stepped towards the tapestries and hidden door, Iasg stopped, turned around, and grinned. "Nae harm in ye asking for a dance. But that's all ye'll be getting." Flann, and his warriors, roared with laughter and then settled their shields on brawny arms.

"Eyes forward. They know something is up. Watch for signs of movement," shouted Flann.

Followed by her guards, Iasg descended the stone steps slowly. Traps or deliberately loose treads were always a possibility. Slippery mosses and fungi were a certainty. Iasg nodded to the squad's leader and then to the door at the bottom of the stairwell. Two hefty warriors with broad, muscled shoulders stepped forward and slammed the door. At first, it resisted but then cracked and finally surrendered with a screech of hinges.

On the other side, two guards caught with their pants down, standing over a young female, reached for their weapons. Iasg's knives took each in the throat. As they clutched at the spurting blood, Iasg snarled, "Finish them. They don't deserve a quick death, but we're in a hurry." From the cries of agony, the men's death might have been quick but was certainly not painless.

"We're here to free you. If you can stand and walk, do it," called out Iasg, in a rich northern burr, while her group smashed through the wooden cages. "We'll carry any too weak to walk. So don't be worried. We'll nae be leaving any behind." As she gave the cells a' final inspection, Iasg spotted the girl and boy huddled in a gloomy corner. Iasg walked over and smiled. "Let's go. You're safe now." The girl sobbed and looked down at her belly.

"My father will disown me and cast me out. I have no future."

Beside her, the boy, who looked several years younger, stepped forward and politely said, "I thank you for the rescue, but I'll not leave my sister."

Iasg cupped the girl's chin with a small, almost childlike hand. Tears streamed from deep green eyes, and choking with emotion, she said, "I'll nae be leaving you. I don't know your ma and da, but I'd be proud of you if you were mine. You'll never be an outcast. If not your kin, then you'll live with me. Now come on. We're not out of this snake pit yet."

I wonder how Beacán will feel about adding to our family, she thought as she followed the brother and sister up the stairs.

＊＊＊

Flann heaved a sigh of relief as Iasg emerged from the Hall. In contrast, Uallachán's garrison commander swore as he watched the shield-wall's two ranks slowly and steadily retreat towards the ramparts. All held their tight formation, and all kept a javelin poised. The children were carried or ushered by Iasg and her ten warriors ahead of the shields. Flann exhaled with relief when he heard the pad of small bare feet on the battlement's stone steps.

"The rear rank will stay with the children. Bind them to you if needed," shouted Flann.

As Flann's men obeyed, the garrison commander shouted, "Attack!" It was not a wise decision. As Uallachán's warriors charged forward, a volley of fifty javelins met them. The commander was the first to feel a spear's iron spike plunge into his chest and explode from his back. Stunned, the advance stalled, and a debate ensued on who was in command.

"One child to a man." Flann rolled his eyes and smiled at several female warriors who bristled at the order. "Or a woman." At a flicker of movement from Uallachán's warriors, he shouted, "The rest of us will defend the wall until they are safe." Having raised a sufficient level of courage and support, the newly promoted leader of Uallachán's garrison ordered her men to attack.

Flann's detachment had received fifty javelins from those carrying the children and threw them at the charging enemy. Ironically, the recently promoted garrison commander met the same fate as the former. She died grasping the shaft of a spear that quivered synchronously with her last breaths. Yet both leaders were better off dying in battle than left to face Uallachán's wrath. The rest of the warriors chose to retreat, hurling impotent curses.

Serendipity plays its part in all human activities—especially in battles. In the skirmish with Caher Conri's garrison, Flann's warriors had suffered little more than skinned knees and knuckles—mostly from climbing the walls. The Goddess of Fortune, forever in her sister's shadow, could not resist the temptation.

One man picked up a javelin and tossed it at the last of the retreating Ráth Na Conall veterans. He had no great skill and had not even bothered to watch its path. As Flann placed his hands on the parapet wall before starting his descent, the iron spike caught him in his side, and he slumped across the fortification.

On the beach, Iasg screamed, "No!"

In the skies, the Goddess of Fortune fled before her sister's wrath found her.

***

The children squealed with joy when their feet felt the sandy beach. Then they stared in awe and trepidation at the great triremes bobbing on the gentle swell. All had never seen boats bigger than small fishing *currachán*. "Everyone on board!" shouted Thrasius. "The tide will be against us soon."

That prompted another round of discussion among the young ones, since they had never met a Greek before. Flann's warriors each took a child on their shoulders and waded into the water. Soon, each boy and girl was lifted into the ship. Once aboard, they stared wide-eyed at the sailors, some of whose bodies were as dark as blackthorn.

∗∗∗

Unaware of Flann's fate but sure that the warriors had made their escape, Brighid turned her mount around to face her riders. About to order the retreat, she suddenly stopped. A look of childish mischievousness appeared on her face, followed by a smile of triumph that said, "I'll show her."

"I see no reason to abandon Caher Conri and allow Uallachán to recover the ráth. Only a few defenders remain, and the walls are solid and defensible. We will occupy and hold the stronghold for Clann Ui Flaithimh."

Fainche and Maolán stared at Brighid in disbelief. "Those are not our orders. We've done our job. We should leave," retorted Maolán through tightly clenched teeth.

Startled by her second-in-command's unexpected opposition, Brighid's eyes narrowed, and her lips thinned. "I'm as much a rígan as my sister. This is *my* decision, and these are *my* orders. We take possession of Caher Conri."

"I've had enough of serving foolish leaders. I'll not add another to that list." Fainche's eyes glared at Brighid. "I will take my riders and return to Ráth Na Conall." Then she looked at Maolán. "Will you join me?" Torn between his loyalty to Brighid and love for Fainche, Maolán looked miserable and angry.

"I have to stay with *her*."

"Treasonous bitseach!" spat Brighid as Fainche and her ten riders rode for the berm.

"If you say anything more, I, too, will ride for Ráth Na Conall, and more will follow me." The fury in Maolán's eyes stunned Brighid. Had she lost a good friend?

<h1 style="text-align:center">CHAPTER 17</h1>

At twenty-four, Cairbre was two summers younger than Maine. A head taller than his brother, Cairbre shared his brother's blue-grey eyes, copper-red hair, and the mass of freckles that covered their faces and bodies. Deemed cleverer than Maine, although that bar was set low, Cairbre preferred the company of his string of horses to that of men, and especially his brothers.

As he trudged through the mud and heavy rain to Chrúachain's Great Hall, Cairbre's demeanour showed he was unhappy. Maine had made his decision on Uallachán, and as usual, it likely paid only lip service to any inputs from his brothers. Cairbre considered his older brother's obsession with trusting only one opinion—his own, a significant weakness. He and his brothers disagreement as to how to take advantage of that flaw kept Maine on the throne.

Now, sitting opposite Maine, Cairbre shifted his arse to stop the creeping numbness and provide a distraction from the discussion on tactics and strategy. He deemed the conversation futile and a waste of his time. *Get on with it, brother. I could be with my horses.*

"Take one thousand men and accompany Uallachán on his return to Caher Conri. Despite Uallachán's incompetence and weaknesses, it remains the strongest ráth in the southwest. Secure the stronghold for the Connachta. It will make a good base for our future plans once the winter has passed and cannot be allowed to fall to the bitseacha."

Cairbre raised an eyebrow in surprise. It actually was a good strategy. "Reconnoitre the lands around Ráth Na Conall, as far north as Cnoc Duíginn, but hold Caher Conri until the main army arrives."

"Uallachán?" queried Cairbre.

"He's an arsehole and full of his own importance. Still, he has nobles who can likely raise a substantial army. That may be useful to us. Do not go out of your way to antagonise him or his chieftains." Maine paused, and his eyes hardened. "However, if he attempts to interfere, dispose of him."

***

"Where is my sister?"

After riding hard for two sunsets, Fainche stood before Danu, several members of the Chomhairle, and Glaisne. Steel-blue eyes met glittering emeralds, and neither flinched nor gave way. As the tall rider's eyes swept the room, she saw worry and anxiety on most, except Glaisne. His lips and chin were covered mainly by his hand, but the dimple on his cheek suggested he was not unhappy at Brighid's absence.

Fainche coughed to clear her throat and wished she had sipped some water beforehand. "Brighid, along with Maolán and the remaining riders, remains in Caher Conri. I disagreed with her decision to hold the ráth and withdrew my riders."

"Rut the Hag!" exclaimed Conchobhar. "Why? She knew the plan."

"*She* reached a different conclusion than Danu," said Fainche.

"Not remaining with my sister could be considered disloyal."

"Yes, it could. Possibly that's why she called me a treasonous bitseach," retorted Fainche, her cheekbones now flushed red.

"Awww, shite!" Conchobhar shook his head in disbelief.

"I told you once that I would never serve a foolish leader again. That remains true for me—and my riders." The threat did not go unnoticed.

Beacán touched Danu's hand, bent his head to her ear, and whispered, "You need to resolve this *now*. I will kill her if that is your wish. But you will certainly lose Curraghatoor's riders."

"I might lose my sister." Danu's words were full of pain. Yet her rose slumbered, and that gave her hope.

"She made her choice. We cannot leave Ráth Na Conall weakened. There is nothing *we* can do." Beacán reluctantly looked at Draighean. The porcelain mask gave no hint of the Sidhe's emotions, but her eyes glittered with fury… and disappointment. There would be no rescue from that source.

Danu inhaled deeply and slowly exhaled and once more held Fainche's gaze. "I thank you for your report. All around this table appreciate the strength that you, and your riders, add to Ráth Na Conall. We would not wish you to leave because of this incident." Danu paused and rubbed a finger along her lips. "If there is any fault, it lies at my feet for being unsympathetic to my sister's ideas."

On her other side, Glaisne muttered, "No."

✳✳✳

The forced smile on Uallachán's face was for Cairbre, who rode alongside him. His visit to Chrúachain had left him very unhappy. *Have I been usurped?* The fact that behind him and his one hundred marched a thousand Connachta warriors seemed to shout, "Yes!"

Astride a nondescript, mud-brown mare, he walked at a leisurely pace at the head of his guard. Uallachán's poor judgement of horseflesh matched that of his failings with men. As he looked to his right, his jawbones clenched, and his back teeth ground on each other until he had an aching jaw. Cairbre rode a magnificent chestnut animal that stood at least two hands taller than his. Worse, he rode with an ease that screamed of his enjoyment of riding.

The pace Cairbre set from Chrúachain to Caher Conri meant the journey took less than a half-cycle of the moon. Uallachán and his men were tired and irritable. Uallachán because of chafed thighs and the travel sores across his arse. His men, unused to walking long distances, had gathered an array of blisters on their feet that made the journey constantly painful. Their awkward gait to compensate for the cysts brought temporary relief. The cost was sore joints. In contrast, the Connachta warriors seemed to relish the march as a welcome break from Chrúachain.

Still, once past the next hill, Caher Conri, decent food and beer, and a cot to sleep on awaited. Yet what were the decorations embellishing the berm's apex? What reason did the garrison have for flying banners from the guard posts? A few hundred paces from the earthworks, the revelations became clearer.

"Shite!" muttered Uallachán's shield-man.

"Rip them down!" Uallachán screamed. Most were unsure as to which of the blemishes their king referred to. The flapping gold and black flag of Clann Ui Flaithimh or the red and black banner of Conall Mac Gabhann raised on the remaining uprights of the smoking ruins of guard posts? Or perhaps he meant the skulls of the defence's former garrison. They were spiked on spears and arrayed along the dirt embankment. The wind whistled eerily through the sunken black holes of their eyes and out of their jaws. Any flesh had long been consumed by the ravens who sat defiantly on each of the heads.

Fear paralysed Uallachán. He felt his triubhas and dillat wet. What of his fortress? Did a new king sit on his throne? *Control yourself.* Uallachán glanced at a grim-faced Cairbre and wondered if his head would soon join the band of the dead. He opened his mouth to shout an order, but a glare from Cairbre stopped him.

Cairbre turned on his dillat and roared, "Uallachán's men will open the gates and secure the gateway. The rest stand ready."

Anxiety rippled through Uallachán's warriors. Left with no choice, they unstrapped scíatha from their backs, gripped spears, and moved forward at a measured pace. True to form, Uallachán slowed his mount to allow his men to advance ahead of him. Cairbre shook his head in disgust. Fortunately for Uallachán, the only resistance he encountered was the heavy oak gates, which Brighid's riders had braced with timbers.

* * *

The rider galloped through the gates of Caher Conri and came to a halt before Brighid and Maolán. "Warriors have breached the berm entrance and march on Caher Conri." The young woman looked at the grey sky. "They'll be here before meán lae."

"That's not long to prepare," said Maolán. It was mid-morning. "We should have posted riders beyond the berm."

"They're only Uallachán's men, and they're afraid of me," snapped Brighid, angry at Maolán's undisguised criticism. The rider shook her head.

"Over a thousand warriors are marching towards our gates. By the banners, the vast majority are Connachta."

"The Hag's tits!" exclaimed Maolán and glared at Brighid. "What is your plan?"

"Mount up. We'll gallop for the berm and escape."

The messenger shook her head. "You don't understand. Their numbers, the position of Caher Conri, and the berm mean they have cut off the possibility of any retreat to the north, east, and west. There is only south."

"No."

On the ramparts, Brighid looked around her, vainly hoping for inspiration. To the south was the coastline and a long tramp home, but they would have to abandon the horses. Tears misted Brighid's eyes as she thought about leaving her cherished black mare. Did she have a choice? How many riders would she lose if they confronted Uallachán and the Connachta? She wondered what Danu would do.

"Set fire to anything that will burn. After that, we'll descend the walls and make for the coastline and home. Load up with as many weapons as you can carry. Burn the rest."

Angry stares stabbed Brighid, and curses filled her ears. For many, their mounts were family, and they had been asked to cast them aside. Given a choice, most would prefer to die in battle with their horses.

"I'm sorry. I made a terrible blunder." Tears streamed down

Brighid's cheeks, and she choked on her words. "Say your goodbyes. I leave your friends' lives in your hands."

✶✶✶

The billowing smoke and destroyed gates of Caher Conri suggested that Uallachán's troubles might not be over. Even the rain seemed to hold back to allow the flames to wreak more damage. On the battlements, no spears glinted, and in the guard towers, no men peered down or shouted demands for identification. No booted feet thumped on the stone steps and walkway, and there was no noise from weapons and shields being readied.

The only sound was the *kraa kraa* of the conspiracy of ravens who swooped and soared over the ráth. Uallachán's paranoia was such that they seemed to mock him. Uallachán flinched and rubbed the back of his neck as he felt the eyes of Cairbre bore into his back. "Take fifty men and secure the fort," he snapped to his shield-man.

A short time later, his protector reported. "The fort is deserted. The garrison has fled or is dead. Forty horses remain, but they lie in the courtyard." Red-faced, Uallachán stormed towards the Great Hall, hoping for some respite. At the same time, Cairbre entered the yard.

A great wail of "No!" echoed off Caher Conri's walls as Cairbre spotted the carcasses. "The ruthless bitseach!"

Uallachán cared nothing for what he perceived as useful beasts. All he saw were the burning ruins of Caher Conri. Anything constructed of wood was smoking embers. The roof was gone in the Great Hall, and the supporting beams were charred and weakened beyond repair. His precious throne was no more than a pile of ash. The ráth's grey stone walls were blackened from the smoke and, without wooden braces, leaned ominously.

Having violated many, Uallachán experienced a glimpse of how that felt. Yet it did not prompt a change of heart or sympathy for his victims—only a burning rage that demanded vengeance. "The hostages?" he asked of his shield-man. The man shook his head.

"They are gone, my king. I suspect they were the purpose of the raid."

Uallachán's screams and curses echoed off what remained of the stone walls of Caher Conri. Yet Uallachán's and Brighid's trials were not over. In Ráth Na Conall, Draighean called a winter storm. The occupants of Caher Conri and the forty trudging along the coast were deluged in hail, sleet, and freezing rain.

Ignoring Uallachán, Cairbre set his men to cut timber. Shelters were needed and not just for the present. Samhain, and with it winter, would arrive in a half-cycle of the moon.

✳✳✳

Seven sunsets following Fainche's return to Ráth Na Conall, Brighid's bedraggled and dispirited band slogged up the long path to the gates of the stronghold. As they crossed the entrance, Brighid turned to Maolán. "The fault and shame are mine to bear. Take our riders to their quarters and see to their needs." Brighid hesitated. "When you judge them ready, help them find a new mount." Maolán nodded, turned abruptly, and marched after the riders. Any compassion he might have had for Brighid had died with his horse.

Shoulders slumped, insults of "stupid bitseach", "spoilt princess", "never a queen", and many more far less subtle resounded in Brighid's ears. Her earlobes and the back of her neck burned in shame and anger at her stupidity. Only a grim determination not to suffer greater humiliation held back a waterfall of tears.

"They're waiting for you." The disappointment in Beacán's eyes almost crushed Brighid, but she set her jaw and crossed the chamber's threshold.

"Why, Brighid?" asked Danu.

"You know why, sister. You just won't see or admit it." Brighid eyes flared defiantly, but for the briefest time. "I made a mistake. I regret it. The responsibility is mine."

"You lost forty horses and almost forty riders. Fainche has

threatened to take her riders and serve another rí. How can anyone trust you?"

"I said I was sorry, bitseach, but maybe you want my head on a spear. Then you'd be free to play rígan and rí with your pet."

"Enough!" shouted Danu.

"Yes, it is, sister." Brighid turned to Aulus and Thrasius. "It is winter, and the seas are too violent. At Bealtaine, I would like a ship to carry me home." Brighid took a measure of satisfaction at the stunned silence. About to exit the room, she turned and tossed another brand onto the fire. "By the way, there are a thousand Connachta warriors camped around the ruins of Caher Conri."

"Stop!"

Draighean's voice shook the timbers of the Great Hall and threatened to burst the eardrums of those present. The bone-chilling eyes that swept the room were accompanied by a single word: "Out!" None queried its meaning, and all, apart from Danu and Brighid, scurried from the room.

The Sidhe glowered at Danu and Brighid. "Your behaviour, and I mean both of you, is intolerable—and public." Draighean pointed long accusing fingers. "Work this out in private. Your roses bind you together until death. If you are not together in this mission, Ráth Na Conall will fall, its people will be slaughtered or enslaved, you will dishonour your father and mother, and embarrass the Sidhe, Mongfhionn."

The Sidhe drew herself to her full towering height and flung one final spear. "I will not be a party to any of that. You have one cycle of the moon to convince me that you are worthy of the support of the Aes Sidhe… and me. Otherwise, I shall return to my sisters and leave you to your petty squabbles and a fate *both* of you will fully deserve."

CHAPTER 18

It was a procession of the grateful, the hostile, and the surly. Under Danu's orders, messengers traversed Uallachán's domain. They demanded that the mothers and fathers of the rescued children present themselves at Ráth Na Conall. Any who failed to appear would be deemed to have disowned their offspring. Furthermore, they would be declared enemies of Danu and Brighid.

In Ériu, women fought alongside men in battle. Their rights and those of their children were prescribed in the Fénechas. The Law was not perfect, since gold and power corrupt even the best of intentions. Still, it was a brave or foolish man who dared to challenge his hand-fast partner when it came to their children. A mother bear could learn lessons from Gaelic mothers. Hence, the intemperate mood of men given no choice but to make the journey to Ráth Na Conall.

Optimistically, Danu perceived the situation as a means to educate errant members of Clann Ui Flaithimh on the foolishness of their loyalty to Uallachán. Reflecting on Draighean's harsh words, she persuaded Brighid to greet the parents and their retinues—most travelled with servants and fifty to one hundred warriors. Brighid redefined "greet" as intimidate.

Thus, at the ends of the forested passes to the north of Na Comaraigh, Brighid's riders and Báine's chariots met the travellers in full battle array. Fainche's mounted warriors did likewise at the southern corridor. The tension between the two formidable women had not re-ceded. Brighid still bristled at what she considered Fainche's disloyalty; Fainche could not forgive Brighid for the deaths of the horses.

The throng was shepherded along the winding path to the eastern entrance of Ráth Na Conall. Most, nourished by Uallachán's propaganda, expected a dilapidated ráth. Instead, they stared, open-mouthed, at a new, expanded stronghold.

Before the heavy oak gates and arrayed along the last thirty paces of the dirt track, fifty tall, hard-faced warriors stood to attention. Red and black plumes sprouted from the acorn-shaped nubs of helmets and fluttered in the light breeze. Few, however, saw past the eyes of the swooping black ravens painted on red shields or the javelins hefted as if ready for battle. Some glanced to the side and the perimeter ditches and wished they had not.

The thumping sound of *bodhráin* drew the travellers' eyes to the parapets where warriors stood shield-to-shield. In one of the eastern gate's guard towers, Onchú smiled. Re-establishing the tradition of the drums was Brighid's idea. Perhaps seeing an uncontentious issue, Danu had heartily endorsed it.

The younger children from Niúig were overjoyed at the opportunity. None more so than Aoife and her brother. With unbridled enthusiasm, if not great skill, they used knucklebones to pound their bodhráin. Onchú grimaced as he recalled the ditches of the old fort and surmised where the bones had originated.

"Welcome to Ráth Na Conall, home of Danu Ni Conall and Brighid Ni Conall, the daughters of Conall Mac Gabhann, Rí Ruirech of Clann Ui Flaithimh and Mórrígan Ni Cathasaigh, Rígan of Clann Ui Flaithimh and also known as An Fiagaí Dorcha." A tremor of fear permeated the crowd at the mention of the Dark Huntress. The voice of Onchú boomed from the ramparts.

"I see that the people of this land remember An Fiagaí Dorcha. It is said that Conall's daughters favour their mother." Further anxious whisperings rippled through those at the gate. "Uallachán lied to you. Conall, Mórrígan, and their children live and reign over a great kingdom and tribe in the land of Gaul."

Onchú inhaled deeply and exhaled. Few would like his next words. "You will enter the fort with a bodyguard of ten and two servants. Then you will be escorted to the Great Hall to meet your children. The remainder of your entourages will be escorted to the barracks behind the fort. They will be provided with food, drink, and a cot to lie on." Grumblings and angry chatter rose up from a small cluster of chieftains.

"Who are you to give orders to nobles?" The arrogance in the voice was unhidden, but the crowd afforded the man anonymity.

"Thus speaks a coward who hides behind women. Stand clear, identify yourself." Silence followed, and Onchú growled, "Maybe not such a brave man. I am Onchú Ó an Cháintigh, Rí of Carn Tigherna. You may have heard rumours of my death." More whispers percolated through the throng. "There will be no exceptions to our demands. If you wish to challenge us, our warriors will welcome the exercise."

A loud female voice rose above the rumbles of impotent protest. "You will agree to the rí's instructions, *now*. I want to see my children."

* * *

The condition of the children rescued from Caher Conri had improved immeasurably. All were clothed in clean *léinte*, triubhas, and soft boots provided by Cináed's people. A few sunsets of safety, good food, and the company of Aoife, and her friends, had returned the laughter of childhood.

Yet the brother and sister rescued by Iasg peered at those entering the Great Hall with fearful looks and nails bitten to the quick. Sitting at the high table with the Chomhairle, Iasg looked on with equal anxiety. She knew it was wrong but found it challenging to wish the siblings reconciled with their parents. Beacán, sensing his partner's unease, followed her gaze to its subject and smiled.

The twins rose from their seats, and Danu spoke. "I am Danu

Ni Conall, and this is my sister, Brighid Ni Conall. We are the Rígana of Ráth Na Conall. In this land, we, *and only we*, represent Clann Uí Flaithimh and have the full authority of our father and mother." Danu's eyes swept the audience. "Make no mistake. My sister and I will purge this land of Uallachán and his evil—with or without your help."

To those watching, it seemed as if the dark curling sigils on the twins' faces throbbed and flowed. Memories of An Fiagaí Dorcha gave already pale faces a sickly hue. Sitting beside the rígana, Draighean chuckled. *A little terror goes a long way. Time to raise the anxiety level.* The Sidhe stood, threw back her hood, setting loose long black tresses that touched her arse, and probed the congregation with obsidian eyes.

"I am Draighean of the Aes Sidhe. Oppose Ráth Na Conall, and you oppose me." Deep maroon lips curled into a cruel smile. "And, unlike the rígana, I have no mercy." Savouring the dread and to universal silence, Draighean sat down.

Danu's demeanour was grim as she pointed to the children. "Your young ones were badly used and kept in appalling circumstances. Each one is brave beyond any who sits or stands in this Hall. I hope they will find joy and peace reunited with their parents and families." Floods of tears met screams of happiness as children were reunited with their parents.

Brighid's face became a dark mask of anger as she observed that only half of the parents had claimed their offspring. Danu placed a hand on Brighid's arm. The gesture ended swiftly when Brighid jerked her arm away. "Patience, sister. It was never going to be simple. *We* will deal with this." Brighid wondered at Danu's choice of words. Did she also speak of their fractured relationship?

Danu signalled Báine and Fainche and exclaimed, "A room with food and beverages has been set aside for the reunited. There will also be a Feast of Celebration and bonfires when the sun sets. Please follow my captains. My sister and I will join you later."

Danu then addressed the remaining parents in an icy voice. "We will resolve *your* difficulties when they have departed."

At Danu's nod, Brighid stepped forward and glared at the remaining parents. "I heard but could not believe that some would disown their offspring because of what was done to them by Uallachán and his men." Brighid paused before roiling passions overwhelmed her. "It is not their fault. It is yours. How did you expect children to resist men with evil intent?"

Brighid swept the room with eyes that spoke of imminent retribution. Mothers and fathers recoiled under the scrutiny. Gritting her teeth, Brighid added, "I urge you to reconsider and show yourself worthy of your children. Do not spurn their love for and faith in you." Trembling with promised wrath, Brighid sat down to rising discord between mothers and fathers.

Danu's cheeks flushed red, and she spat her words through lips thinned by anger. "*I* have heard there are those among you who surrendered their offspring to Uallachán but not under duress. Rather you voluntarily gave your sons and daughters into vile hands to curry favour with a depraved monster. You knew how they would be despoiled."

"Only the presence of your children saves you from being taken outside and staked—and that is too merciful a death." Anxious glances from the nobles confirmed more than enough red shields in the Great Hall to prevent escape or enforce retribution.

The sigils on Danu's face turned black as night. "Those who have had time to reconsider and wish to be reunited with their children may do so now." She took a deep breath as if her following words stuck in her throat. "These are perilous times. I will not count the delay against you." A handful of chastised parents crossed the floor to claim their offspring.

"But know this, my sister and I, the Sidhe, and the druids will know if harm comes to any child. And you will suffer agonies far beyond your comprehension." Having asserted some control over her temper, Danu smiled and pointed to Fainche, who remained at a side exit. "Please join the others." After nodding to Scolai, Danu took her seat.

The black-cloaked druid stood and pushed the garment's hood from his head, revealing a shock of red hair. "At least now we know he's not bald," said Conchobhar, prompting chuckles. A severe look from Danu brought a dip of the head and a mumbled if unrepentant "Sorry" from the fort's battle commander.

"I am Scolai, Leader of the Druids at Ráth Na Conall. I interpret, arbitrate, and administer the Fénechas. In respect of the Law, my judgement is final. Anything I say has the consent of the rígana and the sanction of the Druidic Councils of Ériu and Albu." The Druid looked on those remaining with barely concealed contempt.

"*You* do not deserve the Goddess's blessing of children." The Druid paused as if to order his thoughts. "Any woman present wishing to sunder the bonds between themselves and their hand-fast partner will be given sanctuary in Ráth Na Conall, if accompanied by their offspring. I will ensure that you receive all that is due to you under the Law.

"To those who remain uncontrite, you disgust me and are unsuitable fathers and mothers. In accordance with the Fénechas, your children will be taken from you and will become wards of the rígana…" Scolai paused as if to say something distasteful, "… and the Sidhe, Draighean, until they are adopted by those who will cherish them."

The lady who stepped forward had long, braided plaits of corn-blonde hair. Her frame was large, but her height meant that she carried her weight well. Firmly muscled arms and faded scars suggested she had once fought as a warrior and likely a formidable one. Not instantly beautiful, she had an allure that grew with intimacy.

In a firm voice, she spoke. "Men and druids…" she looked behind her, "… and even sisters have betrayed us before. Do I have the word of the Rígana of Ráth Na Conall and their mother, Mórrígan, that you can and will protect us?"

Onchú dipped his head to Danu and whispered, "The lady who spoke up at the gates."

"You have my word and that of my sister. I can safely say that, on this issue, our mother will fully support us," said Danu.

The lady looked behind her and nodded. "Take your hands off me, arsehole!" and counter shouts of "Bitseacha!" and "Striapacha!" ensued as three women broke from the diminishing group of nobles. They joined the spokeswoman and then, in tears, all ran to embrace their children.

Only the presence of Ráth Na Conall's shields prevented their hand-fast partners from causing them harm. The angst of the men was understandable. Under the Law, the nobles had just lost half of their wealth—cattle, gold, and lands.

As she left the chamber, the spokeswoman turned and shouted to the men remaining, "You well know that I have fought at your side many times. In the future, if I have to fight against you, I will show no mercy."

Danu turned to Onchú and Conchobhar. "We should get better acquainted with the lady."

Draighean stood, blackthorn staff in hand, and looked at Danu and Brighid. "Enough! May I strike the rest of these loathsome people down? I can make it so their children know, hear, and see nothing." There was nothing in Draighean's expression that suggested she was unserious. To the Sidhe's and Brighid's evident disappointment, Danu shook her head.

"My sister, the Sidhe, and likely most of my Chomhairle wish for your death in a quite unpleasant and prolonged manner. Make no mistake. There is nothing that you or your retinues could do to stop us from carrying out the sentence."

The nervous glances exchanged between the group drew an unnerving smile from Danu. "I am not of this mind." At the sighs of relief, she held up her hand and said, "Yet." The disquiet returned. "From this day, you are enemies of Ráth Na Conall and outcasts of Clann Ui Flaithimh. You will take your men and leave this fort immediately. If you cause any trouble, you and your warriors will be put down like rabid animals.

"At dawn, my sister's riders and chariots will seek and kill any found in our lands." Danu paused and looked at Brighid, whose face told that sunrise could not come soon enough. "You should understand that I consider the territory of Clann Ui Flaithimh to stretch from Niúig to Caher Conri."

* * *

Beacán smiled, looked into Iasg's pools of green, and put calloused hands over his partner's. "I am not that unobservant, and you should not torture yourself over what I may or may not think. From what I am told, the girl is brave, and the boy is courageous and loyal. If you wish them to join our family, I have no objections and every reason to see you happy."

"Thank ye, Beacán." A tiny hand squeezed Beacán's, and she led him towards the brother and sister. Midway, Iasg stopped and clapped a hand over her mouth.

"What?

"I just realised that I don't know their names."

Beacán roared with laughter. "If only all problems were solved that easily."

CHAPTER 19

394 B.C.— Feast of Samhain

"Will we have enough room for everyone?" asked Brighid.

Two sunsets before the winter feast of Samhain, Brighid watched the arrival of the third king. This time it was Labhraidh Loingsech from Ráthgeal. Like the kings before him, Aodh from Clárach and Sláine from Cnoc Duíginn, he arrived with family, servants, and a large warband. Like those before him, he also protested loudly the "request" to limit his guard to ten warriors inside Ráth Na Conall. The complaint was political theatre. There was not the remotest prospect of Labhraidh allowing a large, heavily armed force to enter his hillfort of Ráthgeal.

"In a few sunsets after the festival, we'll freeze our arses off and be knee-deep in snow. Given the heavy furs everyone's wearing, we're more likely to run out of storage space. An enterprising thief could make a fortune in one night here," growled Onchú.

Brighid detected the humour in the tone and thanked the Goddess. Under the care of the druids and his daughters, Onchú's physical recovery had progressed well. Any remaining twinges and aches, he laid at the feet of getting old. To everyone's delight apart from Eithne's, he had officially adopted Naomh and Úna.

A frown rested on Brighid's lips. The same could not be said about Flann. He had barely survived a spear in the back at Caher Conri and lay on the cusp between life and death. Brighid could sense the bean-sidhe standing at his cot. Once again, she looked at Onchú and bit her lip.

Onchú's mental well-being and the bouts of depression that sometimes consumed him concerned the rígana. The loss of his sons and Carn Tigherna, the horrendous treatment of Eithne and his daughters, and his capture and torture at Uallachán's hands brought deep emotional scars and guilt. Only time and love would heal those wounds.

Although he had threatened, and with good cause, Onchú remained loath to sever the bonds of hand-fasting because he still loved Eithne. As for Eithne, pragmatism and self-preservation kept her with Onchú—although, according to gossip, not in his cot. Brighid put a hand on Onchú's and squeezed. Whether he noticed the touch was unclear. Standing nearby, Eithne marked the contact and read it through her twisted lens.

***

As Danu descended the guard post, she sighted Glaisne and his brother, Aodh. A broad smile parted her lips, for she enjoyed Glaisne's company and was delighted to see him. However, when Aodh and Glaisne returned from Clárach, a blind man could see that neither were comfortable in the other's presence. Perhaps it was understandable. Aodh had recently put down a rebellion by his brother, Cúmhaí.

Both men were unmistakably at odds in the square before the Great Hall and made no attempt to disguise their quarrel. Did Aodh perceive Glaisne as a threat? Surely not. Glaisne had assured Danu that he had no ambitions for the throne of Clárach. It was, perhaps, one pledge that had a kernel of truth.

As Glaisne stormed away from his brother, he considered his future. He was bored with the simpering daughters of Clárach's nobles, constantly strewn in his path by fathers seeking wealth and influence. Thus, he satisfied his carnal needs in the company of striapacha or gullible young, lowborn girls. The latter, enamoured at his status, willingly spread their thighs. Both groups gave him pleasure without consequence.

However, in Danu, Glaisne saw a path to greater power than Clárach's throne and wanted to dominate and possess her. Glaisne's brow furrowed as he saw Brighid walk across the muddy yard. She was his one obstacle. How could she be removed from the game?

As if feeling Danu's gaze, Glaisne turned and looked upwards. Even to Danu, the instant smile on Glaisne's face seemed disingenuous. *Perhaps he has much on his mind.*

✶✶✶

In the intimate reception chamber, Danu took her seat, clasped her hands, and nodded to Beacán, Brighid, Conchobhar, Draighean, Fainche, and Onchú. Alongside Fainche, two others sat and were plainly ill at ease. According to Fainche, the man and woman were the most senior captains remaining at Curraghatoor.

Both were uncertain why they had been invited to the Samhain celebrations and wary of the potential consequences. Under Crónán and Torna, Curraghatoor had positioned itself as an enemy of Ráth Na Conall. That the Rí of Carn Tigherna faced them across the table further raised their apprehension. Yet the invitation had left no room for a refusal. Better for them to accept the judgement and punishment of the Rígana of Ráth Na Conall than all at the fort.

With a quick cough to loosen her voice, Danu gave what she hoped was a reassuring smile to the uneasy duo. "Welcome to Ráth Na Conall. I hope you enjoy the celebrations with us and that this is the first of many future visits." A slight blush of pink appeared on cheeks, which, until that moment, bore more resemblance to those of corpses. "I called this meeting to discuss Curraghatoor, represented at the table by Fainche and her two comrades from the fort." Like an infection, curious glances flitted from face to face.

Danu looked at Onchú. "I'm sorry. Carn Tigherna is gone and is unlikely to be rebuilt." Danu flinched at the pain on Onchú's face but continued. "Curraghatoor, however, is a stronghold without a king, and that cannot be allowed to persist. It represents a threat to Ráth Na Conall."

Turning to those from Curraghatoor, Danu summarised their

position. "Even with your oversight, without a king, Curraghatoor will inevitably fall either to outlaws, Uallachán, or a rival and possibly un-friendly monarch. In the absence and unlikely return of Íar Mac Dedad, the fort needs a strong leader." The three from Curraghatoor nodded in agreement.

"What are you proposing?" Fainche looked at Danu and Brighid with rising disquiet. "I trust you're not suggesting me for that role. I love Curraghatoor, but I'm no rígan."

Danu smiled and shook her head. "While I think you underestimate your qualities, no, not you." Danu smiled at her sister, who returned the gesture. "But you, Onchú Ó an Cháintigh, I can envisage as the new Rí of Curraghatoor." From the folds of her gown, Danu withdrew and set a heavy gold ring on the table. "This is the seal of the Rí of Curraghatoor. My sister and I have authority from Íar Mac Dedad to pass it to whomever we judge worthy."

Gasps of surprise and then silence fell on the room as those around the table considered Danu's proposal. "Only one question needs to be answered. Onchú, will you accept the throne of Curraghatoor? For my sister and I have the power to crown you."

✳✳✳

"Gentlemen and ladies, welcome to Ráth Na Conall. The feast of Sam-hain will commence next sunset, but we have urgent business to discuss. We have confirmed that Maine Athramail, Rí Ruirech of the Connachta, and his brothers support Uallachán's rebellion. Furthermore, one thou-sand Connachta warriors, under the command of Cairbre, are encamp-ed at Caher Conri."

Taking a sip of wine from a red-figure pottery cup, Danu contin-ued. "It would be folly to believe that Uallachán is in command. Thus, effectively, Maine Athramail has invaded our lands. Our expectation is that a much larger Connachta army will invade the southern kingdoms after the winter. Maine will enslave the people of southern Ériu and re-place its ríthe with those more amenable to servitude."

Danu paused before speaking. "I propose an alliance of the southern ríthe to throw back the aggressors and punish them for their insolence."

"Why is this Ráthgeal's or any of the kings' concern?" asked Labhraidh. "There is a well-known enmity between Chrúachain and Ráth Na Conall. My hillfort on the eastern edge of Ériu is protected by mountains on our western flank. Undoubtedly, Ráthgeal could field the biggest army of the southern kings. But why should I commit to a fight that is not of my making? Even with my warriors, we would be massively outnumbered. Indeed, I doubt this fight is winnable."

Labhraidh lifted his hands. "Convince me otherwise."

"When have you ever known a ravenous beast who, after vanquishing one victim, did not look for the next to consume?" asked Danu. "Maine's ambition will not be constrained to the southwestern kingdoms. He will continue to plunder and pillage the monarchies until he is forced to withdraw. Furthermore, he will add the armies of the defeated to his own, making him even more powerful.

"Where better to face him than in the fields surrounding Ráth Na Conall? Wound him severely, and Maine will be forced to withdraw or face incursions on his northern and eastern borders." Danu searched the sceptical faces of the ríthe before her and endeavoured to tamp down her frustration.

"Who will stand with Clann Ui Flaithimh?"

"I stand with Ráth Na Conall," said Onchú.

"That's all very well for a king without a kingdom," retorted Labhraidh.

"My apologies. Did I forget to mention that Onchú will be crowned Rí of Curraghatoor after the festival?" said Danu, her green eyes glittering in the torchlight.

"Apologies, my arse! Do you have any more well-timed announcements?" growled Labhraidh, and his brown eyes narrowed. Had the Rígana of Ráth Na Conall inherited the cunning of their ma and da?

"Perhaps," said Danu.

"Uallachán has made clear his intentions towards Clárach. The support of the Connachta will only feed his ambitions. Clárach and its nobles and chieftains will fight alongside the rígana," announced Aodh. To Danu's disquiet, it seemed as if Glaisne was poised to object to his brother's statement. A sharp word from Aodh kept him in his seat and his mouth shut.

Sláine shuffled in his seat before speaking. "Cnoc Duíginn has little choice but to align with Clann Ui Flaithimh. We are in the path of any army from the land of the Connachta. We will be washed away like small pebbles in the tide without allies." Taking a deep breath and then exhaling, he added, "Yet, if I am honest, my army is small. I can add far fewer warriors than the other kings present."

"The Rí of Cnoc Duíginn's support is very welcome, and I am sure there are other strengths you will bring to the alliance." Danu dipped her head to Sláine and looked once again at Labhraidh. Her expression needed no words.

"Did the rígana omit me on purpose?"

The tone of rebuke in Draighean's voice was unmistakable. All seated around the long table started as, chameleon-like, the tall shadow detached itself from the chamber's wall. "Your armies *may* cause the Connachta to pause and consider potential losses, but they will not fear you or shrink from testing you in battle." Draighean paused and smiled at Brighid. "I, and Brighid, can make them fear for their lives—day and night." Dark-red lips parted in a ghoulish smile. "Plus, Maine and his brothers no longer have my sister and their mother, Medb, to protect them."

Combing long dark tresses with pale fingers, the Sidhe first held Labhraidh's eyes. "I remember friends and enemies, and their kin, for an exceptionally long time—in this world and the next. Please do not take my words as a threat, more a statement of fact." Draighean glared at Sláine, who shrank visibly in his chair. It was as if the rí knew what was coming. "As for Cnoc Duíginn, your father betrayed the queens' father and my sister, Mongfhionn. She made sure his time on this earth was brief and his sojourn in the Otherworld eternal."

"Shite!"

Those around the table heartily endorsed Labhraidh's exclamation. He looked at Sláine with mild amusement and a modicum of disgust. The current rí, and his ancestors, nurtured a reputation for eccentricity. That focused mainly on cultivating an environment of nakedness in the hillfort. Thus, the men of Cnoc Duíginn strutted around like peacocks displaying their manhoods. In this, they were not alone, for the kingdom's females of all ages eagerly demonstrated their freedom from garments.

The tactic was unsurprising and quite clever. None of the ríthe and their offspring was particularly handsome—far from it. The family inheritance was thin hair, pock-marked faces, and bodies covered in freckles. Thus, the males made the most of their only impressive attribute—their manhoods. As for the women, their lure was the size of their breasts and the friendliness of their thighs. Like bees to honeysuckle, there was no shortage of men and women who wished to partake of what was on offer. Also, and more importantly, the custom sustained the remote fort's population from its inevitable decline.

Labhraidh chuckled, recalling the disconcerted look on Sláine's face when an impish Brighid announced that, with more curling designs on his body, he would fit right in with her clann's *Cinn Péinteáilte*—Painted Ones. With a "nod and a wink" to Danu, Brighid playfully added that her ma, sister, and she often preferred to fight naked in battle. The statement increased Sláine's angst. Losing the attraction of Cnoc Duíginn's long fostered quirkiness was something never considered previously.

Judging her sister to have stretched the limits of hospitality, Danu intervened. "Stop teasing our guest and *ally*, Brighid. He has travelled a long distance to be with us, and his experience as the Rí of Cnoc Duíginn is of great value. We should respect that."

Danu gave Brighid a look of reproach and smiled at Sláine. Brighid muttered her apologies, although few missed the sly wink that passed between the sisters. It was doubtful whether Sláine caught the gesture. His attention had been diverted by the particularly heavy-breasted serving wench directed to his side by Danu. Observing the banter between the girls, Beacán hoped it was a sign of fences being mended.

Labhraidh dipped his head to Beacán's ear and whispered, "The rígana are impressive. Being so young, they wield the art of diplomacy like sword and scíath." Beacán nodded and chuckled when Labhraidh added, "I will need to have my wits about me when in discussions with those two. I fear that I will always be outnumbered, especially since the Sidhe is ever-present." A throaty laugh told both men that Draighean was well aware of their conversation.

"My dear Sláine, I agree with Danu that you underestimate your value to this cause," said Labhraidh. "Your web of spies and connections across Ériu is the envy of many kings, including myself. Most of us tend to stay isolated in our *rátha*." Sláine beamed at the flattery, but Danu looked curiously at Labhraidh and wondered at the direction of the conversation.

"Am I right that you have royal friends within the Ó Neills in northern Ériu?" Sláine nodded, although this time warily. He, too, questioned the destination. "Perhaps, as your contribution to our alliance, you might consider sending envoys to the Ulaid in the north, apprising that clann of a potential opportunity."

Danu smiled and admired Labhraidh's skills. That said, she was not sure she would ever totally trust him or his ambitions. She shrugged. *He likely thinks the same about Brighid and me.* "Can I assume that you will join our alliance, Labhraidh, Rí of Ráthgeal?" The king tugged on copper-red whiskers.

"That depends."

"May I ask on what?"

"Who will be the battle commander?"

Silence fell at Labhraidh's words. The topic had been studiously avoided in the discussion, presumably since none wished to promote their personal ambitions or insult the other kings. Yet all were aware that the issue was critical. Danu wondered if Labhraidh was about to put his name forward. If he did, how could she refuse him?

"Are you suggesting yourself?" asked Beacán.

Danu heaved a sigh of relief that she did not have to pose the question and muttered a heartfelt, "Thank you, uncle," under her breath.

Labhraidh's demeanour changed swiftly, and those around the table tensed. "You know it makes sense. Ráthgeal can contribute the largest number of warriors, and I am the most experienced in warfare. Without my warriors, this venture will fail. It makes no sense that I put my warriors and chariots under the command of…" Labhraidh smiled at Danu and Brighid, "… and I mean no offence, two untried girls."

Icy silence, and cheeks reddened by embarrassment, followed Labhraidh's words. Danu knew that he had a compelling argument, but her gut told her it would be the wrong decision. She felt the anger and heat rising from Brighid, but more ominous was the murderous look in Beacán's eyes. *The Hag, everything had been going so well.*

Danu feverishly searched for a persuasive argument. "The main battle will be fought around Ráth Na Conall. All, except Sláine and you, are familiar with the terrain and have proven battle credentials—here and in Gaul." In desperation, Danu looked at Aulus, but he shook his head almost imperceptibly as if knowing what she was about to say.

The hand waved as if in dismissal and Danu's smile spoke of arrogance. "Perhaps, Brighid, we should avail of the two thousand mounted and shield-warriors and fleet of quinqueremes our father, the Rí Ruirech of Clann Ui Flaithimh, has put at our service."

Beside her, Brighid whispered, "No."

Labhraidh rolled his shoulders. Neck bones cracked and popped as his head rocked from side to side. "I am very disappointed, Danu. Obviously, being a good fidchell player is not passed down from father to daughter." Labhraidh looked at the kings and others.

"If she cannot negotiate her way out of a simple challenge, of what use will she be in the heat of battle?" Labhraidh looked directly at Danu. "Desperation is never a good strategy. Ráth Na Conall will have been destroyed, and your head mounted on a spear long before your father's reinforcements would arrive."

"You should leave while you still can," growled Beacán.

With a shake of his head and a voice that held sorrow, Labhraidh responded. "You know I'm right." Then he looked at Draighean. "And you, too."

"Beacán has given you good counsel." Draighean looked at Labhraidh. "To assess Danu's mettle was not unreasonable and possibly necessary. Yet there was a better way. You chose the trial badly. Leave. Perhaps you might live long enough to die in Ráthgeal."

Rising from her seat, Danu felt her knees buckle and blood drain from her face. Only the firm grip of Brighid forestalled an undignified fall.

"I think this makes my misjudgement quite minor, sister," whispered Brighid.

"Bitseach!"

In the pit of her stomach, Danu knew Brighid was right.

CHAPTER 20

The Great Hall was packed to the doors and, failing to contain all, the raucous crowd spilt into the market square. Tradition had it that Samhain was when the curtain between the dead and the living was at its thinnest, allowing spirits, spectres, and unnatural beings to visit for a time. Hence, great bonfires were lit to ward off those with evil intent. Nevertheless, whether freeman or slave, all intended to have a great time feasting, drinking, and rutting.

A pale-faced Danu twisted braided hair and then her fingers at the high table. She sipped cautiously from a cup of wine diluted with cold spring water, but its contents spilt onto the table. "Put the cup down, Danu," hissed Brighid. "You're making our guests nervous." Then, she added, in a softer tone, "What's done is done. Put your mind to what needs to be accomplished."

Danu and Brighid were resplendent in simple but intricately embroidered sleeveless, Greek-style chitons, each clasped at the shoulders with emerald-encrusted pins. Fine enough to be transparent, the material caused ripples of gasps among those present. Not because the sisters were naked underneath, but because it confirmed to all that the curling symbols were not confined to their arms and faces.

Beside the rígana sat the kings and beyond them the Chomhairle. Recently, the Council had expanded to include Aulus, Báine, and Fainche, and the leader of the druids. A tear rolled down Danu's cheek, yet not for herself. Flann had still not recovered sufficiently to attend. There were, however, two more absent from the table—Beacán and Iasg. Danu frowned when she recalled her earlier conversation with the duo.

"An assassin's dream," was Beacán's summary of the festivities. And so, senses on high alert, the lions prowled the Hall.

A commotion at the Hall's entrance drew Danu's attention. She stiffened, and Brighid's hand went immediately to the blade strapped to her thigh. Onchú, seated next to Danu, chuckled. "I doubt anyone with ill-intent could get through the ring of steel surrounding this feasting hall… or the two shadows that weave in and out of the revellers."

With a nod of his head, Onchú directed Danu's and Brighid's attention to the entrance. Cináed and his hand-fast partner, Ceara—a handsome woman from whom Aoife had clearly taken her looks—walked down the central aisle. Behind them followed the leaders of the artisans and tradespeople. Several paces from the high table, Cináed and Ceara stopped and bowed deeply.

"I have been informed that there is a tradition from the first days of Ráth Na Conall which has not been honoured." He smiled at the perturbed glances shared between the sisters. "It is time to correct that omission." Cináed turned around and nodded to the rear of the hall.

To loud claps and cheers, a beaming Aoife and her brother, Cass, walked slowly down the aisle. In outstretched hands, they carried two large platters. Each had an object covered in a red or blue cloth. From the strain on their faces and set jaws, the gifts were quite heavy.

Finally, they stood beside their ma and da. Cináed looked down and beamed proudly at his daughter and son. "You have done well." He turned to the rígana. "If you allow, they will complete their duty." At a nod from Danu, Aoife and Cass walked to either side of the platform, mounted the few steps, and stood behind the queens. It was then that Aoife discovered the flaw in their plans. They were too small, and the throne chairs too tall to allow the completion of their task.

Setting her tray down on the table in front of Brighid, Aoife whispered, "Would you mind kneeling, my queen?"

Onchú roared with laughter. "It seems that the highest must bow before the lowliest."

With a smile, Danu and Brighid pushed their seats back and knelt. The crowd fell silent in anticipation and then gave a resounding approval as the rígana stood. On each head was an ornately engraved helmet, embellished with gold, silver, and copper. Long, flowing plumes fell from the swooping gold raven that crested each covering—blue for Danu and red-gold for Brighid.

"I think ours are better than ma's and da's," whispered Brighid. Sweeping Aoife up into her arms, a misty-eyed Brighid said, "Thanks." Danu did likewise with Cass, but the dam she had built to hold back her roiling emotions breached, and she could not prevent a cascade of tears.

A red-eyed Danu looked at Cináed and the host behind him. "I can find no words better than a simple 'thank you'. We will wear these helmets with pride." Then Danu dipped her head to Cináed. "Please, take your place at the high table—and your hand-fast partner. You have more than earned your seat." Brighid whispered in her sister's ear, and Danu smiled. "Aoife and Cass are also welcome. Although I suspect they would prefer to be with others much closer to their age."

✳✳✳

"I see our strong-minded lady has a bodyguard. Do you know her name?" Iasg looked in the direction of Beacán's gaze and smiled. The tall, curvy spokeswoman was in animated discussion with Conchobhar.

"She's called Aoibheann," said Iasg. "They certainly haven't been more than a pace away from each other this night or since she first arrived. I think they like each other… a lot."

Beacán dipped his head in the direction of several well-armed warriors. "And *they* have not let her out of their sight, either. Brighid and Danu rightly think the lady's strong defence of the women from Caher Conri has put her in danger. Bodyguards have been assigned to her, so perhaps Conchobhar is merely doing his duty."

Iasg stopped, shook her head, and looked into Beacán's eyes. "Are ye really that daft or jesting with me?" She pointed to the couple and said, "That conversation will end in his or her cot tonight, and not because of duty."

"At least that will be two people we won't have to worry about," said Beacán.

"Explain. Ye've been on edge all day," retorted Iasg.

"An attack on Ráth Na Conall is unlikely. There are too many warriors. But this celebration is perfect for an assassin: high-profile targets, crowds, drunken carousing, and few inhibitions as to partners. I could kill half the nobility in this room and be gone before the alarm is raised. An attractive female slayer could seduce, rut, and slit throats with reckless abandon. We'd never know the true death toll until meán lae."

"So much for enjoying ourselves. Do ye see any possible victims or assassins?"

A perturbed Beacán shook his head. "We mingle, swap jests and tales, and hope we get lucky. And we watch each other's backs. You and I have made quite a few enemies."

✶✶✶

"Time to show our guests our toys," said Danu. "Most doubt we can survive a sustained attack by the Connachta, especially now."

"I hope Aulus has had enough time to train his teams," replied Brighid. "This would not be the appropriate occasion to miss the targets."

Danu stood on Ráth Na Conall's now crowded ramparts. In a voice improved and steadied by Draighean's less worldly talents, she called out, "Many of you have seen and wondered about the unusual machines that stand on our ramparts. There is one large ballista for each corner and guard post and four that point to the north, south, east, and west. All can be moved to face our enemies. We also have one hundred smaller ballistae which are much more mobile but just as deadly."

Danu looked at Aulus, who had generated a high level of curiosity in the hillfort. Most had heard of but never seen a Roman. The men marvelled at his burnished bronze armour and shield; the women wondered about what was barely concealed by the short red tunic. From what Brighid had told Danu, Aulus had no shortage of rutting partners and few complaints of dissatisfied lovers.

"Your turn to shine, Aulus," said Danu.

Gasps of awe, shock, and fear followed the squeal of skeins, the crack of wood, and the sighs of fiery bolts. Hurled as the sun slipped below the horizon, the flaming missiles flew east, west, north, and south towards stacks of timber. At the centre of the ruins of the old Ráth Na Conall was a massive mountain of cut trees soaked in pitch. When struck by a series of projectiles, the wood burst into flames, and a huge bonfire lit up the skies. Immediately around the fort, hundreds of smaller fires followed as they were set alight.

"It seemed fitting that the new Ráth Na Conall should pay homage to the old," said Danu. Then she smiled at the ríthe. "And it seemed too good an excuse to miss the demonstration of our latest weapon. In the morning…" Danu paused and laughed. "Or perhaps after a night of eating, drinking, and rutting, meán lae or later might be more realistic, we shall demonstrate the full capabilities of the ballistae. But I think you get my point."

Aulus smiled, happy that his teams and the ballistae had performed as expected. In truth, he had little doubt in their capabilities. Although how they would perform in battle would not be tested until after the winter. That environment was very much different. Head down, he walked towards the steps that led to the market square and his assignation with a particularly well-endowed young woman. Life was good.

However, Aulus found his path blocked by Aodh and Sláine. "We would like to discuss how our rátha can be similarly equipped," said Aodh.

Aulus smiled. "Danu and Brighid foresaw your interest. I am

instructed to support Clárach, Cnoc Duíginn, and Curraghatoor, to the best of my abilities, without compromising the security of Ráth Na Conall."

✳✳✳

It was not that he was inept or a stranger to violence and murder, whether deliberate or accidental. Rather, his familiarity with the concept of stealth was tenuous. Therefore, he had contracted with another to join him and carry out his client's wishes. As it happened, she was less qualified than he in the art of secrecy. Still, her eyes told that she would kill without mercy and enjoy the experience. His plan was to use her as a shield while he killed the target. Coincidently, that was her plan, too.

Who could the target possibly be? Beacán and Iasg weaved through the boisterous and increasingly drunken crowds in the Great Hall and market square. As meán oíche approached, many became less inhibited about concealing the desire to rut. They also became less discriminating about who to consummate the act with and threw aside thoughts of privacy. Beacán had concluded that the kings and queens were unlikely objectives. The ring of steel around each royal consisted of veterans, who were well aware of the stakes.

The lesser nobles and chieftains were also of little concern. Their existence was one of constant danger and manoeuvring for advantage. In a crowd like this, most accepted that someone would attempt to knock them from their perch. Similarly, they would also have targets in mind.

So who? Who, beyond the royals and the nobles, would someone pay gold to have murdered? Iasg sensed the mounting frustration within Beacán and saw it reflected on his face. For a brief moment, the expression changed to concern infused with a hint of anger.

Iasg turned to follow Beacán's gaze and saw an unsteady and somewhat befuddled Danu being fawned over by Glaisne. Danu's initial abstemious behaviour had been swept aside by feelings of failure and inadequacy—and Glaisne's persistence. Brighid and Báine were nowhere to

213

be seen, which surprised no one.

A squeeze on Iasg's wrist jerked her from her musings. Her eyes followed Beacán's line of sight and fell on a couple. Of average height, he had brown hair and a shaggy beard. She was the more striking of the two. Long, golden hair, in two thick braids, swung in tandem with the upward roll of her arse cheeks. Not as tall as the man, she was just as lean.

Iasg did not recognise either, but there were many strangers in Ráth Na Conall during Samhain. Still, what set the pair apart was their gait. There was no unsteadiness and no stagger or over-correction for having consumed too much beer. In a forest of swaying trees, their mien was marked by determination.

At a nod from Beacán, Iasg languidly crossed the floor and settled behind the pair. Anonymous as ever, Beacán moved parallel to the man. Giving a credible impression of being drunk, he lurched several times into the presumed assassin. Several foul-mouthed curses were followed by a shove that apparently made Beacán stumble. With slurred complaints, Beacán rose unsteadily and staggered alongside the killer.

As the scene played out, the female was the first to sense danger and moved closer to her comrade. *Well, that settles that. They're working as a team.* Still, until a move was made, Iasg had no idea of their target. She and Beacán had little beyond raised hackles and gut feelings to support their suspicions. A shriek of delight momentarily distracted Iasg. She heard the deep laugh of Cináed surrounded by his family, enjoying the celebrations.

"The Hag's arse!" Iasg had uncovered the assassins' target and, at the same time, lost the female assassin.

Beacán had come to the same conclusion as Iasg. With the assassin in his sights, he moved to intercept until Aoife cried, "Look, da! It's Beacán." It was followed by, "Where's Iasg?" Startled, the killer hesitated for the briefest of moments. In his trade, few did not know the name of Ráth Na Conall's ghost… or his female partner. After their night of slaughter and escape from Uallachán's clutches, their reputations had soared.

Now, the assassin looked into cold green eyes that seemed to flicker with tongues of fire. Instinctively, he gripped the short-bladed knife, palmed it in his hand and moved to attack. Beacán's speed fooled him, and he looked into empty space and the startled eyes of Cináed and Ceara. An observant captain nodded, and several shield-warriors detached from the walls, placing themselves in front of the family.

The killer felt Beacán's breath on his neck. How did the bastard get behind him? "You're going to die. That is not in question. How quickly and painfully I kill you is. Whose gold paid for your services?" The would-be killer calculated his chances of escaping through the crowd of revellers. Most of them remained oblivious to the scene unfolding. His body betrayed him.

"Wrong choice," Beacán growled low into the man's ear. The razor-edged blade slipped effortlessly and efficiently between the cutthroat's ribs and into his lungs. By the time the bean-sidhe wailed, Beacán had tossed the corpse onto the floor of the Great Hall.

Furious at herself, Iasg scoured the Hall, searching for the female assassin. *In her place, what would I do? Flee or fight? There's no gold for fleeing and every chance of being tracked down.* Iasg stared at Cináed's group and the shields who stood guard before them. "Shite!" she snarled, spotting the owner of the corn-yellow braids circle in a wide arc around the small shield-wall. There was no chance of Iasg intercepting the killer and even less probability of anyone hearing her scream a warning.

Iasg's hands slipped under the folds of her léine and pulled two throwing knives from the sheaths strapped to her thighs. "Bloody eejits!" she snapped as she dashed past a group of drunkards who cheered and leered at the flash of pale thighs. She reached the platform where the high table stood as the blonde killer moved to strike at Cináed's back. The distance was uncertain as Iasg loosed both knives and prayed to the gods of her people.

Two shrieks cut the air. One was Ceara as she watched the red stain on Cináed's back blossom as he stumbled to his knees. The other was the assassin as Iasg's knives punched into her back, pitching her onto her face. She was immediately set upon by Báine and Brighid, who had appeared, flush-faced, from Brighid's nearby quarters. Báine grabbed the assassin's braids and twisted her head around. Blood seeped from the killer's lips.

"You're not dead yet, bitseach. You will tell me who paid your wages, or my friend, Brighid, will have you staked, and we will watch you die very slowly and very painfully." Fear almost paralysed the murderer's voice, for she was well aware of Brighid's reputation. The assassin's voice was faint, so Báine lowered her face to hear.

Brighid looked into the assassin's eyes. "Báine has spoken on my behalf, and I will not break her promise. You will not be put to the stake."

Relief flooded into the killer's gaze but was halted by the curl of Brighid's lips and her words to the shields who stood close by. "Take her to the nearest bonfire and throw her on it. Make sure she burns until the bean-sidhe comes. No one lives who hurts my family and friends." The assassin's screams were lost in the revelries.

Brighid turned to Báine. "I can't believe that bastard went this far. I must tell Danu."

A finger softly brushed Brighid's cheek, and lips were pressed together. "I understand. Go. We'll find each other later."

✷✷✷

"He will be fine. Thanks to Iasg, your partner suffered only a long and not very deep cut. My druids have tended to that, and he may not even have a scar to boast about. Likely, Cináed has had graver injuries farming." Scolai gave Ceara and her children what he hoped was a reassuring smile and walked away.

"We are in your debt, my lady," said Ceara.

"I'm nae lady," chuckled Iasg. "Just call me Iasg."

"Perhaps you, Breacán, and your children would join us for the rest of the night's festivities. We're not overly exciting." Ceara laughed. "Except perhaps Aoife."

Iasg laughed, and Ceara thought the sound reminded her of the sound of the sea tumbling pebbles. "I think Beacán and I have had enough excitement for this Samhain. We'll be delighted to join ye."

CHAPTER 21

In the scheme of things, rutting was not a major thing among the Gaels. By the time most girls had passed their sixteenth summer, their *maigh-deanas* was little more than a fond memory. The act was natural, people enjoyed it, and men and women of all ages pursued it with reckless abandon at festivals. On such occasions, the choice of partner was often arbitrary, influenced by opportunity, state of inebriation, and the ability to perform.

In the deep night and early morning, as the fires of ardour waned and, like the bonfires of Samhain, turned to ash, Danu lay disappointed—and unsatisfied. Too much wine and a yearning to leave queenly responsibilities aside for just one evening had lowered her defences and inhibitions.

Glaisne proved to be a selfish lover, reminding her of the men and boys who had tried to spread her thighs in the fields and forests around Lugudunon. Their only interest—frantic rutting to a climax and the expending of their seed. Mission accomplished, they moved on to their next conquest. Save Glaisne's clear desire to dominate, he had been no different.

His lack of thought for her needs deeply disappointed Danu. *Perhaps I expected too much.* This was not the first time she had been penetrated. After their first bleeding, even the daughters of kings found themselves pursued by fumbling boys and drooling men.

That Danu had managed to hold out until sixteen summers was due to her hope of finding the right partner. She wanted someone who would measure favourably against her da. Each time, she had been disappointed. All she could remember was that it was over quickly, and her lover—did any justify the description?—was gone. With each failed tryst, the pedestal she sat her father on grew higher, and the chance of satisfying her expectations diminished.

She recalled deeply embarrassing talks with Mòrag Ni Artair, the voluptuous and, until her hand-fasting with Torcán, quite promiscuous queen of the Cinn Péinteáilte. Mòrag had no problem graphically educating an adolescent Danu on what she had a right to expect from a relationship. In detail that mortified Danu, Mòrag explained that Torcán had been a poor, self-centred lover at first. But with patient instruction and the withdrawal of sexual favours, he had become a talented and attentive lover.

Being a practical woman, Mòrag also showed Danu techniques to compensate when her rutting partner proved a disappointment. Now, as Danu lay naked—and worse, alone—on a sweat-dampened meadowsweet and straw bed, she burned with anger and unfulfilled desire. Glaisne had slurred some excuse and departed soon after his "duty" was done. Thus, Danu made full use of Mòrag's wisdom.

Panting harshly, long fingers plunged into the lush auburn triangle, pushing her labia aside and taking the place of his manhood. With the other hand, she twisted and pulled on stiff, prominent nipples. She first uncovered and then rubbed and squeezed her sensitive pink pearl until she spasmed and her skin flushed pink. Covered in a sheen of perspiration, she moaned loudly and climaxed.

With a sigh of regret for a lost moment, Danu grabbed the wolf fur, earlier cast aside, and pulled it over her. As the warmth from the room's fires receded, the chamber would become cold. *Perhaps I need a slave to keep the flames going.* With a deep breath, Danu tried to settle her mind and embrace sleep. In her mind, she began to list and reflect on

Glaisne's shortcomings, which she had previously chosen to overlook.

A hand slipped down, over her belly, and into her luxurious bush. A quick scratch and she fell asleep.

* * *

An abundance of farts, furry tongues, headaches, and roiling bellies greeted meán lae. After the Samhain celebrations, the residents and guests of Ráth Na Conall had slept well beyond the dawn but now slowly came to life. Usually, the festivities would last for days, but winter and war were on the horizon, and preparations had to be made. Perhaps, if alive, they could celebrate Bealtaine at a more leisurely pace.

After more demonstrations of the ballistae and assurances of Aulus' help, Sláine had departed the fort. Onchú and Curraghatoor's two captains were mounted and about to leave, accompanied by one hundred riders. Danu hoped the garrison at that ráth would be amenable and accept their new rí. She dreaded to consider what would happen if Onchú was rebuffed. *I can't have another blunder.*

Danu, Onchú, and Brighid approved Fainche's request to remain at Ráth Na Conall, ostensibly to act as a liaison and command Curraghatoor's remaining hundred riders. Few were deceived as they observed the growing affection between her and Maolán.

From the walkway, Danu observed Aodh and Glaisne cross the square and stride in her direction. She watched Aodh walk towards the ramparts and saw him abruptly stop and make it plain to his younger brother that he was not invited to the conversation. The scowl on Glaisne's face made him look quite ugly. As she heard Aodh's footsteps on the steps, Danu unconsciously slipped a hand under her heavy fur and scratched between her legs.

"Shite!" Danu looked around, hoping that no one had observed the indiscretion.

Aodh's face wore an expression of paternal concern. She had seen the same look on her da's face—many times. The king's demeanour had initially seemed gruff to Danu, but she was fast learning that appearances could be deceptive. Over the Samhain celebrations, she had come to respect how the king treated everyone fairly. Could she ask for more from a neighbour?

Clárach's rí gazed upon Danu and wished for better siblings or that he was ten summers younger. He pulled on his full beard and whiskers, scratched the scar on his left cheek, and tried his best to smile. Still, Aodh had no time to be subtle and resorted to stern bluntness.

"On Na Comaraigh, when the five with Glaisne were slain, what was his reaction? How long did he mourn? Did he give vent to his anger? Did he ask for an eiric for their families?"

That Danu had to think of an appropriate response gave Aodh his answer. He shook his head. "I thought not. Did he mention that they had been his friends since birth? Or that the girl was of noble birth and promised to him… and he to her?" Aodh drew in a great breath and slowly let it out. His face held great sadness and anger.

"Glaisne's heart lacks a level of compassion, and maybe that is his father's and my fault. If it served his purpose, Glaisne could walk away from those close to him without a thought."

Aodh straightened his shoulders, and it seemed that his words burdened him greatly. "I will not stand in the way of Glaisne and you. If that is what *you* desire, then so be it. But *you* will be a better queen than he a king. All I ask is that you accept him for what he is. Not what you want or perceive him to be."

About to turn about and descend the steps, Aodh said, "My brother Cúmhaí was open about his wish to be Rí of Clárach. He was foolish, but I admired him for his honesty. Glaisne's desire is no less, but he keeps it deep within him. Perhaps now he has a better kingdom in his sights, and my throne is safe from his ambitions."

With abruptness, as if wishing an unpleasant conversation to end, Aodh added, "I have commanded Glaisne to return to Clárach with me and stay there until Imbolg. He cannot refuse. The alternative is to be accused of treason. Perhaps, with the Goddess…" Aodh looked around and smiled, "… and the Sidhe's help, the winter months will provide perspective for both of you." The Rí of Clárach dipped his head and left the walkway.

✴✴✴

By the following sunset, Ráth Na Conall's guests had departed. Draighean approached a solitary Danu, deep in thought on the ramparts. "Well, your recent conversation with Aodh was forthright. My respect for him has risen." Danu's cheeks flushed red, not from the cold but with fury.

"My conversations are private. Remember that in the future, Sidhe," she retorted.

"You are a queen. None of your conversations, save the bedchamber, are private or ever will be. And even the bedchamber is not guaranteed," countered the Sidhe, although she was pleased that Danu showed no sign of backing down. "Your actions are public as well. I suggest you bury your pride and visit the druids. They have salves to remedy what ails you."

"What?"

"Come, come, Danu. Are you that blind? I am not the only one who has seen you scratch between your legs and with increasing frequency. Although I may be the only one to confront you." Draighean towered over her ward and glared at Danu. "Learn your lesson and the next time, choose your rutting partners more wisely."

The Sidhe turned to walk away but stopped and, with an evil chuckle, said, "You can say goodbye to that auburn bush between your legs. It will need to be scraped—at least for this winter." Another thought slipped into Draighean's mind, and with a parting shot, she said, "Burn everything you and he touched, *now*! Those little bastards move quickly and get everywhere."

Danu gripped the wooden stockade. Her knuckles turned white, her fingernails bled, and her fingers screamed for release. Fuming and fighting to control a bubbling cauldron of emotions, tears streamed down her cheeks. The feirdhris between her breasts throbbed and called to its partner.

From Danu's lips, there came a long, undulating howl. Startled, those in the fort and the farms beyond ceased their chores to stare at the figure on the ramparts. The fur cloak lay abandoned on the walkway. Arms were outstretched and lifted to the sky, and the curling designs on Danu's body flowed like rivers of power.

The scene ended with a great cry of "Tuilí!" as Danu collapsed to the wooden rampart.

"Now that was unexpected," mouthed Draighean as Brighid pushed her aside and rushed to kneel beside Danu.

Nervously, Brighid reached out to embrace her twin. Her eyes were met by a stare of sheer savagery and obsidian eyes. *The Hag preserve me. She's just like ma… and me.* The sigils on Danu's face flowed and she shook with unchecked power. Horrified, Brighid watched as her sister's rose blackened to match her own. Unable to resist, Brighid's feirdhris and curling designs throbbed and flowed in tandem with her twin's, and she, too, cast off her cloak. In a huddle on the walkway, the sisters held each other, rocking and moaning.

"Shite, Danu! I'm supposed to be the dark one. Come back to me. Please come back. I will not lose you."

Brighid gripped her sister's shoulders and hugged her even tighter. A deluge of hot tears soaked the walkway as both sobbed sorely. Sensing her sister's turmoil had peaked, Brighid kissed Danu's forehead. "We need a distraction and change of scenery. Aoife has been pestering me to go riding. Perhaps the three of us could go. If anyone can cheer us up, it's Aoife."

Danu smiled and nodded. "Agreed. But first, I must consult with the druids." As she rose shakily from the parapet, Brighid bent down to pick up her sister's cloak. A firm hand stopped her. "No." Danu looked around and spotted her servant. "Please. Burn the robe and everything in my bedchamber."

As the twins walked along the rampart to the steps, Brighid turned to Danu. "Sláine will be so disappointed he left early." Both giggled like young girls, and everyone in the fort heaved a sigh of relief.

＊＊＊

Following Danu's pointing out his lack of success in bringing people back to Ráth Na Conall, Neasán's status had rapidly deteriorated. Concurrently, and to his chagrin, the authority of Cináed had risen steadily, buttressed by his success at encouraging the settlement's former farmers and trades return.

However, Danu had decided it was unfair to rub Neasán's nose in the shite by ordering him from the fort. Thus, he had been given generous quarters in the newly constructed hillfort. Yet bitter and angry at his demotion, Neasán made sure everyone he conversed with knew of his unfair treatment at the hands of the rígana. Few took him seriously and many openly mocked him.

Several sunsets after Samhain and about to enter his roundhouse, Neasán found four warriors at his side. They commanded him to appear before the rígana. Protesting his innocence of any wrongdoing, he struggled to keep up with the pace of the warriors. He had the distinct impression that they would have enjoyed dragging him through the mud had he tried to resist.

In the Great Hall, Danu and Brighid sat on the carved chairs that served as their thrones. To either side were Scolai and Draighean. Conchobhar and a glowering Báine stood several paces away. The grim looks on the rígana's faces suggested that Neasán's day would worsen. "You are accused of hiring assassins to murder Cináed. How do you plead?" Danu spoke, and her voice was as cold as the snow-capped peaks of Na Comaraigh.

"I deny it. Where is your proof? Where are your witnesses?" A bead of sweat rolled down Neasán's brow and was quickly joined by another… and another. His eyes glanced furtively around, hoping to find a path from his predicament. All he could see was the score of guards who stood against the long walls or blocked the exit. He felt his shirt damp with perspiration.

"The assassin confessed before she was tossed onto her pyre… alive," rumbled Brighid, barely able to restrain her desire for retribution.

"She lied. I am innocent of this accusation."

"No, she did not. We spoke with the assassins' acquaintances. The pair were not well-liked, and their comrades took little encouragement to disclose how the man had boasted of the gold he had been paid to murder Cináed and who had bought his services." Danu held the trembling man's eyes. He saw no signs of mercy.

"You are declared an outcast of Ráth Na Conall and Clann Ui Flaithimh. Your possessions and gold have already been seized and will be used to compensate those you have wronged."

"No!" gasped Neasán. "Please, no."

Danu nodded to the captain of the guards. "Expel this creature from the fort." Then Danu turned to Báine. "Is your vehicle waiting?" The chariots' leader bowed. One last time, Danu addressed Neasán. "If I were you, I would make haste. Meán lae is not far off, and at that time, *she* will be given leave to pursue you."

✳✳✳

Nuadha shivered in the early chills of winter. That he had survived was a surprise. It gave him a glow of accomplishment and a sense of satisfaction never experienced under Uallachán's tutelage. Cast out from Ráth Na Conall and Clann Ui Flaithimh, although the latter had little meaning for him, he moved from cave to hollow tree to holes scraped in the ground.

With Samhain well past, the winter frosts, snows, and winds reduced his options for shelter. Armed with little more than a hand axe and a knife, the dirt had become too hard to dig, and he did not wish to break the only weapons he possessed.

As the wind howled around him, Nuadha's teeth chattered uncontrollably. He whispered, "Thank you," for the heavy cloak Beacán had given him and pulled the woollen garment closer. Truthfully, he had expected to be stripped and thrown down Ráth Na Conall's hill. That would have been his fate had Brighid and Draighean had their way.

Yet, and a surprise to him, Nuadha held no enmity against anyone at the ráth. Only thoughts of Uallachán brought anger. His future, although hazardous, held the potential for survival. Had the roles been reversed and any of Danu's Chomhairle captured by Uallachán, their fate would have been dire, painful, and mortal.

The food sack given to him when expelled from the hillfort was empty. His belly growled once more, reminding him of his foolishness. He had greedily consumed the bread, cheese, and meats. His rationale that he needed to eat to keep his energy high and body warm was reasonable. It was, however, a lie. Nuadha's nature tended to gluttony, which could not be unlearned in a few sunsets. Water was not an issue. Those at the fort had given him several waterskins, and springs were abundant.

Too late, he learned that he needed to be a scavenger of berries, fungi, and roots to supplement and extend his store of victuals. His stomach hurt from the lack of quantity and the vomiting and retching caused by choosing the wrong fruit or mushroom. That said, he discovered that some mushrooms had pleasant aftereffects.

On this day, Nuadha stumbled along the southern foothills of Bod Carraig in the general direction of Caher Conri. Yet that was not a destination he wished to reach. He pondered whether travelling northeast, away from both Ráth Na Conall and Caher Conri, might be the better choice. If he survived the winter, he would revisit his options. He kept to forested terrain because the ancient trees provided shelter from the wind and the canopy mitigated the driving rain and sleet. The woods also reduced the risk of meeting anyone. Nuadha well knew that an outcast had few friends.

On occasion, he prayed to the Goddess for shelter, although not with any hope of receiving an answer. Measured in the balance, Nuadha knew his final path lay in the direction of the Otherworld, not Mag Mell.

He berated himself for his cowardice and submission to Uallachán. Yet he cursed his brother more and with a passion and venom he had never experienced. Nuadha sighed. Would he now have the courage to confront his sibling or buckle under and submit?

Head down, Nuadha staggered onward. Another loud growl from his belly reminded him of the need to stop and forage for food. At least the detritus of the forest floor was easier to dig in than frozen earth. Fresh meat was out of the question. He had no idea where to find fowl or small animals and had no snares to trap them. Nuadha snorted. Even if he had traps, he had no idea how to use them.

As the sun disappeared below the horizon, he stumbled into the clearing. More accurately, he fell over the stump of a fallen tree. In the gloom of dusk, he discerned the outline of several buildings. He froze and strained his ears for any sign or sound of life, but none came. Relieved, he took a cautious step forward, and it was then the heavy smell of smoke and decay filled his nostrils. Shaking his head at the likely explanation, he made for the most prominent structure and hoped enough remained to provide shelter for the night. In the morning, he would explore.

CHAPTER 22

394 B.C.—Midwinter

Uallachán shivered in the corner of the ruins of Caher Conri's Great Hall and cursed Cairbre. His only consolation was that at least he had food and beer. The fort's stores of grain and meat had been destroyed by Brighid. However, Cairbre, who sensed an imminent and severe winter, supported Uallachán in supplementing their stores. Therefore, between them, they bullied the handful of forts on the promontory into sharing their stores.

That said, self-preservation proved to be the limit of Cairbre's cooperation. Before the winter storms gathered momentum, his thousand warriors had cut down trees from the nearby forests and erected rough, but weatherproof, shelters along Caher Conri's walls. Hence Uallachán's foul mood and curses.

While Cairbre lived in relative comfort, protected from the winter, Uallachán's men proved to be as hopeless as their rí. Not wishing to expend the effort to build solid shelters, they ridiculed the Connachta and constructed little more than flimsy tents from the debris of the fort. Their only good decision was to set the coverings against Caher Conri's inner walls. As the light, powdery snow turned to heavy flakes and a north-easterly wind howled through the ruins, many regretted their sloth.

Appeals to the Connachta to give them refuge proved futile. It appeared that neither Cairbre nor his warriors valued Uallachán or his men. Indeed, in Cairbre's mind, the winter might remove a thorn in his side.

★★★

Danu pulled the wolf-fur cloak tighter and thanked the Goddess for its protection from the bitingly cold wind. She squinted at the bleak yet beautiful white vista before her. It was largely unsullied, apart from the tracks of predators who had yet to hibernate and now searched and dug for sustenance.

Bloody claws and ribs, starkly visible through skin and fur, testified to their lack of success. Occasionally, the white expanse was spotted with red when raging hunger could not be satisfied, and the dash turned on its weakest members. The very young, the sick, and the elderly were culled and devoured. As it had always been, the strong would replenish the packs with the advent of a new mating season.

Only the dead know the cry of the mná-sidhe. Still, Danu imagined that the howling of the wind and wolves was a pretty accurate reflection. "I'm sure they will be fine." Conchobhar read Danu's expression perfectly. Buried beneath drifts of snow were the farmsteads and round-houses of those who were now part of Clann Ui Flaithimh. The heat stored in thick thatched roofs had kept the buildings visible for a time. Not now. All was silent and white.

She watched Báine, with Brighid at her heels, pace the walkway, carving a calf-deep track in the white powder. The chariot leader's ruddy face wore a mask of fear, as did Brighid's. How were Aoife, and Báine's adopted family? Conchobhar and Aoibheann huddled further along the parapet, as did Beacán and Iasg, Fainche and Maolán.

Onchú and his family were stranded at Curraghatoor. To Danu's relief, Onchú's claim to the throne had been accepted by Curraghatoor's garrison. *At least I got one thing right.* She commended the lone rider who brought the welcome news but wondered at the messenger's sanity. A journey which in normal times took less than a sunset, had taken seven times that as he fought the weather for every step.

Further along the rampart, Draighean and Scolai were in a heated conversation, with the druid gesticulating wildly at the landscape. Only the Sidhe seemed immune to the winter storms.

"Shite! The bitseach!"

Everybody's eyes turned to Danu, apart from Draighean, who smiled as if knowing what was coming next.

"To the Great Hall. Now!" bellowed Danu.

***

"Are *you* responsible for this?"

Danu glared at Draighean, knowing perfectly well the answer. The Sidhe nodded, savouring the expressions of horror and anger from those around the table. She did not speak. She did not have to. Her demeanour shouted, "What did you expect?"

"You should have consulted with us," said Danu.

"You would have refused."

Draighean raised a hand to curtail anyone's voiced disapproval. "Without Labhraidh's warriors, Maine's armies will crush you as easily as they will the cornfields around Ráth Na Conall. You will be dead, and Uallachán the puppet Rí of the Connachta. Is that what you want?" Draighean's lips curled into a snarl as she seized Brighid and Danu's gaze.

"If it is, then take the triremes and return to Lugudunon. At least you will spare your parents the pain of your death."

"But…"

"I have given you a chance to survive, if not to win. What you see is but the tail of the winter they experience. The Connachta and Uallachán are suffering many times worse. They will be lucky to dig themselves out by the middle of spring." The Sidhe enjoyed watching the realisation that her actions, although reprehensible, made perfect sense. As the faces around her settled into resigned acceptance, Draighean looked at Danu sternly.

"What *you* are contemplating is the right course of action. Yet ask yourself. Would you have come to it much sooner—together? A pair of roses is much stronger than a single stem. What will it take, and how many will die before you accept this?"

"By the Hag, what is she bloody well talking about?" roared Conchobhar. The irony of Draighean's alter ego being the Hag did not occur to the commander.

"People will die if they have not already done so. Those in the fields and forests need to be brought into the fort, along with all provisions and cattle." Brighid dipped her head to Danu. Both felt the feirdhriseacha between their breasts throb in harmony.

"How? Deep drifts of snow already constrain movement around the fort. And, with the arrival of the kings and nobles who fled Uallachán, the ráth is already full. We are fortunate that the weather prevented their full armies accompanying them, although that will change after Imbolg," said Conchobhar.

Danu gripped Brighid's hand for strength. "We use the Great Hall and its attached buildings, the roundhouses, barracks for the riders and warriors, and any trade buildings. If we run out of space, we erect tents in the square until we can build additional, solid accommodations. There is no shortage of trees, and hard labour will keep everyone warm. Better the people living within the fort in any circumstance than leaving them to freeze to death outside." Beaming faces and a round of applause greeted Danu's words.

✳✳✳

"It's so cold, da. Can we put another log or piece of peat on the fire?"

Tears streamed down Aoife's flushed cheeks as she snuggled closer to Cináed. Cows, dogs, plough-horses, and humans all crammed into the largest of the farmstead's roundhouses in the hope of conserving warmth. The stores of cut wood and turf bricks had dwindled to an alarmingly low level.

Cináed and his oldest sons had tried to forge a path to the woodshed, but the snow was too high and packed hard. The only good thing was that drifts blocked the window and door holes, reducing the impact of the harsh winds. In truth, Cináed feared for his family and for those on the neighbouring farms. He hoped that the Goddess smiled on the people, for he could see no escape.

"I think I hear something, da," snuffled Aoife. Cináed smiled and hugged his youngest closer to him.

"It's just the wind, Aoife. Just the wind."

"No, da. Listen."

Above the wind, the faint refrain of hunting horns sounded. Still, Cináed remained unconvinced. *The wind plays tricks on our senses.* Ever the optimist, once Aoife had her hopes raised, she refused to hear any nay-saying. *Perhaps the burning flame of hope in her eyes will melt the snow.* Cináed shook his head at such nonsensical ramblings. His job was not to dash dreams but to lessen the inevitable disappointment and provide hugs when wishes and prayers went unanswered.

Hence, both Cináed and Ceara nearly jumped out of their skins as the snow blocking the roundhouse's entrance shattered. They watched Maolán kick his way through the remaining snow and stand before them. On his heels followed Báine, who was immediately jumped on by a hysterically happy Aoife. Wiping the tears away, the charioteer smiled at Cináed and Ceara.

"Sorry we're late."

"Not late. Just in time. Aoife had faith in you." The relief on Cináed's face was undisguised.

A long howl from the forest interrupted the conversation. "Our troubles are not over," said Báine. "Your wagons are waiting to be hitched. Load your family and any food onto them, and tie the livestock to the carts. They are to be driven to the fort. Danu and Brighid have decreed that everyone is to be brought to the stronghold for safety."

Báine and Maolán took Cináed to the side. "We need you to remain with us. Only you know the exact locations of your people and the newest arrivals. It took a score of warriors from dawn to meán lae to cut a path from the ráth to your farm. Other teams—almost the whole population of the hillfort, both civilians and army—are branching out from this trail. But without your knowledge, we're just guessing."

Maolán looked to the skies and the angry clouds that threatened more snow. "Time is running out." Then the wind died, and an eerie silence fell across the land. It was broken by another long howl… and another… and another.

✳✳✳

Compared to the humans, theirs was a short life. She had been his partner for most of his life and now lay dead at his feet. Instinctively, he knew the winter snows and storms were unnatural. He had lived through many severe winters, but none like this. He knew the land had been unnaturally cold for many human generations. Yet this was different.

Teeth bared, he growled at those of the pack who saw his mate as no more than food. He sympathised with them but would tear out the throats of any who tried to feed on her emaciated carcass. Then he let out a long howl of loss. His next call was for vengeance.

The alpha, known as Silverback because of the broad stripe of silver-white along his back, knew that a lone band would be slaughtered, skinned, and their pelts used to keep the two-legs warm. The time to draw the packs together had come.

The dash took up his song, barking and baying. Rival groups around the pack and in the forest took up the call and sought permission to move closer. The humans had considerable numbers and iron teeth, but the predators knew the land. They also had no choice. They needed food, or they would die. It was that basic, that simple. As was the fact that Ráth Na Conall was the only source of meat remaining.

✳✳✳

The six carts pulled by oxen and plough-horses, with cattle ambling behind, moved slowly and steadily towards Ráth Na Conall. They were the last families to be rescued before night fell and it became too dangerous to continue.

On the following dawn, more bands would set out from the hillfort to resume the operation. Likely, several more sunsets would be needed to complete the mission. After that, it was doubtful that any who

233

remained unfound would survive the snow and freezing cold. Imbolg would be celebrated before their bodies were found and respects paid at their funeral pyres.

Torches fluttered in the deep blackness. Maolán thanked the Goddess for the silver-blue moon that broke the darkness but shivered. It was known as the Mourning Moon to the Gaels—not a good omen. He heaved a sigh of relief and watched the pale white mist of his breath escape as the silhouette of Ráth Na Conall finally came into view.

The increased level of snorting from the score of horses and the growling and barking from the handful of wolfhounds raised Maolán's unease. "Tighten up! Move faster!" he shouted. It was as if the wolves, stalking the carts, sensed this was their last chance of the evening. At least the ground was frozen hard, and once the solid wheels cut through the snow, they found purchase.

Earlier attacks on the human wagons had produced limited success, bringing down some cattle and a few horses. Silverback growled. With each win, he lost wolves as they stopped to feed on the warm carcasses. Others were killed by the iron wielded by the humans. Each cart was heavily protected by two-legs on horses and others with spears positioned in the vehicles. The wolf developed a grudging respect for the Leader. He was a wise man and had protected his pack well. *He had to die.* Silverback howled to gather the wolves for the final attack.

"No matter what happens, keep moving towards the fort. Do not stop for anything or anyone," ordered Maolán. Reluctantly Cináed agreed, guiltily thankful his family were already within the stronghold's walls. The sound of many beasts yipping and barking came closer and closer. "Protect the wagons or die!" roared Maolán. His command was answered by a howl of challenge from Silverback.

The powerful wolfhounds, sensing the presence of the wolves' leader, knew their duty. Moving silently, the dark shapes ran until the alpha was in sight and then attacked. With Silverback's attention concentrated on the wagons, the swiftness and savagery of the hounds' attack took him unawares, and he barely escaped their snapping jaws. The beasts were well-fed—a critical advantage against wolves weakened by malnutrition.

Perhaps, if they had prowled the edges of the packs, they would have caused much more damage and death. They fought bravely but were overwhelmed by the dash's members and other groups who surrounded Silverback. The hounds' blood stained the snow black as they lay with their throats ripped out and steaming innards spilling onto the white powder. The wolf growled. *Had their sacrifice been deliberate?* The wagons drew closer to the fort.

The heavy shape sprang from the shadows, knocking Maolán from his mount and into a snowbank. Unmounting the two-legs was not difficult. The rider had little to hold onto. The horse was immediately swarmed and brought down, thrashing out with bony hooves until exhausted. Several riders turned to give assistance but were stopped by Maolán's shout.

"Get the civilians to the fort! Die if you must."

Sword and mace in his hands, Maolán swept in circles at the constantly moving ghosts surrounding him. Standing on the snowbank, Silverback growled low and menacingly at Maolán. *He's a fine beast and would look good draped across my shoulders.* The fiery white glow of the wolf's eyes was hypnotic, and Maolán shook his head to focus.

Will he fight or send his troops in? If the alpha fought and Maolán killed him, he might survive the night. Several barks, and Maolán had his answer. He laughed at the wolf's strategy. Send in the weak and, when they had sapped the prey's strength, deliver the death bite. It was a peculiarly human tactic.

Maolán thrashed at first, but now he twitched with each new bite and felt the steady spurt of blood from a torn artery pump in rhythm with his fading heartbeat. He had been resigned to death when he had fallen from his horse but had taken many with him. Now he would suffer the same fate as his mount. *Perhaps that was how it should be.*

Silverback stood over him and howled. Maolán thought the sound was beautifully melodic. A bloody snout hovered over Maolán's neck, and he felt warm drool drip onto it. Another howl, the baring of fangs, and Maolán's throat was gone.

Yet not before he whispered, "Fainche."

∗ ∗ ∗

The mood of the meeting on Ráth Na Conall's ramparts was sombre. After three sunsets and diminishing success, the search for survivors of the cold had been abandoned. Cináed reckoned about fifty were missing—three full families. All in the room prayed that their end came by the weather and not wolves' teeth.

A band of riders departed at dawn to search for Maolán. They returned by meán lae, bringing only his mace and reports of a blood trail to the forest. Fainche would not be consoled and wailed as they put Maolán's blood-stained mace into her hands. Her cries and tears only ceased when she collapsed to the floor.

"Are we safe?" asked Danu. "Surely our efforts will be rewarded and those within the fort protected from beast and weather?"

As Conchobhar paced the fort's walls, his face and hands were scoured red raw by the wind. He looked sorrowfully at Brighid, who stood beside Danu. The news of Maolán's death had devastated Brighid and her shoulders, burdened with guilt at their unresolved arguments, slumped.

Conchobhar shook his head. "I've talked with the returning riders, those rescued, and the ráth's hunters. The wolves continue to gather under the alpha. That is exceedingly rare but understandable. What other source of food is there?" Broad shoulders shrugged in resignation. "They have no choice but to attack. I think they will strike soon, before malnutrition weakens them further, and most likely at night when they have the advantage."

Conchobhar looked to the rígana. "Arm everyone, bar the youngest children. Take the infants and the very young to the Great Hall and bar the doors." Conchobhar turned to face Aulus. "Your ballistae may be the difference between life and death for the fort. But you will be firing into the darkness." Aulus nodded, scratched his shaven head, and rubbed his chin.

"My men and women will be ready."

✦✦✦

Aggression among the wolves was not unknown. Indeed, it was a necessary trait for a pack leader. Still, Silverback had been unwell for several days and now snapped and bit at any who came close. Wiser heads among the dashes recognised the signs. It was feared and known among the packs as the "madness". Once bitten, the infection spread like wildfire and the numbers of its victims multiplied.

Yet Silverback remained powerful—indeed more so with the ferocity of the madness—and in charge. No other pack leader had the strength or confidence to challenge him. That said, instinct told the giant wolf his death drew closer. Those with the disease had short lives and unpleasant endings. If he was to feed the packs, the massed dashes needed to attack when the moon was high.

✦✦✦

In the fort, all shivered, although not because of the cold. Around the ráth, thousands of eyes glowed white and seemed to float eerily above the earth. It was no surprise that the wolves would attack at night. Darkness was their natural environment. From the forest, Silverback howled, and his call was taken up and harmonised by the packs. The wailing and barking seemed to last an eternity to those in the fort. Yet it was only a brief period before the night fell eerily silent.

"Ballistae!"

The shout from Aulus needed no further explanation. The great war machines' skeins squealed, and wood strained. Iron-tipped bolts, wrapped with pitch-soaked cloths, were quickly dipped into braziers, slapped into grooves, and shot into the darkness. The smaller bolt-throwers stayed silent, knowing their time would come soon. Fiery missiles slammed into the oak and pine trees on the forested foothills turning them into huge torches. Around the hillfort, coronas of light and fire sprang up.

"Oh, my ma's tits!" muttered Conchobhar as he watched the dark mass of beasts lope towards the fort. He had never imagined that so many wolves existed. Then he roared, "Light the braziers! Steady the wolfhounds!" Around the parapets and inside the walls, hundreds of fires were lit. From a distance, the fort looked as if it was on fire.

"Lock shields. Heft javelins. None pass." The harsh clang of iron rims sounded around the ramparts. Two ranks of scíatha stood resolute on the walkway. A much smaller reserve, led by Báine, Beacán, and Iasg, and supported by the hounds, stood alert in the square. All prayed to the Goddess that they would not be needed.

The wolves effortlessly bounded up the slopes towards the walls of Ráth Na Conall. Above the thunderous crack and crash of the ballistae, all—large and small—now in action, came the wailing ululations of Draighean, Danu, and Brighid. In the moonlight, all three stood on the north wall, naked, and arms stretched upward. The curling symbols that swathed their bodies absorbed the blue-white light of the moon and flowed like silver rivers.

Draighean swept her staff it in a wide circle. In the ditches and berms around the fort, blackthorn burst through the snow. Brighid and Danu glanced at the Sidhe with mounting concern. The demi-goddess fought to maintain the winter in the north while urging the blackthorn to sprout. Yet perhaps the most critical battle was keeping the Hag under control—or at least at bay. The strain visible on the normally marble-smooth face did not bode well.

Silverback howled at the unearthly trio. Countless volleys of missiles had visited unimagined violence and pierced his army's ranks, cleaving limbs and pinning many to the trees, the earth, and each other. *One day, the two-legs will destroy themselves.* He banished the crescendo of painful whimpering from his thoughts. There was little he could do to combat the witches or barbs, so he barked and snapped at those whose minds were weakened. He cursed the fort's halo of fire that took away the advantage of night vision. Urging the beast-host forward, he sensed they were close. But to what? Victory or annihilation?

"The blackthorn may slow them, but it will not stop the beasts," said Conchobhar. "Their hides are too thick, and their paws are well used to the brambles and thorns of the wildwood."

Conchobhar looked at Aoibheann and smiled. She had made it clear she intended to stand and fight on the wall and looked comfortable in the armour and chainmail he insisted she wore. Given the unusual circumstances of the trio's performance on the parapet and the introduction to the war machines, Conchobhar thought Aoibheann had coped surprisingly well.

Danu stretched to pick up the bow and quiver of arrows, resting against the palisade. She smiled at Brighid's look of scepticism. "Time to see if we've inherited our ma's ability to send an arrow to its target in the night," she rasped, her voice husky with the strain of the incantations. Brighid chortled and took up her own bow and quiver.

"Let's see which of us kills the big bastard that leads them."

Silverback snapped at the black shafts that sprouted from his fur and cursed the witches who stood, dark silhouettes against the burning braziers. He saw the flowing rivers of power that swirled over their skin and hesitated for the first time. *Who were they? How could they see in the dark? Was their mother part-wolf?* The humans' barbs were an irritation and did little to slow Silverback. Several bounds, and he crested the berm protecting the fort. Strong rear legs launched him at the wooden stockade.

"I hope there's a decent seanchaí in the fort," said Brighid as she watched the tide of wolves flow over the berm with apparently effortless ease, and jump the fort's ditches. At Danu's raised eyebrow, she added, "A naked Sidhe, two stark-naked rígana, and a massive wolf attack. Even a half-witted poet or storyteller could make an epic ballad from that material."

Danu grinned at her sister and then picked up and balanced two short-hafted axes in her hands. "My concern is whether our beautiful designs are as effective as chainmail." To her left, Draighean chuckled before flexing the curved knives that had appeared in her hands.

Brighid shook her head. "I hope she teaches us that trick. Where did she hide those?"

The flickering torches and brazier flames attributed a nightmarish element to the horde that leapt the perimeter ditches. Hurled from the parapet, hundreds of javelins pierced tough hides and wounded many. Yet they only killed a few. The injured, unable to climb the wooden stockade, howled in frustration. They yelped as pack members dug long talons into their flesh, using them to leap upwards.

"Clever bastards," muttered Conchobhar.

Around the fortifications, the sound of fangs and claws biting and scratching for purchase on the timber grated on the garrison's ears. "At times like these, don't you wish for smooth stone walls?" said Brighid, thinking fondly of the almost glacial high walls of their home of Lugudunon.

"Remind me the next time we rebuild," replied a sarcastic Danu.

About to add more, Danu spotted the first snouts and paws struggling to scramble over the fence and heard the frantic scraping of rear legs seeking purchase on the wood. A step forward and Danu's axe completed the short arc that cleaved the beast's skull. All along the walkway, warriors—men and women from thirteen summers up—stabbed at the snarling, slavering tide flowing over the walls.

Silverback's strong hind legs propelled him upwards, and claws hauled him over the stockade. Landing on the wooden walkway, the huge wolf snarled and snapped at any two-legs. Drool and foam flew as he bit and worried any who crossed his path—man or beast. Hearing the voices of the witches, he turned in their direction.

The alpha howled for support, and the dashes came to him as he pushed towards the rígana. He knew the packs needed to keep moving.

They could not stand and fight. That was a strength of two-legs, not wolves. Speed, the isolation of the weak, and strong jaws and teeth were their weapons.

On the broad parapet, the front row of the red shield-wall pushed forward, giving no gap for more beasts to surmount the stockade. Iron stabbed and slashed the muzzles of Silverback's army. Thrown back from the fence, their shrieking increased. Many, unable to defend themselves, found themselves preyed upon by those who had yet to climb the ramparts. It was the wolf way.

Finally stemming the assault, the two ranks of shield-warriors on the walkway formed a run, encircling the battlements. It was reinforced by a hedge of spears more deadly than blackthorn spines. Large groups of wolves charged around the arena, snapping and biting. It was an army with deep reserves of stamina, for the wolves' way of life relied on enduring beyond any other animal. Still, Silverback knew that caught between two human walls, his army would run until eventually exhausted and then die. Already the attack on the fortress walls had slowed and soon would cease.

Wolfhounds howled in the ráth's courtyard, wanting to join the attack. Silverback growled and cursed any beast that would serve man. Where was their pride? His brief diversion from the walkway's battle made the great wolf bare his teeth. It looked as if he was smiling. *A weakness.* Once more, the alpha's call summoned his army, and like a general, he issued orders. Like a surging river, the wolves charged along the walkway and, with incredible discipline, ignored the humans.

Danu twisted her head around frantically. "What's happening?" she yelled at Brighid. A shrug of Brighid's blood-splattered shoulders was her reply.

Twenty paces away, Aoibheann clapped a hand to her mouth and shrieked, "No!" On the western ramparts, a crashing wave of beasts slammed against a section of the shield-wall. Taken unawares, men and beasts cascaded from the walkway and tumbled into the courtyard. But that was not the danger. Howling, Silverback gathered his followers, and they bounded along the parapet towards the gap in the shield-wall.

"The Hag help us!"

A blood-splattered Fainche, intent on using Maolán's mace to smash any wolf's skull who came close enough, referred not to the hundreds of wolves falling into the market square. Her eyes were fixed on Silverback, who, followed by over a hundred others, had leapt the gap between the defences and the Great Hall. The building's sloping thatched roof provided a much better purchase for claws, and Silverback scrambled upwards before starting to tear at the thatch. Others followed his lead.

"Rear rank, to the square!" bellowed Conchobhar.

✷✷✷

Beacán looked at Iasg and Báine. The emotion on his face was new to him—a father's anxiety. Yet he could not let his fear overwhelm his need to command. That was a sure path to tragedy. He roared, "Master of the Hounds, control your dogs. Give them targets to kill instead of abandoning them to their own natures. Mimic the wolf pack—isolate and destroy." A chastened wolfhound leader dipped his head and began to whistle orders.

"Báine and Iasg. Take half of the reserve and enter the Great Hall. Protect the children," snapped Beacán. Turning to the remaining warriors, he said, "We will hold the entrance to the hall. We will die rather than let any beast past us."

In the Great Hall, Aoife wondered at the scratching noises coming from the ceiling. Then she watched dust particles and flakes of straw float down like a soft snowfall. Soon heavier chunks of thatch fell, crashing to the slatted wooden floor. Now, through increasingly wider gaps, she could see the myriad stars of the winter sky. The scene unfolding fascinated Aoife, and she wondered how such a thing could happen. A low growl from one of the holes and the appearance of a dark muzzle answered her question. Aoife turned to her mother and pointed. She did not have to say any words.

"Everyone to the platform. *Now!*" Ceara looked anxiously around the hall and at her defenders. Mothers, either pregnant or with young children, those between childhood and adolescence, and the elderly and the frail. An ashen-faced Flann gripped a spear and hauled himself to his feet.

Ceara heaved a partial sigh of relief at the racks of spears. *Foresight or premonition.* Then she called out, "Anyone who can hold a spear, grab one. Overturn the long tables and chairs. Drag the braziers to the platform. Bring anything that can be used as a barricade. Quickly! We have little time."

The first thud on the timber floor ended the preparations. The young wolf, eager to prove his mettle, fell through the gaping hole in the roof. His only reward was pain, the dull crack of ribs, and a broken spine. Paralysed, he whimpered and waited for death. The adolescent had misjudged the drop, but he was not the only one to make that error and soon had several companions. A few fell into the still glowing firepits. Silverback howled, and the packs learned. Using the Hall's great oak crossbeams, they reduced the descent to a manageable drop.

Ceara looked along the line of her defenders. All wore grim, determined faces. She knew the mothers would fight fiercely and show no mercy to protect their children. They would die if needed. Her concern was for the young boys and girls and the elderly, whose spears, gripped in weak, untrained hands, wavered uncontrollably. "Use the table and benches to steady your spears. Hold firm," she shouted. It was as if a challenge had been issued. At the sound of Ceara's voice, the wolves turned and attacked.

Spear tips toppled the braziers, spilling glowing embers onto the floor before the high table. Yelps filled the room as the initial rush of animals found hot cinders stuck to their paws. Scrambling for purchase on the wood, they slid into open firepits or crashed against the platform's edge, only to be impaled on leaf-shaped iron spearheads. At a howl from Silverback, the wolves surged forward again.

Screams, both animal and human, filled the air. Blood splashed Ceara's face, but this time it was the one who stood by her as a heavy silver wolf snapped, and fangs ripped an artery. Staring into its white eyes, she swore and stabbed at the beast, carving a gash along its snout. Silverback howled and retreated a few paces.

Ceara sensed that the great animal was unwell. Foam flew when it shook its head, and it seemed as if its back legs were not fully coordinated. *Shite, no! Not this, too.* Frantically, she glanced around to see if any had been bitten. Another beast before her distracted her attention. Arm muscles burned, and she lunged.

When the front doors burst open, Ceara was horrified. More wolves would make their defence impossible. "Báine!" shouted Aoife. Ceara's newly raised hopes were abruptly dashed when the huge wolf jumped and slammed into her, knocking her over. Her spear fell, clattering to the floor beyond her reach. She watched the powerful beast close on her. Drool flowed from its mouth, splashing her face as it straddled her. Its maw opened, showing rows of teeth interspersed with long fangs. The beast howled and then yelped in pain and surprise.

"Stay away from my ma, tuilí!"

Clumsily but as firm as her small hands could grip, Aoife stabbed once again at the beast's face. Taking a pace forward, she edged the beast away from her ma. Across the hall, Aoife heard a shriek from Báine and quickly prayed to the Goddess for rescue. Yet Aoife proved once more to be wise beyond her years. She watched the beast circle and then turn to advance and noticed its back legs were stiff as if frozen and its mouth slack. Weak barks from the beast pointed to it having difficulties breathing.

Silverback knew his time had come. The madness had run its course. He snorted that his end would come at the hands of a small female human. Yet she was brave and perhaps it was fitting that she should be the one to deliver his death. Mustering his strength and uttering one last howl, he advanced on Aoife and was gratified she showed no sign of retreat. *She will be a leader among the two-legs.* The lunge of the spear was guided by the Goddess, but the courage that propelled it belonged to Aoife. The leaf-shaped spearhead bypassed the wolf's teeth, plunged down the beast's throat, and into its heart.

∗∗∗

The last wolves were put down or driven off as the dawn skies approached. In one part of Ráth Na Conall's public square lay rows of bodies—warriors, mothers, the elderly, and children. Given the penetrating cold, decaying corpses were not an issue, and there was no great urgency to burn the bodies. The departed were already in Tír Tairngire, Tír Na nÓg, or Mag Mell. Yet it was not good for the residents of the hillfort to be reminded of the attack. Thus, Danu ordered the funeral pyres to burn day and night.

Alongside Conchobhar, Aoibheann rubbed a smudge of blood from her cheek and thanked the Goddess for the lives of her son and daughter. "The wolf pelts will keep the tanners busy and everyone warm for the rest of the winter," remarked Conchobhar, absent-mindedly scratching at bite marks on his forearm. Aoibheann looked anxiously at Danu.

At Aoibheann's glance, Danu's eyes widened. It was common knowledge that a substantial number of the wolves were infected with the madness. "Report to the druids, Conchobhar," ordered Danu. Conchobhar stopped scratching and, about to protest, looked at the faces of Danu and Aoibheann. Nothing on either of their faces said he had a choice.

CHAPTER 23

At first, it was the victims of bites from infected wolves. There was little anyone could do, except make them comfortable and hold their hands until the mná-sidhe took them. The druids had no remedies save roots and plants that dulled the mind and lowered the pain. Those with good friends who had sharp blades met the bean-sidhe on their own terms. The funeral pyres burned, and kin and friends wept.

Danu and Brighid stood at the foot of Conchobhar's cot. He had fought the madness for a cycle of the moon, but eventually, it overwhelmed him. Normally calm and organised, he swung from bouts of clarity to loss of memory, anxiety, confusion, and agitation. Beset by constant hallucinations, sleep deserted him. At his side sat Aoibheann, her face haggard from not eating or sleeping, and her eyes red from continual crying. She looked at Danu.

"Why?"

Danu had no answer. She sensed the presence of the bean-sidhe, for, at one time, she had been at death's door. A hoarse whisper caught her attention. "Come closer, my queen." The hazel eyes seemed brighter, and behind them, the mind clearer. Hope rose in her breast, but the man she had grown to love shook his head.

"It is not to be, Danu. The bean-sidhe awaits."

A cascade of tears splashed Conchobhar's chest. Pain reared up in his eyes as he fought for clarity. Gripping Aoibheann's hand, he placed it on Danu's and whispered, "My love is your new battle commander." The room fell silent until Aoibheann screamed, "No!" and fell across her lover. The bean-sidhe had guided Conchobhar beyond the veil.

∗∗∗

Inside and outside the hillfort, skinned wolf carcasses and splashes of red broke the stark whiteness of the landscape. Shielding her eyes from the unrelenting glare, Danu tramped around a snowbound hillfort rampant with disease.

"What price will you pay for victory?" Danu recalled Draighean's words. Was the blood cost too high? Was this all her fault?

The druids under Scolai were overwhelmed. Even Draighean had volunteered her hitherto unrevealed healing skills. The Sidhe railed against what she deemed the barbaric practices of the druids. That said, Danu strongly suspected that, for many under Draighean's care, her remedy was a sharp blade and a meeting with the bean-sidhe. But was that good or bad?

Danu brushed the back of her hand across her nose and winced at the pain from inflamed and broken flesh and the unrelenting flow of snot. She coughed, spitting up a melange of blood, phlegm, and other pale-coloured fluids and wiped her mouth with the linen rag she now carried. *The people cannot see my weakness.* At first, her pain had been sharp, like the stabbing of a broken rib but now, her constant companion just throbbed and throbbed.

Brighid had not moved from her cot in three sunsets. Danu shook her head and sneezed to clear her nostrils. On her earlier visit, she had to fight her way through an atmosphere thick with stale sweat and bodily wastes. How did Báine sit by Brighid's cot from sunrise to sunrise and not succumb? That she would have no one, save Brighid, to sit by her cot and mop her brow brought tears to Danu's eyes.

Keeping her roiling stomach under control, Danu had held Brighid's moist, limp hand and forced herself to make conversation. As with her previous visits, Brighid gave no response. Only the steady rise and fall of breasts told of her sister's fight for life. Danu took hope from the mutual throb of their feirdhríseacha.

As Danu gazed around the fort, she knew her family's story was not unique but was repeated hundreds of times, whether slave, freeman or noble. The sounds of disease and mourning filled her ears from sunrise to sunset. Even during the night, they were unrelenting. The tears of mothers and curses of fathers, helpless to prevent the cries of babies and children too young to understand, filled the air. For the people, loyalty to the Goddess stretched almost to breaking.

Danu's muscles ached. Stooped and with teeth gritted, she walked around the parapet. The great wolf fur draped on her shoulders seemed an unbearable weight. This morning the burden of her armour had been too much, and it lay abandoned on her bedchamber floor.

Following the wolf attack, she and Brighid had tramped the walkway together, morning, meán lae, and evening. Now she was alone. Those with the strength, a diminishing number, waved and cheered her presence. She traded sympathies and hopes for their well-being. In a dark time, she became their beacon of light and hope. It was a terrible burden to bear, and, alone in her chamber, Danu wept and wished for the arms of her ma and da.

It should not have been a surprise to her, and for that, she cursed her inexperience and, in unwarranted penance, flogged her mind. *Why was I not more prepared?* The fort overflowed with people of all ages, from newborns to those not far from crossing the veil. Conditions, at first cramped, soon became unsanitary. Infection did not refuse the invitation. The first wave of death came from those bitten by wolves that carried the madness.

Yet that tragedy proved a small part of the tithe Fate levied. Coughs and snuffles grew into a raging torrent of pain, fluid-filled lungs, and wasted bodies. Disease, and rotting, blackened fingers and toes from the frost, ravaged the residents of Ráth Na Conall. Those in the newly built shelters outside the fort fared better. Angry eyes soon dulled to hopeless resignation. Prayers and sacrifices to the Goddess peaked and then ceased. What use had she been?

Hundreds of bodies lay wrapped in shrouds outside the perimeter. Few looked at them, taking consolation that their loved ones were in a better place. Paths were cut in the snow to small clearings. In those glades, the funeral pyres burned from sunrise to sunset. The stench of burning flesh was abhorrent, but it was a reminder that, for the moment, they had survived. Clothes, property, and shelters were burned to stem the path of the disease.

"When?" The fur fell from Danu's shoulders and, with arms raised, she reached up to the skies.

"Soon," replied the Goddess. "But first you need rest."

With a wave of the Goddess's hand, Danu slumped to the walkway and rolled over its edge.

✳✳✳

"Don't you think you've slept enough?"

A startled Danu's eyes opened to see what appeared to be a healthy Brighid. *Thank the Goddess.* In the background stood Beacán, Iasg, and Draighean. *Maybe I'm not alone.* "How long?" she croaked.

"Since your impressive dive off the rampart?" asked Brighid. "You were lucky we had the snow." The relief in Brighid's voice was unmistakable. "That was about seven sunsets ago." Brighid pursed her lips and looked like she was considering something for the first time. "Strangely, that was also when our troubles began to recede… and quite rapidly at that.

"I'm sure you're starving. Hot food and drinks are waiting to be served." Brighid's nose crinkled. "But perhaps a bath first. You stink," she added with a grin. "Then you can get dressed and eat with the rest of us."

A pale leg slid from under the furs, and bare toes felt the wooden floor as if testing her strength. Brighid turned to the others and smirked. "I told you she's a stubborn bitseach."

CHAPTER 24

393 B.C.—Imbolg

Imbolg was celebrated without further drama or tragedy. The faint fragrance of spring, carried on a breeze rather than a howling wind, refreshed the spirits of those within Ráth Na Conall. The snows were in retreat, and farmers praised the Goddess as the first green shoots of new life forced their way through the icy crust.

"Soon, we'll be knee-deep in mud," grumbled Brighid.

In a small side-room off the Great Hall, four women met. A decision had to be made. "We don't know you. Yet you are highly, if tragically, recommended. Flann would be my logical choice for commander of the garrison. Yet he remains several cycles of the moon from being fully fit. Indeed, he may never be the warrior he used to be."

Aoibheann held Danu's eyes without flinching and ignored the presence of Draighean. Since Conchobhar's death, a hardness had crept into her intense blue gaze. Only the lady's deep love for her children tethered her to sanity. Danu awaited a response, but it did not come.

Yet something bothered Danu. Something scratched at a scab in her memory. Her sigils and the rose between her breasts throbbed as if sharing a jest. Both twins' senses had acutely improved since their performance on the ramparts. Deep within her, Danu knew that Aoibheann had a secret and she did not want it brought into the light. A whisper from Brighid brought a smile to Danu's face. It broadened when she saw wariness in Aoibheann's eyes.

"Your style of dress has changed with the better weather. I cannot recall seeing you in a sleeveless léinte—until today." Aoibheann's eyes widened imperceptibly to anyone but the three before her. "Indulge us. Please remove the pelt, stand, and turn around." Anxiety, although well-controlled, flickered on the lady's face. Resignedly, she laid the fur draped over her shoulders on the seat.

"Even I missed that," said Draighean, revelling in her ward's perception.

"The design on your right arm is quite rare, my lady. Indeed, I know of only one other woman, and a fierce one at that, who bears that particular tattoo. It is a sigil worn only by warriors of the Ulaid's famed Cróeb Ruad. Is it not?" said Danu.

Beside her, Brighid slapped the table with glee. "I knew it!"

Aoibheann nodded and smiled, although her eyes held sadness at something long lost. "My older sister, Bláithín Ni Neill, wears its twin. A ridiculous fight over an even stupider man sundered us." A tear rolled down her cheek. "Is she well?"

"She is the rígan of Ráth Cavares in Gaul and the hand-fast partner of our uncle, Brocc," said Brighid.

Only by grasping the back of her chair did Aoibheann overcome the shock of Brighid's declaration and an unseemly collapse to the floor. "But what of Cuán Ó Neill?"

"You were right in your assessment of that man. Cuán fomented a rebellion against our father. An assassin killed him—although not one paid by my da." Brighid's eyes smouldered at the memory but then grew sad at the rift between the sisters.

"The arsehole!" growled Aoibheann, and another tear rolled over her cheek. "Such a waste, a sundered relationship, and all for nothing."

"The Goddess has strange ways of guiding and rewarding her people," said Danu. "When you win a great victory for us over Uallachán and Maine, you have my promise of a sea journey to the Great Sea and a celebration of sisters reunited."

"I assume you're offering me the honour of leading Ráth Na Conall's army?"

Danu looked at Brighid and nodded. "Based on our knowledge of your sister and that design, we'd be stupid not to. Well, Battle Commander, how will you ensure we can keep our vows—to our people and you?"

"I'm curious. Why did you hide the symbol? Most carry it with pride," asked Brighid.

A long, sorrowful sigh preceded Aoibheann's answer. "I, too, married an eejit. Afraid that the combination of my northern accent and tattoo would upset Uallachán, he ordered it covered at all times. He was quite forceful in his insistence." It was only then that Danu noticed the faint shadows of repeated bruising. She growled. Aoibheann shrugged. "I had young children."

Aoibheann straightened her shoulders as if wishing to draw a line under the past. She looked at the rígana and her eyes narrowed before she said, "Sisters who are close often make the same mistakes."

"Very true," murmured Draighean.

✳✳✳

As she stumbled through the broken-down gateway, the waif slipped, landing in a pool of slush. She swore at the icy water that numbed her arse. Perhaps fifteen summers old and skeletal, she wore a haunted look. The demeanour was unsurprising. She bore a burden no child should ever have to carry on her shoulders.

She was the last of her family. At the height of the winter, when all seemed lost, her ma and da had laid the girl on her cot. Then they swathed her in all the furs and coverings the family possessed. The remaining food, milk, and water were set within her reach. Finally, each of them, older brothers, sisters, parents, and grandparents, said a prayer, kissed her, and walked out into the whiteness.

At winter's end, she found her family huddled together and frozen in death. Several cycles of the moon passed before her family thawed enough for her to pry them apart and drag them to the pyre she had built. During that time, she visited them every sunset and with each sunrise, her tears and guilt at surviving increased. It was not the girl's fault, yet she assumed the responsibility for her family's fate.

That it did not crush her, even when she longed to throw herself on the roaring funeral fire, testified to her strength. She cursed the Goddess but perhaps the Goddess had made the right choice. There were too many memories and ghosts at her home, and she decided to move on.

Her shouted curse made Nuadha look up from chopping firewood. He watched the intruder rise from the pool of slush and brush lumps of ice from rags that hung on a scrawny frame. Whether male or female, he could not determine. For her part, she had not seen or talked to anyone in a long time. Thus, the presence of Nuadha startled her as much as she did him. She had thought the ruins of the farmholding deserted.

"May I shelter for the night?" she called out. "I will cause no trouble and am not a thief."

A girl. Was that good or bad? A torrent of memories cascaded through Nuadha, and none were pleasant. For a long time, he had buried any remembrances of the abuse and pain Uallachán and he had inflicted on others of her age and younger. Now in the shape of one emaciated child, his past came back to haunt him. He looked skywards. *Why? Why tempt me like this? She does not deserve to be my trial.*

The girl was observant, her sense of smell sharp, and her intuition flawless. "I can hunt and set traps. If you can build a fire, we could share roasted meat for our evening meal."

Clever little witch. Yet there was no malice in Nuadha's thought, which surprised him. He chuckled for the first time in many summers and liked the sound. Nodding to the girl, he said, "Yes, for the night." Then he looked at her drenched rags.

"There are dry clothes in the small hut. They're from the previous owners. Better you change than I waste my stock of herbs to stop your nose from ceaselessly running and your lungs from filling with fluid."

Nuadha looked around at the main roundhouse. "My home is not much, but it is dry when it rains."

She smiled, and for her, it was the first since her family departed. "Thanks. Are there traps?" Nuadha dipped his head. "Good, I'll change and then start laying the snares."

CHAPTER 25

Maine paced the floor of Chrúachain's Great Hall. His face was flushed red but with anger rather than the icy northerly winds, which scoured all exposed flesh. The winter had been the severest anyone had known. Maine blamed the witches at Ráth Na Conall, which, while accurate, was not due to any deduction or insight of the Connachta king. He simply needed someone to blame.

Even the clann's seanchaithe could not recall stories of any similar season. Great drifts of hard-packed snow made movement impossible. Thousands of dead from the cold and disease had broken the spirit of the people and weakened the Connachta armies. One further consequence was the focus of Maine's current ire—the delay of the Ráth Na Conall campaign.

The festival of Bealtaine would be celebrated in two cycles of the moon. In Maine's calculations, he should have already breached Ráth Na Conall's walls and destroyed Conall Mac Gabhann's bitseacha and legacy. Maine had planned to celebrate Bealtaine, watching Ráth Na Conall burn and seeing Conall's daughters' heads on spikes.

However, instead of bogs and ground hardened by winter frosts and able to withstand ten thousand pairs of boots, Maine looked out on fields knee-deep in slush and mud. The Connachta army could not tramp through this terrain without making the ground worse. He swore openly at the Goddess, and that was imprudent.

Something had to be done. A start on the campaign needed to be made. Maine had thick tresses of red hair and long red whiskers like his brothers. He twisted and pulled on the latter, perhaps in the hope that pain would be his inspiration. It did not work, and so instead, he rumbled, "Cairbre had better follow my orders."

***

Cairbre strode through the muddy quagmire of Caher Conri's courtyard and grimaced as his *bróga iallacha* quickly became sodden. His winter boots showed signs of rot, and yet he was fortunate. Most of his men did not have the luxury of additional pairs of footwear. Many had been reduced to walking barefoot in the harshest winter in memory. Hence, flesh rotted instead of leather. A considerable number had blackened toes and foul-smelling feet. Most were missing toes, but better that than disease. Still, his veterans had kept a spare pair of *bróga* to use in the battles ahead.

The stench of decay and infection as Cairbre entered the ruins of Caher Conri's Great Hall made him gag. Even the brisk wind that flowed through the ruins could not dissipate the smell. In a far corner, isolated from his men, Uallachán was partially visible under a mountain of furs. Still seething at his neglectful treatment, he scowled as Cairbre approached.

"Get your men on their feet." Cairbre's nose crinkled, he shook his head, and his lips curled into a sneer. "Kill any who cannot stand and fight, which I suspect is most of this rabble." Cairbre continued, "Send messengers to the nobles still loyal to you. Command them to assemble here in a cycle of the moon. We march on Cnoc Duíginn."

Uallachán roused himself and stood, albeit shakily. He had had little exercise during the storms, apart from going for a piss and, from the pungent smell surrounding him, he had abandoned that some time ago. As Cairbre departed the ruins, Uallachán cursed the Connachta king and called his shield-man. "Check our warriors. Send the unwell to Mag Mell." As he spoke, it dawned on Uallachán that he had become little more than a messenger for Maine and Cairbre. *Could this get any worse?*

✷✷✷

"We need to know the situation in Cnoc Duíginn. They are our forward eyes, yet we have heard nothing from Sláine." Palms on the solid oak table, Danu spoke. Her tone was business-like, yet the anxiety in her eyes could not be hidden.

"Sláine, like his father, cannot be trusted," growled Draighean.

Around the table from Danu and Brighid sat most of the Chomhairle. Onchú would arrive from Curraghatoor in two or three sunsets. Scolai had demurred from attending the meeting, asserting that dealing with the aftermath of war, not the battle, was his job. Cináed, fully occupied with rebuilding the community and planning the planting of crops, had sent his apologies. Danu would brief him later.

All looked up at the opening of the chamber's door. Swollen with winter dampness, it dragged and scraped the floor. Danu dipped her head in acknowledgement of a dishevelled Báine's muttered apologies. Brighid smirked, ignoring the glare from Báine.

The room's mood was sombre. Yet there was relief that the tribulations of the winter were behind them. Ráth Na Conall had once again become a hive of activity. While remaining overcrowded, inside and outside the fort, the bustle was one of purpose, not despair. For those who had decided to make the hillfort's domain their home, temporary dwellings were transformed into permanent structures.

New barracks were erected for warriors sworn to the nobles and chieftains allied with Ráth Na Conall as they began to drift in. Traders and artisans plied their crafts. The smell of normality—freshly baked bread, cooked meat, and peat fires—finally expelled the stronghold's miasma of death.

"I need someone to go to Cnoc Duíginn," said Danu.

"I'll go," responded Beacán.

Danu shook her head. "No. Aoibheann is still settling into her new role, and until Flann is fully active, we both need your counsel." Danu

257

chuckled. "Besides, uncle, you would hate a journey in these conditions." Danu rubbed her chin as if considering something that had just occurred to her.

"However, if you wish a break from the fort, you could ride to Clárach. It is a much shorter distance, and the ground through the forests is firmer. Perhaps Iasg and you could call on Aodh. The time to draw our forces together nears." Beacán dipped his head.

"Well, I guess that leaves me," said Brighid. The look on her face spoke of a task she considered dreary, but Danu was not fooled.

"Sister, you have begged incessantly to get away from the boredom of the fort. Make the preparations and take ten riders with you. That should be enough for protection but not to raise suspicions." A movement caught Danu's eye. She turned, smiled, and said, "Your concern is noted, Báine. Yet the land between Ráth Na Conall and Cnoc Duíginn remains a quagmire and definitely not suited to chariots."

✶✶✶

From the heights of Cnoc Duíginn, Sláine looked down on the force assembling at the foot of the mountain. His stomach felt empty and nauseous, although not through any lack of food or the presence of disease. The irony of his predicament made Sláine smile. The Rígana of Ráth Na Conall expected him to deliver forewarning of the Connachta advance. He doubted they expected that signal to be Cnoc Duíginn in flames.

He scratched the stubble on his chin, which was the only place on his body where hair flourished, and considered the armour laid out on his throne. What was the point? Sláine's strength was in his network of spies and informants. Cnoc Duíginn's garrison numbered fifty and had never fought more than minor skirmishes. The Connachta and Uallachán's force numbered over two thousand warriors.

Make a deal. It was an alternative Sláine had to consider, but what did he have to bargain with? He had no significant numbers of warriors to add to the Connachta and no vital intelligence. Maine's spies and informants would know as much as he. A thought, although not his own, slipped into his mind. *Your father betrayed Conall and the Sidhe, Mongfhionn. That did not go well for him.* Sláine sighed and turned his deliberations to the safety of his people.

Cnoc Duíginn had a secret—a labyrinth of tunnels and hidden doorways in the fort's thick stone walls. Most led to the silver mines or the marshes north of the hillfort. The pathways were known only to a small, trusted group. Sláine turned to his shield-man. "Use the tunnels to evacuate the elderly and the women and children. A score of the warriors will lead the way; the same number will protect the rear." Sláine's stalwart companion nodded and barked orders to his captains.

"You, my king?"

The Rí of Cnoc Duíginn shook his head. "I will play the hero for a time."

The shield-man had served Sláine since they were both young men but had never been sure of the king's character. As he considered Sláine's words, he wished he had devoted much more time to understanding the man. "No matter what, I will remain at your side, as will ten others. The great cauldrons are filled. They bubble and smoke on the battlements, and the braziers glow. Even a clag has its day."

Sláine chuckled. "You'll have to help me with the armour. I don't recall ever having worn it."

✳✳✳

Beacán and Iasg borrowed several of the smaller, hardier horses from Báine's stables. As the mounts forged a path up the slippery slopes of Sléibhe na Clárach, they were glad of the animals' stubborn temperaments. Aodh's shield-man met them at Clárach's gateway and beamed approvingly at their choice of transport. Beacán recognised the broad-shouldered, muscular warrior from the Samhain festival. Big then, swathed in thick winter furs, he looked gargantuan.

"Aodh waits in the Great Hall." A scowl appeared on the face of Aodh's second-in-command. "And so does Glaisne."

Aodh sat at a large table laden with huge platters of meats, cheeses, fruits, and beverages. "Come, rest your legs and arses. Eat." Warmed by blazing firepits and glowing braziers, the large chamber was pleasantly warm and scented with peat and pine. Before long, Beacán and Iasg had little choice but to remove their outer furs. On the periphery of his vision, Beacán observed a sullen Glaisne lounging against the wall.

"How did ye fare during the winter?" asked Iasg.

"It was rough. Worst winter even the oldest of the tribe could remember. More deaths than usual." Aodh's face broke into a wry grin. "It's not all bad, though. The men and women were sequestered together for a season with nothing to do but keep warm and rut. I expect a good harvest of babies around Lugnasad."

The king held Beacán and Iasg's gaze. "We heard about the wolf attack and the disease that followed. I am sorry for your losses and especially that of Conchobhar. Isolated at Clárach, there was little my people could do but pray to the Goddess on your behalf."

"I know you would have helped if you could. We faced the storm, and our steel is forged stronger for it."

"You will stay overnight as my guests. I've invited my chieftains and nobles to eat with us this evening. It will let you get the measure of them, and we can discuss the levy of Clárach's armies." Aodh stopped, tugged on his long whiskers, and looked at Beacán. "A few will be the fathers of the ones killed on Na Comaraigh."

"The Hag's tits!" exclaimed Iasg, glad she had hidden a few knives in her garments. Beacán shrugged. Sadly, this was nothing new for him.

Aodh shook his head. "Most hold Glaisne to blame for their deaths, but just be aware. Parents can be irrational when it comes to their children." The king played with the ends of his blond whiskers as if unhappy to broach a subject. "Many chieftains are also unhappy that Labhraidh withdrew his support."

Beacán nodded. "I will address their concerns." In a lower tone, he added, "We have not heard from Cnoc Duíginn. Have you?" Aodh shook his head. Beacán added, "Brighid and a small band of riders leave in two sunsets for the fort." Aodh's head turned sharply to where Glaisne had stood but he was gone.

Glaisne's hearing was sharp, unsurprising, given his inclination for eavesdropping. Thus, his sudden alertness when Aodh's and Beacán's discussion turned to Cnoc Duíginn and Brighid. Even whispered words echoed off Clárach's walls.

I can use this. Glaisne had thought his ambitions to possess Danu and Ráth Na Conall thwarted. In his mind, he reasoned that the Goddess had opened a new door for him. Danu's would-be consort smiled to himself. He had the chance to separate that bitseach, Brighid, from her sister—permanently.

✳✳✳

Cairbre and his second-in-command looked with unconcealed disdain at Uallachán's warriors as they staggered closer to Cnoc Duíginn. The enforced march from Caher Conri, compounded by appalling land and weather conditions, made Uallachán's army look pathetic. They also walked a good one thousand paces behind the Connachta.

"We should let Uallachán's rabble bear the brunt of any aggressive defences and traps Sláine has prepared."

Yet the thought of the interminable crowing Uallachán would inflict on him should he overcome Cnoc Duíginn decided the matter for Cairbre. With a roar of *"Ionsaí!"* and keeping to the cover of the thickly wooded slopes, the Connachta attacked. Like Clárach, Cnoc Duíginn's main defensive strength was that it sat a stone-grey pimple on a mountain top. Its walls were thick and solid but should have been a spear's length higher. The ditch encircling the hillfort had, over many summers, filled with refuse, and many of its wooden stakes had rotted.

Sláine glanced at his shield-man and shrugged. He had been a poor steward, and Cnoc Duíginn's likely fate would be it razed to the ground. As the shouts of the Connachta became louder and siege ladders banged against the walls, he turned to one he considered a friend, grasped his hand, and said, "Thank you. Now burn the tuilithe."

Around the ramparts, men shouted defiantly and overturned the cauldrons and braziers. Sláine savoured the screams from below and the fragrance of burning Connachta flesh—if only briefly.

***

Two sunrises later, Sláine, dressed in a light tunic, stood on the broad stone ramparts of Cnoc Duíginn. He shivered in a blustery northern wind and the chill of the dawn. As he looked to the rising sun in the east, Sláine prayed silently to the Goddess, thanking her for his warriors' sacrifice.

To his left, eleven heads were spiked on spears lodged in cracks in the walkway. All had satisfied, proud looks frozen on their faces. And why not? They had killed or injured over two hundred Connachta and were now feasting in Mag Mell. For many generations, the clann's seanchaithe would remember the Battle of Cnoc Duíginn.

Cairbre and Uallachán stood ten paces to the side. The Connachta king had a perturbed look on his face. Sláine was undoubtedly the weakest of the ríthe, yet he had taken a terrible toll. For his part, Uallachán scowled at a victory which should have been his.

Sláine's consolation was the look of disappointment on Cairbre's and Uallachán's faces. The hillfort, apart from the small band of defenders, was deserted. Sláine watched the axe-man step forward and indicate the freshly cut tree stump. *At least I'm to be spared torture before death.*

The Rí of Cnoc Duíginn knelt, but before laying his neck on the wood, he looked up at Cairbre and grinned. *The Ulaid forces assemble on your borders. My revenge will be when Chrúachain burns.*

The smile drew a look of consternation from Cairbre. Few considered Sláine to be a brave man. What else could they be wrong about? As for Sláine, he died quickly and with the scent of pine as his final memory.

***

Cnoc Duíginn's messenger heaved a sigh of relief as he galloped away from the hillfort's final stand. The overthrow of the fort had provided the diversion that secured his escape. Now he cantered south towards Ráth Na Conall, grumbling at the mud and great pools of melted snow that slowed his progress.

As sunset approached, the envoy spotted a lone rider coming from the west. He moved at a quick canter and was apparently on a path to intercept him. The messenger quickly checked his weapons and slowed to a fast trot. At twenty paces, the stranger waved and shouted, "I am Glaisne Mac Aodh, Prince of Clárach, and am heading to Ráth Na Conall. If you're travelling in that direction, two swords will be better than one."

The evening meal passed with pleasant conversation, and Glaisne expressed his deep sorrow at the fall of Cnoc Duíginn. The envoy, pleased by Glaisne's sincerity, bade his companion goodnight, and sought a piece of dry land to sleep.

On the next sunrise, Glaisne mounted his horse and rode in the direction of Cnoc Duíginn. By his reckoning, he was a sunset ahead of Brighid and her riders. *Plenty of time to put my plan into action.* The messenger from Cnoc Duíginn, his throat cut, never rose from his bed.

Having finally arrived at Cnoc Duíginn, Glaisne had no knowledge of the power structure between the Connachta and Uallachán. Thus, he assumed Uallachán to be in charge and asked to be taken to the Rí of Caher Conri. For his part, and still smarting from Cairbre's contempt, Uallachán had no intention of alerting Cairbre to Glaisne's news.

CHAPTER 26

Brighid's mud-splattered riders finally reached the foothills of Cnoc Duíginn's mountain perch five sunsets after departing Ráth Na Conall. The landscape between the two rátha was a mix of flat or gently rolling pasture, cropland, and forests. In normal times, the ride was pleasant and, at a canter, could be travelled in two sunsets—less at a gallop. In the aftermath of the harsh winter, the land resembled the bogs covering much of central Ériu.

Sunset drew near as the party entered thickly wooded foothills. "We'll make camp here and get an early start for the fort in the morning," said Brighid. Sheltered by tall oaks and pines, the glade she chose gave protection from wind and rain and allowed for the comfort of a few small campfires. It had no other saving graces, and that made Brighid nervous. She imagined Beacán's disapproval and shouted orders as she dismounted.

"Dig traps and plant stakes around the perimeter. I want three on guard at all times: one to watch the horses and the others to patrol the boundary. Keep your weapons at your side."

Despite the precautions, Brighid slept fitfully, suffering a series of nightmares, each with increasing foreboding. She fought unsuccessfully to wrestle meaning from the dreams. Her body experienced waves of pinpricks as her senses reached out beyond the camp, searching... but for what? In her half-sleep, she wished Danu, her ma, or even Draighean were with her and could help unravel the visions. Her mind finally exhausted, Brighid drifted into sleep.

Dawn arrived, and the flushed pink horizon soon gave way to purple-grey clouds and drizzle. A smell, faint yet unmistakable, tickled Brighid's nostrils—woodsmoke, pitch, and roasted flesh. *Shite!* "On your feet. Mount up. *Now!*" Instinct and muscle memory came to the aid of the riders as they swung up and onto their mounts. Most grasped a small scíath in one hand and a mace in the other—blunt force trauma being practical and effective. Horses nickered and snorted. Long ears rotated, sweeping the forest.

The enemy was not artful. Loud shouts and the sounds of men crashing through forest floor greenery and debris announced their presence. *The Hag's arse! Did an army surround them?* Brighid's speculation proved to be not far from the mark. Uallachán had sent one thousand men into the foothills.

"Make the tuilithe pay! Ní ghéillfear, nó cúlú!" The battle cry of Clann Ui Flaithimh rose into the air and was immediately joined by the *kraa kraa* of ravens who rose from the forest floor.

Around the circle of riders, bodies formed a berm of the dead and dying. Many had skulls crushed by lumps of iron. Others lay maimed by javelins whose trembling wooden shafts were the only signs that the mná-sidhe had not taken them. Brighid pulled the last arrow from her quiver and scanned the battlefield for signs of Uallachán.

Frustrated, she screamed, "Coward!" before placing the barb in the eye of an attacker. Five of her band remained. From their lofty position, the riders fought bravely but in vain. Horses screamed as they were hamstrung, and they and their partners pulled to the forest floor and slaughtered.

Salty tears stung Brighid's eyes as she cried for her men and their horses. *Not again!* Her black feirdhris pounded furiously, and her arm muscles burned as she constantly swept her short-handled axes at any movement. Thigh muscles begged for relief from the constant pressure needed to control and position her mount. A whispered prayer to the Goddess and an "I'm sorry" to Danu escaped her lips.

Men shrieked as she slashed faces to the bone. Yet for each who fell, another replaced him… and another… and another. She felt her horse wet with sweat and blood. The mare shuddered under an onslaught of blows and then collapsed. Standing on its back, covered in gore, and bleeding from a multitude of cuts, Brighid shouted, "Ní ghéillfear, nó cúlú!" before leaping into the throng.

Uallachán's orders that she must be taken alive prolonged the battle and proved costly as warrior after warrior fell to her axes. It was, perhaps, one of the most incredible stands in Clann Ui Flaithimh's history. *Where's a seanachaí when you need him?* Brighid's ghoulish grin and the unearthly ululation from deep within made the warrior hesitate. Her axe rose and cleaved his skull. Too late, the glimmer of a smile made Brighid wary. The blow to the back of her head pitched her forward into the slush of blood and mud, and a nauseating blackness descended.

In Ráth Na Conall, Danu sat bolt upright in her cot and screamed, "No!"

✳✳✳

Ice-cold water roused Brighid. A fist to her mouth split her lip and almost sent her back into oblivion. Around her, she saw the skulls of her riders hanging from the attackers' belts. She noted each of their faces and promised retribution. Then she gasped in horror at the heads of the horses, each hacked off and spiked on spears. "Barbarians!" she mumbled through bloody and swollen lips and prayed there was a place in Mag Mell for the mounts.

Brighid inspected Uallachán's face. Bloated through gluttony, it resembled a sweating beeswax candle. His sour breath and heavy body odour made her stomach churn. *How could anyone follow such a man?* As his pale blue eyes took in her body—some kind person had relieved her of her armour and clothes and bound her wrists—a lecherous smile formed on his thin lips.

"So nice to finally meet one of Conall's daughters." The gloating expression added to the roiling in Brighid's belly.

"Póg mo thoin! You one-armed tuilithe."

The blow to her head almost broke Brighid's jaw, and she wondered if she still had a complete set of teeth. "My men and I have looked forward to enjoying your company." Uallachán paused and considered his next move. With one transaction, he could change the outcome of the game. "However, I have a proposition to save your, and maybe your sister's, skins." Brighid looked at him warily while tamping down the revulsion in her belly.

"What?"

"Become my hand-fast partner and reign as my rígan. Admit it, we are alike. Your bloodlust and fondness for terror make you my equal. By my side, there would be no sister to restrain your natural instincts and talents." For the most part, Brighid's expression looked carved in stone, except her eyes narrowed. Uallachán smiled triumphantly. *She's considering the offer.*

"Come closer," Brighid whispered through bruised and bloody lips. She shuddered when lank strands of hair stroked her cheeks as Uallachán lowered his head. The last sound Uallachán heard in his right ear was Brighid's snarl before her teeth sank into it, and she ripped the flesh from his head. Her mouth bloody, Brighid spat the ear at a screeching Uallachán's feet.

"Go rut a goat. That's about your level, although definitely not a pleasure for the goat."

The shriek of fury almost burst Brighid's eardrums. The knife to her chest took her back to the darkness.

✳✳✳

A pale-faced Danu appeared distracted as the Chomhairle gathered, along with representatives from Clárach and Curraghatoor. The agenda had only one item: to plan for the Connachta attack, with all agreed that the battle would likely commence before the feast of Bealtaine. That way, whoever was victorious could hold a grand celebration. It was the way of the Gaels.

Draighean watched Danu with growing concern. Danu's face showed extreme pain, shadows of bruises appeared to grow more definite, and blood trickled from her lips. But what was the source of her agonies? Before long, the others present followed the Sidhe's stare. Mutters of "What is going on?" rippled around the table.

The explanation sought never came. Danu rose, pounded the oak table with her fists until the wood was stained with her blood, and screamed, "Betrayed!" That she collapsed shortly after saved Danu from causing more injury to herself. Draighean, the fastest to react, ordered Danu's shield-men to carry the rígan to her chamber. The Sidhe, Beacán, and Iasg followed in their wake and were quickly joined by Aodh, Aoibheann, and Onchú.

With no apology, Draighean ripped open Danu's delicate linen gown. "The Hag!" swore Beacán, Iasg bit her fist, and the Sidhe uttered dark oaths of vengeance. Across Danu's body, bruises and cuts appeared as if she had been kicked and punched repeatedly. Yet compared to the open wound that materialised, all other injuries paled into insignificance. Draighean swore in an unearthly language as she watched Danu's pink feirdhris turn black, and its petals drip blood.

"Brighid is betrayed!" Gathering her strength, Danu threw off the hands of those who tried to restrain her and suddenly sat up. Mercifully, she then succumbed to unconsciousness.

"Who? Who does she speak of?" asked Beacán.

Aodh turned to Beacán. "Following your visit, Glaisne evaded the Clárach sentries and has not been seen for many sunsets. I fear my brother's intentions are revealed."

Draighean turned to Beacán and Iasg. "Danu's connection to Brighid is much deeper than I or anyone anticipated. Each appears vital for the other's survival." Battling emotions totally foreign to her, Draighean's eyes became dark and glacial. "If Brighid dies, the blood tie will be sundered, and Danu will suffer the same fate. Ráth Na Conall will fall, and southern Ériu will be enslaved.

"The druids and I will manage Danu's physical condition. But only reuniting Danu with Brighid will preserve both lives." The Sidhe drew herself up and looked at Beacán. "Take as many as you see fit. Ride quickly to Cnoc Duíginn. I will firm the ground for your ride. Kill any who get in your way. Bring back Brighid." A grim smile appeared on the Sidhe's red lips.

"Then I shall dispense retribution."

***

The sharp pain near her heart made Brighid sob. By lying very still on the damp dirt floor, she slowed the blood flow and reduced the agony, although not by much. She thought of Danu and the pain she had suffered when the axe buried itself in her chest. *I'm sorry, Danu, but how could I understand—until now?*

As the cell door opened, Brighid's neck bones crunched like shingle as she twisted to get a better view of her visitor. Glaisne entered, full of hubris and grinning broadly. At his heel were two beefy warriors. Brighid laughed. Yet the act sent her body into agonising pains, and the chest wound opened. She felt the iron ankle shackles and chuckled.

"Even like this, you fear me and rightly so."

"Bitseach. I fear neither you nor your stupid sister. Danu will submit to me, Ráth Na Conall will be mine, and you will be dead."

"She may be infatuated with you, but that will pass. Do you seriously think you'd be anything more than a token rí? If so, you're an even bigger fool than I imagined." Brighid coughed and spat blood from her lips. "If you think Danu will kneel before you, you obviously don't know my sister. She is much stronger, more cold-hearted, and measured than me. I am the fire to her ice."

Brighid laughed painfully, gritted her teeth, and struggled to sit up. "Do you think that Danu does not know of your treachery? She sees everything I see, knows everything I know, and feels every blow, broken bone, and wound as if it were her body." Brighid paused to let the pain recede and inhaled deeply. "And you have not considered the Sidhe, Draighean."

In the gloom of the cell, Glaisne shivered as he felt Brighid's eyes darken and bore into him. "Glaisne of Clárach, you are a dead man, and your path has one destination—the Otherworld." Disconcertingly, Brighid glanced over Glaisne's shoulder. "The bean-sidhe stands behind you. She knows your death is near."

Brighid winced as Glaisne took a step forward, intent on adding more bruises to Brighid's body. He stopped only because the cell door swung open and Cairbre walked in, followed by Uallachán. The Connachta rí snarled, "We have rules for the nobility. You will not touch the Rígan of Ráth Na Conall."

Glaisne did not know Cairbre and, infuriated at being interrupted, looked to Uallachán. "I am Cairbre, Rí of the Connachta. *I* command here. Look at *him* again, and your head will join those on the walls." Glaisne's Adam's apple rose and fell several times. He gulped, stammered an apology, bowed, and kneeled. Cairbre chuckled, and it was not a pleasant sound.

His face, already like thunder, looked even more fearsome in the flickering rushlights as Cairbre turned to face Uallachán. "Why did you not inform *me* of her capture? A foolish omission and one for which a price will be paid. Brighid is a valuable piece in this game and her fate is in Maine's hands—not yours." The cell filled with the silence of promised retribution until Brighid coughed raggedly.

By the light of the torches, Cairbre observed the naked form of Brighid. Many bruises and lacerations covered her body, but the swirling sigils and black feirdhris intrigued him. While the symbols swathing Brighid's body appeared dormant, the rose pulsated as if gathering strength. And that made Cairbre wary. The designs brought long-buried memories of his mother to the front of Cairbre's mind. Many things were spoken of Medb and her appetites, but none doubted her powers—at least none who lived.

He looked into Brighid's eyes, but even in the half-light, Cairbre could not hold her intense gaze. A smile parted Brighid's lips, revealing blood-stained teeth. Cairbre looked at Uallachán's ravaged ear and smiled. She had fought with everything she possessed. However, of more concern to Cairbre, nothing in Brighid's mien spoke of defeat. Everything pointed to a mountain lincse biding her time before striking.

"Even in this state and in this gloom, I can see the danger in your eyes. I will not free you from this cell, but this I will do." Before exiting, Cairbre barked an order to his shield-man. "See that the rígan's wounds are tended to."

***

With a glance upward, Brighid sent a brief prayer to the Goddess. Yet she had doubts about her standing with that deity, and therefore the supplication lacked conviction.

"I'm not sure why you peer at the ceiling when I am standing over here." The voice held tones of mocking, rebuke, and humour. Yet there was no doubting its authority.

"Oh, shite!"

The laughter that filled the cell was deafening, and Brighid wondered how it was not heard everywhere in Cnoc Duíginn. "I think I like your family because of their honesty, although it is sometimes quite brutal and irreverent. I pride myself on having not wiped your line from the face of the earth. Fate claims that it is he who tempers my wrath. I disagree."

"Why are you here, Goddess?"

"Your father is my Hand, and your mother is my Huntress." The pause that followed seemed to last a long time but likely was brief. "You and Danu have a place in my plans and whatever counts as my heart. But, like your ma and da, you have tribulations to overcome before your roles are revealed."

"Are you going to spirit me from this cell?" The Goddess smiled at the tremor of hope in Brighid's voice and shook her head.

"No. Why would you wish to spoil the stories of others? That's just selfish." The Goddess paused, and Brighid imagined her deep in thought. "It's all about the blood, Brighid. Many, and some that you hold dear, will give their lives for you. Others' bodies will be broken because of their loyalty to Danu and you. Your mother and father never forgot any who suffered for them. They knew that the blood spilt was more precious than gold—or the accumulation of power. They made me a better Goddess. Follow their example." Brighid felt the presence withdraw, and then came a laugh.

"But remember, you're not immortal, and Fate is fickler than I. You can die."

"Great motivational talk, Goddess."

"Sarcasm was never your da's strong suit and obviously is not yours."

"Bitseach!"

Brighid stood and flexed her muscles, which was a surprise. Her pains had not gone but had receded to a manageable throb, and her shackles lay on the cell floor. She looked upward, smiled, and said, "Thanks."

∗∗∗

Draighean paced the floor of Danu's chamber. The Sidhe was infuriated by her apparent impotence and the realisation that she actually needed the humans to be truly terrible. Was this the lesson Mongfhionn needed her to learn? Only as partners could man and Aes Sidhe reach their full potential. Pride made Draighean snarl at the thought.

Then she looked at Danu and barely held back the single tear that demanded to be freed. Danu tossed and turned in her cot. Scolai's druids gave her potions made from herbs and flowers, which eased the pain and made her drowsy. Since her collapse, the druids' leader had kept a vigil at Danu's side. Draighean appreciated that, although she would never admit it. Instead, she grumbled, "Charlatans," when in Scolai's company.

Perhaps it was wishful thinking, but Draighean observed a lowering of the pain and possibly more rapid healing of the bruising that swathed Danu's body. The wound in her chest glared accusingly at Draighean. *What could I have done to prevent this?* Yet its edges seemed to draw closer, and Danu's breathing had steadied, which, in turn, ameliorated Draighean's temper.

✳✳✳

Five sunsets had passed since Brighid's conversation with the Goddess. Cairbre had ignored her since their first meeting, although he kept his promise about tending to her wounds. Uallachán came daily to taunt and promise her and Danu vile retribution, but he was never permitted into the cell. For her part, after the first time, Brighid refused to acknowledge his presence, and that drove the heat of his rage higher.

For the hundredth time, Brighid scrutinised the walls of her prison, and for the hundredth time, she saw nothing that might help her escape. A scraping sound drew Brighid's attention to the far wall of the cell. Quickly, she looked around for a weapon but had to make do with a wooden platter.

"This should be interesting."

Crouched and ready to spring, Brighid peered at the mould- and grime-encrusted wall. In the gloom and the glow of a single rushlight, hearing proved more useful than sight. Did she imagine the scraping sound and that it grew louder? She quickly dismissed as wishful thinking that several stones moved.

Yet even after furiously blinking to focus her vision, Brighid could not ignore her perception that a section of the wall moved and apparently with purpose. Several blocks crashed and fell into the cell, and a patch of black, the size a small person could squeeze through, replaced the hewn rock. From it emerged a small head, and as he stood, a second face appeared.

"The Hag! Who are you?" Brighid looked at the two—a boy and girl. They were no more than fourteen summers and obviously related. Their features reminded her of someone, but a solution to that mystery eluded her. "Did you bring clothes?" Brighid bit her lips at the stupidity of the question. *Really! My death is imminent, and I want something to wear.* The girl chuckled and looked down at her and her brother's bodies— both were naked.

"I am Sláine Mac Sláine."

There was a deep sadness in the boy's eyes as he grasped the girl's hand. "This is my sister, Daráine." He took a deep breath to steady himself. "This cell is regarded as the toughest to escape from and is the logical place to imprison dangerous enemies. My father…" Sláine's voice trembled, "… being wise, knew that a change of king could see him incarcerated in his own dungeon."

The boy pointed to the opening. "He provided an exit route should that happen. My father's intentions were often misconstrued, but were always honourable. My sister and I were tasked to remain in Cnoc Duíginn's hidden passageways and help any left behind." The young man smiled. "You're lucky. Our food ran out several days ago, and we were about to leave." Daráine tugged at her brother's hand, and he nodded.

"We must leave immediately. Cairbre would prefer to use you as an edge in negotiations with your sister. However, Uallachán and his men have not been backward in describing how they intend to make you suffer. From what I have gleaned, your fate will be decided by Maine and, by repute, he is unsubtle." A noise outside the cell made Sláine start. "Sister, go first. Quickly."

With a flash of a white arse, Daráine disappeared. "I will go next." The young man dipped his head to Brighid. "You are stronger and will be able to replace the stones quicker than me." The young Sláine grinned. "Cairbre and Uallachán will think you spirited away by the Goddess."

Brighid looked upwards. "That may not be far away from the truth."

＊＊＊

The one hundred veterans who accompanied Beacán had no qualms about dying to save Brighid. All had sworn to make Uallachán and the Connachta pay a heavy price. None were horsemen. Beacán had chosen shield-warriors rather than cavalry based on their ability to fight a bloody ground retreat. Hence, all were delighted to dismount and scratched and rubbed travel-weary arses.

"Where do we start? The mountain is huge. Cnoc Duíginn is built of rock," said Iasg. "And there's the small matter of thousands of enemy warriors."

"Brighid is well-trained and knows she has to escape. In which direction is the question." In his mind, Beacán visualised the hillfort and surrounding terrain. "The Phortaigh Na Cullen marshes to the north is the sensible choice. Only the bogs would give her an advantage." Beacán prayed to the Goddess that his choice would be the right one and then turned to his band. "We will climb halfway up the mountain and then go north. Walk quietly and no fighting unless we have to."

✷✷✷

The tunnel was low, narrow, and stank of damp earth and decay. Breathing harshly at the exercise and residual pains, Brighid heaved a sigh of relief as a pinprick of light appeared ahead of them and a puff of wind lifted her lank tresses. As the trio crawled closer to the daylight, a melange of smells tickled her nose—brimstone, the air after a lightning storm, and decomposed vegetation. She smiled. Young Sláine was clever, for they neared the marshes. Hope fluttered in Brighid's breast, and only the low height of the tunnel prevented her from dancing a celebratory jig.

Emerging from the shaft, Brighid inhaled deeply and turned to smile at Daráine and Sláine. The wide-eyed look of panic on their faces shocked her and she swung around to shouts of, "There she is!" The growl from Brighid's lips made the adolescents blanche. They watched the sigils on her body begin to flow like black rivers, and retreated at the ululating howl that flowed from her mouth. Its origin seemed that of the Otherworld.

"Go back into the passageway. They look for me, not you. I will make their bodies and souls pay the price. I may not win here, but I will beyond the veil."

But the two shook their heads and stood by Brighid's side. "We will fight."

Not far away, Beacán faced Iasg and his face cracked into a grim smile. "At least we know where she is!" Then he turned to his warriors, pointed in the direction of the wailing, and said, "Kill all who stand in our way. Save the rígan."

The howling from the mountainside startled Uallachán's men and shredded the veils that protected their minds. Still, at spearpoint and with threats of punishment, their advance resumed, and the two hundred trudged upward, closing on Brighid's small band. Grasping a thick branch, Brighid turned to her rescuers.

"Fight with everything you have, teeth, nails. Gouge their eyes out. Make them pay. Make them kill, not capture, you."

Fifty paces from their position, another sound entered the battle. Instead of taunts and threats of brutality and violation, panic rippled through the ranks of Uallachán's men. Javelins sprouted from chests, sword and axe blades glinted as they were swung and carved deep gashes in flesh. Blood and gore splashed friend and foe.

Brighid turned to Daráine and Sláine, who trembled but stood firm. "Stay here. Do not move until you hear from me." Then the rígan howled and ran towards the fight. She had people to kill and vengeance to serve.

∗∗∗

"How many did we lose?" asked Brighid.

The battle had been a fierce if short skirmish between a warband who fought for someone they loved and a larger force compelled to fight. Brighid, Beacán, and Iasg, along with Daráine and Sláine, sat around a campfire in the northern bogs and counted the cost.

"Four dead. A score injured, although only one's wound is mortal," answered Beacán. He sported a new scar on his face. Iasg, nursing a blade slash to her shoulder, swore good-humouredly at the warrior who patiently sewed the tear. "The dead sit in the feasting halls of Mag Mell, and none will have any regrets."

"We will take care of the dead's families." Brighid's words were less of a query and more of a statement of intent. Beacán nodded and looked at Brighid curiously. His niece had changed. Something had been lost, but more gained. He turned to Sláine.

"Are your people dead?" Sláine shook his head.

"My father ordered the people evacuated through the tunnels before Cairbre attacked. Only ten plus my father and his shield-man remained. The civilians and warriors will have used the marshes to make good their escape and should now be in Curraghatoor." The new Rí of Cnoc Duíginn set his jaw. "My father and his guard died bravely and took many with them." A tear rolled down a dirty cheek, leaving a pale track.

Beacán put his arm around the young man's shoulder while Iasg did the same with Daráine. "I'm sure he did," said Beacán. "My regret is in not having known him better."

The young man sighed. "It's a pity that often it's too late when we recognise the true worth of those we know."

CHAPTER 27

393 B.C.—Spring

A shocked Brighid looked at her sister and turned to Draighean. "She will recover, won't she?" The Sidhe nodded, although Brighid saw an uncharacteristic uncertainty in her demeanour. "Shite! All her suffering. It's my fault."

"Hardly, sister. My foolishness encouraged Glaisne and delivered you into Uallachán's hand. Can you forgive *me*?" Danu's voice lacked strength yet was clear. Her emerald eyes burned fiercely, which made Draighean heave a sigh of relief. "Please put some furs behind me. I wish to greet my sister but not on my back." Danu moaned and gritted her teeth as several servants carried out her wish.

"Nothing to forgive. We both made mistakes and greatly underestimated this 'gift' from Mongfhionn. We have a lot to learn about it and each other." Brighid sat beside Danu and gently hugged her. Then she smirked broadly. "It must be really sore on your arse when I go riding," Danu chuckled.

"Now that you mention it."

"Now, what shall we do about Glaisne?"

"Surely he won't be so stupid as to show up at Ráth Na Conall."

***

Despite antagonising Cairbre and being encouraged to leave Cnoc Duíginn, ego and hubris would not permit Glaisne to doubt or postpone his plan to be Rí of Ráth Na Conall. That said, the rebuffed embrace and coldness of Danu on his arrival took him by surprise.

He saw doubt in Danu's eyes at his tale of Brighid's capture, torture, and likely death. Repeated attempts to comfort her were spurned; guards barred him from her bedchamber. Oblivious to the signs, Glaisne congratulated himself on containing his anger at his future queen's dismissal of his affections. *She'll come round when she's done grieving.*

On his way to a meeting with Danu in the Great Hall, Glaisne's one concern was how to forestall the inevitable destruction of Ráth Na Conall by Maine. How could Ráth Na Conall's pitiful defences withstand the combined might of the Connachta? Yet the fort was to be the future throne of his kingdom or perhaps a rebuilt Caher Conri would be better. Cairbre, and likely Maine, had no respect for Uallachán and would be unlikely to come to his aid. Thus, an assassin's blade should be sufficient to add Caher Conri to his domain.

Glaisne smiled as his ambitions expanded. *Do I actually need Danu?* How likely was it that her father would seek to avenge his daughters? He inhaled and exhaled slowly, donned a façade of care and sorrow, opened the door, and stepped into the room.

That Danu was not the sole occupant disturbed Glaisne. Opposite him and raised up on a platform stood the high table. One thing was evident, there was no seat for him. At the centre were the thrones of Danu and Brighid, although only one was occupied. Glaisne could not resist a smirk. Flanking Danu, and seated on carved chairs, were his brother, Aodh, and Onchú of Curraghatoor. A young boy also sat among them. Who was he? None had friendly eyes.

Beyond them, Glaisne recognised Beacán and his partner, Iasg. Glaisne shivered. That man had death in his eyes, and his partner constantly fingered her knives. Behind Danu, like a black raven of death, stood Draighean. The remaining seats were occupied by the druid leader, Scolai, Flann, Báine, Fainche, Aulus, and Cináed. A tall woman with braided blonde hair he did not recognise also sat at the table.

Glances to his left and right revealed Danu's shield-warriors standing erect along the walls. Heavy drapes to the stone floor hung behind them. He flinched as the door was slammed shut behind him and its locking bar rammed into place. A glance to his rear saw warriors block the exit. *What the Hag is going on?* Yet Glaisne's audacity refused to acknowledge his peril. Head held high, he strode towards the table, stopping ten paces from the plinth.

"There does not appear to be a seat for me. Perhaps one of the slaves can bring one."

"You will not need one." The simple statement from Draighean prompted beads of sweat to form on Glaisne's forehead.

"If I may summarise. You watched my sister captured, tortured, and allegedly executed," said Danu. Her voice held a paradox—the cold ice of the highest mountain top and the hot fury of a funeral pyre. "Did you take any steps to aid or comfort her?"

"Thousands surrounded her. I had no choice but to observe and report back."

Beacán looked at Onchú. "As I recall, thousands surrounded us. Yet we slew many of Uallachán's chieftains." Beacán's eyes turned back to Glaisne. "Are you a coward?"

Flustered and with cheeks flushed red with anger, Glaisne shouted, "I am no coward! I had no choice. I could do nothing for Brighid but had information on the Connachta that needed to be brought to Ráth Na Conall." Glaisne looked to Aodh. "Brother, will you speak on my behalf?" Aodh shook his head, and his face showed disappointment, sorrow, and anger.

Glaisne's eyes widened. Had his brother had thrown him to the wolves? These beasts were hungry for vengeance. Anger bubbled to the surface as his mind railed against what he saw as a great injustice. He opened his mouth to protest but was halted by Danu's raised palm.

"Did you speak with my sister?"

"How could I? She was imprisoned and surrounded by many guards."

"That is unfortunate—on many levels."

Rising from her throne, Danu descended the platform steps and walked towards Glaisne. Eyes, so deep a green as to appear black, locked onto Glaisne's. The dagger in her right hand glinted in the light of the braziers and torches. Glaisne's Adam's apple bobbed up and down, and more beads of sweat formed on his brow. *She's mad. The death of Brighid has driven her insane.*

"If you had spoken with my sister, she would have told you that all she sees, I see. All that she feels, I feel." Danu smiled, and the look froze Glaisne's blood. "My sister and I also share a gift from the Sidhe, Mongfhionn. Brighid also has a feirdhris between her breasts. Each flower is connected with the other. That each rose throbs is a sign that each of us lives. Mine still throbs. How can that be if my sister is dead?" snarled Danu.

In desperation, Glaisne raised his hands and sought allies on the high table. "Clearly, the queen is distressed. The death of Brighid has driven her to the precipice of madness." Glaisne looked to Scolai. "Surely you can see she needs rest and isolation. The burden of a crown is too much for her to bear." Scolai shook his head. Glaisne mistakenly took it as a sign of agreement.

"Ah, now you say my sister is dead," said Danu, looking like a spider at the centre of its web. "Which is it, dead or alive?" Glaisne's mouth flopped open.

"She must be dead... my love. I'm sorry." Glaisne endeavoured to infuse his tone with compassion. Danu ignored his words and looked over his shoulder. Glaisne shivered. In Cnoc Duíginn's dungeon, Brighid had done the same—and saw a bean-sidhe. "What is *your* opinion, Brighid?"

From behind the tapestries, Brighid emerged and padded bare-footed towards Glaisne. He refused to hear her soft steps or turn around in the vain hope that this was simply a nightmare from which he would soon awaken. "It is good to see you again, Glaisne. Our last conversation in Cnoc Duíginn's dungeon left many unanswered questions between us."

Brighid's words hissed like a viper in his ear. A sharp blade pricked his lower back. The trickle of blood dispelled any hope that he was dreaming. If he needed further evidence, Danu's knife piercing the skin under his chin provided it.

Caught on the horns of a dilemma, Glaisne considered fighting a last stand. He was, after all, an accomplished swordsman, and it would be a noble death. The lack of weight on his belt ruled that option out. He had left his sword in his quarters. Still, if he asked, someone would probably give him a sword if only to prolong the sport. Glaisne exhaled and made his decision. He fell to his knees, grovelling and pleading for his life. Around the Hall, oaths of disgust resounded.

"My sister and I have discussed suitable deaths for you. My uncle, Beacán, tells me that the famed Persian could torture and dismember a man, piece by piece, for at least seven sunsets before permitting him to cross the veil," said Danu.

"Brighid, as you know, has always favoured staking. That said, Báine is extremely upset at your treatment of her love. Brighid assures me that Báine can remove your skin by dragging you behind her chariot. And you'd still be alive when we cut your manhood off and gut you. Yet time is not on our side. We have a war to fight." Danu turned to Brighid. "The choice is yours, sister."

✳✳✳

The Goddess nodded in approval. It was a death that their mother, the Dark Huntress, would wholly endorse. Stripped and spreadeagled between two posts, with ankles and wrists bound, Glaisne alternately begged for mercy or screamed insults.

A killing arrow's flight away stood Brighid and Danu. Bow staves strung, they each plucked shafts from quivers and took turns to shoot.

Undoubtedly the best archers in Ériu, the rígana's misses were intentional or due to a sudden gust of wind. The latter they understood as allowing the Goddess her say.

They took Glaisne's balls first—one each—demonstrating their skill and wrath. Several shafts followed, each calculated to cause maximum pain but not death. As the sun set on the horizon, Danu nodded to Brighid, and a final two arrows sped towards Glaisne, along with a prayer to the Goddess.

The Goddess smiled on her rígana, and the barbs that flew to Glaisne's eyes appeared to take an eternity to arrive before bursting through his eyeballs and exiting his skull. Yet although Glaisne's wounds were mortal, they were not to be the end of his suffering. Knives glinting red in the sunset, the twins opened his chest and cracked his ribcage before ripping out his still-beating heart.

Across the plain before Ráth Na Conall, the wind carried the final judgement of Danu and Brighid.

Do mo dheirfiúr—for my sister.

CHAPTER 28

"There's only one path they can take—the river plain between Bod Carraig and Na Comaraigh. The valley could be considered narrow at five thousand paces wide. Once navigated, the battle will be on the pastures north of Ráth Na Conall. The battlefield is bounded by a ridge that spurs off from Na Comaraigh and follows the Abhainn na Siúire river to the east. Even the Connachta army will look small in that expanse." Aoibheann sat down and joined the grim faces of those around the table.

"When can we expect our guests? And how many?"

Danu looked at Beacán and Iasg. "Fortunately, apart from the nobles and chieftains, they will be on foot. They should arrive at the tip of Bod Carraig in a half-cycle of the moon. From there, it will take two, maybe three, sunsets before they're at our gates." Beacán tugged the ends of his beard. After several seasons' care and attention, he was proud of its thickness. More importantly, so was Iasg.

"As to their numbers. We should plan on receiving fifteen thousand. Uallachán's army is about three thousand strong. It's much less than he wanted, but thanks to Brighid, he no longer commands the absolute loyalty of his people. Many now fight on our side."

Beacán stopped, smiled, and dipped his head to Brighid. "Nor do they fear him as much as Brighid." The rígan glowed in her uncle's praise. "My informants tell me that the rest of the enemy comprises the

Connachta led by Maine, Cairbre, and another brother, Cet."

Onchú smiled. "By my reckoning, that means we're outnumbered by seven to one. Not wonderful but not as bad as I had anticipated."

Beacán nodded. "Agreed. Without Labhraidh's warriors, our shields number about two thousand, and we've only twenty chariots." Danu's cheeks flushed at the reminder of her diplomatic failure. Brighid glared at Beacán in Danu's defence. Hands raised, Beacán said, "Sorry." Unity, not more cracks, was needed.

"We have three hundred riders, *uncle*." Brighid's interjection and emphasis pointed to her not having forgiven Beacán.

Danu beamed at her sister. "The riders and chariots give us an important edge in the open plain before Ráth Na Conall." A quick cough drew everyone's attention to the presence of Draighean. Danu dipped her head and smiled. "And, of course, the Sidhe provides her unique brand of assistance."

"Thank you. Although I was not fishing for compliments. The mobile forces provide a contrast between the two armies. However, their presence constrains what I can do with the elements. Horses and chariots do not like icy, rain-soaked, or muddy battlefields." Draighean pursed her lips and waved a hand dismissively. "I will find a solution."

Danu noted that Aulus had been uncommonly silent during the meeting. "Is something bothering you, Aulus?" The Roman chuckled and shook his head.

"Like those around this table, I've been pondering tactics. With your permission, I would like Beacán and Iasg to ride with me to Na Comaraigh when this meeting is concluded. I have an idea." Beacán looked quizzically at Aulus and dipped his head.

As the meeting broke up, Danu signalled Cináed to stay behind. "You are likely wondering why I requested your presence in a discussion on battle plans." Cináed smiled and nodded. "Aoibheann, Brighid, Draighean, and I would like to talk with you. I think you will get an answer to that question."

***

Uallachán's Caher Conri force passed the tip of Bod Carraig as the sun began its descent. As he looked around, Uallachán's eyes fell on Cairbre, Cet, and Maine. The Connachta army marched five hundred paces to his rear. His angst was understandable, and Maine's strategy clear. He and his warriors were expendable. Since Cairbre's symbolic slap in the face at Cnoc Duíginn and Brighid's escape, Uallachán's standing with Maine and his brothers had plummeted further.

Yet that did not fully explain Uallachán's anxiety. Unlike the Connachta ríthe, riding at the head of his army had never been a position of comfort for him. His warriors' duty was to protect him. How could they possibly achieve that if he placed himself in danger by riding ahead of them? Uallachán's inclination tended towards giving orders and watching them carried out—all from the safety of his pavilion and guarded by a fence of one hundred hard men.

The sly looks and mocking quips that passed between the Connachta ríthe raised the heat in Uallachán's cheeks. He recalled ignoring similar behaviour on his last visit to Chrúachain. At that time, their contempt for him had been clear, but foolishly he chose to ignore the obvious. Now, even a blind man could grasp that he and his army were to be sacrificed. And that he was impotent to prevent it.

Behind Uallachán, Caher Conri's men and women joked and, with puffed out chests, bragged about how they would teach the witches of Ráth Na Conall a bloody lesson. "Eejits!" spat Uallachán. Could they not hear the laughter and scorn of their ally? His veterans knew the first to be sacrificed in battle were those in the front ranks. Their angry stares and curses pommelled Uallachán. Glory and plunder were not in their future, only a painful death and journey to the Otherworld.

True to form, Uallachán's thoughts pivoted to self-preservation. How could he find a way to cheat the Goddess?

***

On the outcrop that jutted from the northern slopes of Na Comaraigh, three stood and waited. The ridge followed the eastward path of the Abhainn na Siúire river for about twenty thousand paces before it turned south, drawing level with Ráth Na Conall. The chest-high wrinkle of land effectively defined the battlefield.

As sunset fell and the campfires of the invaders flourished in the valley between Bod Carraig and Na Comaraigh, Aulus and Beacán watched from their lofty post.

"You're sure this will work?"

Aulus laughed. "It's war. Of course it won't work. At least not in the way we expect. Are your people ready?" Beacán dipped his head. "I hope you chose the fastest runners."

A muttered string of oaths was Beacán's response, and Aulus chuckled. It gladdened him that Iasg remained, albeit very reluctantly, at Ráth Na Conall. A family should not lose both parents. The Roman looked up at the sky and prayed to Apollo and Mars that the moon would remain behind the clouds.

"You'd best get in position and wait for the signal."

Beacán nodded and trotted off.

***

Two women stood naked on the ramparts of Ráth Na Conall, the ageless Draighean and Danu, one of the two she now considered her wards. Draighean looked upwards and spoke one word. "Bitseach!" Whether she referred to the Goddess or the Sidhe, Mongfhionn, was unclear to Danu. Perhaps it was both. Yet there was a smile on her full lips that looked black as night. Danu looked inquisitively at Draighean, and the Sidhe shook her head.

"Just a message to an old friend, who is much wiser than I believed." Draighean turned to face the Bod Carraig valley. "Shall we begin?" On a mound in small clearing close to her riders, Brighid mirrored them.

Apart from the normal sentries and a smattering of kings and nobles, the northern walkway was empty as the pair reached up to the skies and began an opera of sorts. In the first act, the beautiful harmonising of the twins and Draighean calmed all—even those in the enemy's camp. The voices were low and ethereal, yet none had difficulty hearing them. Steadily the volume grew, and for those in the Connachta's camp, the ululations took on a dark and despairing theme. The dirge foretold of terrible deaths and the Otherworld.

Men and women cried out for the horrors to stop. Some beat their heads bloody against wooden posts. Others stuffed their ears with anything soft and malleable. Their efforts were futile. The trio glowed with a power that flowed through the curling designs on their bodies.

The death song intensified, and from the forests and mountains, another howling joined the refrain. Hundreds of wolf dashes lifted up their heads and yowled. Many drew closer to the Connachta encampment, determined to follow those who had once vanquished them. It was the wolf way. Soon, the hounds of Ráth Na Conall joined the chorus.

In the Connachta camp, Cairbre turned to Maine and Cet. "Battle has begun, brothers." He ground his teeth and firmly grasped the bone amulet his mother had given him as a boy.

✳✳✳

At Aulus' shout of "Forward!" one hundred warriors hauled the smaller, yet no less lethal, ballistae to the crest of the ridge. Others lugged sacks of bolts and overflowing buckets of pitch. Coarse rags were bound around the shafts and in the shadow of the range, fires were lit.

Aulus knew that the distance to the enemy camp was too far to accurately strike specific targets. Yet, with the advantage of the ridge and lobbing the bolts high into the air, he thought—he hoped—he could reach the encampment.

"Dip, light, and loose!" Aulus bellowed and ten thousand fiery missiles shot into the air.

To the Connachta camp, they looked like the fiery tails of shooting stars. Many cheered the good omen, and for a moment, the beauty diverted their attention from the horrendous wailing of witches, wolves, and hounds. Then the screaming started as Serendipity chose her victims.

A tithe of the flaming bolts slammed into men and women, instantly turning them into living torches. The brimstone stench of burning hair and the smell of charred flesh wafted across the camp. The awful sound of shrieking battled to overwhelm the ululations of Brighid, Danu, and Draighean.

The majority of the bolts punched holes into the army's woollen pavilions and tents. The coverings were flammable and close to each other. Thus, the fires jumped from shelter to shelter, spread rapidly, and devoured all in their path. A few errant missiles thudded into oxen and the supply wagons.

As the screams of pain from man and beast reached a crescendo, Aulus turned to the ballistae teams. "Your job is done. Dismantle the ballistae and run for Ráth Na Conall." Aulus glanced towards the burning camp. "Apollo go with you, Beacán." He smiled and mouthed, "And the Goddess," before turning to another group of five hundred. "Rest for now. At sunrise, you too will enter the battle."

***

Maine howled at the impudence of Brighid and Danu to dare attack his great army. That he and his brothers were surprised by the attack perturbed Uallachán. Did the great ríthe of the Connachta honestly expect no raids or resistance from Ráth Na Conall and its allies? Did they believe Danu and Brighid would prostrate themselves before him and beg for mercy? Had they learned nothing from Cnoc Duíginn or Brighid's raids?

In his head, Uallachán scoffed at Maine's fury. *I have more insight into the rígana.* Still, Maine had not asked his counsel and pierced deeply by his reduced status, Uallachán's bruised ego would not permit him to volunteer anything. *Let them suffer.* While Uallachán's anger towards the Connachta kings was in his mind, his face could not conceal his thoughts from them.

Yet even Uallachán's senses were slow to fully recognise the extent of the current danger. The splashes in the waters of the Abhainn na

Siúire, he took as fish jumping out of the river to feed on flies or the filling of pails to douse the fires. Thus he did not notice Beacán's band traverse the river. The stream was one hundred paces wide for most of its length and at its deepest barely came up to the chest of an average-sized man. Hence it proved to be no challenge for those wading across.

Midway across the river, Beacán smiled and mused he should get to know Aulus better. *The man's tactics were superb.* He hoped that the Roman would remain at Ráth Na Conall after the current troubles instead of boarding one of the triremes and returning to Gaul. Beacán grimaced and flexed his shoulder and arm muscles to avoid cramps. The two clay pots he and everyone in the band carried seemed heavier with each step, but they needed to be kept out of the water.

The fires from Aulus' barrage were quickly doused by the Connachta with earth and water. Beacán's nose sampled the scents of small cooking fires and campfire woodsmoke drifting over the river. He heaved a sigh of relief. The night was pitch black and the moon hid behind clouds. In the darkness, only the cooking fires and the smell of livestock shite were Beacán's guides.

Like him, Beacán's band were naked save for the weapons' baldrics and belts, buckled across shoulders or on waists. As they emerged from the river, Beacán hissed a rebuke, silencing the ripple of comments directed at the white arses and breasts of the female warriors and the flaccid manhoods of their male comrades.

None objected to the earthy flattery and insults, but Beacán knew that sound carried far on a still night. All laid their pots carefully on the grassy verge of the riverbank before slipping back down the slope and applying mud to their bodies. As the raiders moved towards the supply wagons and livestock pens, they were practically invisible.

Hundreds of wagons sat in a score of circles, guarded by unhappy warriors. Does anyone volunteer for guard duty? At the perimeter of the supply encampment, Beacán's group laid their clay pots aside and moved silently towards the sentries. Throats were efficiently slit and blades slipped between ribs until only the oxen and livestock remained alive.

The sound of pottery vessels breaking against wooden carts jarred against the silence of the night. On its heels followed the pungent smells of pitch and pine and then a whoosh of flames as brands plucked from the campfires were hurled onto the vehicles.

"Retreat!" bellowed Beacán. Amid stampeding cattle, the warband dashed to the river and safety. Indeed, the only casualties that night were several warriors trampled by the livestock.

CHAPTER 29

Brighid looked at Báine and tried to smile reassuringly at the charioteer. "Be careful," she mouthed and then shrugged. When had Báine ever been cautious? Then she looked across to a grim-faced Fainche.

"Let's get in place."

Fainche nodded, and three hundred riders moved as one towards the entrance of the river plain. Passing between a pair of man-high standing stones, they spread out left and right before coming to a halt fifty paces later at a second, similar pair of tall rocks.

"Now we wait," Brighid called out.

* * *

A fractious, ill-tempered, and sleep-deprived Connachta camp awoke as the sun rose above the horizon. The witches' songs, flaming missiles, fires, and Beacán's raid on the encampment had infuriated and rattled Maine and his brothers. The "what did you expect?" expression on Uallachán's face did little to endear him to the kings.

Beacán had successfully degraded much of the Connachta's supplies and driven off their livestock. For the first time since he departed Chrúachain, Maine acknowledged the effectiveness of Danu's and Brighid's tactics, if reluctantly. Yet he remained convinced that defeating his army was a delusion on their part.

Thus, except for those who landed and cooked fish from the river, the meal that broke the army's fast was basic. Capriciously, the beer barrels had taken only minor damage. Gulped back on partially full bellies, whether that was good or bad was debatable. With promises of great plunder, a grumbling Connachta army formed up and marched towards the eastern end of the river plain.

Once again, Uallachán found his army placed ahead of the combined force. Maine and his brothers rode at the front of their warriors but well behind those from Caher Conri. "Tuilithe!" spat Uallachán. That he and his men were the sacrificial goats caused great merriment among the Connachta. Still, the angry stares from Uallachán's men were for the Rí of Caher Conri—not the Connachta ríthe.

The simplest of all long-range weapons, slings could be mastered by a child, were highly transportable, and used ammunition found lying on the ground or in riverbeds. The five hundred with Aulus carried pouches filled with lead and iron slugs. As the mid-section of the Connachta passed Aulus' position, he shouted, "Now!" Five hundred rose to the ridge's crest and began the storm. Given the distance, as with the ballistae, there could be no targeting and an improbable chance of a killing strike. But Aulus' goal was to create chaos. Death was a bonus.

A long wail of pain and anguish rose from the Connachta army. The slugs, ignoring Uallachán's contingent, rained down on Maine's warriors. There was no warning for the opening volleys and little time to react or bring their shields to bear. Skulls were cracked and exposed flesh bruised. Fighters pushed comrades out of the way to escape the slingshots, disrupting the formation.

The ríthe and chieftains bellowed orders to move to the northern side of the valley, beyond the range of the slings. Maine swore as his helmet was neatly removed by a missile. With a flick of the Goddess's hand, the next slug slapped against his skull, and he tumbled from his mount.

"Retreat! Move north and east to the valley's end," bellowed Cairbre.

With a tenuous grip on order, Maine's forces staggered towards the standing stones. For his part, Uallachán stared at the tall rocks, perplexed.

He could not recall any such boulders at that location before this day. On the ridge, with ammunition exhausted, Aulus grinned and shouted for his five hundred to run for Ráth Na Conall.

The two pairs of standing stones were deliberately staggered with a gap of one hundred paces, separating each set. As Brighid approached the western-most monuments, she shouted for her riders to dismount and walk up the gentle incline. Each rider carried two quivers containing twenty-five arrows. Half of the riders smoothed red and white fletches, nocked the black shafts to the cord, and drew back the bowstring. The other half held the reins of their partners' horses and waited their turn.

"Wait until they pass the markers. Make your arrows count," shouted Brighid.

As the front rank of Uallachán's men passed the fluttering red ribbons, marking the beginning of Brighid's killing zone, waves of arrows rose into the air. Pierced by several shafts, Uallachán's horse screamed before it collapsed. Thrown to the ground, Uallachán rolled to the side, narrowly avoiding being crushed by the beast. Around him, men and women clutched at arrows that suddenly sprouted from their bodies.

Thousands of black shafts cast a shadow over the enemy before descending. The first wave decimated Uallachán's ranks. The second fell on the front rows of the Connachta, who immediately halted and took what cover they could. Cairbre cursed as he watched the auburn-haired Rígan of Ráth Na Conall calmly direct her riders to retreat to the far set of rocks. He turned to his brother, Cet.

"That one's battle tactics are commendable. It's a pity she's not on our side."

"The Hag's arse! *You* should have killed her when you had the chance," snapped an angry Cet.

The space between the standing stones was deliberate and allowed two chariots, armed with scythes, to pass side by side. Howling like a bean-sidhe and with braided white hair flowing behind her, the apparition that was Báine gripped the side of the cret with one hand and hefted a javelin in the other. The vehicle drove through the first set of stones and then wheeled sharply to the left for a short distance before crossing between the second pair of pillars.

Báine grinned. Aulus and Brighid had carried out their tactics perfectly. Chariots are terrifying, but to be effective need space to operate. The arrows, ballistae, and slings had achieved that outcome. Uallachán's rabble—it could hardly be called an army—was in disarray and lacked firm leadership. Faced with the iron-rimmed wheels and cruel spinning blades of twenty chariots, most chose to flee. Yet, having moved northwards to avoid the missile barrages, they had little room for escape unless they climbed the mountains.

The screams of men and women echoed across the valley. Brightly coloured carbaid, with banners flapping, weaved in and out of the chaos. Legless torsos pumped blood onto the grass. Wheels crushed bones. Limbs cleaved by the spinning blades were flung across the field and strewn abroad. A few blades broke and became terrifying missiles that severed heads from necks. Soon the chariots, and the horse teams that drew them, were splattered in gore.

As the drivers steered the carbaid to cause maximum mayhem, the warriors in the crets threw javelins and darts from quivers. Those who were more proficient with bows and had an excellent sense of balance shot more arrows into Uallachán's men and women. Once the missiles were exhausted, the chariots' warriors took up swords, maces, and axes.

The only defence against a chariot attack is to keep one's head, leap aside to let it pass, and throw a spear at the departing vehicle. Few of Uallachán's men had the presence of mind or courage to use the tactic.

After making sure the injured Maine had reached a secure refuge, Cairbre surveyed the destruction and scattering of Uallachán's army. To Cairbre's mind, it was not much of a loss. His concern was the chariots that had lined up two hundred paces away. Tack jewellery glinted and clinked in the morning sun. Horses snorted and pawed at the ground, encouraging the charioteers to go again. *Will they fight or run?* Cairbre turned to Cet. "Bring the best spearmen forward. Tighten up the formation. Leave the tuilithe no space."

***

Báine's chariot rocked back and forward as she looked across the battlefield. Her heart pounded, her breathing rushed, and she felt her face flush. It seemed as if every nerve in her body kept firing. So far, she had not lost any carbaid. Undoubtedly, the Goddess was with her. A long-sword was raised high in the air, and a score of others raised weapons. With a scream, Báine's vehicle leapt forward. Across the plain, vehicles fanned out and stormed towards the Connachta.

On the far side of the standing stones, Brighid's mood swung between anger and anxiety as she watched Báine's disappearing back. "No!" she screamed. This was not the plan. A cough alongside Brighid made her turn to face Fainche.

"The act is foolhardy, but can we let the chariots fight alone? Each of our horses carries six javelins and a similar number of darts. Only we can snatch the brave, if unwise, Báine from the embrace of the bean-sidhe."

"I will kill her myself if any of my horses are injured by those bloody blades," growled Brighid. She smoothed the red-gold plumes on her helmet before settling it over her thick, damp braids, turned on her dillat, and shouted, "Forward!" Three hundred horses recrossed the line of standing stones and galloped towards the Connachta lines.

***

Cairbre squinted as he watched hundreds of Brighid's riders gallop towards his front ranks. He felt the ground tremble under the pounding of several thousand hooves. *Surely they do not intend to attack us.* Traditionally, only chieftains and veterans rode to a battlefield, but they always dismounted to join the fight. From the disposition of these riders, this did not seem to be the case. The chariots would arrive first, but the horses, each the weight of ten men, would not be far behind.

"Let's hope horses have some sense of self-preservation," muttered

Cairbre. He exhaled sharply as his shield-man inspected and tightened his boiled leather armour. Finally, the warrior settled a scíath securely on Cairbre's arm and a spear in his right hand. Only then was the rí allowed to take his place with his men.

Fifty paces from the front row of the Connachta, Báine grasped the foolishness of her action and her responsibility for the chariot teams. She screamed and furiously waved her longsword in the air, signalling the vehicles to turn and retreat.

Yet an integral part of a carbad's terror is the momentum it generates. It is impossible to stop suddenly. Showers of dirt, grass, and mud splattered the Connachta front lines as the carbaid fought to swing around. The clatter of scythes and wheels against shields and the sharp cracks of spears splintering rang out. Impetus prevented two from turning, and they crashed into the Connachta's ranks. Spinning knives and wheels and swords and axes struck the enemy before the teams were overwhelmed and killed.

As the charging Brighid and her riders came into her vision, Báine had the presence of mind to bellow, "Scatter!" She would rather walk into the Otherworld than face the wrath of Brighid if any of her horses were killed or, worse, maimed.

A zephyr of air rushed past Báine's ear. She heard her driver grunt before tumbling from the open cret, a spear protruding from his back. Driverless, the carbad careened and slowed as Báine scrambled to grasp the reins. She had them in her hand when a thud to her side propelled her forward and over the chariot's side.

Brighid knew it was Báine's chariot from its colours. The Connachta, sensing an opportunity to kill the white-haired bean-sidhe, surged forward. Brighid turned to Fainche. "Make the tuilithe pay. Lose javelins and darts and then retreat. Do *not* get into a brawl. I'll see to Báine."

Cairbre stared aghast and furious at the body of his shield-man, a man he considered his closest friend. A shaft of wood protruded from his chest. Many around him had suffered the same fate. No one had expected the multiple volleys of javelins and darts from the Ráth Na Conall cavalry. Or that, under the direction of another impressive female warrior, the riders would refuse to engage. It was not a tactic any had experienced before. Lessons needed to be learned from Conall's daughters.

Under Fainche's withering fire, the Connachta had little option but to retreat several hundred paces to regroup. Gathering his thoughts, Cairbre correctly surmised that the riders likely had a limited number of throwing weapons. Thus, it frustrated but did not surprise him when, having achieved their goal, the horses and chariots retreated.

That they now stood cheering and defiant on the grassy bank between the pairs of standing stones made Cairbre grind his teeth. His Connachta had been outwitted repeatedly since Cnoc Duíginn. The shame of a defeat at the hands of another Mac Gabhann robbed Cairbre of his usual pragmatism. He roared for his men to form, and five thousand Connachta surged towards the standing stones.

Brighid's eyes widened as she watched the Connachta charge forward. She could not believe Cairbre's impetuosity—or the opportunity. "Fetch the reserves of javelins and quivers of arrows," she ordered. Fainche's suggestion to hide extra weapons on the far slope of the mound now seemed inspired. Brighid thanked the Goddess and prayed that Draighean's powers did not flag. *"Do not doubt me, child."* Drawing strength from Danu's feirdhris, Brighid's rose throbbed reassuringly.

The Connachta charge had the result of calming Cairbre's mind, and he examined the land before the tall rocks. The grass seemed a different shade of green to the lush pastures, and as he drew closer to the towering rocks, he could make out masses of tiny white flowers. He saw Brighid mounted at the centre of the Ráth Na Conall force and her mocking smile. *What did she know?*

His mind screamed, "Danger!" He visualised the paths of the chariots and riders when they charged from the standing stones. "Shite!" he exclaimed and bellowed, "Retreat!" It was too late. In a mindless frenzy and smarting at their humiliation, the Connachta's ears were closed to

Cairbre's command. Eager to salvage their dignity and reputation, thousands charged towards the stones. Alongside Brighid, the mná-sidhe awaited.

Momentum slaughtered Cairbre's army as it tumbled over the edge of a deep trench concealed by the profusion of blackthorn bushes. The shrubs' thorny spikes would have been agony enough, but a multitude of sharpened stakes also populated the ditch's floor. Shrieks and curses filled the air. The press from behind turned the Connachta's charge into a cascade of bodies.

In desperation, Cairbre dug his boots into the dirt, hoping to slow his approach to the ditch. He yelled for his men to turn, but many of his chieftains were impaled already. His was a lone and unheard voice. He felt the soft dirt at the edge of the chasm crumble under his feet and saw the face of the bean-sidhe. He twisted around, fighting many others, but the torrent of bodies could not be resisted. The stake punched through Cairbre's flesh, broke his back, and exited his chest. Yet it missed vital organs, and so he clung onto life.

Brighid stood at the far edge of the ditch and looked down at the dead and dying. Behind her lay many bodies of the Connachta. They were the ones who discovered the narrow dirt bridges that traversed the ditches. Too late, they realised the purpose of the standing stones but fell to the arrows, javelins, and maces of her riders. A second ditch protected the eastern pair of tall rocks, and it too filled with corpses. *Danu is really clever.*

A groan from the main ditch drew her attention, and Brighid smiled. *Fate can be cruel… and satisfying.* Cairbre looked up and saw the swirling sigils on Brighid's face and the bow in her hand. "Mercy, please." The faint croak from his blood-stained lips was barely perceptible.

"I have no mercy," growled Brighid, unstringing her bow.

✴✴✴

Brighid passed a distraught Aoife clinging to her ma and paced the floor of her bedchamber. Only assurances that her friend was not going to die and promises of unfettered access to the room reduced but did not stem Aoife's tears. The druids had assured Brighid that Báine was not going to cross the veil. The spear had hit her in the side, but the chainmail had done its job.

The rígan once more turned her wrath on the prone body, or at least that was her intention. Tresses of auburn hair fell across Báine's breasts and tears cascaded from eyes already rimmed red. She felt the steady beat of Báine's heart and the hand placed on her head and smiled. It was the first movement in several sunsets.

"You do know that your head on my breasts is quite painful… and very wet."

"Bitseach! Do anything like that again, and I will have you shovelling horse shite for the rest of your life."

CHAPTER 30

A deepening bruise on his forehead and a thumping headache from the slingshot that had unhorsed him did not improve Maine's temper. He raged at those around him and railed at Cet, his nobles, and chieftains for the Bod Carraig debacle. Worse, his brother Cairbre's ashes cooled on a slumbering funeral pyre. He had been a well-liked king of the Connachta and deserved a more fitting celebration.

"Through *your* incompetence, I have lost a fifth of my fighting strength. Three thousand Connachta warriors and a dozen experienced leaders are dead or severely injured." Foam flecked Maine's lips. "And where is Uallachán? Is he dead? That is no great loss. Or has he simply disappeared? If so, that would show uncommon judgement on his part. Yet we are still over ten thousand strong and have taken the measure of our enemy."

Maine sat back in his chair. Ignominy and the likelihood of a challenge for the throne of Chrúachain stared him in the face should he fail. He had five remaining brothers, and a few of those, including Cet, were supported by avaricious nobles and, thus, likely rivals. He had to win this war.

Slapping the arms of the seat, Maine straightened his back and stood. He was not a tall man, yet his presence dominated. "The garrison at Ráth Na Conall has not been tested. Reconnoitre the land, bridge the ditches at the eastern end of Bod Carraig, and search for traps." Maine glared at his upper command.

"We will attack the fort in three sunsets, or you will lose your heads."

The Connachta army entered the plain of Ráth Na Conall on the fourth sunset. Maine grumbled at another deadline missed but grudgingly respected the rígana's tactics. He was equally confident they could not possibly prevail and that their heads would soon decorate the stronghold's ramparts.

Shrieks of agony from his frontline warriors told that more snares awaited. Maine shrugged. This was not the time for caution, and given the expanse of the battleground, a speedy and complete assessment of the landscape was impossible. Men would die, but that was war. The Connachta army, impressive, and over ten thousand strong, entered the pastureland at a steady march.

*∗∗

"Our guests have arrived."

Brighid found it challenging to keep pace with Danu as she paced the northern ramparts. The elder twin paused from time to time to peer and mutter curses at the tents of the Connachta army that had sprung up like mushrooms after a rain shower.

The rígana wore gowns. It was Danu's attempt to hold onto normality for as long as possible. Although that ignored the curling symbols that swathed both queens' bodies and were evident when the sun shone through the translucent material.

Northern Albu's Cinn Péinteáilte—the Painted Ones—had a long history of applying or imprinting designs to their bodies before battles and ceremonial events. They claimed it endowed spiritual protection and some of the plant dyes used helped blood to clot. The rígana's sigils were given, not applied, would never fade, and throbbed with power. That force now seemed to flow from and into the feirdhriseacha.

The younger of the twins, although not by much, bit her lip. Danu's recent demeanour worried her. Brighid had spoken to Beacán, Draighean, and Iasg of her fears for Danu's well-being. After Glaisne's betrayal and almost losing Brighid, Danu had become more withdrawn and kept an even tighter rein on her emotions.

Still, worse than this, Brighid had often joked about Danu being made of ice. Now her sister's mien held the chill of the snow-capped peaks of Na Comaraigh. Worryingly, her feirdhris, although no longer black, had not recovered its pink colour. Beacán and Iasg counselled that time would heal. Draighean asserted that Danu simply needed to be rutted by a good man. Brighid thought both opinions had their merits.

"I will be fine, sister."

Danu's words jerked Brighid from her musings. Brighid's eyes widened, and concern settled in her eyes. Were their thoughts no longer their own? That could be highly embarrassing. Brighid's cheeks flushed pink, and Danu chuckled. "I promise not to peek. But after this battle, we need to discuss boundaries." With a deep sigh, she said, "It's time for one final meeting with the War Council."

There was little enthusiasm in Danu's voice, which was mirrored by Brighid's expression. What more could be said? All knew the impossibility of the task before them. Few, except Draighean, thought they could vanquish Maine and the Connachta. The critical question was could they make them pay such a high price they would be forced to withdraw?

Danu stopped suddenly, grasped Brighid, and pulled her into a crushing embrace. "I'm glad you are by my side." The voice was hoarse with emotion and nervousness at showing vulnerability. "To the Otherworld with another meeting. This evening, the garrison and people of Ráth Na Conall will feast and drink."

Brighid grinned. Perhaps the ice was melting.

* * *

The battle began before dawn as Draighean and the rígana took their places on the northern wall. Few saw anything untoward about the trio's lack of clothing. Those who remembered the twins' ma as a young and tempestuous adolescent knew the daughters followed a family tradition.

Hands raised, the death chant rose and was quickly joined by the howling of the fort's wolfhounds and numerous dashes of wolves in the forests and mountain slopes. A cold northerly wind rushed through the trees, plucking the tents of the Connachta from their stakes.

A final element made Brighid smile broadly and proudly. Further along the parapet, Aoife sported a small wolf design above her right eye. It had been reluctantly agreed to by Ceara. As the chants rose, Aoife and her band pounded a deep rhythm on the bodhrán.

Standing further along the walkway, Aoibheann uttered a prayer to the Goddess. Her eyes swept along the ramparts. The sight of the double shield-wall, over two thousand warriors, men and women, from Clárach, Cnoc Duíginn, Curraghatoor, and Ráth Na Conall, standing shoulder to shoulder, made her chest swell with pride.

In the square stood a reserve of one thousand. Flann, insistent that he was fit to fight, commanded the unit. That made Aoibheann happy—if she fell, he would take her place. She grinned at the fussiness of the kings' and queens' shield-men, ensuring their charges were properly attired.

The arresting warrior's corn-yellow braids whipped around when she turned and shouted, "Loose the hounds!" It would be the first of many orders she would give that day. Finally, she placed a plain bronze and iron helmet on her head. It had been Conchobhar's, and that gave her comfort.

✶ ✶ ✶

"Shite!"

The grizzled, grey-haired Connachta veteran shivered. He was unsure whether that could be attributed to the sudden biting wind, the ululations from Ráth Na Conall, or the howling wolves in the forest. Swooping and soaring high above the plain, a black cloud of ravens added their harsh voices. Nothing suggested any were good omens.

The timing, before sunrise when the camp had not fully aroused, was perfect. Warriors cursed their interrupted sleep and the likelihood of a rushed or no meal to break their fast. Many stumbled in the morning gloom, searching for the armour and weapons cast aside during a night of rutting whores.

Another sound caught the veteran's attention. Faint at first but getting louder and louder. "Hounds!" he bellowed, but most were too drowsy for the warning to register. Exasperated, he turned to the young warrior beside him. She was sixteen summers old, with long, braided, raven-black hair set against milk-pale skin. He conceded that, with her deep blue eyes, she looked pretty—if a bit skinny for his personal taste.

Seniority, for he had fought many times alongside the Connachta ríthe and their father Ailill, meant the girl had been assigned to him as his apprentice. He snorted in disgust. Whore or slave was more accurate. Yet rutting was less of a priority at his age. She had offered herself to him, although likely due to fear, which did not sit well with him. Instead, he had decided to train her. He had no children. She would be his legacy.

"You will stay by my side. You will never be more than two paces from me. You will watch my back, and I will guide you through whatever comes." The girl beamed and nodded. *She has a lovely smile.* The veteran looked around and pointed to a small copse of oak trees. "Get your scrawny arse up and into one of those oaks. The hounds will be among us soon. By the Hag, if we die today, it won't be by the jaws of a beast."

∗∗∗

Brighid watched Onchú embrace his four daughters and heard them beg and sob for him not to go. The scene made her heart both sad and glad. He was a good man, an honourable man. Brighid's gaze caught a movement in the shadows. The scowling face of Eithne looked up at Brighid, and the lady's lips twisted into a snarl.

Why? What had she done to the woman to deserve such hate? One punch to the jaw hardly earned the remembrance.

All had hoped that being elevated to the queen of Curraghatoor would ameliorate Eithne's mien. It did not. *Perhaps she has always been a bitseach.* Brighid dipped her head in Eithne's direction and grinned at how that disturbed the woman.

"We will have a reckoning, bitseach," she mouthed. Eithne's eyes widened.

* * *

Aulus looked along the northern wall and the twenty tall ballistae that stood sentinel. The weapons' teams laughed and shared the craic and a beer. He looked upwards to a greying sky and prayed to Apollo.

"You look worried, Roman." Whether it was the mocking voice or that Draighean had appeared alongside him without a whisper of sound, he jumped… and then swore. She laughed.

"Have you sent a trireme back to Massalia for Conall's aid?"

A broad smile appeared on Aulus' lips, and he shook his head. "I think you know fine well that was always more of an encouragement to stand firm. Conall and Mórrígan understand their daughters." Aulus paused, and a more sober look took up residence on his face.

"Yet we also know Conall and Mórrígan. If this does not work out well, their retribution will drown Ériu in rivers of blood. That I dread and pray never happens."

"The problem, Roman, is that you pray to the wrong god."

* * *

"Time to get dressed."

Danu's voice held an attractive huskiness from the round of chanting that had begun before dawn. It was now between sunrise and meán lae, and only Draighean sustained the incantations. The harsh, cold northerly wind continued to scour the land, and many in the hillfort draped winter pelts over their shoulders. A purple-grey sky, rolling peals of thunder, and spikes of lightning threatened torrential rain, adding dread to the scene. Draighean had assured all she would not call the rain—unless she deemed it necessary.

Brighid smiled and nodded to their personal guards, who stepped forward, and much to Draighean's disapproval, began to enrobe and arm the rígana. The Sidhe insisted all they needed were the feirdhriseacha and the curling sigils. Danu disagreed, arguing that this was a time to show they were part of their people, and not set apart from them. Brighid agreed.

The younger twin laughed, and Danu's eyebrow arched. "Look at us. Our arms are covered in gold, silver, and copper bands. We wear heavy, jewelled gold torcs around our necks, and on our heads rest ornately embellished helmets worth a king's ransom. Could we be better targets?" A cough drew both girls' attention.

"Not just for warriors but also assassins. Let's hope Maine's people are not as good as Iasg and me," said Beacán.

"We trust you to protect us from such persons, uncle," responded Danu.

"For you, yes. But Brighid will shortly take her place with the riders and chariots. She will be beyond my oversight."

"So, the rumour you've been training several of my riders in the darker arts is untrue?"

There was a note of annoyance in Brighid's voice, but it vanished as she laughed, winked, and strode from the walkway. Beacán shook his head and wondered if anything got past his nieces.

***

Maine wondered at the sharp cracks that carried on the wind and got louder as his army neared Ráth Na Conall. Then he cursed as he spotted the giant flags and banners of Clann Ui Flaithimh and Conall Mac Gabhann flapping in the gusting wind. The harsh *kraa kraa* of swooping black ravens taunted Maine, making him snarl. Everything about this campaign had an unearthly feel to it. As if to confirm his musing, strains of the Sidhe's ululations rose above the wind. It assaulted the minds of the weak—and there were many of them.

"Bitseacha!"

The wolfhounds had struck terror into camp until they were eventually killed. Was it a foretaste of the battle to come that none had retreated? The witch's song continued to unnerve his warriors, and even some of the nobles, as the army tramped forward. Every footstep of the ground was examined for traps and snares. More ditches concealed by blackthorn bushes had been discovered—although mainly by those who fell into them.

Still, Maine's instinct told him that these were meant to be found and lull him into a false sense of safety as they closed on the hill. Where were the witch's cavalry and chariots? The ground was perfect for them. When this was over, he would take the herds of horses back to Chrúachain and train his own cavalry. War had changed.

Maine shook his head and chastised himself for overthinking. He had a great army. What if he lost a few thousand? He would still have more than enough to slaughter those in the ráth. His family's honour would be restored, and a kingdom added to his domain. The possibility of wresting the crown of the Ard-Righ—High King—of Ériu from the Ulaid was within his grasp. Maine grinned, held his longsword high, and shouted.

"Ionsaí!—Attack!"

⁎

"First is dead."

He told her this before they took up their positions in the horde. She looked at the web of scars on his face, arms, and legs and knew he was not a coward. Thus, she ignored taunts of *"Sicín*—chicken!" from the flush-faced arseholes who rushed by, barging her out of the way. She fought against the growing fever that made her face glow and her blood pump faster. Yet she could not resist joining in the chants and the hateful cursing of an enemy she did not know. She never questioned why they fought. The Rí Ruirech had ordered it, and the plunder would set her free.

The odd-looking duo loped along at a pace that placed them between the first and second thirds of the army. Already they passed eejits bent over double, puking and retching, having prematurely exhausted their reserves. She sensed the older warrior temper his pace and mirrored the action. It made no sense to face the enemy exhausted and too tired to fight.

She imagined she heard a shout of "Now!" from the hillfort but thought her mind deceived. They reached the foot of the hill, but the stronghold remained far away at the apex of long wooded inclines. She felt a rush of air and a deluge of blood drenched her head and torso. The young woman grimaced as liquid seeped through her lips and wanted to puke.

A firm grip on her upper arm pulled her to the side, and she glimpsed a long shaft fly past her to claim another victim. The screams and shrieking increased, as well as the stench of loosened bowels. The girl asked the Goddess to remove her senses.

The yellow ribbon fluttering in the wind had caught the observant veteran's attention. Long-honed instincts snapped into action. Yet even he could not imagine the carnage visited on the Connachta. Thousands of iron-headed bolts flung from the tall machines on the ráth's walls gouged bloody trails deep into the Connachta ranks.

Had Maine been warned of these? Why had he not informed them about the weapons? The veteran felt the army give a collective shudder. Their vaunted superiority had been assaulted. The fortunate were those whose heads disappeared in a mist of blood. Others were left missing limbs or spitted together like *sicíní* over a fire. The old warrior shook his head. The beast had been wounded, and hundreds were dead or injured.

As the missiles repeatedly struck into the heart of the Connachta, the veteran thanked the Goddess for their position. He wiped the gore from the girl's eyes and mouth, took her by the shoulders, and shook her roughly. He could not allow shock to overwhelm her mind. Then he bellowed for those around him to push on.

Barely had the towering ballistae ceased their slaughter when the deep *barr-ewww* of a Clann Uí Flaithimh battle-horn blasted out across the killing ground. "Shite!" muttered Maine. "What's next?" The Connachta king did not have long to wait for an answer.

Alternately cajoled and threatened by Maine's chieftains, the

Connachta struggled to regain their shape after the last barrage. Seizing the opportunity, Báine's chariots attacked those who had not entered the forested hills. "Spears forward! Kill the tuilithe!" roared Maine. When the second battle-horn reverberated over the plain, Maine attempted to countermand his order. It was too late, and a thousand Connachta fighters raced to throw up a hedge of spears between them and the army's left flank.

Báine, still suffering from her injuries, had to be tied to the vehicle's cret. Screaming, "Ionsaí!" she led her chariots at the breakaway group. Under Cet's orders, another thousand Connachta broke from the central column and charged to support their comrades. In reply, over a thousand hooves made the land tremble.

"The Hag preserve me from incompetents," spat Maine, rounding on his brother. "What idiocy made you send another thousand to their deaths?"

Ashen-faced and furious, Cet retorted, "On your orders, the first thousand attacked. The chariots did not break their stride and were joined by mounted warriors. What other option did we have?"

"The riders and chariots are a nuisance, a distraction. They would have killed or injured hundreds before exhausting their missiles and had to retreat." Maine gestured at the two thousand Connachta cut off by the chariots and riders. "*You* have likely cost me many more. Do not think and do not give orders. That is my job. The thrust of our attack is the walls of the bitseacha's stronghold, and I have many more warriors than the witches can match."

Maine's brow furrowed. "Another mistake, brother, and your head may be spiked alongside the rígana."

CHAPTER 31

Danu watched her riders and chariots savage Maine's left flank. It was enormously satisfying to hear the Connachta's howls of frustration when the mounted warriors refused to stand and engage. Yet mounting anxiety made her pace the ramparts back and forth. Those alongside knew why.

"The Hag, Brighid. Where are you?"

"Behind you, sister."

Stunned, Danu could do little but stand with a silly smirk on her face. The smile grew wider as Brighid said, "Na Feirdhriseacha fight together as one." A frown fluttered on Brighid's lips. "Besides, as much as I hate to admit it, Fainche may be a better commander than me—although not a better rider."

Behind the rígana, the statuesque Draighean fought to control the features of her usually porcelain-sculpted face from breaking into a relieved smile. "Enough of the sisterly love. We have a battle to win. And I have work to do."

The ghoulish smile that twisted the Sidhe's full lips widened into the awful maw of the Hag. A horrendous voice flowed from the cavernous mouth, and on the slopes of the hill, blackthorn bushes spread and blossomed.

The profusion of scented white flowers camouflaged the shrubs' vicious, long thorns, and the traps dug into the hillside. Casting a satisfied eye on her handiwork, Draighean pulled two curved knives from the folds of her cloak and turned to the twins.

"What is it that you say? Ní ghéillfear, nó cúlú—no retreat, no surrender!" The battle cry echoed off Na Comaraigh's bluffs and across the plain of Ráth Na Conall.

Around the walkway and in the square, men, women, children, warriors, and civilians roared back. "Ní ghéillfear, nó cúlú!" It was soon joined by a new battle cry of "*Na Feirdhriseacha Abú!*" Brighid and Danu wiped tears from their eyes. The last time that chant had been heard was when their da fought on the same ground, and those with him shouted, "Conall Abú!"

Attempting to stem the flow of emotions from overwhelming her, Danu turned to Cináed. The civic leader seemed unsure of his place. "Your work is done, Cináed. My sister, the army, and I owe you and your people a great debt for the labour that dug the ditches. Please find a safe place for you and your family and pray to the Goddess for victory."

Cináed shook his head and pointed to Aoife, who tirelessly pounded her bodhran. "My daughter, although very young, fights with what she can. Your warriors did as much work as my people." Cináed pointed to the mass of civilians, men, and women gathered in the square below. "This is their fight as much as the warriors'. We will stand on the walls with our rígana."

✳✳✳

The veteran swore at the myriad stinging cuts and scratched at the dried blood on his arms and legs. None were severe, but they added up to on-going misery. He looked to his side, where his companion slowly hacked her way through the thick growth of blackthorn.

Until now, the older warrior had given no credence to the gossip that the Rígana of Ráth Na Conall were witches. Yet, looking around at the flourishing draighean, the ominous skies, and the howling wind interspersed with the ululations of the Sidhe and the rígana, he was no longer sure. The unexpected growth slowed the assault's momentum and sapped its strength.

"Keep up," he growled at the girl.

She made an obscene gesture with her middle finger and snapped an angry retort, which was instantly lost in the rumble of voices. He laughed and prayed that she retained that spirit when they scaled the hill-fort's walls. Then he scowled. Maine had neglected to mention the fort had been rebuilt, stronger and in a better location. Still, for the moment, he was content that they had avoided the stake-filled traps.

He saw her pace quicken and grabbed her arm. "Slow down. We do not want to be among those who reach the berm and ditch first. Let the foolish die. We can use their bodies as stepping-stones." The young woman looked shocked at his callousness. He smiled, shrugged, and slashed at the thorny shrubs.

＊

Danu watched the hill's dense profusion of trees and shrubs ripple as the Connachta horde came closer. Only the growing sound from ten thousand raw throats gave their actual position. The ballistae were silent, and arrows and javelins useless. Thus, the defenders waited anxiously and patiently until Maine's warriors finally broke cover and entered the ground cleared around the ráth.

Projectiles—arrows, bolts, and slingshots—rose high against the purple-grey skies and disappeared. Caught in the open, iron rained on the Connachta from an unrelenting dark sky. Missiles found their targets, and the awful screaming began. In the ráth, muscles burned to maintain the barrage. On the hillside, the mná-sidhe shrieked and reaped their harvest.

Leading the assault, Maine and Cet barked orders and forged ahead. Slowly, inevitably, the Connachta reached the walls of Ráth Na Conall. The fort's ditches had been bridged by trees and the dead. Those impaled on fire-hardened stakes, but not yet dead, cried for release. The Connachta kings ignored their entreaties and urged their warriors on. Rickety scaling ladders thumped against the stockade, and metal hooks on ropes bit into the wood.

The only way of knowing how many heads would soon appear over the parapet was to peer over the stockade and look down. That, however, invited a premature death by a spear thrust or thrown axe. Thus, Danu inhaled and tamped down her curiosity.

Danu's expression spoke of unease, and she bit her lip until she tasted blood. How many would they shortly face on the ramparts? The hill the new fort perched on had steep sides, and the fort's high walls added to that. Consequently, the far picture was clearer, and she saw a hill crawling with ants, all intent on killing Brighid and her. *They do not know us, yet they hate us.*

"We need to force a break in the attack. Without respite, we'll be overwhelmed."

Danu agreed with Brighid and turned to Aulus. "Depress the ballistae as much as possible. That should allow you to strike midway down the slope." Aulus dipped his head. "Use all remaining bolts." Danu turned back to Brighid. "Likewise with your bows. Exhaust the quivers. They'll be of no use in dead hands."

Finally, Danu turned to Aoibheann. "Our location gives us a challenge, which I had not foreseen. How can our javelins be best used?"

The tall warrior smiled at Danu's observation. "The walkway is broad, and I have a solution."

As she turned back to the stockade, a thought or suggestion popped into Danu's head, and she shook her head. Less naïve, she turned to Draighean. "Was that you?" The Sidhe smiled but, infuriatingly, gave no answer. Danu faced Brighid, a troubled look on her face.

"What?" asked Brighid.

"You're not going to like my next command."

Brighid shrugged. "The bitseach put the same thought in my head. Do it."

* * *

The girl yelped as an arrow sliced a cut across her cheek. She felt the warm trickle of blood and pouted. "I'll have a bloody scar now." Beside her, the veteran dropped to his knees and shouted, "Down!" Black shafts peppered their wooden scíatha. She cursed as some barbs penetrated enough to scratch their arms and hands. Still, she knew they had been fortunate, which gave her hope. *Maybe the Goddess protects us.*

The sky darkened as a storm of bolts and arrows continued. *Will their missiles ever cease?* She and the veteran could do little but hunker down and find what cover they could. Around them, men and women shrieked and fell. The terror of the thick, iron-headed bolts from the machines seemed to do more damage to minds than bodies. Although given the dead could no longer speak, that was arguable.

In the distance, the girl heard Maine roar orders and drive his army forward as if by the force of his will. She heard him scream with a mix of pain and fury, and—it seemed to her—fear. An arrow had slammed into Maine's left shoulder, spinning the Rí Ruirech around and into his guard. Or where his guard should have been. Bolts had neatly skewered those on his right and decapitated those on his left. Maine rose from the dirt, swearing retribution.

Both veteran and girl heaved a sigh of relief when the barrage ended. Along with the army, they stood, steadied shields, and gripped weapons. The walls of Ráth Na Conall were closer. She could see the roughness of the stockade's bark. When the sun broke through the gloom, she saw the glint of spears and helmets. She imagined she saw the auburn-haired rígana and heard them bark out orders. The young woman wondered what it would be like to be a rígan. Yet, right now, she would take the peace of a roundhouse and small farmstead over a throne.

The girl shivered as the northerly wind bore down on the Connachta. Like whips, the flags and banners of Ráth Na Conall flapped and cracked defiantly. Wide-eyed, she watched a naked figure climb and stand on the thatch of a guard tower. Arms were stretched to the skies, and she heard a song rise upwards. Unlike previous incantations, the young woman thought this one a pleasant melody. It seemed the lady asked for a gift… but from whom?

Her answer came quickly. Dark clouds shrouded the fleeting glimpse of the sun. The atmosphere crackled with tension, and across the hill, a clean, sharp smell, both sweet and pungent, filled her nostrils. Thunder and lightning rolled over the battleground. A splash on her forearm caused the girl to glance down. The droplet was joined by another and another until her arm was drenched.

"Shite!" muttered the girl, and her companion nodded in agreement. The song from the creature on the guard tower no longer sounded pleasant.

Aoibheann's "solution" left the ramparts of Ráth Na Conall awash in blood, although the heavy rainfall ameliorated that. "Javelins!" she shouted. "Front rank throw. Rear rank supply." The simplicity of the order made Danu shake her head in admiration, and she and Brighid hefted their spears. As the first heads appeared above the walls, Aoibheann yelled, "Throw!" Around the ramparts, a thousand warriors threw a thousand javelins, and a thousand Connachta died screaming.

"Sacrificial lambs," spat Aoibheann and threw her last javelin into the open mouth of the latest head to appear above the stockade. At the short distance, there was little chance of missing. She watched the arm's-length iron spike exit with a gush of blood and bone before her assailant fell backwards. Around the walls, shouts of "Out!" told Aoibheann the stocks were depleted. Still, she knew all would keep one spear.

"Cauldrons!"

It was an order Aoibheann never liked giving. She hated the results of its use. Yet what choice did she have? Ráth Na Conall's steaming black cauldrons of boiling oil, pitch water, and embers—even the fort's braziers—were hauled forward and tipped over the parapets. The stench of boiled and roasted flesh and the rising stink of piss and shite assaulted her nostrils. It had been many years since she last fought a pitched battle. This day proved reason enough not to resurrect the custom.

Two mud-splattered hands gripped the stockade, and a breathless, ruddy-faced woman began to clamber over the fence. *Did she have a husband and children? What desperation made her leave them to fight in this war?* Aoibheann shrugged and lunged the spear forward. The woman screamed, "No!" and fell backwards to be impaled on the stakes below. *I pray she has someone to mourn her.* Aoibheann wiped the bloody shaft with a rag, settled her feet, and waited for the next fool.

★★★

The first to crest the stockade were either eejits, hoping to get lucky and set booted feet on the walkway, or the compelled. Those with wiser heads waited and watched. All knew the rule—the army with overwhelming numbers will prevail. Although that was less certain in the siege of a well-defended stronghold.

Maine and Cet stood on the apex of the man-high berm fronting the perimeter ditches and urged their warriors forward. They watched the trench swallow hundreds, possibly thousands of warriors before it was spanned. Now, the ditches filled with water, and bodies started to float in the deluge of rain.

They watched the Connachta assault on the walls blunted and fighters thrown back. There was no demonstration of sword skills and no great acts of valour. Just a brutal, bloody battle for life. Maine's visage told of his fury and frustration. He cursed the rígana's battle plan and their refusal to fight face-to-face until there was no choice. Death by a thousand cuts was their reply to his battering ram.

Cet looked at Maine and shook his head. "After a generation, the Goddess and the Aes Sidhe have turned against us. They favour our enemies. The walls of Ráth Na Conall are as strong as stone. The men of the shield-wall that stands on the parapets are equally powerful and zealous in their loyalty to the rígana." Maine's face spoke of his deep anger at the truth of his brother's words. Cet did not flinch.

"The rígana and their allies have outmanoeuvred and outfought us. Their battle plan has been executed with the zeal of a mother bear

317

protecting her cubs." Cet cringed at the wailing of the Sidhe and swept his arm in a semi-circle.

"Look, brother. Look around this hill. Our warriors slip and slide in a quagmire of mud and thorns. When they crest the walls, they are thrown back." Cet inhaled deeply and spoke again. "We must withdraw. We can assess our force, regroup, and fight at a better time."

Instinct made Maine lash out. The fist caught Cet on the jaw, knocking him to the dirt and almost over the berm. Only the warrior he stumbled against and who fell into the ditch in his place prevented Cet's journey to Mag Mell. Shock paralysed both ríthe for a moment.

"You have lost your nerve and will not betray the Connachta or me. I am not your brother. I am the Rí Ruirech, and you will obey me," snapped Maine.

Cet shook his head and, lisping through a bloody, swollen lip, said, "If you want me to stay, challenge the rígana. According to our ways, one of them, or their champion, has no option other than to accept. Settle this the old way." Maine shook his head.

"I have the numbers. I will destroy them and Ráth Na Conall."

"Not with my warriors. I am a Rí of the Connachta, not your fidchell piece. If you want to die on this mud heap, that is your choice." The disgust in Cet's voice was matched by the glob of spit launched at Maine's feet. He turned to his shield-man. "Sound the retreat. We're done with this battle. Thank the Goddess for this rain. At least it will protect us from the rígana's riders and chariots." Before Maine could object, the horns of Cet's army rang out, and his warriors began to slip and slide down the hill.

"Tuilí! *Cladhartha!*" shouted Maine as a third of his besieging force turned their backs and followed Cet.

CHAPTER 32

"That's a welcome sight."

Brighid pointed to the retreating Connachta while doing an awkward jig on a slippery gore- and rain-soaked walkway. Danu's response was much more measured. "Yes, now we are only outnumbered three to one."

In the brief but welcome lull, before Maine inevitably resumed his attack, Danu considered her opponent. "Maine cares little for his warriors or the dead. We have pierced the bear's self-esteem, and he cannot allow that to stand. He will be more dangerous than ever, and this battle is far from over."

The rígan's words were fateful. From the killing ground came the bellowed orders of Maine's chieftains. With a great roar, once again, hundreds of ladders slammed against the stockade. This time, there were no missiles to break their spirit and Ráth Na Conall's garrison stood, silent, ready, and determined.

Maine's hard-headed veterans pushed the young and gullible before them as a shield. There was no relief when they crested the fence, only a rough shove that bundled them over to be sacrificed. The tactic was cold and pragmatic and likely led to an eternity in the Otherworld. However, it proved effective, and Maine's experienced warriors tumbled onto the walkway. Behind them, hundreds more followed.

The cry of euphoria took Danu's attention from wrenching free the axe-head she had buried in her foe's chest. Draighean's curved knives slashed and ripped, spraying gouts of blood over a Sidhe who had discarded her cloak. No blood stained her body, but it drenched a walkway already slick with entrails and gore.

The growing corona of bodies around Draighean were unceremoniously rolled over the edge of the parapet by defenders, needing room to manoeuvre and fight. Shouts of pain and curses flowed from Ráth Na Conall's army as Connachta blades found their enemy's flesh. To the Connachta's dismay, those killed or injured were quickly replaced from the rear shield-wall. In turn, warriors from Flann's reserve and the citizens' militia took their place.

Danu and Brighid circled back-to-back, hacking with short-hafted axes, and battering all who challenged them. Spines were broken, and skulls cracked open by the iron bosses of shields. There was no shortage of opponents for the twins or their burly shield-men. Yet many, howling with victory at what they saw was a killing strike, found only disappointment and death as the rígana's curling sigils turned blades away from mortal cuts.

Brighid grimaced as she felt the edge of another blade add a new scar to her mounting collection of cuts. She felt her body slick with blood and her muscles ached with the exertion. Her ears rang from the continual strikes of weapons on her helmet. Only the steady rhythm of her feirdhris in harmony with Danu's rose confirmed that her sister thrived. Yet there was no doubting the weariness that crept into the beat.

"Drink deeply from the well of strength that flows within you. You have reserves beyond your understanding." The Sidhe moved towards the rígana, slaughtering any who got between them. "We need to end this. The garrison is exhausted. Many are dead or mortally injured. The reserve is used, and many on the parapet are farmers with pitchforks."

Danu's jaw set, and she hardly recognised the voice that thundered across the hill, "Ní ghéillfear, nó cúlú! Throw the Connachta tuilithe back!" A roar of "Na Feirdhriseacha Abu!" was the response. In a far corner of the hillfort, Aoife stepped forward, lifted an aching arm, and began to strike her bodhran. Soon, a score of others joined her.

Brighid smiled and turned to Danu. "Should we be concerned that we have fostered a future rígan?"

Danu chuckled. "Would that be so bad?" Then she turned to Brighid and Draighean. "Let's finish this. No mercy!" With blades dripping blood, like a whirlwind the three howling apparitions spun along the northern rampart, sending hundreds to Mag Mell. In their wake, Beacán and Iasg followed, dispensing unseen judgement.

✱✱✱

None could ever accuse the Connachta Rí Ruirech of cowardice and he had one thought, one goal. To kill the rígana and redeem his tribe's honour. Maine did not trust flimsy rain- and gore-soaked ladders that were liable to break without warning. Instead, along with his personal guard, he slowly scaled the stockade.

Muscles strained and nails broke as he clawed closer to the summit. As he reached the top, Maine reached over his shoulder and grasped the hilt of his longsword. As he swept the weapon from its sheath, bodies bundled over the fence slammed into him. His one-handed grip on the stockade was weak, and howling in anger, Maine fell into the awaiting slop of gore and guts. Thinking him dead, the Connachta attack faltered and horns sounded the retreat.

"Over the wall!" croaked the veteran, "I'll hold them back." The young girl stared aghast at the blood-covered man she loved. She had never known her father. To her, this man had become her true da, and she was not about to abandon him. She shook her head. He smiled in admiration and said, "I haven't the strength to make it over the stockade. Please. You have to go. *Now!*"

The boy, a young farmhand, whose hand bore the callouses of working a plough, was unused to war. He grimaced at the taste of blood that was not his own, his head pounded, and his body ached for respite. The enemy, although in retreat, fought hard and died bravely. He could sense the impatience of thousands of mná-sidhe who surrounded the hillfort and awaited the warriors assigned to them. He saw the pair, an older man and a young girl, fighting a desperate battle for survival. He heard the man shout, "Go!" and watched her shake her head.

The veteran stumbled to his knees. Blood flowed from many cuts, and the only surprise was that he still lived. His armour was in tatters, and his helmet lay a few paces away. Whether it had been tossed by him at a foe or knocked off was unknown. The old fighter used a cracked scíath as a club. The young man saw admiration in the eyes of those who closed on him. He had fought well. The bodies surrounding him told that tale.

He watched the young girl straddle his body, which was now sprawled on the walkway. She swung her gore-encrusted spear at any who sought to end the old warrior's life. He heard the man's hoarse whisper, "Please go," and again saw the girl shake her head and set her jaw.

"I won't leave you, father."

The girl's reply would forever haunt the adolescent's dreams. He watched his comrades close in and shouted, "No!" The girl looked into his eyes without understanding. She did not see the blow that cleaved her head from her shoulder, which was a mercy. Yet, in a final moment, it seemed she recognised the boy's intent and smiled. "Thank you." The young man fell to his knees and wept for a girl he would have liked to have known… and might have loved.

A hand on his shoulder made him turn and look into the chestnut-brown eyes of Aoibheann. "She died fighting for one she loved. Honour her memory, and you will become a fine man."

✳✳✳

The veteran looked much younger and more handsome than she recalled, and his grip firm, if gently so. She did not recognise the verdant green pastures they walked across or the city that shimmered on a distant hill. The soft nudging of the bean-sidhe at her side seemed at odds with the awful tales told of the creatures. In this, the girl was half-right, for their destination was Mag Mell and an eternity with the one she called father—not the Otherworld.

CHAPTER 33

Maine was bull-headed, single-minded, and a survivor. He lived, following his fall from the stockade, due to the thick carpet of bodies lying at the foot of the defences. His head throbbed, although not from pain, but from his feverish search for a path to avoid a humiliating defeat. Cet's words came to him as he recrossed the ditch and berm and Maine laughed aloud. He reclimbed the great dirt bank, opened his arms wide and bellowed.

"Choose a champion, daughters of Conall. Fight me for your throne."

"Shite!"

The sentiment was heartily endorsed by Aoibheann, Beacán, Flann, and the ríthe on the walkway. Fury simmered in Draighean's eyes along with resignation. Danu and Brighid stared at their Chomhairle. "What? We won. He retreated. What's more to be said?"

"You have no choice. One of you, or your chosen champion, must accept Maine's challenge. Leader against leader is a tradition among the Gaels. The Goddess will choose the victor," said Beacán.

"It's a bloody stupid tradition. Does all this blood and death count for nothing?" snapped Brighid and then turned to Danu. "I'll do it." Danu shook her head.

"You're a horse-fighter, Brighid. This is more in my domain." Brighid's jaw set, and her lips parted to protest. "Please, sister. Trust me."

Draighean placed her hands on Danu's shoulders. *"Trust the feirdhris."*

✶✶✶

Relieved the fighting was over, the two armies glowered at each other but fought with insults and taunts, not blades and bludgeons. The Connachta, having stared defeat in the face, once again considered the result a foregone conclusion. How could a mere girl overcome a battle-proven Rí Ruirech of the Connachta? Those in Ráth Na Conall bit their lips and chewed the insides of their cheeks.

A long eerie howl reverberated from the northern wall of Ráth Na Conall, and the Connachta looked fearfully upwards. "She has an amazing sense of balance," said Beacán to Iasg. The object of his admiration, Draighean, stood on the tips of the stockade's posts, black cloak flapping in the gusty wind.

"You know the rules, Sidhe. You cannot interfere in this duel," shouted Maine. Draighean's disconcerting response was a peal of mocking laughter.

"Fool. I have no need to interfere. It was not I you heard but Danu, Rígan of Ráth Na Conall and of Clann Ui Flaithimh."

"Witches' tricks. Iron will remove her head," snarled Maine, "…and yours."

The heavy gates of the stronghold protested as they were unbarred and swung open. One hundred warriors marched down the eastern pathway. All were from the queens' shield-wall. Their comrades had either died on the hillfort's walls or lay injured and tended by Scolai's druids. As the red and black scíatha of Clann Ui Flaithimh marched into view, a chill rippled through the Connachta. Some grasped weapons and settled shields on their arms.

Amid the scíatha, back straight and head held high, walked Danu. Brighid had woven Danu's lush auburn tresses into two long plaits, with each presenting her silver-blue highlights. Synchronised with the sway of her hips, each tail tapped the rolling cheeks of her arse as she glided forward. Apart from the crown of hair, Danu was naked. The only armour

Danu wore was the curling designs that seemed to flow with each step taken. At the centre of the tapestry, a deep scarlet feirdhris throbbed to the beat of her and Brighid's hearts. She carried a blade strapped to her thigh and two short axes—one in each hand.

"What is this trick? Do you mock me? Send out your champion." Maine pointed his spear at Danu. "A well-padded arse and good tits won't stop me from spitting you like a pig, bitseach."

Wariness resided in Maine's eyes, for Danu's steps showed no hesitation. Deep green eyes seemed to stare past his and into his soul, and full lips moved as she sang softly. The battlefield was a quagmire of mud and blood, yet Danu barely left a footprint. Maine shuddered and muttered, "Witch!"

"Shite! The man's a fool. I'd be scared shiteless of her," remarked Beacán. Brighid said nothing but smiled coldly, lifted her bow, and put a black shaft to the bowstring.

"You will break all the norms of Gael tradition if you kill him.'

"If he kills my sister, he dies. That is *my* tradition."

Duels are dances with blades and generally follow a pre-determined set of rules. Danu's lips curled upwards in a smile made unsettling by her blood-stained teeth. She was a handspan taller than Maine, but the advantage was more cerebral than physical. Maine's body was stocky and thickly muscled, whereas she appeared soft and curvaceous. He was a mighty bear; Danu was a lincse.

Combatants usually walk in a circle to get the measure of their opponent. Maine proved to be no exception to that custom. As he circled to his left, he expected Danu to move in the opposite direction. That she did not, choosing to face and close on her enemy, startled him. In her hands, the axes whirled constantly and mesmerisingly. Maine blinked to focus, and instinct made him bring his scíath across his body. *How adept was the bitseach at throwing the weapons?* Danu smirked as if she knew his thoughts, and that infuriated Maine.

The spear lunged forward with lightning speed. Shouts of "Yes!"

from the Connachta broke the silence. Maine felt the leaf-shaped spearhead tremble and watched a red droplet fall from its tip. He looked to his front and poised for a second, killing strike but Danu was not there.

"It will take much more than that to kill me."

Maine whirled around to see Danu lick a thin line of blood from her forearm. The axes kept spinning, and Danu stepped towards Maine. *How could the bitseach move so quickly in this quagmire?* Maine's face flushed, and sweat formed on his brow.

"Finish him. Don't play with him," muttered Beacán.

Draighean shook her head. "You need to train her to be merciless… like you."

"She's not like me. And for that, I thank the Goddess." Yet as Beacán watched, Danu's eyes and her feirdhris darkened, and he shuddered.

The crowds gasped as Danu hurtled towards Maine. The speed and number of axe strikes on Maine's shield—too many to count—stunned the Connachta king. Long shavings of wood floated to the mud, and Maine stumbled backwards until his feet found purchase in the dirt. A roar, a scíath bash, and a backhanded fist stopped Danu's attack, propelling her into the air. She landed in the mud and ruefully rubbed a bruised cheek.

Maine grinned, and the Connachta ranks roared. He stomped forward, stabbing, and slashing with the spear. Danu retreated to the edge of the fighting circle. "There is no escape, bitseach," growled Maine and quickly reversed his grip on the spear. He slammed the butt-end into Danu. Or at least, that was his intent. Instead, he heard one of the Connachta gasp and collapse into the mud.

"Too slow," mocked Danu, and the axes began to spin again.

The audience gasped when they heard the solid thunk of the blade as it buried itself in Maine's shield. The respite was short-lived as another axe spun through the air. Maine grunted as the axe split the right edge of the scíath and bit deeply into his shoulder. "Striapach!" Tossing the shield aside, he grasped his spear in both hands and advanced on Danu.

"You have no weapons, bitseach."

"Fool. I am the weapon."

Maine's confidence rose as Danu backtracked and then moved to the side. "There is no escape. The circle will not part for you. Kneel and die." Silence fell on the two armies and those on the ramparts of Ráth Na Conall until a small voice shouted, "Na Feirdhriseacha Abu!" and the crowd took up the chant.

Danu smiled. "Thanks, Aoife." Then she charged. A broad grin settled on Maine's lips. The king imagined the rígan dangling helplessly from his shaft. Instead, Danu's naked feet thudded on Maine's discarded shield. She rose up into the air, accompanied by a screech worthy of the bean-sidhe. The flash of a dagger caught Maine's eye, but the information proved too late.

Mud splattered onlookers as Danu slid between Maine's legs. The upwards thrust of the blade sliced through Maine's balls and manhood as she passed between his legs. Warm blood splashed her hand and flowed down her arm. The king grimaced at the sudden, acute agony and dropped to his knees.

In a blur of motion, Danu stood before a pale, shocked Maine. She grasped his long hair and twisted it until he gasped and could do nothing but look at her. The face before him was as terrifying as the Hag. Her eyes were obsidian black, as was the feirdhris that throbbed between her breasts.

"Do it, bitseach! I won't beg."

In stunned silence, those from the Connachta and Ráth Na Conall watched Danu draw her blade slowly across Maine's throat and listened as he choked on his blood. As Maine pitched forward, Danu walked deliberately to one of her axes, and grasped it in a bloody hand. A spark of life remained in Maine. It ended when, with unnatural strength, Danu brought the blade down on his neck and cleaved his head with a single blow.

As she lifted up Maine's head by his hair, Danu howled and tossed it into the midst of the Connachta. On the walls of Ráth Na Conall, she was answered by Brighid's wailing.

On Ráth Na Conall ramparts, Beacán shook his head and looked at Draighean. "It seems you have your wish, and they are together—but for what purpose?"

CHAPTER 34

Battered, discouraged, and angry at the stupidity of their leaders, the Connachta gathered on the northern bank of the Abhainn na Siúire. The army numbered less than half of its original strength. Over the next half-cycle of the moon, infection and disease would likely take a further tithe of the injured. Sullen eyes watched the messenger gallop into the camp.

The envoy had expected feasting and celebrations of victory. Instead, the atmosphere spoke of despair and defeat. Around the camp-fires, no jests or boasts of epic battles, or talk of plunder were heard. Only the sound of whetstones grinding iron broke the silence. Yet the herald did not comprehend that the activity was not to sharpen blades for an attack. Rather it was to defend the position when inevitably, the Rígana of Ráth Na Conall decided to dispense further retribution.

Passing tents arranged by family and clann, the herald counted many gaps as he walked his mount to the kings' pavilion. The wind that blew across the battlefield wafted the taint of dead and decaying flesh into his nostrils. Only the flocks of ravens and dashes of wolves seemed happy with the table laid before them.

Tall, brawny guards nodded to the messenger, a willowy young man of eighteen summers, signifying his permission to enter the pavilion. As he approached the entrance, the envoy shuddered as if realising that the "honour" of the mission might be fateful for him. He carried an unwelcome message from Chrúachain. Yet he vowed not to shirk his duty and, with a deep grunt and a sharp exhalation, pulled the tent flap aside and entered.

Where was Maine? Cet, his demeanour troubled, sat on the central chair. He signalled the messenger to speak.

"I have a message for the Rí Ruirech," said the messenger.

"Tell me. I hope it is good tidings."

The messenger gulped. "No offence, but I should first give it to the Rí Ruirech."

Cet frowned, and the envoy looked nervously around. "My brother, Maine Athramail, is dead, executed by Danu Ni Conall, Rígan of Ráth Na Conall. My brother, Cairbre, died in battle. We lost—badly. By succession, I am Rí Ruirech. Now, what is your message?"

Blood drained from the messenger's face. *I'm a dead man.* The young man steadied his breathing and spoke. "Your brothers, the ríthe, request your immediate return to Chrúachain. Ten thousand Ulaid Cróeb Ruad warriors have crossed the Black Pig's Dyke. More are reported to be following in their wake." The herald paused. "When I departed Chrúachain, the Ulaid were five sunsets from sighting our walls." Pain filled the envoy's eyes. "I departed the fort ten sunsets ago. Likely the siege has already begun." The young man crossed his hands behind his back and awaited his fate.

Cet walked across the tent and stood before the envoy. "It seems that the Connachta's trials are not yet over. You are courageous beyond your years to bring this news. Rest and eat. In two sunsets, we will march."

⋆⋆⋆

In Ráth Na Conall, the celebrations for the festival of Bealtaine, which was still several sunsets off, began early, and who could blame the warriors and civilians for the liberty taken? Still, on the walls of Ráth Na Conall, shield-warriors stood alert, the ballistae teams inspected the machines, and the armourers were busy replenishing the stocks of weapons and missiles.

Around a table in the Great Hall, the kings of Clárach, Cnoc Duíginn, and Curraghatoor sat and savoured a victory few had thought possible. Beyond them, the nobles and chieftains of the clanns ate, drank, and swapped stories. Seanchaithe moved among the tables, collecting tales that would become part of their clann's lore.

Yet there was a nervousness in the guests' eyes as they looked at Danu and Brighid. Under the hearty celebrations wafted a ripple of unease. What were the ambitions of Na Feirdhriseacha and how safe were their kingdoms from Ráth Na Conall?

✷✷✷

Finally escaping the increasingly raucous festivities, Brighid threw her arms around Danu. Both sisters were battered, bruised, and sported fresh scars but otherwise were healthy. "What does it mean, Brighid?" Danu twisted her fingers at broaching a topic they had avoided since Maine's execution. Both of their roses remained black with pink tips.

"I don't know. The Goddess told me that we would have challenges to overcome like our ma and da. I think we're meant to face them together."

The twins watched the early summer sun drift towards the horizon, flushing the sky with tints of gold and red. "In a different way, perhaps, but you need to heal as much as I, sister," said Brighid and then laughed. "Neither of us are role models for a balanced life. But then maybe that is what the Goddess wants." Brighid grasped Danu's hands, looked into her sister's eyes, and pronounced her remedy.

"You need to get rutted by some of those handsome chieftains that watch every move of your sinuous hips." Danu's eyes widened in shock, and Brighid laughed. "I have a love. It may not last, but I have someone to hold in the dark hours of the night. You need the same." Brighid's brow furrowed. "But before I can enjoy my lover, I have a duty to perform."

✷✷✷

That night, few in the ráth were lonely. Companionship of every variety was freely available. Yet one, by her own designs, walked alone. She had no need to be cast out but had made herself an exile. An obstinate clinging to the past infected her mind and body. Her shoulders slumped under the burden she had placed on them. *What else can I do?* screamed her mind.

The hand clamped around Eithne's throat caught her unawares and threatened to crush her larynx. Eithne saw only dark liquid sigils and no mercy in Brighid's face, and the blood drained from her face. A prick to her belly made her glance down, and she saw the dagger in Brighid's hand. She felt blood stain her white léine and gasped, "No."

"You have every right to be angry at your sons' deaths and the violation of you and your daughters. But you should have mourned, taken the succour of friends, and let time heal. Instead, you blame Onchú for the pitiful life you now lead. It was Uallachán's men who killed your sons. It was his men who raped and abused you, not Onchú." In the moonlight, Brighid's eyes glittered ominously.

"Added to this, you listened to and believed gossip that accused me of rutting Onchú. That is false, as anyone who knows me would confirm. I greatly value his counsel, not his body." Brighid's voice grew colder as she pressed the knifepoint deeper.

"You still have choices. Personally, I'd prefer you leave and let Onchú and his daughters live in peace. Scolai will see you receive your due under the Fénechas. Yet Onchú is honourable and, sadly, still loves you. He will undoubtedly accept you back into his arms and cot."

Brighid twisted the knife's point, causing Eithne to gasp. "Make your choice. For I promise, I will end you rather than see Onchú miserable."

CHAPTER 35

Nuadha reflected that he had always lived a solitary life but never one chosen by himself or voluntarily. Now, as he laboured to rebuild the farmstead, stone by stone, thatch by thatch, he was not alone, and it was by his choice. He chuckled. Of course, apart from the girl, there were the spirits of the smallholding. Their appearances carried the terrible abuse they had been subjected to before their tormentors had tired of their entertainment value and killed them. For all that, they appeared benign and happy to see their home restored.

Much leaner and fitter, he could wield an axe and split logs without collapsing at the effort. After numerous disappointments on his own, the young girl had taught him how to trap and hunt. Thus, occasionally they enjoyed fresh meat. As the morning sun rose and its light broke the room's gloom, Nuadha splashed ice-cold water over his face, shivered, and smiled. Then he walked to the other cot and nudged the bare foot that escaped the coverings. A grumbled curse was his reward, and he laughed. She was not an early riser.

His life was of his choosing, and that was uniquely satisfying. A noise in the yard caught his attention. Buried deep in the dense forest, they did not have many visitors. Most had lost their way and needed directions. Apart from the girl, none were encouraged to stay. He was never unfriendly or antagonistic and was happy to share their meagre rations, but his demeanour made his preference clear. His young guest agreed with him. People always brought trouble with them.

The stranger's face and clothes were splattered with mud, and his unkempt hair was a mass of tangles. Pale blue eyes darted to and fro. Dark stains on a torn shirt pointed to a recent and bloody fight. One foot dragged the mud as he made his way, slowly and painfully, towards the roundhouse. The man's body spoke of fear and anxiety, and in his right hand, he gripped a long dagger. The stump of his left arm hung limply. Yet damaged or missing limbs were not uncommon among farmers or warriors.

As Nuadha moved outside his home, instinct told him to grab the axe that rested by the doorway. The visitor kept moving closer in the direction of the entrance, ignoring the lean farmhand who stood in his path. "Stand aside. I need food, drink, and a cot to rest on." A movement behind Nuadha brought a leer to the stranger's face. "A bit older than I prefer, but I'll have her, too."

The arrogant, familiar tone prompted recognition and caused Nuadha's shoulders to slump. His mind swept back to harrowing times, but only for the briefest moment. He smiled at the victory and gripped the smooth axe shaft firmly. Its blade was honed sharp and glinted red as he turned to the girl. "Stay inside, no matter what happens." The tone was authoritative but caring, and she nodded and withdrew into the gloom. Anger at the insult flared in the intruder's eyes.

"You had only to ask, and I would have gladly shared our food. However, I don't much care for demands or commands—anymore." Steel-grey eyes held the intruder's gaze. "Or threats to my companion."

"How dare you. Do you know who I am? I will have you flayed alive for your insolence." Foam flecked Uallachán's thin lips as he spat his words.

"How do you propose to do that? Even here, in the depths of the forest, it is known that your army is destroyed and scattered to the wind. Maine and Cairbre are dead. Cet travels to Chrúachain to lift the Ulaid siege, but before he departed, he put a bounty on your head. He did not take the loss of his brothers well, and you make a useful scapegoat.

"Although, of more concern to you should be that the riders of Brighid Ni Conall scour the land for you. Any who give you succour, even as an act of mercy, place themselves in peril. Yet I will share my food." Something about the voice and the eyes made Uallachán stop, and it was as if he saw Nuadha for the first time. Yet what he witnessed confounded him.

"You. You're dead."

"How would you know, *brother*? Did you look for me? Did you inquire about a ransom? No, you tossed me aside as being inconsequential." The bitterness in Nuadha's voice was unmistakable, and fear settled in Uallachán's eyes. Where was the submissive, spineless sibling he had lorded over? The lean body held a whiplike tension in muscles hardened by labour.

"We will rebuild my kingdom, and I will rule once again," shouted Uallachán.

Nuadha shook his head slowly. "Eat, drink, and move on, brother. The demons who travel with you are not welcome in my home." Nuadha stared at Uallachán and added with grim finality, "And neither are you."

✳✳✳

Labhraidh Loingsech, Rí of Ráthgeal, paced back and forward on the stone floor of his chamber. The festivities of Bealtaine were over, and he had time to consider the news the messenger had delivered. A great victory over the Connachta by Danu and Brighid and their allied ríthe. He groaned as he remembered his last conversation with the rígana. How could he have made such a grave misjudgement? Yet who would have predicted the outcome?

He scratched his whiskers and muttered, "If they can defeat the Connachta, how safe are the walls of Ráthgeal? What are their ambitions. Shite!" The rígana's mother and father had started with a small warband and, by all accounts, now ruled a powerful kingdom. Were the ambitions of the daughters like their parents? "The Hag!" Labhraidh's belly soured at the realisation he would have to make amends. What would be the price of that?

The shadow broke from the wall and stood before Labhraidh. "You!"

"I warned you, Labhraidh, but you thought you knew better than me." Draighean's eyes glittered in the light of the firepit. "Ráthgeal will make peace with Ráth Na Conall… but not with you as king."

"No!"

✳✳✳

"Horse!" shouted the lookout on the northern wall.

"Interesting," said Draighean. "The beast is riderless and yet appears to know where to go. Maybe it escaped from the corral during the battles and now returns." The Sidhe squinted as if to sharpen her focus. Since Draighean's sight was better than any human, beast, or bird, this was an affectation to comfort those around her. Deep red, almost black eyes tracked the horse as it galloped closer. "The mount's mien speaks of purpose."

As the gates swung open, the horse trotted in, slowed to a walk, and came to a halt before the Great Hall. It snorted, tossed its head, and dragged a hoof through the dirt. "There is an old soul within its breast," said Draighean and, filled with curiosity, followed the small group who walked to the Hall.

"Now that is strange," said Beacán. He pointed to the plaid woollen brat draped across the horse's shoulders. Danu raised an eyebrow, and her uncle smiled. "The last time I saw that garment was when I gave it to Nuadha just before casting him out."

"Misplaced compassion, uncle," said Brighid.

"Something that you are unlikely to be acquainted with," growled Beacán. The rapid and deepening flush to Brighid's cheeks gave Beacán hope that redemption was not beyond his niece. A cough focused everyone's attention on Danu.

337

"There appears to be a sack bound to the horse's neck."

Sighing, since no one seemed overly enthusiastic to uncover the sack's contents, Danu walked up to the horse. She smoothed its neck and mane and whispered soothing words in its ears. Grasping the collar of the rough hessian bag, she pulled the neck apart. Revelation was quickly followed by revulsion and a barely controlled gag reflex as Danu emptied the bag's contents onto the dirt.

"We no longer need to worry about Uallachán," said Beacán.

The head of the despot stared at them, a look of malevolence and surprise frozen on its face. The cause of Uallachán's demise was not hard to deduce. A sharp blade had almost split the skull in two.

"We should have executed Nuadha, not cast him out," said Brighid.

Danu nodded. Yet she was not entirely convinced that she had made a misjudgement. "We shall see, sister, but it does seem that we will not be returning to our ma and da just yet."

The End

TECHNICAL NOTES

Ériu (Ireland) 400 years before Christ was an island on the periphery of the then Celtic empire, which was subsequently conquered by the Romans. Yet its location did not mean it was isolated. Phoenician traders as well as Pytheas the Greek, a merchant and explorer from the port of Massalia (modern-day Marseille) voyaged to the north of Ireland and Scotland.

That traders did land in Northern Ireland was evidenced by the discovery of the skeleton of a Barbary ape in Emain Macha (Navan Fort). Carbon dating set the ape in the time period of the novel. Whether Romans landed in Ireland remains the sub-ject of heated academic debate. Personally, I take the view that it is probable that Roman traders, if not their legions, did set foot on Irish soil.

In the time period of the novel, which is late Iron Age, Ireland still suffered from the lingering impacts of a centuries long cold snap. This was deep enough to dry out many of the bogs that covered the centre of the island. Times were harsh and brutal. Also pre-400 B.C. there was a great blurring of reality and mythology. Hence, why this novel is "historical fantasy".

There were hundreds of chieftains and minor kings (ríthe), a much lesser number of rí ruirechs (king over kings), and a single Ard-Righ (High King). That said, the title of "High King" was likely no more than who won the last major battle. Even the legendary Brian Boru, although given the honorific, was unlikely to have controlled all the territories of Ireland.

One thing is certain. When not fighting each other, which seemed to be the national pastime, the Gaels had an undoubted talent for art and design. The storytellers, or seanchaithe, were revered. This, however, proved to be a two-edged sword. It was only when St. Patrick and his ilk arrived circa 500 A.D. to convert pagan Ireland to Christianity, that history was written down and that retelling was unlikely to have been dispassionate.

A word on the Aes Sidhe and it will be a tiny word because there are great volumes written about mythical Ireland. The Aes Sidhe, or the People of the Mounds, were demi-goddesses and probably descended from or were the remnants of the Tuatha Dé Danann (People of Danu). Less kind interpretations say they are fallen angels or come from the Land of the Dead.

The Tuatha Dé Danann were banished to the Mounds (underground) when defeated in battle by the mortal Sons of Mil. However, do not feel too bad for their predicament. Being demi-gods and goddesses they soon set out to build a fantasti-cal world that happily resides side by side with our own. Per-haps it was the first or original parallel universe.

Finally, a brief word about the mysterious creature known as "The Hag". Undoubtedly, the Hag is a powerful deity in Celtic mythology and not to be messed with. One source de-scribes the Hag as a "legendary granny" although I am very happy that my grandma was nothing like her! Some say that, in Irish mythology, she, not Danu, was the mother of the god-desses. Wise, cunning, harsh and brutal, she is always a men-ac-ing creature—and ugly, unless she wants you to see her differ-ently.

In *The Dog Roses* and the *Conall* series, of which this novel is a spin-off, the Hag is represented as a powerful entity. She perpetually strives to break through and dominate her current sidhe host. The Hag gives her host an additional strength or power boost but this comes with a considerable potential downside. The motivation of the Hag is pursued in more detail in The Blood Queen, another spin-off from the Conall quintet.

MEANING OF NAMES/PHRASES

Ardtráthnóna	Midday
Aes Sidhe	Race of demi-goddesses
An Fiagaí Dorcha	The Dark Huntress
Ard-Righ	High Queen
Bealtaine	Festival (Summer)
Bean-sidhe	Banshee (calls the dead)
Bitseach	Bitch
Bitseacha	Bitches
Bodhran	Irish drum
Bodhráin	Irish drums
Caisearbhán	Dandelion
Caomhnóirí	Personal guard
Carbad	Chariot
Carbaid	Chariots
Ceannairí céad	Leader of one hundred
Chomhairle	Council
Cladhartha	Coward
Cret	Chariot basket
Cróeb Ruad	Ulster warrior class
Currachán	Small boats
Dillat	Horse blanket
Do mo dheirfiúr	For my sister
Droimníni	Drumlins
Dún do bheal	Shut your mouth
Eiric	Payment/compensation

Faighean	Vagina
Feirdhris	Dog Rose
Feirdhriseacha	Dog Roses
Fénechas	The Gael Law
Fine	Clann/extended family
Finte	Clanns
Geasa	Promises due/quests
Imbolg	Festival (Spring)
Ionsaí	Attack
Léine	Dress
Luí síos	Get down
Maighdeanas	Hymen
Meán lae	Midday
Meán oíche	Midnight
Mná-sidhe	Plural of bean-sidhe
Na Feirdhriseacha Abú	War cry
Ní ghéillfear, nó cúlú	No retreat, no surrender
Póg mo thoin	Kiss my arse
Ráth	Fort
Rátha	Forts
Rí	King
Rígan	Queen
Rígana	Queens
Ríthe	Kings
Rí Ruirech	King over kings
Samhain	Festival (Winter)
Scíath	Shield
Scíatha	Shields
Seamair óg	Shamrock
Seanchaithe	Storytellers
Sicín	Chicken
Sicíní	Chickens

Sidhe	Demi-goddess
Sláinte mhaith	Good health
Striapach	Whore
Tuilí	Bastard
Tuilithe	Bastards
Ulaid	Men from Ulster

DRAMATIS PERSONNÆ

CLANN UI FLAITHIMH/RÁTH NA CONALL

Aoibheann

Aoife

Báine

Beacán Ó Cathasaigh

Brighid Ni Conall

Cass

Ceara

Cináed

Conchobhar Ó Deargáin

Conall Mac Gabhann

Danu Ni Conall

Flann

Iasg

Maolán

Neasán

Scolai

CAHER CONRI

Nuadha Ó Dubhghaill

Uallachán Ó Dubhghaill

CURRAGHATOOR/CARN TIGHERNA

Crónán Mac Dedad

Fainche

Naomh Ni Onchú

Onchú Ó an Cháintigh

Torna Mac Dedad

Úna Ni Onchú

CLÁRACH

Aodh Mac Aodh

Aodh Mac Eochaidh Fionn

Cúmhaí Mac Aodh

Glaisne Mac Aodh

CONNACHTA

Cairbre

Cet

Maine Athramail

CNOC DUÍGINN

Daráine Ni Sláine

Sláine Mac Sláine (father)

Sláine Mac Sláine (son)

RÁTHGEAL

Labhraidh Loingsech

THE SIDHE

Draighean

Mongfhionn

LOCATIONS

Abhainn na Siúire (River)

Albu (Britain)

An Bhearú (River)

An Mhuir Cheilteach (The Celtic Sea)

Bod Carraig (Cock Rock)

Caher Conri (Uallachán's promontory fort)

Carn Tigherna (Onchú Ó an Cháintigh's hillfort—old)

Chrúachain (Maine Athramail's stronghold
and Connachta reli-gious centre)

Clárach (Aodh Mac Aodh's hillfort)

Cnoc Duíginn (Sláine Mac Sláine's hillfort)

Curraghatoor (Onchú Ó an Cháintigh's hillfort—new)

Emain Macha (Macha Mong-Ruad's hillfort
and Ulaid religious centre)

Ériu (Ireland)

Massalia (Marseille, France)

Na Comaraigh (Mountain west of Ráth Na Conall)

Niúig (Minor settlement east of Ráth Na Conall and Aoife's home)

Phortaigh na Cullen (Bogs northeast of Cnoc Duíginn)

Sléibhe na Clárach (Mountain on which Clárach sits)

Ráthgeal (Labhraidh Loingsech's hillfort)

Ráth Na Conall (Danu's and Brighid's hillfort)

The Great Sea (The Mediterranean)

ABOUT THE AUTHOR

Born in Belfast, Northern Ireland, internationally published author, David H. Millar is the founder, owner, and author-in-residence of 'A Wee Publishing Company'—a business that seeks to promote Celtic literature, authors, and art.

Millar moved from wet Northern Ireland to Nova Scotia, Canada, in the late 1990s. After ten years of shovelling snow, he decided to relocate to warmer climates and settled in Houston, Texas. Quite a contrast!

An avid reader, armchair sportsman, and Liverpool Football Club fan, Millar lives with his family and Bailey, a Manx cat of questionable disposition known to his friends as "the small angry one"!

Millar is the author of the five volume, ancient Celtic-based, *Conall* series. *The Dog Roses* is a spin-off from the series.

KEEP IN TOUCH

Comments and feedback will be greatly appreciated. You can find me at any of the following:

FACEBOOK
https://www.facebook.com/aweepublishingco

GOODREADS AUTHOR PAGE
https://www.goodreads.com/DavidHMillar

INSTAGRAM
Author.DavidHMillar

TWITTER
@DavidHMillar

WEBSITE/BLOG
http://www.aweepublishingco.com/